AFTER MOSES
WORMWOOD

MICHAEL F. KANE

After Moses Wormwood

by Michael F. Kane

www.michaelfkane.com

© 2021 Michael F. Kane

ISBN: 978-1-7341723-7-9

Cover by Evan Cakamurenssen

Books by Michael F. Kane

After Moses
After Moses Prodigal
After Moses Wormwood
After Moses Virtus
After Moses Sanctum   *To be released*
After Moses Book 6   *To be released*

Contents

Acknowledgments

As always I must thank wife, Heather Kane, and my mother, Stephanie Kane. They've both spent countless hours in editing and for that I am forever grateful. How they've put up with three of these things at this point is beyond me.

Next I must thank my writing group. Jordan Kincer, Conner Poulton, and Nathan Hewitt have read, critiqued, and given me a hard time when needed. I'm quite sure After Moses would not exist without these guys.

Finally, I must say thank you to the God that made me. Being a creator, He saw fit to make me in some ways like Himself. Made in His image, I too have the desire to craft new worlds with the breath from my lips.

Parent's Guide

I include a parent's guide in my novels to let parent's know what kind of content their kids are reading. By all means skip this if you you're not in that category. Potentially minor spoilers ahead.

Violence
Typical science fiction violence. Gunfights, physical scuffles, and ship battles. One character is shot and attended by a doctor. The wound and treatment is described in realistic terms. A graphic death in a previous book is retold.

Language
Infrequent mild language, limited to hell, damn.

Alcohol/Tobacco/Drugs
A few scenes take place in bars where alcohol is present. Characters have a wine over dinner.

Sexual Content
Nothing of note.

Other Negative Elements
The story centers around terrorism and corruption in government. Evil men are after all drawn to the corridors of power...

Chapter 1: The Warlord of Metis

The Ceres Incident marked the beginning of a new age, or perhaps the ending of the old. The detonation of a nuclear weapon over the dwarf planet opened the eyes of the colonials to the fact that the universe was changing. Pieces that had been slowly shifting into position for many years were now in play.

The solar system would soon succumb to the chaos.

The story of mankind isn't a story of nations or politics, at least not entirely. It's a story of individuals and how they shaped that history through the centuries. A story of ambition and pride, love and loss. And in those days, bitterness. Bitterness as civilization ground to a halt and loved ones were caught between those great wheels.

But this is not a story about the end of humanity. For those trapped in the web of that era were extraordinary men and women. Rather, it is the story of how one age of history gave rise to the next and the hardships endured in the birthing pains.

As in the Ceres Incident, the crew of the Sparrow was again the fulcrum on which things turned. As they began a new phase in their journey, they were caught between the twin hammers of the colonial governments and the Abrogationists.

But that is a story we even teach to children now.

Aleksandra Iwanski
Author of The Ages of Humanity
Died 204 AM

"So what was this guy's name again?"

Matthew Cole turned to look up at his partner, Abigail Sharon. Her exo-suit shone pale in the half-light. "You were at our briefing. You know his name."

She scratched the back of her head. "I don't know. I think I've forgotten."

He turned back to the imposing stone wall in front of them and the squat keep beyond. Framing all of that, the enormous disc of Jupiter filled the sky, a gigantic sentinel from this close vantage point. Say what you want about Metis, but Jupiter's closest moon of note had a spectacular view of its massive overlord. It blotted out seemingly half the sky. The striped reds, oranges, and whites of the gas giant's endless storms wove a hypnotic pattern across its surface. Metis, an irregular lump of dirty ice a little less than forty miles at its widest, spun its way around Jupiter at a ridiculous speed. Matthew dreaded looking at how much fuel it had taken to match orbit with the dust speck.

"You haven't forgotten, and you know it well," he finally said.

Abigail chuckled. "I just wanted to hear you say it again."

He groaned. "You had better get this out of your system now because you're going to get us killed once we step into those walls."

"Yeah, yeah. Just say it once with a straight face."

He frowned. "His name is Warlord Dan, and he—" Abigail snickered. He just raised an eyebrow and continued. "And he rules this moon with an iron fist." He turned and gestured at the small city of thirty thousand they'd just walked through. Filled with crumbling lives and dilapidated

2

brick buildings, it was like stepping back in time three centuries. Electricity was a luxury for these poor souls.

"I can see that," Abigail said. "But his name is Dan. And hearing you say Warlord Dan will never not be funny. We're going to topple this clown, right?"

He sighed. "You know that's not the job."

"That's not what you said about that bomb."

"This isn't the same thing," he snapped. "We can't fix everything."

They walked in silence for thirty seconds. The gate loomed large in front of them as they approached it. Abigail nudged him in the shoulder and nearly knocked him over. "But we can try, can't we."

"You're going to be the death of me, you know that right?"

"You're the saint, not me."

"I'm not—"

A bright light flicked on, and Matthew raised his hand to shield his eyes. "Stand where you are!" a voice called from above. "What business do you have with Warlord Dan."

Matthew heard the soft exhale from Abigail, but she managed to hold her laugh this time. His gaze lifted to the top of the wall, where a pair of guards held the searchlight on them. He didn't fail to note the guns trained on them either.

"We have a meeting with the warlord," he called out.

"State your name."

He glanced at Abigail. "Freelancer crew. Rex Fisher."

There was a quiet moment in which the only thing for Matthew to do was rock on the balls of his feet and worry about the decision to use a fake name. Matthew Cole was a well enough known name after all the trouble at Ceres a few months back that they doubted the warlord would agree to the meeting. Which meant inventing an imaginary freelancer named Rex of all things. Ridiculous.

"Alright. We've got you here. Stand where you are when the gate opens."

The giant steel door in front of them slowly parted with the groan of old hydraulics. Four more rifle-toting guards stood in the gap. "No need for the hostility," Matthew said. "We're here on invitation of the warlord."

The lead guard walked up to Matthew and stood entirely too close for comfort. Matthew regarded the uniformed thug with a cool eye. His pressed green military uniform was clean and neat, but he could see signs of wear at the cuffs of the sleeve. Then the stench of alcohol hit him in the face.

The man sniffed loudly and backed up. He gestured to his men. "Disarm them."

Matthew stiffened, but then obediently handed his revolver to the scraggly bearded guard that reached for it. The man stowed it in a pouch on his hip. If things went badly, Matthew would have to figure out how to retrieve it. Which hopefully wouldn't be necessary. Ideally, there wouldn't be any shooting. Unless Abigail got her way, that is.

"Umm... What about her?"

Abigail crossed her arms. Matthew shoved a thumb in her direction. "She doesn't go without the armor."

"What's that supposed to mean?" The youngest looking guard was staring at her armor with wide eyes.

"It means she'd be just a head in a jar without the armor. Do you want to be the one carrying the head?"

Every set of eyes turned to Abigail. She shrugged. "It's true. You can carry my shield for me, though." She pulled her shield from her back and tossed it to the nearest guard. The heavy steel nearly took him to the ground. She gave him her sweetest smile and walked toward the open gate.

The head guard didn't look pleased. "Hold it right there. I didn't say that—"

"There's like twenty of you," Abigail said, giving her eyes a lazy roll. "At this point, you're keeping the warlord from his busy schedule."

The guard turned to Matthew. He only shrugged. "Don't look at me. She doesn't listen to me either. She's right about one thing, though." He gestured at the gate. "Time's wasting."

He left the befuddled guard and followed Abigail. Given the state of the town behind them, he'd expected a barren fortress of stone and steel. Instead, the interior courtyard was filled with flowering plants, smooth polished columns, and flowing water.

"Must be a man of fine tastes," Matthew muttered to Abigail.

"It fits what we know of him," she whispered back.

A man in a distinctly old-fashioned suit and a ridiculous little mustache approached and bowed low. "Greetings, Mr. Fisher. I am Braxton, Warlord Dan's majordomo. And who is this vision of loveliness that has arrived with you?"

Abigail giggled. "Name's Miriam. And this vision of loveliness is Mr. Fisher's security."

Braxton clapped his hands together. "Wonderful. Now, if you would please follow me this way."

He led them around the central keep through the manicured park area. Matthew noted the mature trees. This place had been well maintained for generations for them to be so old. They passed down a long passage flanked by elms, up a staircase and out onto a veranda. Braxton gestured to a table and chairs. "I'm afraid you'll have to wait for His Excellency. He is with the children right now."

Matthew resisted the temptation to look at Abigail. So far, so good with the plan. "The children?" he asked, knowing full well what the majordomo meant.

Braxton smiled. "My master delights in bringing the village children in to see his personal zoo. He has one of the most exquisite collections in the solar system. Perhaps you would like a tour yourself when your business is over."

"We might take you up on that offer," Matthew said.

"Please, sit and enjoy yourselves. While you wait, may I bring you something to drink? Perhaps a glass of wine from Freeport 12 or..."

"Two cherry sodas, thank you."

Braxton's lip twitched at that, but his smile never faltered. He bowed once and left. Unsurprisingly, he left the nervous guards. Abigail nodded at the one carrying her shield. "You can just set that down, you know." The look of relief when he leaned the heavy piece of equipment against the wall was unmistakable. She chuckled and shared a quick look with Matthew.

He inclined his head a fraction of an inch. For once, everything was going surprisingly well. Now it was Grace's turn to get to work.

For Grace, the most awkward part was that she was clearly the oldest member of the tour group. At fourteen, most of the kids were half her age. They were bouncing about and jabbering like the monkeys they were hoping to get to see in the Warlord's zoo. She shoved her hands into her jacket and shivered. It was cold out here. Frost shimmering on the ground.

"Where are your parents?"

She looked up at the guard that had approached her and shrugged. "They dropped me off. Said they had stuff to do."

"They are supposed to sign you in."

"Okay." Maybe if she stared at him long enough, it would make him uncomfortable.

"Are you going to go get them?" He shuffled in his boots.

She could practically taste the victory. "They're gone. Look, they can sign the form when they pick me up. Are you going to let me into the zoo or not? The warlord wouldn't want me to miss it, would he?"

The guard looked around as if worried someone would overhear. "Fine, just don't tell anyone. Paperwork is very important."

Grace resisted the temptation to say any of the half dozen retorts that came to mind and just smiled serenely. A few minutes later, the group was herded through a small side gate. It was like stepping into a different world. A weird, well-manicured one for tourists, complete with bright colors and signs showing the way to animal exhibits. The guards ushered them across a flagstone courtyard to a small podium. Grace hung at the back of the group, aware that she was at least a head above the next tallest kid.

A man with a graying beard and monocle stepped up to the podium. "Welcome, beloved children of our benevolent Warlord Dan. He is most pleased that you are here. For on this day, he shares his most precious treasure with you. He hopes that you take great delight in touring the zoo today. Now, do we have any first-time visitors to our Warlord's collection of Earth animals..."

A bunch of hands went up, and Grace lost all interest. She kept a loose ear out as he gave a stirring and exaggerated history of Metis, about how, as Moses disappeared and the solar system descended into ruin, Dan's great-great-grandfather seized control of the Jovian Wildlife Park and Zoo, turning it into a blessed kingdom of peace and happiness.

There was a word for that level of crap. Actually several, but Matthew had managed to beat most of those creative words out of the crew's vocabulary.

Grace quietly marveled at the strange forms all the colonies had taken. This one had been built solely for tourists. A few monkeys and

6

an elephant under a spectacular view of Jupiter was all it had, yet somehow it had managed to spawn a dictatorship. Crazy really.

"And now our wise and most excellent leader, the Warlord Dan wishes to have a word with you, children..."

That was Grace's cue. She turned and stepped over to the nearest guard. "Hey," she whispered. "Where's the nearest bathroom?"

He put a finger to his lips. "You'll have to wait until after the Warlord's speech," he hissed back.

"I'm not going to make it that long." She squirmed at her knees to get the point across. "Look, Mr., please. Don't make a girl wait."

He bit his lip. Behind them, the Jerklord had taken the podium and was yammering on about how great Metis was. Grace managed to work out a tear that dripped down her cheek. That did the trick. "This way," the guard whispered. "We have to be back before the tour starts."

He led her around a corner near the entrance to a pair of restrooms. She smiled, full of fake gratitude, and hurried in. She gave a ten count and then cracked open the door. The guard had his back turned. Poor guy.

She reached out and caught him with her bracelets and threw him into the wall. He dropped like a sack of rice. Grace hurried over to him and rolled him onto his stomach. She pulled his arms behind his back and zip tied them together, did the same to his ankles, and then gagged him. With a flick of the wrist, she lifted him into the air and deposited him in the boy's room.

Too easy. The warlord's speech should be finished at any moment now. She crept to the corner and watched as he bowed politely to the children and turned to go. The bored guards herded the children into the park without any more fanfare, unaware that they'd lost one of their own.

She crept across the now deserted flagstones and followed after the tour group, taking the first turn in the opposite direction and breaking into a jog. She had a destination to reach, deep within the zoo, and time was ticking.

Yvonne gave just a touch to the maneuvering thrusters and frowned at the readouts. This orbit was not working out very well despite all the math she'd done to find it.

"Hey Yvonne," Davey called into the comm. "Why are we drifting?"

One final touch of the thrusters and they settled into the corrected orbit. "Because Metis is way too close to Jupiter. If there's a true geostationary orbit for us to park in above that keep, I don't have the numbers to crunch it. There, is that any better?"

There was a long pause. "It looks like it. No, wait. We're drifting again."

She grumbled and pulled up a screen of orbital information again. The plan had been for them to park in orbit above as overwatch, with Davey in the Sparrow's rear-facing thumper. They would keep it trained below on the off chance that things went badly. Despite how small Metis was, and how subsequently low that orbit was, it was still a long shot to make. At best, Davey might be able to take potshots at a few vehicles if there was a chase. As it was...

"If I pull the trigger, there's no telling what I'll hit," he murmured.

"I see that." She touched the thrusters again. Left unattended, they would be over a very different part of Metis in just a few minutes and completely out of firing range.

"So what's causing this?" Davey asked. "Has to be Jupiter. I've never seen it this close."

"That's most of it, yes. Metis is well within Jupiter's geostationary orbit and barely outside the Roche limit."

"Rash what now?"

Yvonne smiled. She'd never imagined the single physics class she'd taken all those years ago at the University of Ganymede would come in useful during her daily life. These days she used that knowledge more than her medical degree. "Ask me later if you want a science lesson. I think part of it is also that Metis is oblong. The mass, and thus the gravity, isn't equally distributed. The gravitational center may not be quite where I think it is."

"So you're saying you can't fix it."

She sighed and flipped the extra monitor off. "Probably not, no." She sat back in the pilot's seat, eyeing the primary monitor showing their deteriorating orbit.

The comm went silent for a long minute. Yvonne stared out at the stars. In the distance, a bright spot crept across the sky. One of the Galilean moons probably. She'd bet on icy Europa given how it shone with

8

reflected light. Another world, like this one, where the people lived in anguish. Matthew liked to talk about the inertia of civilization, and some days it was pretty easy to feel.

"We better hope they don't need us," Davey said. "No way I could hit a shot from this range without us being perfectly still."

"I know," she said. "But knowing them, you're going to have to."

"I don't like leaving Grace without backup," he muttered.

It had been hard to get him to let Grace out of his sight after Ceres. "She's not the one I'm worried about," Yvonne said. "I'm worried that Matthew and Abigail will decide to liberate Metis from the illustrious Dan."

Davey chuckled. "Remind me to change my name if I ever decide to become a tyrant. Dan is almost as bad as Davey."

She adjusted their orbit yet again. "If you go bad, I'll just have Abigail sit on you and call it a day. Stay alert back there. If we hear from them, we'll have to improvise."

Matthew was relieved when the majordomo returned after only a few minutes. He took another sip of his half-finished cherry soda.

"Finally," Abigail grumbled under her breath. "I hate waiting."

Braxton made a half bow. "Allow me to introduce my liege, the honorable and most excellent Warlord Dan." He stepped aside to reveal the man behind him.

Matthew wasn't quite sure what he was expecting. Probably someone that looked a little more evil. Or at least a little bit intimidating. Dan was neither of these things. Instead, he was a middle-aged man with a poorly fitting second-hand military uniform from one of the Martian colonies covered with self-awarded medals. His receding hairline ended in one of the worst comb-overs Matthew had ever seen. He met Abigail's eyes in warning. He could see that she was barely keeping it together. The warlord might not look like much, but looks weren't everything. He inclined his head respectfully to Dan and waited to let the other man speak first.

Dan eyed them curiously then nodded to his guards. The men backed off to the edges of the veranda. That was a good sign. Matthew kept one eye on the guy that had his gun. Just in case.

"Welcome, freelancers, to my humble abode." He smiled a broad and wholly fake smile. "I hope that you have enjoyed your stay on Metis so far. You'll forgive my tardiness. My first priority is the children. They are our future, after all."

"Of course," Matthew said. He lifted his glass and gave it a swirl, making the ice clink. "Your hospitality would make the Emperor of Venus himself blush."

The fake smile softened into something more natural, but it still hid something sinister behind it. "Your flattery is observed but since you speak truth, I'll allow it. What was your name again? Rex Fisher, I believe?"

Matthew nodded. "And this is my partner, Miriam."

"You appear quite the formidable pair, that's for sure," Dan said, eyeing Abigail closely. "Now as to our arrangements."

"We're ready to provide additional security for your shipments of—"

Dan waved him off. "I'm afraid that's entirely out of the question."

Matthew cocked his head at the sudden shift. "I'm not sure I understand. If you've wasted our time coming out here, I'm going to be an angry man."

"Not as angry as I. You've lied about your identity, Matthew Cole."

Matthew felt his blood freeze solid. This was a bad thing, but it didn't necessarily mean it was the worst thing. Not yet.

Dan continued unabated. "After all the trouble you and your crew have gotten into in the last year, did you honestly think that I wouldn't recognize you? What other gaucho and earthtech suit clad woman could appear on my doorstep? My men recognized you the second your ship dropped you off."

Abigail was giving him a told-you-so look. So this wasn't going to be an easy job. He drained the rest of his cherry soda, unwilling to let it go to waste, and then shrugged. "Fame has its drawbacks." He turned to Abigail. "Make a note that we can't take any undercover jobs anymore."

"It would have been fine if you had just left your hat on the Sparrow like I suggested."

"What about you and that tin can?"

"Head in a jar, remember?"

"And I don't go out without my campero."

"You two can have your little spat later," Dan cut in. "On this world, Warlord Dan is the law, and he does not take lightly to being deceived.

10

You will tell me why you are here, or my men will cut you down where you stand."

Matthew sighed. "I thought we were here to talk about a security job."

Dan made a show of looking annoyed. "Please don't insult me. We all know the famous gunslinger priest isn't going to run security on a third-rate moon. Tell me what you want, or you both die."

He turned to Abigail to stall. "What do you think?"

"I think this job was terrible and you're firing Benny when this is over."

"Good idea." He glanced around the veranda again just to be sure of where his gun was one last time. "Okay, you might not believe me, but here's the real reason we're here..."

Grace slipped through the zoo, following the map in her head that she'd memorized over the last week. She only spotted one or two other people. Since outsiders were only rarely allowed into the Warlord's zoo, there weren't any guards except for the ones with the tour group, and only a few workers going about their daily tasks with the animals.

If she were being honest, she'd love to take her time here. She passed a pond filled with tall pink birds she'd never imagined and an enclosure with a giant black cat that looked like it could take her head off if it wanted. On the streets of Ceres, she and Davey had only seen stray dogs or cats, and occasionally some bats that lived in the tunnels. This place was pretty wild. Pity it was owned by a terrible human being.

She turned a corner into an alley between exhibits and found the door she was looking for. Locked, unfortunately. She tested the door for give. She could rip it off its hinges if it came to it, but it was probably better to keep quiet for as long as possible. Time to pull out the lockpick set she carried for just such occasions.

The lock was mostly designed to keep the curious out rather than the determined, and after less than a minute of testing it with a hook pick and tension wrench, she switched to a rake and had it open in seconds. She stepped through into a storage room, hand fumbling for the light switch. Supplies and food for the animals housed in this enclosure.

She found the door into the pen itself, which was thankfully unlocked. Inside was a neat and proper fake woodland, complete with plastic trees, some real shrubbery, and a bubbling stream of water. The perfect habitat for the last known breeding pair of red foxes in the solar system.

Grace frowned and looked around the enclosure. Where were they? They had to be here somewhere. A short, high-pitched voice barked behind her. She spun on her heels and spotted the male crouched low and staring her down.

"You're kind of cute actually," she murmured. "Except for the bared teeth. Put those away. I'm on your side." She reached out and grabbed him with her bracelet. It let loose a shrill howl and thrashed in the air. Okay, bad idea. Somebody will hear the racket. She pulled a small dart gun out from beneath her jacket and aimed down the sights. With a puff of air, the dart hit its mark. It took nearly a minute for the thrashing to stop as the light tranquilizer took effect. From another jacket pocket, she retrieved a strong fiber sack. Gently she bagged the fox. "You'll be able to breathe, I promise. Now, where's your mate..."

She laid eyes on the den entrance. The hole in the ground was obvious now that she saw it. She peered down into it, wary of getting her face to close. "You in there?" she asked.

To her surprise, a series of sharp barks came from deep inside, and for the briefest of seconds, she glimpsed a flash of red. Quick as lightning, she snatched it, and despite a good deal of scratching and howling, she was able to haul out the vixen and tranquilize her as well.

"You could have come easy," Grace grumbled, "But no. You had to fuss." She carefully laid the fox beside her mate in the bag and gently threw them both over her shoulder. Time to get out of here.

A sneeze from behind her made her jump to her feet. On the other side of the enclosure's glass wall stood the entire tour group of children along with the half dozen guards. Most of the kids were smiling. Most of the guards were wide-eyed, mouths dropped open in shock.

Grace sighed. "Aww man..."

He'll tell the truth, Abigail thought. That's what he always does. When cornered, Matthew will tell the truth, hoping that his enemies will

12

be decent in spite of all evidence to the contrary.

"We're here for your red foxes," Matthew said, just as expected.

Warlord Dan raised an eyebrow. "Our red foxes? What are you... Oh don't tell me that professor sent you. It was him, wasn't it? What's his name? Professor..." He trailed off, making a hand spinning gesture with his hand.

"The client is irrelevant," Matthew said. At least he'd had the presence of mind not to directly incriminate the ecologist from the University of Ganymede, though his hasty interruption was as good as pointing a finger. "The question is, are you willing to make a deal, or do I set loose the Shield Maiden on you?"

That was her cue. Abigail straightened to her full height and towered over the nearby guards. Not that she wanted a fight right now. Matthew was a sitting duck out in the open.

"Please. Don't insult me," Dan said. "You can't possibly fight your way out of this."

"Hmm," Abigail hummed. "I like these odds. I was just telling Matthew on the way here that I wouldn't mind ending your little regime." She narrowed her eyes in a deadly threat. "Which I will do, by the way, if this comes to blows. I'm sure the ancestor of yours that was brave enough to take over a zoo would be incredibly disappointed if you lost it to a single woman."

Matthew laid a hand on her arm. "Easy. There's no need for that if the Warlord gives us what we came for." She could see the corners of his mouth slightly turn upward. She also saw his hand move beneath his poncho. His comm. He'd turned it on so Yvonne would know they'd run into trouble. "So what will it be? Can we work this out like civilized people, or do we fight it out like the animals you keep?"

"You're a century too late for civilized, priest," Dan said. He turned and pointed at a trio of towers visible on the far wall past the zoo. "See those turrets? Each one has a shoulder-mounted thumper aimed at this veranda." He turned to face Abigail. "There would be some collateral damage, but I have little doubt that's more than enough firepower to take down even the famous Shield Maiden. And once you're gone, the priest will be easy enough to dispatch."

Abigail felt her insides coil up on themselves. This might be a problem.

"Davey," Yvonne shouted into the comm, "Do you have a target on those towers?"

He peered into the scope. "Yeah, I see them. But at this range and with the orbit being screwy—"

"You might take out the keep, or the zoo, or innocents in the town instead."

"Right." He took the controls for the thumper and gently tried to sight in on one of the towers. It was an impossible shot to make with any confidence. "Yvonne, what are we going to do?"

"I'm thinking." She paused and he heard her sigh through the comm. "Hang on. I'm going to give you that shot."

Suddenly Metis spun out of view and the engines roared. Wait. She was burning the main engines and not the maneuvering thrusters? What was she doing?

"Yvonne..."

"I said hang on. You're going to get that shot. You'd better not miss."

He gripped the controls and felt the sweat bead on his forehead. "Well, when you put it that way, there's hardly any pressure at all."

"Stop her!"

Grace sprinted blindly through the zoo, clutching her burden desperately to her chest. The foxes weren't big, but together they had to weigh fifteen kilos, making running an awkward affair. She'd carry them with her bracelet, but then she'd be defenseless when she ran into the warlord's goons. From the shouts behind her, they were gaining.

She slid around a corner and ran past an exhibit of monkeys. If they missed her turning the corner, she might be able to slip away undetected.

The monkeys all clustered at the edge of the glass and started shrieking at her.

"Traitors," she muttered and started running again. If she didn't find a way to lose them, she'd have to switch to carrying the foxes with her bracelets. There was no way she could keep this up.

A pair of guards ran around the corner, weapons drawn and trained on her. She skidded to a halt. "Hey, don't shoot! Your boss wouldn't want his foxes to get hurt." She left out the part about her being bullet-proof, but they didn't need to find out about that until later. As it was, the guards shared a quick look. Behind her, she heard more enemies. "And now we're all here to see the monkeys," she said. "Great."

The monkeys kept howling, clearly having more fun than Grace and the guards combined.

She was going to have to surrender for now. Close quarters like this were dangerous, and too many of her foes had closed the gap. She might be able to take out a gunman, but even one in grappling range was a deadly threat.

"I'm setting the bag down. No one freak out."

Then there was a sound like an explosion in the sky above, and a hurricane of wind flattened all of them to the ground.

Abigail was the only one on the veranda to keep her feet. A quick look at the sky showed a rapidly decelerating Sparrow. Its downward-pointing engines created the terrifying backblast that lashed at the keep and zoo.

"Yvonne, you mad woman." Abigail dove for the poor guard that had taken her shield and reclaimed it. Those thumpers weren't going to hold their fire for long. She had to get Matthew and get out of here.

With a deafening roar like thunder, the Sparrow leveled out, its nose pointing slightly at the sky as it circle-strafed around the compound.

Thump, thump, thump went the rear-mounted main gun. Each blast was followed by the cacophony of shattering stone as the towers surrounding the keep were blown apart in quick succession. So much for that threat. With the engines no longer pointing straight down, the wind had subsided, and the warlord's men started to regain their footing.

She plowed through them, sending them scattering like billiard balls.

Matthew had regained his weapon as well and dropped a few particularly ambitious thugs before turning on Warlord Dan. The man squeaked and ran into the zoo with Matthew hot on his heels. Abigail leveled her shield and turned on the remaining guards rallying against her. It looked like she had her own work to do.

Matthew caught the fleeing despot in less than two hundred feet, tackling him to the ground in front of a warthog exhibit. Dan's eyes went wide with fear as he tried to scramble away from Matthew, but it turned out the man was neither in good shape nor much of a fighter, but rather a glorified zookeeper on an ego trip. In a matter of seconds, Matthew had him pinned to the ground.

"Wait! Don't... Don't hurt me!"

"Why would I do that?" Matthew asked. He rolled the man over onto his face and secured his hands behind his back with a plastic tie. "I still have to make sure we get what we came for, and besides, I need some collateral to make sure your men behave." He hauled Dan to his feet, giving him a gentle nudge back toward the veranda.

Above him, the Sparrow drifted on its landing thrusters, rear-mounted thumper pointed at the keep. Maintaining firm hand on his prisoner, he flipped his comm on. "Nice flying Yvonne. Good shooting, Davey."

"You guys okay down there?" Yvonne asked.

"Fine for now. I've taken the illustrious warlord into custody, and—"

"Have you heard from Grace?" Davey interrupted.

"I'm okay, too," Grace interrupted from her own comm. "I had to beat up a bunch of guys, and there's a tour group of terrified kids running around down near the monkeys."

"Do you have the breeding pair?" Matthew asked.

"In the sack over my shoulder," she said. "I'd like to get them out of here. I'm afraid I'll hurt them running around like this."

"Okay, round up the kids and stay put. We'll come to you."

They'd nearly made it back to the staircase leading up to the veranda when the majordomo, Braxton, stepped out of the bushes where he'd been hiding. "Oh, thank God," he said. "You're not going to let him go when you leave, are you?"

Matthew raised an eyebrow. "I thought you were his right-hand man around here."

The man stroked his mustache. "Please. This fool holds us all in terror, but there's not many around here that wouldn't mind seeing him take the boot."

Dan struggled against Matthew's grip. "Braxton! How dare you—"

Matthew gave him a good shake. "That's enough of that." He gave the majordomo a hard stare. "Come on then. Looks like you get to help me disassemble a kingdom."

By the time they reached the veranda, Abigail had made a pile of unconscious or injured guards, and the rest were sitting quietly in a circle. "They had an awful lot of bark," she said. "But I wasn't impressed with the bite. Looks like you caught the big fish. What do you think the people in the city will do with him? I bet they hang him." She stooped over to look him in the face. "No, that would be too easy for Warlord Dan. Maybe they'll feed him to his pets. I bet even the vegetarians will make an exception for this guy."

Dan trembled and covered his head with his arms.

"Well, you got your wish, Abigail. We've knocked a third-rate dictator off his throne. Now we're left with the consequences and clean up. Dan, figure out how to get your lackeys to surrender, or I give you to Abigail. Braxton, anything you can do to help would be greatly appreciated."

Matthew pinched the bridge of his nose. He could already feel the beginnings of a monstrous headache.

Half a day later, officials from both the University of Ganymede and the Vatican showed up on Metis. Truth was, Matthew didn't know who else to call. The crew of the Sparrow wasn't really equipped to help the people of Metis set up any form of self-government, and those were the only two institutions in the Jupiter Neighborhood that were near-universally trusted.

Four shuttles set down in the open area between the city and the former zoo. After a quick meeting with the delegation from the church bringing humanitarian aid, Matthew and Abigail turned to the group from the University.

"Professor Jerome? We uh... Have your foxes. And a lot of other specimens." Matthew took his hat off and ran a hand through his sandy hair.

Jerome Whitlock, an older man with a pair of square spectacles, chuckled in response. "I see. We'll take stock of what's here in the next few weeks and do what we can to protect any critically endangered species."

Abigail jabbed a finger at the stone wall behind them. "We went ahead and returned the foxes to their pen. Have you thought about leaving them here and maybe working with the people of Metis to reopen the Jovian Wildlife Park and Zoo to the wider public?"

The professor tapped his chin thoughtfully. "It's a good thought. Perhaps the University can make this happen. I'm going to insist on taking the foxes with me, however. We've been working on a sustainable and self-sufficient nature preserve on Ganymede. We need a medium-sized predator for the food chain we are hoping to build. If we can save the red fox, it may just be the perfect link in the chain."

She nodded. "I'll take you to them."

Matthew watched her lead one group of scientists away. Unfortunately, he had others to meet with. Along with the ecologists, the university had sent a pair of economists, a handful of political scientists, and anyone else they thought would have the knowledge and expertise to help the people of Metis get back on their feet. Matthew didn't really have a lot of input on the matter, but between the church and the academics, Metis was going to get the fresh start they needed to govern themselves for the first time since Moses' disappearance.

At long last, he dragged himself back to the Sparrow. In the common room, Davey and Grace were catching up on the radio program they'd missed in all the action. Matthew made sure to lay a hand on Davey's shoulder as he passed. "Good work out there today." Davey nodded, but Matthew could see the hint of a smile.

He found Yvonne in the cockpit. "Have you finished solving all the solar system's problems yet?" she asked.

He laid his hat on the console. "No, but somehow everyone thinks that's something I'm capable of accomplishing. We've started to develop a bit of a reputation." He gestured out the window at the keep in the distance. "They wanted to know how I thought the warlord's wealth should be split amongst the population he and his family have spent a century plundering. I don't have those kinds of answers."

Matthew noticed that she was getting more streaks of gray in her hair. Maybe the stress of the last few months was getting to all of them. Yvonne regarded him quietly for a moment. "Perhaps people just want to believe in that East Wind that Whitaker wanted you to be."

18

The Wind of Change.

He decided to shift the subject. "I don't think we can do undercover jobs anymore," he mused.

She laughed. "Matthew Cole. The least personable celebrity in the solar system."

He eyed her. "That bad, huh?"

"To the outside world, yes. To your crew? Well, we know better."

It was better to just ignore that. "How do the books look after this?"

"Black ink, with plenty to spare." She pulled up the monitor and flipped through a few sheets to show him their finances. "We've got enough to pay back the operations loan that Dominic bought out."

Matthew nodded. They'd been working jobs hard for the last few months to get into a better financial state. Money hadn't exactly followed their fame. Despite the Emperor of Venus' invitation, Matthew was insistent on not heading that way until they had the cash on hand to pay him back. He looked at the numbers and did some quick math in his head. "And it looks like we'll still be in good shape afterwards."

"You know he's not going to take the money, right?"

He grimaced. "Yeah, I know."

They sat in silence for several minutes as Matthew finished his perusal of their finances. To his mind, Yvonne was still working miracles. The number of things she'd taken over and made her own astounded him on a daily basis. Even now that she was no longer a virtual prisoner on the Sparrow, she still worked harder than anyone else on the ship.

"You know," he said quietly, "with that bounty removed, you don't have to stay with us. We want you around, of course, but you're a doctor and—"

"Don't be an idiot, Matthew Cole," she snapped. "This is my place now."

"Hmm." And as expected, the moment her bounty was mentioned, the air in the room chilled. "I wish you'd tell me how it happened. I'm grateful, of course, for your sake, but I can't help but think there's more to the story."

She stared out the window. "It's fine. What happened is... private."

"And if you change your mind and need a willing ear, I'm on your side."

"I know that. And I won't. Are you through interrogating me?"

He sighed. "Yes. I've been up for over a day now. As often as I promise myself not to let this happen, it keeps happening." He stood. "Good night, Yvonne."

She muttered in response, and he left the cockpit for his cabin, too tired and bewildered to try to puzzle the mystery out any further.

Yvonne stared out the window for over an hour, her emotions twisted in a labyrinth that was impossible to unwind. She'd spent months trying.

If Matthew was still asking about what happened, then that meant he hadn't thought to look at the Sparrow's security footage of that day. The day Kudzu died and she regained her freedom.

It was a terrible idea. She knew it was, but she couldn't stop herself.

Quietly she stood and closed the door to the cockpit. Everyone else was asleep by now anyway, but an iron grip had closed around her heart. She turned the monitor back on and pulled up archive footage from the security cameras. It took her only a moment to find the timestamp.

There it was, as if it was yesterday. Her pulling the trigger and screaming at Kudzu, impotent in her rage. And then Piggy finishing the job. She looked away, part of her shocked at the violence of it all. Part of her disappointed it hadn't been her to end it. Piggy had set her free, but he'd denied her the closure she craved. Her lip curled in frustration as she watched the scene play a second time and made her decision.

Matthew would never understand. He'd be worse than Bishop Elias had been. Love your enemies and all. They'd even forgiven Grace's grandfather, Arthur Morgensen, of all people. But Kudzu wasn't Arthur Morgensen. Kudzu had been a monster. A murderer. She saw in her mind Tomas dead in their clinic as she saved the ungrateful animal's life.

No, Matthew would never understand, and he could never be allowed to see this footage. She grabbed a data chip and downloaded the video. Then she deleted it from the Sparrows archive.

Yvonne slipped the data chip into her pocket. It was better if they all just went on with their lives. Tomas and Kudzu were both gone. The loose ends had all been sorted.

And if any more reared their heads, she would deal with those ghosts herself.

Chapter 2: Lanterns in the Firmament

---◁◊▷---

My father, Emperor Dominic the Second of Venus, was one of history's more colorful characters. His love for grand stories and adventure is well known at this point, and I must stress that these accounts are true. Some have called my father a silly man, and a weak leader.

I won't argue the first, after all I grew up in the same household as him. But I must protest the latter.

What makes a good leader? Is it the one who's iron will can set the policies they see fit despite great opposition? One whose honeyed tongue eases all foreign powers?

Or is it one who does right by their people and is in turn loved?

My father perhaps wasn't the greatest at managing finances. He was a poor legal scholar. And he drove nearly all of his advisors mad, myself included. But he was a man whose eyes were clear, an idealist, more suited perhaps to poetry than wielding absolute authority over an entire planet. But then I fail to see what is so wrong with this. It is said that in Paradise, poets will have flames upon their heads.

If this is true, even now they bear the embers of those fires and are more precious than gold.

Julia of Venus
Daughter of Dominic of Venus
Died 140 AM

"Something is wrong with the clocks."

Davey looked up from the book he was reading on his tablet. Grace was standing frowning at the idle display on the entertainment monitor in the common room. "What do you mean?"

She pointed at the screen. "It jumped forward two seconds when the frameshift cut off. It does that sometimes. I've been watching for it."

"Maybe it's just adjusting for local time. Maybe the colonies can't stay perfectly lined up or something."

She shook her head. "It's always forward. Every time. Never once back."

He set the tablet down and stood from the couch. Part of him doubted her, but then he knew better than to second guess Grace on something like this. She was always good at watching the little details. "Okay, if that's the case then we're losing time."

"Just a few seconds a year. Maybe a minute. No, something is wrong with the clocks, I think."

"So go ask Matthew about it."

"Ask Matthew about what?" Yvonne said, coming from the aft ladder. She had a tub full of vegetables from her garden in the hold. Davey spotted his favorite, tomatoes, which meant dinner would be good for the next few months if she had a plant producing.

Grace explained the problem with the missing seconds. Yvonne nodded. "You're right. We're losing time."

Davey stopped short. "Wait, what?"

Yvonne set her tub on a counter and Grace hurried over to help her unload it. "We are losing time," Yvonne repeated. "In a sense. I explained this to you two a few months ago and you've already forgotten."

"We never asked about the clocks," Grace said, opening the fridge to load the produce.

"Not the tomatoes," Yvonne warned. "Those stay out or you ruin the

22

flavor. No, I explained some science about time."

Davey snapped his fingers. "Relativity. Something about time not always being the same depending on speed and gravity, right?"

"There you go." Yvonne smiled and handed a sack of peppers to Grace. "So why is the clock jumping forward?"

"Because..." he trailed off trying to make the connections. "While frameshifted, we're going fast. Like a fraction of the speed of light fast. So on a long trip, like Metis to Venus, time is going slower for us and the Sparrow's clock adjusts forward when we reach a destination."

"Very good," Yvonne said. "I said we were losing time, and in one sense we are. The rest of the universe rolls along at a normal rate while we go slightly slower. But you could also say we're gaining time because we're skipping forward in tiny little jumps. After years of living on a ship, a freelancer might add a couple hours to his life according to the calendar."

"And now my head hurts," Grace said.

"I doubt it makes much difference to daily life," Davey said. "A second here or there won't matter."

"For most things, no," Yvonne agreed. "There are some technical applications that require high precision timing and positional accuracy where those tiny slivers of time matter, but for everyday life, it makes little difference." She'd finished putting up the produce and leaned against the counter. "If Moses had ever worked out interstellar travel before he left that would be a different story."

"How's that?" Grace asked.

"Well the faster you go," Yvonne said "or the higher the gravity for that matter, the slower time goes. The closer you get to the speed of light, the more exaggerated the effect. At two percent the speed of light, relativity is a novelty. At ninety percent it's extreme."

"It's like one-way time travel," Davey mused, his mind spinning at the possibilities. "You can only travel to the future."

She nodded. "More or less. But Moses never got that far, despite all his promises that we'd colonize the stars."

"Pity," he said. "I'd like to get on a ship and drive around for a while at close to the speed of light. Jump far into the future and see what it's like a thousand years from now."

Yvonne smiled "And then you leave your world behind forever and never see the rest of us again."

"And you sucked all the fun out of that," Grace said. "Okay, I hereby declare the clocks to be functioning as expected. I'm heading to the cockpit. Venus is one of the cooler landings to watch."

Davey made to follow her but was stopped by Yvonne's hand on his shoulder. "Need something?" he asked, suddenly uncomfortable.

"Don't ever let anyone tell you that you're not intelligent, Davey."

He looked at his feet, unsure of where this was going.

"You're a bright young man. Quick to learn and adapt and understand. It's not your fault you never had a fair shot at an education. You got dealt a bad hand in life, but that doesn't make you stupid or less intelligent."

He shoved his hands in his pockets. "It's not a big deal. I'm fine with it. Really."

"You don't have to be," Yvonne said. "You're young and can still choose your own path."

Suddenly, Davey wanted to be anywhere but here. "Thanks, he mumbled," feeling his face turn red. What else did she expect him to say? She was overselling it. He knew that. He knew his limitations. He stepped past her to follow after Grace.

"Think about it," Yvonne said.

"Sure, I will," he muttered and intended to do no such thing.

Matthew pushed the flight yoke forward a few degrees and dipped the Sparrow into the upper reaches of Venus' atmosphere. The deck beneath his boots began to vibrate as atmospheric drag exerted tremendous forces on the hull. Friction would slow them down, which would save money on fuel. The flip side being they'd have to spend more to take off again.

Of course, if this was anything like their usual trips to Venus, Emperor Dominic would insist on filling their reserves himself. As much as he didn't like handouts, Matthew knew he should be thankful. And then there was Yvonne, who practically plotted reasons to come to Venus because the handouts kept the ink black.

Grace bounced into the cockpit and landed in the copilot's seat. "Venus sure is beautiful," she declared, eyeing the pale golden horizon beneath them.

He took in the readouts and relaxed. They were right on course for the city. "The Morning and the Evening Star. For thousands of years, the people of Earth thought it was special too."

"What do you think the emperor wants?"

He sighed. "Honestly, I have no idea. His message a few months back said he had a project he wanted to partner with us on. Your guess is as good as mine, but knowing Dominic it's going to be something dramatic."

"So what you're saying is, everyone else will love it and you're going to hate it." She gave him a glare intended to pin him in place. She picked that skill up from Abigail, and just like when that look came from her, he ignored this one too.

A moment later Davey joined them, but he didn't seem to be in a talkative mood and they all sat in silence watching the entry. By the time Yvonne shooed Grace out of the copilot's seat, they were in the thick of the atmosphere and rapidly descending. When they were in range, Matthew commed ahead. "Discordia tower control, this is SPW 5840 looking for a landing pad."

"SPW 5840, we have you on our scopes but we're not seeing you on the schedule. Please state your business."

"We have a standing invitation from Emperor Dominic that we're making good on. You may have to check with his people."

"One moment please."

The city came into view. A massive hexagonal-shaped station suspended on air bladders, it floated at an altitude where breathable air was buoyant in Venus' thick soup. Once there had been four such cities, but only two remained, Discordia and its sister, Concordia. The emperors of Venus had worked hard to protect the quality of life of their citizens and it showed. Few in the colonies would turn down a chance to live here.

"Anyone seen Abigail this morning?" he asked.

Yvonne shrugged. "It's barely nine o'clock."

"She usually gets up earlier when we're going planetside."

"Dominic will probably keep us up late demanding stories," Davey said. "She'll be glad she slept in when the welcome banquet lasts half the night."

"You never complain," Grace said, a mischievous tone coloring her voice. "At least not when Claudia is around."

25

Davey rounded on her. "Hey! I didn't give you any problems over your little boyfriend from Ceres. Claudia is a friend."

Grace's face turned red. "Jason isn't my boyfriend and, yes, you did give—"

"That's enough," Matthew cut her off. If this line of conversation continued, someone was going to bring up—

"Are you looking forward to seeing Julia?" Davey asked.

And there it was. Matthew adjusted the Sparrow's heading slightly as a strong crosswind set in. "Has the fact that I'm a priest been entirely forgotten?"

"Former priest," Grace said. "You're an eligible bachelor these days."

"Technically not true. I've not been laicized."

Davey threw up his arms in exasperation. "I don't even want to know what that means."

"Actually, I think you can legally marry," Yvonne said. "According to Pope Krupnik anyway. Celibacy is still encouraged but not strictly mandated anymore due to—"

"Why do you even know that?" Matthew asked. He looked at the comm begging tower control to give him landing permission. Anything to end this conversation.

"I was curious," Grace said, "and had Yvonne look that last part up. I say you're an eligible bachelor and need to keep your mind open to the possibilities." She winked aggressively.

The comm crackled and Matthew breathed a prayer of thanks. "SPW 5840, this is Tower Control. You are cleared for landing at the Royal Hanger. Enjoy your stay."

"Thanks, Tower." Matthew finished the approach to the city. The hanger was on the trailing side of the city at the moment, making landing an easy task. With a gentle bump, he set the ship down on the deck. "Someone go beat on Abigail's door. It's time to start the day." In hindsight, he was glad she'd slept in. The last thing he needed was her heckling him as well.

The portside airlock opened and Abigail followed Matthew out into the spacious hangar. She stifled a yawn as she shielded her eyes from the harsh glare of the overhead lamps. At the bottom of the ramp stood four crimson armored security guards. And behind them...

Oh great. Ms. Legs was here. Julia, eldest daughter of Emperor Dominic the Second, stood with a smile on her face. She wore a crimson and silver coat over an ankle-length skirt. The whole getup had a light and airy look, more like she was dressed for a picnic than business.

Matthew nodded to the guards. "All weapons have been left behind on the ship, as usual. And the Shield Maiden has special permission to wear her armor in public on Discordia." They parted and allowed Julia to step forward.

"Well, well, Matthew Cole," she said. "You and your crew can't seem to stay out of trouble, can you?"

He took his hat off and bowed politely. "Believe it or not, we try to keep ourselves out of the limelight. There have just been complications lately."

She smiled wryly. "Is that so? I'm starting to think that dad is right about you. But I'll let him speak for himself" She smiled at Abigail. "Ms. Sharon, I hope you're doing well."

Abigail honestly did her best to return the smile, but she had a feeling it was more like a pinched grimace. "Well enough, for all the difficulty it is keeping Matthew alive. That's quite a trick on some days. I thought you spent most of your time on Concordia. I wasn't expecting you to greet us today."

"My term as Concordia's Trade Minister ended six months ago and I'm currently serving my father in an advisory role. When I heard of your arrival, I dropped what I was doing and came this way." She looked past them at the opening into the Sparrow. "Is the rest of your crew here? You are all invited to brunch in the palace gardens. Sadly, my father will not be able to join us until the evening as he has prior engagements."

Matthew shared a quick glance with Abigail. "I'll get the rest," she shrugged and turned back toward the Sparrow. Unsurprisingly, the other members of the crew were lurking just inside the open airlock.

"Ha, told you Julia would be here," Davey said, and then grunted as Grace elbowed him.

"Come on," Abigail grumbled. "Your faces aren't going to stuff themselves." She spun on her heel and marched back down the ramp, not really caring if her manners were lacking. There was a whisper behind her back but she decided it was better for everyone if she just ignored it.

"It's good to see each of you again," Julia called to the group. "If you'll all follow me, please."

Abigail didn't fail to notice the guard falling into place behind them. As they left the hangar via a long-arched hall, Davey nudged her. "See the pikes those guys have? You should get one of those. A shield is cool and all, but a pike...?"

Abigail eyed the long slender weapon the guards carried and the wicked curved blade at the top. "Remember the Swiss Guard at the Vatican? All pomp and circumstance, and if you look at them wrong, precision and death. I guarantee you the guns come out when things get nasty."

"Right. But you could have a giant blade and a giant shield." She frowned at Davey, but he just shrugged. "I'm just saying it would be awesome and you should keep your options open."

The hallway emptied out into a large garden, the same one that had held Julia's disastrous thirtieth birthday party not quite two years ago. Then, it had been filled with costumed guests. Now it looked like a good spot to curl up for a nap. High above, yellow light filtered down through skylights onto rows of hedges and cool fountains. An open grassy area was set with tables and a dozen or more palace servants ran about setting places with utensils.

"Brunch will be ready in about half an hour," Julia said. She placed a hand on her hip. "You'll have to forgive the wait. You didn't exactly give us much warning."

"This really isn't necessary," Matthew insisted. "We've had breakfast already and—"

"It was cold oatmeal," Abigail said. "Please don't let Matthew's humility interfere with your generosity. We're starving freelancers and when someone offers real food, we take it."

"Amen to that," Yvonne muttered. Davey and Grace both nodded. Thankfully, Matthew bit his tongue and let the matter slide.

Julia gave them a mischievous smile. "Matthew's overdeveloped sense of propriety has no power here. You're welcome to enjoy the gardens until then. I'm going to see if any of my brothers and sisters are free to join us." Abigail nudged Davey at the same time that Grace did, and he nearly fell to the floor. The Venusians nearby, including Julia,

28

were polite enough to ignore them.

Matthew just gave them all a tired glare. "I'd like to get through today without mortal embarrassment, if that's okay with the rest of you."

Brunch was everything you'd expect at the palace of an emperor and Yvonne had scarcely eaten so well in her life. There were smoked salmon toasts with herbs, fried eggs on ratatouille, asparagus frittatas, and more that she wouldn't have been able to try if she had a week of breakfasts.

"Are you sure you weren't expecting the pope himself?" she politely asked Empress Vivian.

Vivian was only a few years younger than Yvonne, the youngest of her eight children being three years younger than Grace. "The crew of the Sparrow are friends of the throne and will be even closer if my husband has anything to say on the matter."

"We've been wondering what this was about."

"I'm afraid you'll have to wonder a little longer. Dominic would be crushed if I blabbed about his grand idea."

Some ways down the table, Davey and Grace sat with the younger batch of imperial kids. "I notice that one of your children is absent," Yvonne said. "Claudia, I think her name was."

"Claudia just started her first term at the University of Ganymede three weeks ago." Vivian took a sip from her tea. "She was fortunate to have made the required marks. They don't grant special privilege to anyone, not even the imperial family. Which I'm thankful for. We don't practice primogeniture here on Venus, and someday when my husband abdicates to his chosen successor, they will have to stand as private citizens on their own merits."

That was something that Yvonne could respect. It also pleased her that even the richest in the solar system couldn't just buy their way into her alma mater. "Claudia is due a congratulations on her achievement then, though I think the younger crewmen were looking forward to seeing her."

"Claudia was quite disappointed that the Sparrow didn't make it here before her departure. I think she may have been hoping to see a certain young man."

"Is that so?" Yvonne asked, drinking from her coffee. And what glorious coffee it was. She wondered if the Sparrow could afford it. "Pity."

"Pity indeed," Vivian said and laughed.

For a moment, Yvonne felt like a mother sharing a conspiratorial moment with another mother. It was a surreal thought. In some ways, she was like a mother to the rest of Sparrow, but it was a job she was ill-suited for. Nurturing had never really been in her nature. If she and Tomas had been able to have kids, he would have been the one the kids ran to when they skinned their knees. There was more to mothering than simply doting upon injuries and hurt feelings but she had learned none of that. Matthew was good at the parental role, his time as a father in the church had prepared him to deal with, well, all of them. For the briefest moment, she imagined a future where Tomas was on the Sparrow with them. It would have been perfect, for all of them.

Vivian was saying something. "I'm sorry," Yvonne said. "I missed that last part." She'd been caught daydreaming, of all things, and in polite company.

Vivian was courteous enough not to miss a beat. "I was saying that there will be other times. And that she wasn't my only daughter to take an interest in the Sparrow's men."

Yvonne glanced down the table to where Matthew sat sandwiched between Julia and Abigail. Julia looked like the only one that was enjoying herself. "I hope she doesn't get her hopes up."

"Are he and Ms. Sharon together then?"

Yvonne nearly choked on her frittata. "Excuse me. No, they aren't, but some days I wonder at the possibility. I mostly meant she shouldn't get her hopes up because Matthew Cole is..." She searched for a word that was both polite and accurate. "Romantically challenged." She smiled so the other woman knew she was joking, but they were both interrupted before she could respond.

"My friends, it is good to see you all!" Yvonne turned to see Emperor Dominic the Second, entering the courtyard with a cadre of guards. The brown-bearded man wore a bright crimson tunic with a silver sash. Yvonne appreciated the strange styles of Venus. It was one of the few places in the solar system that had a truly new culture, rather than endlessly iterating on a lost homeland.

Vivian stood and went to her husband at once. "What are you doing here? You have your meeting with the Warszawan Prime Minister!"

Dominic made a dismissive gesture. "That can wait. We all know we'll both sign the treaty as soon as the adjustments are made. This is far more important." Yvonne smiled at the way he avoided Vivian's keen glare.

Matthew stood as the man approached him and dipped his head respectfully. "We appreciate the invitation. We've had some business to finish up these last few months and are sorry about the delay."

Dominic extended his hand to him, and Yvonne noticed that Matthew hesitated for a split second before taking it. "I said to come at your leisure," Dominic said. "But please continue your meal. My children, I'll have to ask you to part the waters for me. I need to speak with the freelancer and his crew."

The younger royals grumbled as they made room across the table from Matthew. Vivian and Yvonne also moved closer to where the business would be occurring. A servant tried to approach Dominic with food. "No, thank you, Cecil, I'm fine for now, but something to drink would be wonderful." He turned to Matthew. "I believe you owe me a story of your recent adventures. I'm rather looking forward to hearing the details on how you saved Ceres."

To his credit, Matthew took a breath and dove right in, rather than protesting. The tale was amended on occasion by other crew members, particularly the parts where Matthew wasn't involved, and on occasion Dominic had questions. But at length he finished the tale. Satisfied at last, Dominic sat back and stroked his thick beard. "Amazing. Even better than the news stories. They entirely left out Grace's part, and that seems to have been the beating heart of it all."

"We thought it best to protect Arthur by keeping her out of the public eye," Matthew said.

"That was wise, but I am glad to know the true story. Consider your debt repaid."

"About that," Matthew said. "I'd like to pay you back for the loan. I appreciate what you saved us in interest. If a freelancer can't stand on their own two feet, they won't be in the business long."

Vivian chuckled, and placed a hand on her husband's arm. "I told you this was going to happen, dear."

Dominic crossed his arms. "I laid out the terms. I bought your loan in exchange for an account of your most recent exploits, which you have paid in full. I won't take one penny from you."

At this Yvonne gave Matthew a look. "And I told you that was going to happen."

She hoped Matthew wasn't going to insist on a fight he was destined to lose. Instead, he nodded. "Then I'll have to offer you my thanks."

Dominic smiled. "Now about this idea I've had for a while. It's a big one. And I want you and the Sparrow to be the face of it." The table quieted down and all eyes turned toward the emperor. "What if there was an organization for the freelancers. The good ones. And I don't mean the ones that are good at their jobs. I mean the moral heroes out there fighting the good fight, like you guys. Any citizen that wants to ensure that they hire an honest freelancer, those that make the solar system a better place, would be able to put in their request to the organization."

"Like the League of Heroes in Splendid Sam." All eyes turned to Davey. He turned red and shrank into himself as he realized who he had interrupted. "Sorry."

"Precisely like the League," Dominic said, growing more excited by the minute. "And just like the League has its champion in Splendid Sam, our organization will have its champion too. What do you say, Matthew Cole?"

Yvonne wasn't surprised to find out that the emperor was a fan of pulp radio dramas, not with the way he romanticized adventure. Nor was she surprised that Matthew had gone still as stone, probably mortified that he was being asked to be part of this.

It was a funny thing to watch the slow evolution of the gruff former priest. Once a quiet and private man, he kept getting drawn into the thick of things, like the universe just couldn't leave him alone. And somehow he made things better. Perhaps it was the rare mixture of strength, and gentle compassion. In a universe where the weak were crushed, he was an anomaly who transformed those around him. Abigail was once little more than an armored ruffian, only mitigated by the fact that the people she beat up were usually the bad guys. Now she looked for excuses to be just the sort of hero Dominic wanted to fill his organization with. And Davey, he wasn't even recognizable from the dangerous young man that had first stepped foot on the Sparrow.

For a moment Yvonne wondered if she was any better off. Then she saw in her mind Kudzu's broken body on Ceres and decided that wasn't the case. Maybe if circumstances had been different. She'd never asked for Tomas to be murdered.

But Matthew was like Tomas. An upright and moral man. And Yvonne knew good and well that he wouldn't turn Dominic down. He might complain and insist there was a better man for the job, but Matthew was the worst judge of his own worth. Even Whitaker could see what everyone else saw.

Those gathered at the brunch table watched Matthew as the silence dragged out. At last, he swallowed. "You've got the wrong man, Emperor. You're gonna need someone that's good in front of cameras and I'd just as soon avoid the attention."

"Don't listen to him," Yvonne said sharply. "Of course he'll do it."

"Don't you think I have a say in this?" Matthew asked.

She met his gaze without flinching. "You seem to think you'll say no. At least hear him out before you refuse." She knew quite well that if this was a serious endeavor Matthew would eventually agree to it. The man couldn't do the wrong thing if he wanted to. And this was the kind of thing he'd been born for.

He was silent for a good minute before continuing. "There's a lot to talk about before I come anywhere near agreeing," Matthew said. "Which I've not done."

"Yet," Yvonne said.

He ignored her and turned back to the emperor. "What's your part in this?"

"Financial sponsor and public relations. I'll pay for overhead. I can also help negotiate with the Broker's Alliance. I offer you my lawyers and accountants to make the backend work. But I need you to be the figurehead. The face of the organization. I also want you to vet potential members. I imagine you can call to mind prospective candidates as we speak."

"I can think of a few, but you may be disappointed to find that there aren't many freelancers with clean records."

"Not at all." Dominic folded his hands together on the table. "You'll be able to offer crews a second chance at being the good guys. You've made quite a stir the last few years. We may find them flocking to your rallying call."

Matthew laughed darkly. "They'll be disappointed to discover that money doesn't come with the kind of fame I bring."

"But fame is enough for some. And for others, the chance to do something new will be even better. The colonies haven't had much hope since Moses left. Our death sentence was signed. It was always just a matter of how long it would take. Give enough men a chance to be heroes though, a chance to make a difference... Why, we might just be granted a stay of execution, at least for a time."

Matthew looked at each of his crew as if for confirmation. Yes, we will follow you down any road, Yvonne thought. We trust you. He seemed to hold Abigail's gaze for a second longer before she smiled and nodded.

"Alright," he said. Let's go somewhere more private and talk. Abigail and Yvonne. Come with us. You're as big a part of this as I am."

Dominic smiled. He was going to get his League of Heroes or whatever they ended up calling it. Matthew had as good as made his decision. Yvonne was hardly surprised.

Part of Grace wanted to be annoyed that the adults had left her and Davey behind. Then she thought about how boring their conversation was going to be. Probably all talk about money and rules and business.

Which meant that Matthew was going to be doing whatever Yvonne thought best and Abigail would regret being there. Grace had been around enough conversations on the Sparrow to know how this was going to go.

She was startled from her train of thought when someone sat beside her at the table.

"Hello, Grace."

It was Nicolas, the member of the royal family closest to her own age. She gave him a blank look.

"I just came to see if you wanted to—"

"Do you remember that time at your sister's birthday that you made fun of my dress?" She narrowed her eyes. "Because I remember."

Nicolas' mouth hung open. "Oh. Right. Maybe later then."

"No, I don't think so. Have a good life."

He practically ran away. Grace just smiled smugly.

"He's not come back to the ship," Davey said.

Abigail frowned at that. "Okay thanks, I'll find him." She groaned and put her comm away. She'd tried calling Matthew an hour ago, but he wasn't answering. He'd either left his comm somewhere, which was unlike him, or was trying to avoid everyone, also unusual. This meant he was in a particularly bad mood. Maybe he was in the gardens.

It had been a long week. Endless meetings hashing out the details of how the organization would function. Emperor Dominic had been periodically present, but he was a busy man and it was Julia who had really taken over the task from that end. A lot of the groundwork had been laid before they'd arrived, but Matthew and Abigail were needed for their expertise on the way the freelancer business worked. Yvonne of course was brilliant and managed to slide right into place, offering excellent suggestions. And then there were the other advisors Julia had brought in. A pair of lawyers to write up the charter, an accountant to go over the financial plan, and more.

Abigail was exhausted, but she thought that this thing might just work. Only now, their brave leader had up and disappeared sometime after dinner. A voice in the back of her head insisted that he obviously didn't want to be found, meaning he wouldn't be happy to see her. But she was going to ignore that.

The garden looked empty too. She heard a sound behind her.

"Good evening, Shield Maiden." Julia curtsied, her skirts swishing softly at the motion.

Abigail was annoyed that, of all people, she ran into the one person on Venus that inexplicably rubbed her the wrong way. But then that wasn't quite true and she knew it. "Good evening, Julia," she said, doing her best to keep her tone cheerful and polite. Hopefully she didn't overdo it. "What brings you out to the gardens?"

Julia raised an eyebrow. "I was looking for our friend Matthew, but he's made himself scarce. And by your reaction I suspect you were doing the same."

"Guilty as charged. He's not on the ship, not in the dining hall, the conference rooms, the gardens. I'm out of ideas. Know anywhere else quiet he could disappear to?"

Julia crossed her arms. "There are observation platforms to view the clouds, the library, or perhaps he even left the palace grounds." Suddenly she snapped her fingers. "Or there's a small chapel here. Down past the receiving hall. I can't imagine a better place for a former priest to sequester himself away."

"Right. Thanks." Abigail paused awkwardly for a minute. "Well I guess we can head that way together."

"That's alright. I'll let you check on him." Julia smiled softly. "I misjudged you, you know. I had assumed you were just the hired muscle. Turns out you're a consummate professional. If you hadn't been here to give advice, things would look quite different."

A compliment was the last thing Abigail was expecting. But that meant she had to return it. Blasted social expectations. "I misjudged you too, you know. I assumed you were just eyelashes and a pair of legs." Julia laughed awkwardly, and Abigail realized she probably didn't even know that she was a paraplegic. Who knows how she interpreted that one? "What I mean is that this wouldn't be possible at all without you. Your father may have had the idea—"

"Stolen from radio dramas."

"Right. But you made it happen." She paused. "Has your father always been like that?"

"An idealistic dreamer? As long as I can remember. That's why the last emperor chose him as his successor. I was nine at the time. We had to drop our last name, and dad even changed his first to follow in his predecessor's footsteps. None of my brothers or sisters really remember his coronation."

Abigail wondered if her own father was rotting in prison. Probably. She felt the old familiar tug of guilt but there wasn't anything she could do about it now. "Well, I'm glad he's the one running Venus. I'll... uhh, go check on Matthew I guess."

Julia curtsied again and left. Abigail watched her for a minute and then turned to reenter the palace. The guards eyed her as she passed but let her be. The Sparrow crew had been given near free run of the grounds, outside of certain high security areas. It also made the place start to feel like home, the way they were treated. She walked through the long halls to the receiving room and then continued past it. Julia said the chapel would be around here somewhere.

There. An open set of double doors led into a small room filled with pews. A simple stained-glass window adorned the back of the room. It was backlit and cast colored light across the chamber. On the front pew Matthew sat, his hat off, and his head bowed.

He was praying.

All at once she felt guilty for searching him out. She was obviously barging in on a private moment. She backed away from the door as slowly as she could, aware that in the quiet chapel the whine of the servo motors in her suit were painfully loud.

Matthew raised his head. "I hear you back there."

"Sorry, I... I'll leave you be."

"It's fine. Come in."

She walked down the aisle to the front bench and sat on the floor beside it. "I didn't mean to intrude," she offered weakly.

"I'm just looking for a bit of peace," he said. "I never wanted this sort of life. I never asked to be shoved stumbling into the spotlight."

"Any luck?"

He turned to her and frowned. "What?"

"At finding peace."

He sighed. "I don't know. I don't think I've been at peace since my first year at the Vatican seminary. Since then it's been one long string of crises. Some day... Some day it will be nice to retire from this life. I'll miss the travel. But for a little peace of mind I'd happily give it up. And now I'm being asked to do more." He exhaled a quiet laugh. "But I have the peace that if this is the path that God sets before me, then it's the one I should take. At least for a season."

Abigail shook her head. "You make it look easy, you know. Faith. Praying. I was raised in a household that believed God existed, but that was about it."

"You didn't practice then?"

"We certainly weren't Orthodox." She sighed. "Look, Matthew. You can do this. We can do this together."

He stood to his feet. "I know. I'm just... tired. It's been a long week."

Abigail laughed. "No kidding. I never imagined when I laid you out on the street in Kyoto that someday we'd be out to revolutionize the business. Come on. Get some rest. You'll need it for the press conference tomorrow."

Matthew wilted in his boots. "Don't remind me."

The next day, the crew of the Sparrow, dozens of Venusian dignitaries, the entire royal family, and Venus' entire press corp gathered in the palace's receiving room. Dominic's throne had been moved and a podium had been placed on the dais. The room was hectic, chaotic, and, to Davey at least, a completely alien experience.

"I don't understand half of what's going on," he muttered to Yvonne.

"Theatrics," she replied. "Dominic wants to start things off with a bang. What better way to do so than with cameras? By the end of the day half the solar system will be talking about Matthew Cole's new organization."

"But what good is that going to even do?" Grace asked.

"In theory, it softens the freelancers up to the idea. That way as Matthew and Abigail try to recruit some of them over the next few months, they're more receptive. If the public has a positive outlook on this little operation, then the freelancers will want in on it. It will be good for business, as a bonus. Let's go take a seat."

The three of them fought their way through the crowds to a spot near the stage and chose a seat among the quickly filling rows. Davey made sure Grace was on the inside and found himself sandwiched between her and a total stranger, a reporter from a Ganymede news outlet if his badge and lanyard were anything to go by.

Impatient, he looked around the room. The opulence barely even drew his notice after being in the palace for a week. The shining columns of marble, elegant crimson tapestries, and graceful arches were familiar to his eyes. He'd even learned the names of a bunch of the servants and guards. It was weird. He was starting to feel an itch to be back out in the Sparrow. Maybe it was the wanderlust that he'd heard other freelancers talk about. He'd been a little disappointed that Claudia was gone, but then there was always next time. Venus was always going to be a friendly port for the Sparrow.

Emperor Dominic took the stage and the room quieted almost at once. "My friends! I am thankful that you have all joined us today."

Davey noticed he was dressed up in even more elaborate fineries than normal. He tried to imagine a life where you had to deal with that level of overkill on a daily basis. He would hate it, though the money that came with it wouldn't be bad.

Dominic began a long speech about the state of the solar system. The decline of humanity. The dire straits they were all in. All in all, it was a gloomy picture.

"Sheesh, talk about being a downer," Grace whispered.

Davey nodded, feeling it was inappropriate to reply when everyone else's attention was fixed on the emperor.

"But," Dominic said. "We are not without hope, not until the last child ceases to draw breath. And I judge that time is far away and may yet never come. Because today, I announce something new. Something to push back the clouds that have gathered around us. Allow me to introduce my partner in this endeavor." From off stage, Matthew and Abigail appeared and joined him. A murmur rippled through the crowd. The press knew them both by sight after the Ceres Incident. Dominic smiled and continued. "That's right. You know this man for his actions. For the character of his deeds. He is a hero. A defender of the weak. A strong arm guided by a gentle hand." He paused for effect. "And now he calls others of like mind to himself. Today we announce the Guild of Lanterns. We shall fill it with the most exceptional of free-lancers. They will be a light in the dark, upright men and women who will fight for civilization and against the coming night. We will pit the Lanterns against the cartels, the syndicates, the Abrogationists, and any who raise their hand against the good of their neighbor."

The well-behaved crowd lost all sense of propriety as the whole room began talking at once. Davey chuckled. Dominic's flair for the dramatic came in handy at times like this. He gestured to Matthew. "But I will allow the Gaucho to speak for himself."

The room immediately silenced and nearly everyone leaned forward to hear him speak.

Matthew stepped to the podium and looked out over the audience. He met Davey's eyes, if only for a moment, and Davey saw the ghost of a smile pass over his features. Davey knew Matthew had been practicing this speech for several days. Hopefully it came out as well as they all hoped.

"I can't claim half the praise that the emperor heaps on my shoulders. I'm just one man. A failed priest turned freelancer. It's been a long road. A hard one. The truth I've learned is a simple one. We all have our kingdoms, the things we have influence over. Not all of us can change the tide of history or civilization, but we can see to our own little realm. I never asked to be called a hero or to be given a voice among the great. But that's the kingdom I've been given. And by God's grace, I'll uphold that trust."

His gaze fell around the room. "To any freelancers out there that are honorable and true, expect to hear from me. And to those that have faltered and taken the easy road? Now is the time to think about who you are. The guild will need many lanterns, even imperfect ones."

He moved back from the podium and the room erupted in conversation. Dominic stepped back to the microphone and the noise died down. "At this time we will take a few questions from the press."

Every hand in the room shot up and every voice started shouting. Davey saw Matthew's eyes widen ever so slightly in horror and had to stifle his own smile. This was the part Matthew had been afraid of. Looks like those fears had been justified.

By the end of the day, over three dozen messages were waiting for Matthew. Yvonne had been keeping an eye on them as they came in, laughing as she read the subject lines. Most of them were from news organizations demanding interviews. A few were from curious freelancers. One message had a particularly strongly worded subject line. It was from Benny, their broker. To be fair, he had a right to be angry given that they had neglected to talk to him about any of this. There was also a message from Bishop Elias. She moved that one to the top of the pile. Matthew would want to read it first.

There was also one from Whitaker. They hadn't heard much from him since Ceres. With no leads on the last Anemoi piece, he'd probably gone back to chasing Abrogationists and being the generally manipulative villain that he was. If Yvonne had to guess, he would be pleased over these developments. She moved it to low priority. No need to raise Matthew's blood pressure any further. He'd been a knot of stress ever since the grilling that afternoon.

She laid her tablet aside on the bench and looked across the receiving room. The last of the reporters were long since gone, but Matthew and Abigail were still deep in conversation with Dominic and Julia. The kids had wandered off. Probably to the garden. Growing up in underground cities, they were drawn like magnets to live greenery.

Her tablet chimed and she glanced at the next message. Another freelancer interested in talking to Matthew. She knew this one by reputation and moved them before the reporters on the list. He might want to check this one out.

She glanced up as the others approached her. "I've been playing secretary for you, Matthew. It seems you've suddenly become a very popular man. You have forty-three messages to deal with."

"That was the intention," he said. "Are you ready to go?"

She frowned. "We're leaving right now?"

"There's work to do, and time is wasting."

Dominic smiled. "For all his protestations, he has thrown himself into the work. I knew this would be a success."

"It's not a success yet," Matthew cautioned. "We've a long way to go before we can say that. Call the kids Yvonne. Have them meet us at the Sparrow." He turned to Dominic and Julia. "You'll hear from us soon, and often, as we build the roster."

"We're eager to get started," Julia said. "I'll be talking to the Broker's Alliance later this evening."

Abigail grimaced. "Benny isn't going to be very happy with us," she said quietly.

"No, he's not," Yvonne said, waving the tablet. She stood to her feet and smoothed her shirt. "Let's not tarry. I've already got freelancers wanting to talk to you and we can go over the list this evening."

"We'll get to those," Matthew said, holding up his hand. "But I've already got my first candidate in mind."

"Oh?" Abigail asked. "Do I know this person?"

"You've met."

Yvonne crossed her arms. "Has this person shot at us?"

Matthew grinned and shrugged. "Maybe."

Chapter 3: Allies and Enemies

One of the things that most people take for granted is the supply chain that ensures that their daily needs are provided for. The average citizen has a vague notion of the places where food is grown, usually in orbital hydroponics facilities or the occasional surface farm. They know that, unless they are paying a premium, their meat is grown from cultures in labs.

They even know that the equipment that lets them walk with standard gravity comes from a pair of factories on Mars and Ganymede.

But the rest? Total ignorance on the part of the public. Most have no idea of the intricate lines of supply that keep daily life in the colonies moving. Maybe it's better that way. Better not to know you're only a crisis away from starving or suffocation.

And then there are the, shall we say, professionals that deal with earthtech. Militaries, police, freelancers, the Vatican. Either you know where it comes from, or you know better than to ask questions of those that do. That black market is one of the most closely guarded secrets in the solar system.

Boris Metcalf
Freelancer on Titan
Died 103 AM

"This wouldn't be nearly as much of a nuisance if we'd allowed even a day between these meetings," Yvonne said.

Matthew finished shoving the last few things he'd need overnight into his bag and looked up to where she leaned against the doorframe of his cabin. "You don't have to tell me that. Unfortunately, this was the only time both crews would be in the Jupiter neighborhood. You guys will be back from Callisto in a day."

"I just... Look, I'm not a fan of us splitting up."

He zipped the bag and threw it over his shoulder. Just clothes for a couple of nights in case something delayed the Sparrow. It was that chance of a delay that was worrying Yvonne. "I know," he said. "This won't be like Ceres, I promise. We won't make this a habit."

Her features relaxed ever so slightly. "Hurry up then. I'm ready to deorbit."

Matthew stepped out into the hall and rapped his knuckles on Davey's door. "Time to go."

It slid open. "I'm on my way," he muttered around the ration bar that stuck out of his mouth. "There's never enough time in the mornings."

"You've known this was the plan for three days," Matthew said as they walked to the common room. "You could have been packed already."

"You just finished packing yourself!" Yvonne shouted from the cockpit.

"Except I got up early enough to eat something better than a ration bar," Matthew said. "See you soon, Yvonne."

"Stay out of trouble."

He and Davey climbed down the ladder into the hold where Grace and Abigail were prepping the bikes.

"We aren't going to take Vanquisher," Davey said. "Just Matthew's bike."

Grace stopped pushing the chopper toward the lift. "Why not?"

"To save fuel," Matthew said. "We're not going to be splitting up anyway."

She grumbled and returned the bike to its corner. Davey ran to help her lock it down. Matthew joined Abigail at the lift. "You good on this?"

"I don't see what could possibly go wrong," she said. "Gebre'elwa's crew was one of the first to contact us and what I know of her fits."

"Have you guys met?"

She shook her head. "I know the freelancers that frequent Mars pretty well and anyone that worked with Mistress Medvedev, but the shipboard crews and I didn't cross paths that often. Everyone in the business knows her reputation though. Don't worry. I've got the sales pitch. You weren't going to be able to do all of the recruiting by yourself, anyway."

"Deorbiting now," Yvonne said over the intercom. The engines roared as the Sparrow slowed its velocity on approach to Ganymede's surface. In just a few minutes, they were at their destination. Matthew and Davey stepped out onto the lift and mounted the bike.

"Take care!" Grace said. "We'll be back soon. Call if you need us."

Matthew frowned. "It isn't us I'm worried about."

"Don't let Grace do anything reckless," Davey said.

"As if anyone could stop me," Grace replied.

Abigail waved a quick goodbye and activated the lift. The platform lowered Matthew and Davey down, but not to the ground. The icy surface of Ganymede was an indistinct blur around a hundred feet below them. The Sparrow cruised over the colony's outskirts to keep from wasting fuel on landing. "Hang on," Matthew said and gunned the bike's engines. They flew off the platform and plummeted toward the ground. As they approached, the bike's grav plates kicked in and slowed their breakneck descent. Even so, they nearly bottomed out as Matthew fired the brakes and slid to a stop.

The Sparrow pulled up, and the main engines flared brightly as it burned for orbit and Callisto beyond. "There they go," he mumbled.

"I'm surprised you're okay with this," Davey said from behind him.

"I'm not, but we do what we must to redeem the time. Let's get into town."

He turned the bike and drove towards the lights below them. The southern polar colony of Gilgamesh was one that Matthew had seldom visited. Named after the ancient crater basin in which it was built, Gilgamesh was an industrial city, built around one of the solar system's two grav plate factories. Owned and operated by the colony itself, the factory was one of the key pieces of infrastructure that kept life in the colonies possible. Between it and its sister in Kyoto, thousands of grav plates were produced each year to make grav vehicles, outfit ships with gravity, and replace aging colony infrastructure.

Ultimately it was a losing battle on that last one. As the colonies aged, more and more of the grav plates that maintained standard gravity were beginning to fail. They were expensive to replace, and output from the factories was increasingly being divided between the creation of new vehicles and the maintenance of old systems. It was a ticking time bomb, one that, in a generation or two, would throw the solar system into chaos as economies were forced to make hard choices. The pressure was already being felt in cities like Blight that couldn't afford to renew what was lost.

And living in low gravity was more than just an inconvenience. Loss of muscle and bone mass brought a rapid deterioration of health unless vigorous calisthenic regimens were maintained. No way the entire human race was going to be able pull that off.

"I'm guessing that's the factory?" Davey shouted from behind him.

Matthew nodded, exaggerating the gesture so Davey could see it from the back. He slowed the bike so they wouldn't have to shout over the roar of the wind. "Gilgamesh exists to support the one facility." The city was arranged in concentric circles around a massive building visible from miles away. Those rings were punctured by spokes of raised monorails branching outward from the center hub of the factory.

"I thought the factory was mostly automated." Matthew half turned in surprise. "I was reading up on Gilgamesh on the way here," Davey said with a shrug.

"Good," Matthew said. "It's never a bad thing for a freelancer to know the territory. The production lines themselves are automated, but logistics are handled by human hands. Plus, a lot of the plates are modified as needed. Moses may have made sure that we couldn't reverse engineer the production lines themselves, but that hasn't stopped us from tinkering with the finished product."

"I thought we didn't understand grav plates or how they worked?"

Matthew pulled the bike onto a road in an outlying residential area. It looked to be the end of one of the main spokes leading into the city. "We understand the principles involved and most of the math. Grav plates actually aren't all that different from the frameshift devices that move us from place to place."

"They don't seem all that alike to me."

"You'd be wrong there. Both work by changing the reference frame in a shaped area around the device. Gravity and motion aren't so different at a fundamental level."

Davey huffed. "This is about relativity again, isn't it?"

"Exactly. We figured out the math even before Moses left. You can thank Jose Eschevarria, the same physicist that worked out the limitations of the frameshift device in his famous Eschevarria Equations. It's the actual engineering work we can't reproduce. We have no way of manufacturing the atomic level crystalline lattices used in grav plates. At that scale, quantum effects get in the way, and whatever techniques Moses used to get around those inconveniences were lost with him."

The residential areas were growing denser, and now there were other vehicles on the road with them. Davey was quiet for a few minutes. Finally, he spoke up. "Why did Moses keep that kind of knowledge from us?"

"A question for the ages," Matthew said. "The short answer is we don't know, but a popular theory is the invention of the thumper."

"What does that have to do with anything?"

"Moses didn't invent the thumper."

Davey paused briefly before filling in the lines. "We did. We took his grav plates, applied what we knew of them, probably from that Eschevarria guy's research, and made a weapon. So then he hid how to make grav plates from us. To slow us down, I guess. Or maybe punish us."

Matthew smiled, pleased that Davey had come to the correct conclusion. "That's the theory."

"But it doesn't really make sense. It seems... short-sighted. He had to have known we'd make weapons. Why would he condemn us to death for doing the sort of things humans have always done?"

"More good questions. And your guess is as good as the so-called experts. Perhaps he miscalculated. He was an AI, not God. And maybe that's the real takeaway. We're never too clever, never too wise, not to make a mess of things." Traffic ground to a halt as they reached a major intersection. He frowned at the sudden congestion. "It's a good thing we're early because we're going to be stuck here for a while."

Callisto was just a short frameshift away from Ganymede. The furthest out of the four Galilean moons was a dark patchwork of craters beneath them. Yvonne checked her controls and then made a slight adjustment to her orbit. "We'll rendezvous with the Queen of Sheba in just a few minutes," she said.

"Wait, we don't get to go down to the surface?" Grace asked.

"Not this time," Abigail said. "The Queen isn't the sort of ship you take planetside, so we're going to meet her in orbit."

Grace leaned forward to peer out the window. "Why's that?"

"You'll see," Yvonne said. She rechecked their position and used the maneuvering thrusters to rotate the Sparrow away from the moon's surface. She burned the engines for another brief second. "Right about now," she said as she swung the Sparrow back around.

Between them and Callisto was the super-freighter, the Queen of Sheba. The largest part of the ship was an elegant structure easily four times the dimensions of the Sparrow. Behind that, a long spine extended nearly seven hundred meters. Periodic spurs jutted from either side, to which were attached hundreds of cargo containers. Behind that sat the massive primary engine structure.

Abigail whistled. "Can you imagine making enough money as a freelancer that you can afford a monster like that?"

Yvonne smirked. "When you're not running your ship like a charity? Maybe."

Grace leaned forward. "Are those smaller ships on the belly?"

"Probably," Yvonne said. "Super-freighters usually carry a dozen or more single-pilot interceptors for defense. Pick a fight with this one and you'll get swarmed." She flipped on the comm. "Queen of Sheba, this is the Sparrow. Thanks for agreeing to meet us."

"We were in the area," came the dry rasp of an older woman. "I'm glad you could make it before we had to set out for Mars. You're welcome to come aboard. I'll light a beacon at our ventral half-dock."

"Half-dock?" Grace asked.

"It's exactly what it sounds like," Yvonne said, beginning the process of maneuvering beneath the behemoth. "You know how if you push an upside-down cup into the sink, it'll stay filled with air? Think of it like that. Only in a half-dock, the air is trying to escape and is held in with an environmental shield. We'll just slip the top of the Sparrow through the shield and climb out the top hatch."

47

The Queen of Sheba's mass was now directly above them. Yvonne watched the instruments as she guided the Sparrow up toward the beacon and the pair of magnetic clamps. She felt a brief moment of resistance as the Sparrow pushed up into the shield, and then they made contact. "That should do it."

"Are you coming with us?" Grace asked.

"I wasn't planning on it," Yvonne said as she began going through the shutdown sequence.

"Oh come on," the teen begged. "It's girl's day. Besides, you're not stuck here anymore. Enjoy your freedom."

"She's got you there," Abigail said. "You've no need to be a recluse anymore. Live a little."

Yvonne thought about turning her down, wanted to even. Instead, she said, "Let me finish things up here. I'll be right behind you."

Grace turned to leave, but as she passed Abigail, she gave her a thumbs up. "You're right. That was easy."

"Why is it always a bar?" Davey asked. "Have a meeting with a client or ally? Just find the nearest place serving alcohol." They'd located the cozy little establishment a few hours back, and after killing some time, had stepped in to grab a bite to eat before the other freelancer arrived.

"It's a pub," Matthew said. "And where else should we meet Ewan? A shadowy back alley?"

Davey scratched the back of his head. Fair enough. This was as neutral a place as any. He finished the last few bites of his panini. "Given how well thought of freelancers are in polite society, I figured the alley was the way to go. You know. Keep the trash out back."

Matthew grinned at that. "We're trying to change that, you know."

"Pretty soon, we'll be upstanding members of society. We'll get invited to all sorts of fancy functions where we have to wear ties."

"I wouldn't go that far," a new voice said. Davey twisted his neck to see Ewan Hywel standing behind him. The man wore an old fashion bomber style jacket and an easy smile. Davey had once blown a hole through Ewan's ship during a scuffle over a metal-rich asteroid. Matthew had given him strict instructions not to bring up the incident. Which was a serious fun killer, but then Matthew wasn't known for his capacity to have fun.

Matthew shook Ewan's hand as he sat. "How's the captain of the Red Dragon doing these days?"

The man slid into the booth beside Davey. "The Ddraig Goch is still flying, so that means it's a good day." He turned to Davey and snapped his fingers. "I've forgotten your name entirely. Wasn't it you that tried to shoot me down?"

Davey coughed out a laugh and gave Matthew a look. "Davey Long. And if I remember correctly, the Red Dragon opened fire first."

"Aye. We made the mistake of starting a fight we couldn't finish. But that was back when I still thought Matthew Cole was a loser with no friends."

Matthew raised an eyebrow but didn't take the bait.

Ewan continued. "Turns out he was just biding his time before trying to join into a group with all the cool kids."

"And you were the first crew I thought of," Matthew said.

That seemed to surprise Ewan, and he leaned back in the seat. "I've met Dominic. I know about his flair for the dramatic and wouldn't put it past him to just be having some fun. But I guess you're serious about this."

Matthew shook his head. "This is the real deal. We're gathering the best in the business to form a guild, the Guild of Lanterns. The ones that the public knows they can trust."

"Well, that sounds like a hell of a thing." Ewan scratched the back of his head, and Davey thought he even seemed a little nervous. "Look. Matthew. I'm not going to sit here and pretend that the Ddraig Goch is crewed by saints. We've delivered shipments that we knew better than to ask what was inside. I've heard about how you used to be a priest, and it explains a few things, that's for sure. But there's no way we can live up to that standard and still cut a profit."

"We're going to keep things profitable. And we know there are no perfect people out there. Here's the plan," Matthew said. "To start, we're going to recruit about a dozen freelancers. Between the Sparrow, the Red Dragon, and the Queen of Sheba, we'll have spaceboard crews covered."

"Wait, the Queen? You talked the old lady into this already?"

"Actually," Davey said. "She contacted us. Abigail... err, the Shield Maiden should be meeting with her right about now."

49

"And then we'll recruit from around the various hubs in the solar system. A couple from Mars, Ceres, Ganymede, Titan."

Ewan snapped his fingers. "Have you thought about the Jameson brothers?"

Matthew just smiled. "Already on the list. So that's the first dozen. See if there are enough jobs on the market to support us without tripping over each other and fighting for scraps. If it works, we invite more as time goes on."

"So we get the publicity and the glory of being the solar system's heroes. I like it. What is this going to cost us?"

"Emperor Dominic has offered to pay the bills of the organization itself, but I'm not interested in the Lanterns mooching off of a patron permanently. Two percent of every job run as a Lantern. Dominic's daughter Julia and one of my crew members, Yvonne Naude, are going to be handling the paperwork, the business side, talking to press, etc."

"Two percent." Ewan glanced upward as if running numbers in his head. "Easily covered if the public starts looking for Lanterns."

"That's what we hope."

Ewan chewed on his lip for a moment and Davey could tell he was almost sold. "Why my crew?"

"Remember when we met?" Matthew asked. "Over Dione in the Saturn neighborhood? Six years ago."

"That was an outlier," Ewan said.

"I'm not so sure about that, and even if it was, it doesn't have to be. You helped me save a lot of people on that transport and didn't get paid a dime."

Ewan eyed Davey. "I don't know why I didn't see the priest thing coming. Pretty soon, he'll have me confessing."

"He's good at that." Davey took this as a sign that the battle was over. Ewan was convinced.

"I'm not agreeing yet," Ewan said. "Let's just assume I'm going to decline for now. But I'll take a look at whatever paperwork you have. Just in case. I'm sure the dos and don'ts list for the Guild of Lanterns will be as long as the Bible. It probably is the Bible."

Davey laughed and Matthew slid a tablet across the table. "Here's the charter. We can talk through it."

Abigail climbed out onto the top of the Sparrow. The half-dock struck her as slightly dangerous. The indentation that they were nestled into was filled with air held in by a shield, but she could see stars off to the side. It would be quite possible to walk off the edge of the Sparrow and fall out into space, depending on how strong that shield was. A ramp had been lowered down to their hull from an airlock into the Queen of Sheba. An armed guard stood at attention at the door. That was more formal than she was expecting, but this was a lot bigger operation than she was used to.

Grace's head popped out of the hatch. "Whoa. This is kind of scary."

"Be careful," Abigail said.

"Gee, thanks." Grace pulled herself out onto the hull. "I don't have exhaust for brains. I've done more low gee and vacuum than you have."

"Sorry." Abigail stepped over to the hatch and knelt down by the opening as Yvonne appeared. She offered the woman an armored hand.

Yvonne looked at it like she was offended by the idea.

"We all know the ladders aren't kind to your knees," Abigail said. "I'm not trying to be insulting."

Yvonne pursed her lips. "Neither am I, and yet I'm the one behaving like a child." She took the hand, and Abigail gently helped her out of the hatch.

"Watch your step." She said as she led the way to the guard. "Abigail Sharon, here to see Gebre'elwa." Her tongue stumbled over the unfamiliar name, and she chastised herself. Mispronouncing the host's name was a faux pas she couldn't afford today.

"Yes, Ms. Sharon. Please follow me."

The guard thankfully didn't seem offended and led them through the airlock. They were led through a pair of halls and up two flights of stairs. They passed at least a dozen crewmen. Abigail wondered just how many called the Queen their home. At last, they reached the main corridor.

"Check that view," Grace said, pointing behind them.

The corridor stretched unchanging down the entire spine of the ship. Hundreds of meters away, it ended somewhere in the aft structure. "I bet it's not always open like that," Yvonne said. "There are probably dozens of bulkheads along that length that close at the slightest sign of danger."

51

The guard directed them toward the bow. After a short distance, it opened into a spacious bridge. Ten or more crew could comfortably run the various stations, a far cry from the Sparrow's cockpit that got crowded all too quickly. Alone in the center of the room stood a command chair facing the viewing window. The guard approached it. "Ma'am, your guests, Abigail Sharon and crew."

The chair rotated to reveal a black woman a good ten years older than Yvonne. She wore an airy looking white dress. Brilliant patterns of color ran in a wide stripe from the neckline to the hem at her ankles. "Welcome aboard the Queen of Sheba," she said, rising to her feet.

Abigail nodded her head respectfully. "Gebre'elwa, it's a pleasure to meet you." She was ninety percent confident she had it right that time.

The captain chuckled, reading her mind. "Close, but not quite. English speakers tend to struggle with my name. Gebre'elwa is the feminine Amharic take on Gabriel. But I won't be offended if you shorten it to 'Elwa as my crew does."

"'Elwa it is then," Abigail said.

'Elwa looked past her to Yvonne and Grace. "The Shield Maiden I know from her reputation." Abigail felt a stir of pride that one of the oldest and most powerful freelancers knew of her. "Who else stands before me? Is the Sparrow crewed by one man, a priest at that, and a cohort of capable women?"

Grace snorted. "There's also my brother, but we outnumber the men." She inclined her head. "Grace Anderson."

"And what do you do aboard the Sparrow, Grace?"

"Whatever they need. Sometimes that's cooking dinner. Sometimes that's beating up thugs."

'Elwa's eyes narrowed and her head tilted a fraction to the side. "I see. And you?"

"Yvonne Naude. Doctor by trade."

"And that's selling it short," Abigail added. "She's also a pilot, a mechanic, keeps the books, and anything else needed." She ignored the glare that she knew Yvonne was giving her. "I hope you're not upset that Matthew Cole was unable to make it today."

"Only a little disappointed. For all the stir he's caused, I do look forward to meeting him in person. But some other day, perhaps. Enough of the greetings. We have business to attend to. The answer is yes. I want in on your little guild."

Grace snorted. "That was easy."

'Elwa smiled. "Emperor Dominic and I have quite a history. And Matthew Cole is a new and rising star. A chance to partner with two such men for the greater good isn't an opportunity I'm going to pass up on. I'm old enough to have known the solar system when it was tamer." Her eyes twinkled as she stepped past them. "I'm also savvy enough a businesswoman to smell profit. The Queen of Sheba is famous on her own, but the additional prestige and publicity of the Guild of Lanterns will only increase that."

She motioned for them to follow, and the four women left the bridge together. Abigail had a feeling she was going to like the captain of the Queen of Sheba. At the very least, the guild wasn't going to be a hard sale.

"Well, I'm convinced," Ewan said, "but I'll have to talk over the charter with the rest of the crew. They'll get their vote, but I expect them to go along with it as well."

Matthew smiled, quietly relieved. He hadn't really had many doubts that the Red Dragon would join up, but then the whole idea was completely untested, and he could have been way off in his assumptions. "You can send me the signed agreements when you're ready."

"And with that, I think I'll take my leave of you gentlemen. My crew is unloading across town, and, well, I don't trust them enough to stay away for long." He winked. "I'm sure you understand what I'm getting at."

If they were half as good at getting into trouble as Grace and Davey were, Matthew was pretty sure he did. "You have no idea—"

The ground shook, and the floor rumbled as the thump of a distant explosion rolled through the pub. Ewan immediately grabbed his comm and called for his crew. Davey jumped to his feet and ran to the pub's exit.

Matthew was right behind Davey. A distant cloud of smoke rose over the rooftops and into the sky. "That's in the direction of the factory," he muttered. Nobody was mad enough to hit the grav plate factories. The colonies depended on them. He shook the thought from his head. That wasn't true. He knew just who was mad enough to go after something that critical. "Maybe there was an industrial accident."

Davey gave him a look that said he didn't believe it. People were crowding into the streets from the nearby businesses. Ewan ran out the door. "The Ddraig Goch is inside the factory's secure zone. We brought in a shipment of rare earth elements. Rhydian says a fuel tanker just blew up for no reason, and now they're hearing gunfire in the facility."

Davey swore quietly. "Abrogationists."

"I'm going to guess you don't have clearance to get you inside the secure zone," Ewan said.

Matthew stared at the smoke cloud. A second explosion rocked the city. He shook his head. "You offering to get me in there?"

He nodded. "If my crew is in a warzone, they need their captain."

"Davey. Go get the bike. Ewan, we'll be right behind you." He grabbed his comm and sent a message to Abigail. Callisto was too far away for real-time communication, but at least the message would get there in seconds rather than minutes.

Gebre'elwa's parlor was as comfortable a room as Yvonne had ever seen on a spaceship. Thick carpet, luxurious furnishings, and soft light made it an enjoyable place to spend an afternoon with friends. And Gebre'elwa seemed absolutely determined to become just that.

"And then I told the Prime Minister that he could keep his seven hundred tons of synthwool and find someone else to do his dirty work."

Yvonne smiled and took a sip from her tea. "My husband and I actually lived on Tethys during his administration. Needless to say, we weren't fans, but then Tomas never trusted any politician with the airlock controls."

Eventually, he'd grown so disillusioned with authority that he'd even stopped following local politics. That had been a waste of time anyway, given how often they'd moved from one colony to the next. No sooner had they begun to put down roots than a new opportunity would arise and they would move on.

"Has he been gone long?"

Yvonne's attention snapped back to the other woman. "Umm. It's been three years now. Syndicate violence on Ceres."

Gebre'elwa smiled weakly at her. "My condolences. My first husband was killed over twenty years ago by a rival. It took over a decade for the world to settle enough for me to remarry. I chose my accountant, something I haven't regretted for even a single moment."

From across the room where he and Abigail were going over the guild's charter, her husband, Mateo, laughed. "I love you 'El, but that's quite a lie. I have made you regret it on many occasions."

"They're short-lived moments and far enough apart that they are hardly worth speaking of. Unless I need you to do a favor, of course. Is everything forward-facing in the paperwork?"

"For the most part, though I have a couple of questions about arbitration between brokers when both are trying to secure the same job. It's my understanding that you don't mean members to compete with one another."

"We'll have to take another look at that part of the charter," Abigail admitted. "We had lawyers on hand when we wrote it, but no brokers. We missed that detail."

"I work with several," Gebre'elwa said. "Perhaps we can pool resources to decide on a solution."

"We gotta talk to Benny anyway," Grace said. She'd been sitting at the table with Mateo and Abigail, looking utterly bored the whole time. This wasn't exactly the girl's day she had been hoping for. "From what Matthew said, he's foaming at the mouth that we did all this without consulting him."

Gebre'elwa looked at Yvonne in question. Yvonne shrugged. "They have a somewhat adversarial relationship. Trust me when I say that Matthew Cole and his broker are a perfect match for each other. We'll tap his advice when we hit Mars in a few days."

Mateo stood from his chair. "I'll have no objections once the amendments are made."

"In which case, I'll have none either," Gebre'elwa said. "You can tell Matthew that the Queen of Sheba would be honored to join the Guild of Lanterns. We may even be able to provide administrative support if need be. Mateo knows his way around numbers."

Yvonne nodded as she downed the rest of her tea. "I'll put you in touch with Julia. In the meantime—" Her comm chimed. She glanced at it. "It's Matthew. Probably checking in after his meeting." She stepped to the side of the room and answered it. "I'm here."

She had to wait for her message to get to Ganymede and then for his reply. "We've got an emergency. I need you to return right now."

She sucked in a breath of air. The comm was loud enough that the rest of the room probably heard that. "What kind of emergency are we talking about? There are others present if this is a private matter."

"This is as public as it gets," he said after the delay. "The Gilgamesh grav plate factory is under attack. Explosions and gunfire in the secure zone. Ewan's ship is in there, and he's going to try to get us in under his security clearance. I need the Sparrow nearby in case air support is needed."

"We're on our way. Keep us updated."

For a single frozen moment, no one in the room moved as the implications sank in. Horror. Denial. Who was crazy enough to go after the grav plates? Alexander Logan. And the fact that it happened while Matthew was in the area couldn't be a coincidence.

Gebre'elwa snapped out of shock first. She already had her comm out, broadcasting to the whole ship via the intercom. "All hands-on deck. Prepare for emergency departure. Pilots to your interceptors. I want the Queen ready to break orbit when I hit the bridge." She stood and marched from the room, white dress flowing behind her. "Sparrow crew, I'm going to Ganymede. You're welcome to join me." And with that, she was gone.

Yvonne made her decision. "Grace, you're with me in the Sparrow. I want it ready to fly when the Queen enters Ganymede orbit. Abigail, stay with Gebre'elwa for now. We may need to coordinate with her."

"I'll take you back to your ship," Mateo said. "Come with me."

Yvonne and Grace followed behind him. Yvonne tried to push down the rising tide of fear. This was an existential threat to every man, woman, and child. If that factory burned, the colonies' doom would come far sooner than forecast. A single generation was all they would have left.

The Abrogationists would have won.

It took only a few lies and one argument for Ewan to smuggle Matthew and Davey into the secure zone. Davey wondered if the deception pricked Matthew's conscience. There were days when he was still surprised when the Gaucho took objections to a particular course of action. But today he stayed silent, probably because the stakes were so high.

The guards finally let them through with warning to return straight to the Red Dragon. They actually did that, though Davey knew they had no intention of doing just that.

The secure zone was the entire inner ring of the colony of Gilgamesh. After the tall outer wall, there was a wide-open yard, filled with scattered vehicles and ships. Nearly a kilometer further in stood the imposing factory. It had to be the biggest building he'd ever seen, maybe the biggest anyone had ever seen. He was yanked out of his gaping by the distinct popping of distant gunfire. It was sporadic, as if it wasn't a single battle, but several small firefights.

Matthew banked the bike to follow Ewan around a convoy of fuel trucks. Ahead of them sat the Red Dragon, ramp down. Ewan pulled up to a stop and leaped off his bike as two of his own crew ran to meet him. An armed guard stood nearby and eyed the whole group warily. Matthew dismounted and went straight to the nervous man.

"What's the situation, officer?"

The man crossed his arms. "The current security situation is under control."

"That's not what it sounds like to me," Davey muttered.

Matthew frowned at him. "Is there anything we can do to help? We're willing to aid your security teams in any way we can."

"I said we have it under control."

Ewan approached with three of his men. All armed. Ewan gestured at Matthew. "Do you have any idea who this man is?"

"Do you think I care?"

"You should. That's Matthew Cole. Captain of the Sparrow. The man who saved Ceres. I'm sure you've heard of him. He's got more experience in combat than the entire Gilgamesh Colonial Security Force combined."

It was probably true, but Matthew took a step back looking more than a little uncomfortable at the praise. Davey watched as the guard's eyes first narrowed and then widened in shock. "You're that Matthew Cole?" He went from nervous looking to downright upset. "I'll check with my boss. Maybe we could use a hand after all." He grabbed his comm and turned his back on the group.

57

Ewan introduced his men. The tallest was his older brother Rhydian. The other two were distant cousins, Lloyd and Jacob Hughes. "These are my best men in a fight. We try to keep our feet off the ground, but if it comes to it, we can handle our own."

The guard returned. "Come with me. Garrison Commander Mavros wants to see you."

When the bridge of the Queen of Sheba went into action, it was a sight to behold. Abigail stood to the back, doing her best to stay out of the way and not gawk at things. They were a well-oiled machine as crewmen went about their duties, ensuring all drop shuttles and cargo were secured, interceptor pilots were at their stations, gunners in their turrets, and more. Gebre'elwa stood in the middle of it all, issuing orders, a pillar in white.

"Prepare to frameshift," she said calmly. "Percy, proceed."

The stars beyond the viewport blurred out of focus for a brief moment as they transitioned to a fraction of the speed of light. Half a minute passed, and they dropped out of frameshift.

"Bring us around toward Ganymede."

The stars outside began to slowly wheel. The Queen was a massive ship and certainly couldn't turn as fast as the Sparrow could. It would take several minutes at this rate.

Gebre'elwa turned and motioned for Abigail to join her. Feeling more than a little out of place, Abigail crossed the bridge to stand beside the woman. "Yvonne and Grace have the Sparrow warmed and ready to go."

"Very good. I doubt the Queen herself will be of any assistance, but I have Shotel Squadron ready to launch. Have you had any updates from Matthew Cole?"

"Only that they have made it into the secure zone and are in contact with security trying to ascertain what exactly is going on."

"Hopefully, they will know by the time we get there." She turned back to the window. "If the need is dire, I can spare a shuttle and perhaps a half dozen men for the ground. But we have little experience in that regard. The Queen keeps to the space lanes." Ahead of them, a distant Jupiter was slowly coming into view. "I wonder how the Abrogationists went from impotent academics screaming about the evils of mankind to an actual threat."

"New leadership," Abigail said simply.

"Yes, Alexander Logan. I've read of his purported accomplishments. He shall not be allowed another victory. Not today. Humanity may be doomed, but I intend it to last long enough for my own children to die of old age."

"We're ready to frameshift, ma'am."

She set her jaw and raised her chin ever so slightly. "Take us to Ganymede."

Davey really couldn't make much sense of the factory interior. To him, it was all industrial equipment, machinery, and piping. He could walk into the Sparrow's engine compartments to see those sights. It was big, though. Real big. They'd been loaded into some kind of open-top transport vehicle, like a train car, and were traveling down one of the wide lanes for vehicular traffic through the factory. Davey walked to the front of their transport and joined Matthew. "Do you think they'll actually let us help?"

"Maybe. If there's anything we can do."

"I just have a sidearm, and I didn't bring much ammo." He scratched the back of his head. "I was kind of hoping for a normal day."

Matthew chuckled. "That's not really our specialty, is it?"

Ahead, a small tower, illuminated by gold light, rose into the cavernous space. "That's the security hub," one of the guards said. "Commander Mavros is waiting for you."

The grav car barely slowed and banked hard, sliding up to the tower. They unloaded, and the whole group was rushed into a command center on the ground level. Their IDs were checked, but it seemed most of the guards recognized Matthew anyway. Either that or they were too ashamed to admit that they didn't.

Davey didn't even have to guess who Commander Mavros was. The man in charge had been barking orders since they first stepped foot in the room. "Let me see them," he said, his head snapping up to look at the newcomers. "Five men and a runt, huh? You made it sound like you were bringing a small army."

Davey bristled at the irrelevant snipe, but Matthew calmly diffused it. "Six men, all combat veterans. If we can be of service to the colony of Gilgamesh, we will."

The man regarded Matthew for a moment. "Are news reports from Ceres true?"

Matthew's lip twitched. "Some of them."

There was a brief pause. "Fine." He motioned them to the screen. "If you have any bright ideas, now is the time. Otherwise, I want you out of here." They clustered around the screen, which currently showed a map of the factory. "The enemy, whoever they are, is wearing our uniforms. We don't know how they got in. We don't know how many of them there are. They've been steadily pushing deeper into production line one." He marked a massive arm of the factory. "They don't appear to have made it to the Taciturn Assemblers yet, but that's the destination."

"Do we need to know what that means?" Ewan asked.

"It's the part of the line we can't replace. Machines that build machines and sabotage themselves if you try to open them up. They've kept their secrets for a century. If they get damaged, the whole line behind it is useless junk."

"What's the hold up to mounting a counteroffensive into line one?" Matthew asked.

"Friend foe recognition. We don't know who's on our side until they fire back. We're working on a system to tag all of our people."

"Are there workers in the area?"

Mavros shook his head. "Thank God, no. The line was down for routine maintenance."

"Then put us on the vanguard with your best men," Matthew said. "Keep your people out of our way as we sweep through. Anyone we run into will be assumed hostile unless they immediately surrender. We push straight up line one to the Taciturn Assemblers and secure the area."

Mavros seemed to consider that. "That could work. I've got various groups working to clear the area, but it's taking time with the number of hostiles that have popped out of the ground. Harv. Start getting firm locations on teams in line one. We'll need to maneuver them out of the way when the freelancers press through. Captain Ferris. Take your squad and lead Mr. Cole to the Assemblers. If you come across friendlies, assume the worst, but use your best judgment. The less friendly fire losses, the better. Remember the Assemblers are top priority. Make it happen. I don't know how much time we have."

The room flew into action. The freelancers were led back outside by Captain Ferris and his squad. "You'll be under my command," he warned. "I don't think I need to tell you how sensitive this location is." The group simply stared at him. "Good. Everyone armed?"

Davey sheepishly waved. "I didn't wake up this morning expecting a fight. I just have one magazine for my sidearm."

"Let me see." Davey unholstered the pistol at his hip and showed him. "Not a caliber we use. You sure you know what you're doing, kid?"

"Just get him something," Matthew growled.

Ferris nodded. "Have you ever fired an RK-90 before?"

"Only in my dreams," Davey said. "I've got an old 72 I've been dying to upgrade."

Captain Ferris pointed at one of the guards standing outside the building. "Hector. We'll be borrowing your firearm. Mags too." Davey took the weapon and resisted the temptation to smile. "Main difference between the 72 and 90 is the bullpup layout. The magazine—"

Davey had already ejected the magazine and peered into it to ensure it was loaded.

"Never mind," Ferris said. "Let's go."

"Do we have any more updates on the ground?" Gebre'elwa asked.

Abigail shook her head. "Not yet. Can I set up on an open comm link to the Sparrow to avoid having to relay?"

She gestured to the communication console, "Aliah, give her a hand."

It took less than a minute to set up the pass-through line. "Yvonne, you're broadcasting over the bridge. Have you heard from Matthew?"

"He hasn't answered yet," she said. "I'll try— Never mind. He's calling now. Passing his call through."

This was a convoluted set up just to allow allies to communicate. Strong communication lines were something else the guild was going to have to work out. Secure channels would be a necessity in any scenario involving multiple crews.

Yvonne's voice continued over the bridge. "I'm here, Matthew. You're patched through to the Queen of Sheba as well. Give us an update. What do you need?"

"We're working with security to retake control of a critical part of the factory. If you can get Abigail on the ground in the next thirty seconds, that would be grand. If not, maintain overwatch."

"We're still in orbit," Abigail said, frustration beginning to mount. "Sorry."

"I expected as much." He paused. "Wait, you're on the Queen in orbit? Gebre'elwa, can you control Gilgamesh airspace? Make sure no ships arrive or depart until this is over?"

The woman smiled. "It would be my pleasure, Matthew Cole. A proper introduction will be in order later."

There was a burst of gunfire over the speaker. "We'll talk," he shouted. "Things just got hot." He disconnected with a pop.

"I'll guess we'll maintain position in dock," Yvonne said. "Muting the channel."

Gebre'elwa turned to the officer at the communication station. "Aliah. Prep my comm to broadcast on all emergency and public frequencies."

"One moment, ma'am. Okay, go ahead."

She lifted her comm. "This is the Queen of Sheba to the colony of Gilgamesh and all spacecraft in the Ganymede orbit. I am hereby prohibiting all traffic to and from the colony until I have received word from colony officials that the current crisis has passed. All traffic, civilian and official, is strongly recommended to stay away. If you're in my airspace, you will be considered hostile." She paused. "Play that on loop, Aliah." She turned to the viewport. "Launch Shotel Squadron. They are free to devise their own tactics, as long as they are able to respond to any threat to either the Queen or the factory."

Abigail held her breath as she watched the woman effortlessly command those around her. If there was one woman she could choose to be in about forty years, it was this one. She wasn't one to be trifled with, and that was something Abigail could respect.

Davey leaned out of what little cover the open-topped grav car provided and squeezed off a few shots as they passed under a catwalk bridge. The assailants in Gilgamesh security uniforms dove for cover behind equipment. It had been like that the whole trip through production line one as the road ran its back-and-forth route through the machinery. Deadly, nerve-wracking quiet, punctuated by brief moments of terror as they were ambushed from above.

Two of Ferris' squad were down, and from the Red Dragon, Rhydian had taken a bullet to the knee.

"After the next turn, we'll be at the Assemblers," Ferris said.

Matthew glanced at one of the wounded. They'd applied some synth-skin to the wound, but that was all they could do. He shared a quick look with Davey. Davey hefted his weapon in response as they rounded the corner. This machinery looked no different than the rest, but apparently it was the most valuable equipment in the colonies. Davey was pretty sure Matthew would have a moral lesson about appearances being deceiving. It irked him to think that he could probably give some of Matthew's speeches himself at this point.

The gunfire started almost immediately. The driver practically rammed the grav car into cover, and they joined the fight in earnest. For Davey, it was fear and adrenaline, moving cover to cover with Matthew, slowly clearing out the nest of terrorists.

And then, like most fights, it ended as abruptly as it began.

A light haze of smoke drifted through the Assemblers as Ferris ordered his men to spread out in teams and check for stragglers. Matthew rolled a body over and began to go through the pockets on his vest.

"What are you doing?" Davey shuddered at the thought of handling a dead man.

"Looking for clues. Proof that these are Abrogationists."

"Do you think we got here in time?"

Matthew stood. "You'll have to ask the engineers when they get in here to inspect things and take inventory." He walked to the next body. "Or maybe we did." He crouched and peeled the dead man's fingers back from the object he'd clutched in his death embrace. "Ferris. You need to see this."

The captain and Ewan hurried over. "What do you have?"

Matthew handed him a detonator. "We might be surrounded by explosives."

"Lovely. I'll call for a bomb squad. We'll have to comb the whole line." Ferris said.

Ewan eyed the thing with distrust. "I hope this is the only detonator and we're not all about to get blown to pieces."

"You and me both," Davey agreed.

The ground rumbled in a series of distant explosions. To Davey's ears, those blasts sounded like they were on the other side of the factory. All eyes went to Ferris. "Give me a minute," he mumbled as he dug out his comm.

Matthew and Ewan went back to checking bodies. Davey knew he should probably help but didn't think he could handle touching corpses. A minute later, Ferris returned. "Those explosions were in production line two. There's no confirmation yet, but it looks like they hit the Assemblers over there."

Matthew shook his head and kicked a stray pipe at his feet. "Two groups. One as bait. If they succeeded, great. If not, the other would slip past unnoticed."

Davey was too tired to even try and work out the consequences. They'd saved one line and lost another?

"Security cameras have an armed group fleeing. They're trying to break out of the factory."

"Can you get us outside?" Ewan asked. "Maybe we can cut them off."

Ferris hesitated for a moment. "There are escape tunnels that cut beneath the factory. Normally they are sealed with firebreaks every fifty meters. I can give the order for them to be opened. There's a nearby access ramp. The grav car should just be able to fit. We might intercept the combatants at their exit point." He turned to one of his men. "Orville, you're in charge. Wait here with the wounded for reinforcements and medics. I'm going with the freelancers."

Matthew motioned to the grav car. "Lead the way."

"This is your final warning. If you enter Gilgamesh airspace, you will be shot down."

The pilot on the other side was sputtering in rage. Abigail whistled quietly.

"You... You have no right to do this."

"Legally? No. But this is a temporary emergency that will soon pass," Gebre'elwa said. "Until it has, traffic to and from Gilgamesh is suspended."

"Ma'am, they've pulled away to regain orbit."

She smiled. "Wise decision. We will inform you when the crisis has passed." She turned to Abigail. She didn't voice the question, but Abigail answered it anyway.

"Updates aren't good. It looks like they saved the first line from sabotage, but the second production line was hit as well. Matthew's team is trying to cut off that group's escape."

"Hmm. That is dire news. But we'll have to sort the damage later. Hopefully, this will be over soon, and I can stop breaking every law in the book." Abigail was surprised when the woman reached out and laid a hand on her armored shoulder. "Are you... alright? You look troubled."

The touch made her uncomfortable, and she shifted slightly to pull away without making it seem like that's what she was doing. "I'd rather be on the ground, as opposed to playing glorified courier between people actually being useful."

"Enjoy the action while it lasts. My days on the front lines ended decades ago with the arrival of children."

"Well, when mine end, I don't think it'll look like this." Abigail gestured at the bridge around them.

"You never know. Besides. This is less exciting than it looks. Most of my time is spent telling people with specialized skills to do their jobs. Command is hardly as thrilling as sneaking into a bandit den and making off with their leader in the dead of night. Just have a plan before something forces you to change careers."

If that was supposed to make Abigail feel better, it was hardly a success. She'd turned thirty a few weeks back, and while the crew had wisely not made a big deal about it, somewhere in the back of her mind, she knew she was living on borrowed time. One day her suit would take damage that Ivan couldn't repair, and when that happened, it was over. She'd go back to being a paraplegic with no skills but radiation zone safety procedures. There'd be no freelancer empire to retire on like Gebre'elwa had.

She wouldn't even be of any use on the Sparrow.

"I'll think about it," Abigail said and turned back to the monitor, hoping the other woman would get that the conversation was over.

"They're retreating toward loading dock fifteen," Ferris shouted over the rush of air.

The driver had hit the accelerator the second they were outside, and Matthew kept a hand on his campero to keep it from flying off. "Is that close? Are we going to make it?"

"We're almost there. Hang on."

They flung around a corner, the back end of the car swinging wide. Ahead of them, gunfire crackled, and a ship's engines growled in warmup stage.

"There's the getaway vehicle," Davey said. "All part of the plan, no doubt."

"And loaded with grav plates too," Ferris said. "The dock extension has been retracted already."

A smash and grab then. The nature of their plan was getting more apparent by the moment. It had to be one of Logan's. The distance between them and the ship closed rapidly as they blasted across the open yard. They were going to board that ship and keep it from taking off one way or the other. There was no way they were letting the Abrogationists get a full load of—

The landing engines flared, and the freighter lifted its bulk off the ground. Ferris shouted obscenities at the ship as it passed overhead. Their driver hit the brakes and the car crawled to a stop.

"We can head for the Ddraig Goch," Ewan offered. "We'll get airborne quickly, and if that thing is under a full load, I can't imagine they'll make it to frameshift altitude before we can intercept."

"Don't bother," Matthew said. "Abigail? You still with 'Elwa?"

"I am. What's the update?"

"We think the terrorists just took off in a ship. Do you guys have an angle on it?"

"One second. Yes, the Queen has it on the scanners. Patching you back through so you can talk to 'Elwa."

'Elwa's voice came through the comm. "I've sent the ship an ultimatum to stand down, or I will force the issue. I've received no response.

I can take them out of the sky if you want."

Matthew looked at bright flares of light now accelerating away from the surface. "Let me check with the factory official. Ferris?"

The security captain put away his comm and glanced at the sky. "Surprising absolutely no one, it appears our surface to air defenses are down. Convenient. If you have allies that can bring it down, Commander Mavros requests you blow it out of the sky."

"That's a lot of lost grav plates," Ewan said quietly.

"Ninety-five million dollars worth, I'm told. They'll be sold on the black market and funding Abrogationist activities for years to come if we don't shoot it down. The shipment is a loss either way."

Matthew nodded mournfully. "Okay, 'Elwa. Whatever you do, don't let them get away."

"As you wish. Sending my squadron now."

They watched in silence as over the next several minutes, a dozen lights converged on the brighter engines of the freighter. At that distance, they couldn't see the fight, but there were a few brief flashes of fire before a brilliant explosion flashed like a star. Then a lone meteor fell back to Ganymede, leaving a trail of debris across the sky.

"What a waste," Davey said.

Matthew wholly agreed with that sentiment.

"You know, I hate the aftermath more than the fights themselves," Matthew said, his temples throbbing. Yvonne didn't even look over at him as she pulled the Sparrow back into the Queen's half-dock. He continued. "Hours with the Gilgamesh authorities, and now 'Elwa wants a meeting."

"She'll join the guild. She's all but agreed to that."

"Last thing on my mind right now, Yvonne."

"I'm aware of that. I was pointing out the silver lining."

There was a gentle bump as the magnetic clamps gripped the hull firmly into place.

"Sorry you had to sit this one out," he said.

"I'm hardly disappointed that I wasn't required to take myself and the Sparrow into danger when there were capable allies available to do so." She smiled a crooked smile at him. "Although you might apologize

67

to Grace. She was strapped into the thumper, ready to go."

Matthew grimaced, as he helped Yvonne with the shutdown procedures. "I don't like the thought of her stacking up a body count. She's just a kid."

"I'm sure she's broken more than a few necks with those miracles of hers."

"Don't remind me." He flipped the comm switch. "Abigail, we're here."

"About time. We're tired of waiting for you." She cut the call short.

"What's with her," Matthew said, frowning at the speaker.

"I don't think she likes being left on the sidelines."

"And I could have used her on the surface."

"She's the one that needs to hear that, not me,"

He turned to leave.

"Matthew." He paused and she let the moment hang. "Have you considered the timing of this attack?"

"I have. And I don't like it. The Sparrow hasn't been through Gilgamesh since you guys joined. Either it's a coincidence of cosmic scale..."

"Or he waited till we were in town," Yvonne completed the thought. She let out a long sigh. "We both know the answer."

"I wonder..." he said, an idea coming to him. It was a long shot, but then there wasn't anything to lose. He fumbled with his comm for a moment and ignored the puzzled look on Yvonne's face. Jackpot. The call connected and the recipient was in range for real-time communication.

A familiar voice with its stiff British accent crackled out of the speakers. One they hadn't heard since Marion Park in Port Jacobson. "I've been expecting to hear from you and hoping I wouldn't have to be the one to take the initiative. I kept this number active just for you, after all."

Yvonne covered her mouth with her hand and watched Matthew carefully.

"What's the game, Logan?" he said. "Why did you involve us in this?"

"I want you to pass on a message for me. Five production lines at the Gilgamesh factory, one sabotaged years ago by Moses himself when the engineers tried to reverse engineer the Taciturn Assemblers. I attacked two, giving you a fair shot at saving one, which to your credit you did. Though I'm a little sour over the lost grav plate shipment."

Matthew didn't answer. He wasn't in the mood to banter with a terrorist.

"Which gets to your part, of course. I need you to pass a message on to the President of Arizona. Tell him I'm coming for the grav plate factory on Mars. Since you saved one of these lines, I'll have to take out three at that factory instead of the two I had planned on."

"I'm not interested in being a part of your schemes."

"Nor am I particularly interested in yours. This little guild joke of yours is fun and games, I suppose, but you can't seriously expect it to accomplish anything. Humanity is too far gone for that. Be a candle in the wind for all I care, Cole. The ending has already been written."

The transmission ended. "I think you've gotten under his skin," Yvonne said dryly. "He's trapped us, you know."

Matthew thought he knew what she was getting at it but was too tired to acknowledge it. "How is that?"

"We have to play the game. He's directly made a threat to the Kyoto factory after hitting Gilgamesh's. But there's the trick. Why does he want us to pass the message to President Barclay rather than the Prime Minister of Kyoto? It doesn't make sense. He has an angle, and we're going to fall into it."

Matthew closed his eyes. "We go to the Prime Minister first. Give him the warning, and then go to President Barclay a few days later. Logan made a direct threat and we can't in good conscience ignore it. We'll leave for Mars first thing in the morning." He left the cockpit and wished that, for just once, life could be simple.

Chapter 4: Harbor of Disquiet

The attack on the Gilgamesh factory changed that colony forever. Where once its residents lived quiet lives in relative freedom, suddenly, they were the center of intense scrutiny. The secure zone became heavily militarized for fear of future incursions. Status of forces agreements were signed with other Ganymedean colonies, and by the end of the month, the meager security teams became a multinational defense force capable of fighting off any invasion.

Anyone that had to step foot in the secure zone went through countless background checks and invasive interviews to ensure no one with abrogationist sympathies slipped through the cracks. Its citizens were closely monitored, their communications spied on, their lives intruded upon.

It was the ancient struggle between freedom and security. In the name of the greater good, the individual was crushed beneath the boots of necessity. Perhaps they were right, the eleventh hour of humanity was nigh with its impending stroke set to end all their struggles.

Or else they were wrong, and the colonists of Gilgamesh would learn like so many others that fear brings the death of freedom.

Marvin Faust
Political Philosopher
Died 120 AM

"You may as well get it over with," Yvonne said. "We've got a few minutes till we're in position to deorbit to Kyoto."

Matthew groaned. Beneath them stretched the comfortable red horizon of Mars, the planet of his birth. It always felt a bit like home, even if he'd spent most of the last twenty years in the Jupiter neighborhood. Of course, an angry broker was going to make things feel a bit less homelike. "Hopefully, he won't answer."

"Matthew Cole. You wouldn't be nervous about talking to Benny, would you?"

"He might be justified in his anger. This time. And just this time, mind you. You want to give me a moment of privacy?"

"And miss this?" She shook her head. "No, I'm good."

He stared at her, incredulous, and then sighed. "I used to be the captain of my own ship." He placed the call, silently praying that Benny wouldn't answer. No such luck.

"It's about time I got more than a quick message," Benny said, his voice dull. "I'm so glad to know that after four years of working together, you would care enough to agree to a very public hair-brained scheme without even asking my advice."

Yvonne gestured to the comm.

Matthew sighed again. "Hey, Benny. Sorry, it's been a busy few weeks. I thought it would be better to wait until I got to Mars before—"

"Can it, Cole. Let me talk. No. Let me take you on a little journey of anger and eventual acceptance of your irresponsibility."

Matthew bristled at the insult but took a deep breath. "Okay. Go ahead then. Get it over with."

Benny cleared his throat. "I got the news of your new little guild when my, uh, business partner came in to show me the headlines. Im-

71

agine my surprise seeing my star client involved in a massive new undertaking that I had never heard about."

"Hey, did you hear that, Yvonne? I'm his star client."

She pursed her lips. "Don't get me involved in this."

"And don't let it go to your head," Benny said. "Because I was livid. Furious even. I was this close to dropping you right then and there like every other broker you ever had. You have no idea how many brokers warned me away from the dead weight roadkill that was Matthew Cole."

Matthew glanced at Yvonne and couldn't keep the smile away. She rolled her eyes. "Don't look so proud. And stop trying to involve me."

"You were the one that wanted to witness this shipwreck." He glanced back at the comm. "I'm waiting for the turn around here."

Benny drew the pause out for an excruciatingly long time. "But," he finally said, "within the hour requests started coming across the boards for you, or your Lanterns. Which, by the way, I'm not sure I can take that name seriously, Cole."

"Too late. It's done. Job requests are good, though, right?"

"Dozens of them. More than you could do in a year."

Okay. Better than expected. And a little unsettling. "Are they the right kind of jobs? The kind I take?"

"Of course. After that little press conference, everyone is looking for a Good Samaritan."

"They still have to pay us, Benny."

"Yeah, and next year you'll be canceling that as well."

"No he won't," Yvonne said. "I get a say there."

"And at least I know you're reliable. Unlike some people. While you're at it, Yvonne, make sure he doesn't make any more major changes to the business model without asking me first."

"Will do. I'll have to schedule some time to talk to you about this, Benny. There are still a few questions we need to sort out, and we may need to put you in touch with Julia of Venus and a few of the other brokers."

The comm was silent for nearly ten seconds before Benny continued. "What have you roped me into?"

"Something good, hopefully," Matthew said. "Look, we'll be on Mars for a couple of weeks. If you can scrounge up some low-key jobs, that would be great. Nothing too intense."

"Great. I've got thirty you can choose from."

"Give us a couple days. We have to make a few appointments with some politicians and then we'll be free."

"I haven't forgiven you yet, Cole. And remember I'm this close to dropping you."

"No you're not. Talk to you soon Benny." He cut the transmission and grinned at Yvonne. "See. I told you that wouldn't be too bad." She stared at him with a raised eyebrow until a chime on the console announced their window had come up. "Next stop, Kyoto," he said as he spun the Sparrow to burn retrograde.

Kyoto had once been part of Abigail's territory when she was just the Shield Maiden of Mars, so it was her turn to lead as they weaved through the dense downtown district toward the government complex. She hadn't actually been back to Kyoto since that fateful day she'd laid Matthew out on the street. This trip wasn't going to have an equally positive effect on her life. But today they were on the same side. Outside of a quick stop at the capitol complex, they weren't planning on sticking around, which was a pity. Kyoto was one of her favorite colonies.

Unfortunately, the afternoon turned out to be a total bust. As luck would have it, they arrived during a public holiday, and other than an annoying number of tourists crowding the park in front of the Colonial Diet building, the complex was more or less empty. The Prime Minister they'd hoped to see was long gone. Eventually, they got word of a single councilor that was still in his office, but security caught them and escorted them, grumbling, out of the building. Abigail thought about brushing them off. It wasn't like they could stop her. Sadly, Matthew must have known what she was thinking. He patted her arm. "We're here to make friends, not enemies."

Defeated, they regrouped under a grove of Yoshino cherry trees. Sadly, they had missed the pale pink blossoms by only a couple of weeks. Piles of dirty petals still littered corners protected from the wind. "So what now?" she asked. "It'll be a couple of days before the government is back in office."

"We can't wait that long," Matthew said. "There's no telling how quickly the Abrogationists are going to act."

"We could go right to the factory, I suppose."

"That may be the play in the end." Matthew grimaced and leaned his back against the trunk of the tree. "Are you sure you don't know anyone in authority?"

She laughed. "Look, Matthew. I didn't run in the circles of the high and mighty before you came along. The criminal groups knew me. I'm sure all the yakuza clans kept tabs on me. But I didn't exactly rub shoulders with bishops and emperors like you do."

"Okay, fine. How about we go a little lower. Police maybe? Surely you worked with law enforcement."

She snapped her fingers. "I met the old commissioner-general once. He retired a couple of years back, but I guarantee you he still knows people." She dug out her comm. "I should still have his contact information."

Her number led to a secretary. It took several minutes of begging and pleading, as well as a few threats as to the nature of their news before the secretary took them seriously and contacted the ex-commissioner-general on their behalf. To their surprise, he invited them to his home to explain the situation to him.

By the time they reached his estate some distance outside of Kyoto, the sun had set beneath the horizon, and the sky faded to a starry expanse. The grounds of the walled estate were immaculate. A servant led them down the paths to a softly lit outdoor pergola where an older Japanese couple sat reading under the light. They stood at their approach.

Abigail bowed slightly at the waist to each of them. "Konbanwa. Konbanwa."

Ex Commissioner-General Kagurazaka and his wife returned the gesture, if somewhat shallower. He extended a polite greeting in Japanese. She only got about three-quarters of it. Apparently, she was a little rusty. Out of the corner of her eye, she saw Matthew stiffen. He knew a smattering of several languages, including the dead ones that only academics learned, but she doubted Japanese was on that list. Thankfully, he got with the program and emulated the bow Abigail had given. It was only a little late.

Then Kagurazaka switched to perfect English. "It's been some time, Ms. Sharon. Four years, I believe, since you retrieved my deep cover agent from the Onozuwa Yakuza. I believe I have heard your name of late, in relation to the crew of this Mr. Cole." He offered Matthew his hand. Matthew hesitated for just the briefest of seconds and Kagurazaka laughed. "Relax, Mr. Cole. I'm offering a western handshake because I'm meeting with an Arizonan whom I respect."

Matthew took the hand. "Sorry to act like a fish out of water. I've only periodically passed through Kyoto." He paused. "And I wish we were here with better news."

Kagurazaka scratched his graying goatee. "Yes, well, Ms. Sharon managed to scare my secretary, something I've not yet managed to accomplish. Dear, if you don't mind..."

His wife nodded. "I'll go prepare some tea for our guests. If it would make you even more uncomfortable, Mr. Cole, I could prepare a full tea ceremony." The corner of her mouth turned up in the barest of a smile.

"Oh please, don't," Abigail said. "He might not survive that."

"Just something for refreshment then," she said and disappeared into the night toward the house.

"Now then," Kagurazaka said. "What is so important that it could not wait for the proper officials?"

Matthew told him. All of it, including their past association with Logan and the most recent call that Abigail had missed out on. "We're not sure why the message was directed at the Arizonan government rather than that of Kyoto. Given Logan's propensity for deception, we thought it best to warn you first."

The ex-commissioner-general was silent for a long moment. "I see. Since the attack on the Gilgamesh factory last week, we have been increasing security at our own factory. Quietly, so as not to frighten the public. But this is alarming news, indeed. If Logan is so arrogant as to taunt us, perhaps he means a different target entirely so that we misallocate resources."

"That's what I've been saying," Abigail said. "Smoke and mirrors. Feint and counter feint."

"Or else the real target is flexible depending on how we react," Kagurazaka said. "These will be questions for intelligence agencies to sort out and not ones we can answer tonight. I will speak with the Prime Minister in the morning."

"We're heading for Arizona tomorrow," Matthew said. "Do we need to hold off on informing President Barclay and give Kyoto time to prepare a response?"

In the distance, Kagurazaka's wife reappeared with a tray. "No," he said. "The sooner counterintelligence operations begin, the better, and Arizona's Office of Colonial Intelligence is better situated for that task. We appreciate the warning. Now, I believe my wife takes her duties as hostess seriously and will insist on that tea before you leave."

It wasn't an actual tea ceremony, but somehow she made it into an abbreviated cultural experience for Matthew anyway, one in which he convincingly feigned interest. Abigail wondered if, as the wife of a government official, she was used to entertaining foreign guests and had grown accustomed to sharing her culture or if she was actually trying to make Matthew miserable.

She hoped it was the latter. She liked sharing the finer things in life.

Half an hour later, as they left the grounds, she turned and smirked at him. "How was the tea?"

He curled his lip. "I'll stick to coffee, thanks."

When the Sparrow set down in the colony of Arizona on a farm outside the city of Flagstaff, it was always a race to the ramps to get off the ship. Matthew always lost that race since he had to finish shutdown procedures. By the time he and Yvonne stepped out the portside airlock into the bright Martian afternoon, the other three had already walked halfway down the lane between the fields of wheat to the farmhouse.

"I think they're more excited to see my mother than I am," Matthew said as his boots hit the soil.

"The Sparrow has three nests," Yvonne said. "One on Venus in the lap of luxury. One at Antioch, with the meek and needy. But the last, well, the Cole family farm is as special as it gets to those kids."

"Maybe so." Matthew wondered for the briefest of moments at the life he'd missed out on by leaving at eighteen for the seminary on Ganymede. The chance to have his own family and stay in one place for longer than a week. "We'll have to stop referring to Davey as a kid. He's close to twenty, you know."

Yvonne reached her hand out to brush the stalks of wheat as they walked. "You'll have to stop calling him a kid. When I hit sixty, in two months, I'll be able to call all of you kids."

"And you'll have earned that right."

By the time they had reached the back porch of the modern revival

76

style farmhouse, Matthew's mother, Elizabeth, was already trading hugs with the rest of the crew. Grace's seemed longer than the rest. "Save some for me, please," he said.

Elizabeth made a beeline for him and wrapped her arms around his neck. "I'm glad you're home," she whispered. "After everything I heard about Ceres..."

"I'm sorry that we couldn't come right home. Ceres was a wild ride. We've been running ever since."

She pulled back and gave him a look. "I know. That's what the news is telling me. Again. But we don't have to talk about it right now. I'd rather not actually. How is everyone? I know there are a thousand stories to tell."

"There always are," Abigail agreed. "We ended a nearly century-old dictatorship while trying to rob a zoo. That was a fun one."

Elizabeth brushed a wispy strand of hair behind her ear. "I read about Metis. The article didn't mention the crew or ship by name, but I had a feeling it was you."

"It was sort of an accident," Davey said. "Abigail and Matthew got caught, so Yvonne and I had to fly to the rescue. You should have seen the maneuver Yvonne pulled."

Elizabeth laughed. "Most women my age are praying for visits from grandchildren. I gave up on that dream when Matthew became a priest, but you all are the next best thing." Matthew's heart twisted in his chest. The crew was his family and his job took him far from here. But he was glad that his mother had forgiven him for his dangerous lifestyle enough to have accepted them into her life too.

"We'll be around for a few weeks," he said. "In and out on business."

She opened the back screen door. "Good. Am I cooking for the whole crew tonight?"

"That's up to you. We have to head into town for the afternoon, but we should be back by the evening."

Abigail frowned. "Are you sure there's time? Kyoto had us running circles until late in the evening."

"We know people here," Matthew said. "They might not be happy to see us, but that's not ever slowed us down before."

"Oh... Him."

Matthew nodded. Elizabeth pointed at him. "Dinner is at seven. You'll be more disappointed than I will be if you're late." She looked around at the other crew members and then stage whispered to him. "I have enough real bacon for everyone to have three rashers." There was a hearty cheer all around. It was a silly and expensive treat, but Matthew could almost forgive her for splurging on his crew. After all, she wasn't likely to get those grandchildren at this point.

Grace yawned as the magnetic train glided down the tracks into Flagstaff. They'd taken public transportation to avoid rush hour traffic on the way back, but with how many stops the line had, she wasn't sure this was any faster.

"No yawning, Abigail said. "Those things are contagious." She stood in the aisle, a hand on the overhead racks.

"Can't help it," Grace muttered. "It confuses my brain when we land, it's one time in one colony, get up and leave to the next and it's another time entirely. What do you call that?"

"Jet lag is what I've always heard."

She frowned. "What's that supposed to mean?"

Abigail paused for a moment. "I'm not actually sure. Matthew?"

"Archaic idiom," he said without looking up from his tablet. "They used to use jet-engined aircraft on Earth for air travel. Kind of like skyhoppers."

"What are you so engrossed in?" Yvonne asked from beside him.

"Local newspaper. Trying to get a feel for how Arizona is reacting to the Gilgamesh attack."

It was hard for Grace to imagine the scale of disaster that damage to those factories meant. Humanity might have lost a decade or two. With the way things were going, that didn't really seem like much of a change. But the hushed conversations she'd seen between the adults and the looks on their faces were enough to give her a thrill of fear. Maybe she didn't understand things as well as she thought she did. How could the whole species hang by a thread like that?

Abigail broke her out of her thoughts. "So why did your brother stay home today?"

She looked out the window. "He likes it here. And I think he likes Ms. Elizabeth." She lowered her voice and glanced toward Yvonne to make sure she wasn't listening. "They had quite an adventure together the day that White Void attacked."

"Well, it's not like this will be a fun trip anyway. But I bet Elizabeth puts him to work."

"He wouldn't mind that."

Abigail raised an eyebrow at her. Grace sighed. Abigail never really did give Davey enough credit. In her mind, he was still the angry kid with a gun that had snuck onboard over Titan. It bothered Grace, but what was she going to do about it. The train chimed and began to slow down. "This is our stop," Matthew said, standing up. "Downtown."

They piled off the train into the afternoon sun. Low skyscrapers, nothing like the glass and steel towers of Port Jacobson, lined the streets. The station was busy at the moment, but Abigail was easy to follow through the crowd as it parted for her. They followed her down the stairs to street level. Beside the busy street, there was an open plaza filled with food vendors and people.

"I smell tacos," Grace said. She sniffed the air again. "And something with lots of herbs."

"Forgotten about the bacon already?" Matthew asked.

"Never." She didn't mention that, as a kid growing up on the street, there was always room for a meal. Long ago, she and Davey had figured out that the adults got uncomfortable when their former lives were brought up. It was the past anyway, and there was no reason to linger on it. Either way, her mouth still watered at the wonderful smells and nothing was going to stop that.

They crossed the plaza to an open green park surrounded by fancy looking office buildings and a white-pillared building with a dome. "That's the capitol building," Matthew said. "Hopefully we'll be visiting later, but we get to pay an old friend a visit first." He turned toward the closest office building.

They were stopped by armed security out front. "I'm sorry, sir, due to recent terrorist activity in the colonies, visitors are not allowed into any state building in groups larger than two." He glanced at Abigail nervously. "And I'll have to get special clearance for her to enter the building."

"Well, get started on that," Matthew said. He glanced at Yvonne.

She nodded. "Grace and I will find a way to entertain ourselves or else head back to the ship."

And just like that, Grace was relegated to second-class crew member again. Figures. Going with Matthew would have been a snooze-fest anyway. Still, she rolled her eyes and made a show of crossing her arms. Just so long as everyone else knew she wasn't pleased with being automatically excluded. "Let's go then," she said.

She and Yvonne walked back toward the plaza by the train station. "You're not as mad as you're acting," Yvonne said.

"Nah. This will be better anyway. I guess it's still not a girl's day because Abigail is stuck with Matthew, but I bet we can scrape up some fun before heading home. Here. One of those tourist maps." She stepped past a group of people to get a better look at it.

Yvonne squinted her eyes as she read down the list of nearby attractions. "Museum of the First Martians. I've heard they have good exhibits there."

"Already been."

"Really? When was that?" Yvonne side-eyed her.

"A couple of years ago. The first time Davey and I came to Mars. It was actually the day that White Void attacked the farm." She shoved her hands in her pockets. "But I can see why you might want to forget that day."

Yvonne stared at the map. "A lot has happened since then."

Grace mentally kicked herself. There she'd gone and accidentally picked at a scab. Better make it up to Yvonne. "I wouldn't mind going again. That is if you want to go."

"We don't need to waste money on a museum you've already visited."

"It was free. Stop being depressing. Let's go see the old rusted piles of junk. It's only two blocks away."

Yvonne looked at her feet and then smiled weakly. "Alright. Lead the way."

Grace peered at the map again to make sure she had it down and then turned to follow the street that led away from the square. Yvonne sure was touchy these days. Say one wrong thing, and she was either angry for no good reason or turned into a moody loner. Grace had figured getting that bounty lifted would turn her into a new woman, but this wasn't what she had been hoping for. Maybe it would have been more fun to go with Matthew and Abigail.

Arizona Minister of Law Ryan Thompson sat at his office desk with a permanent scowl fixed to his face. As the chief law enforcement officer of the colony, life had been a pain since the Ceres Incident. Previously the only harm Abrogationists had managed to wreak on Arizona was two days of no comms when they took a satellite offline. Now creeping rumors of terrorists were more than a nuisance. They signaled an existential threat.

"Just peachy," he mumbled as he picked up the expensive print newspaper his secretary had delivered an hour ago. The attack on the Gilgamesh factory last week had complicated everything. Editorialists now saw a terrorist behind every politician, even going so far as accusing the Barclay administration of having Abrogationist sympathizers. That made about as much sense as a colony without an environmental shield. Politicians and bureaucrats need a society to stay in power. Radicals that want to end civilization are a threat to that way of life. It was all nonsense. Normally the press had enough healthy cynicism of the political class, but lately, they'd forgotten that power-hungry monsters weren't liable to destroy their own kingdoms. Politics and human abrogation didn't mix. He threw the paper into the recycle bin in frustration.

But the public was afraid, so Ryan Thompson had to look for terrorists under every rock. Oh, they were out there. They'd arrested a couple a month ago that had been digging up water mains, damaging seals so that they leaked before reburying them. Because apparently, a little wasted water would bring about the twilight of civilization.

His intercom buzzed. "Mr. Thompson, you have a visitor."

"I don't remember any appointments this afternoon."

"You have one more in an hour."

"Right. Besides that one. Well, who's here to see me?"

Sheila went silent. Ryan frowned and felt his perpetual headache reemerging with a vengeance. She finally continued. "You remember those visitors you had that one time that you said would never under any circumstances be allowed to see you again?"

He closed his eyes and pinched the bridge of his nose. "Then why are you bothering me about this if you already know my answer? Call security and have them thrown out."

"Sir, we both know how well that works with the Shield Maiden. They claim to have credible evidence of an Abrogationist threat, and I thought that—"

"Then stop wasting all of our time and send them in." He walked to his window and opened the blinds. The afternoon sun peeked between the buildings, lighting up the capital park grounds. When the door opened behind him, he didn't turn to greet them. He could at least deny them that dignity since they never bothered to schedule an appointment. "What do you want?"

"Good to see you, too," Cole said.

"I told you he would be charming as ever," Sharon added.

Ryan turned to face them, hands at ease behind his back. He had to keep some control over this situation and look like he was the one in charge. At least it was just the two of them this time "Forgive me for not rolling out the red carpet for meddlers and mercenaries."

Sharon snorted. "That's an ironic accusation considering you hired us the first time."

"Which is what mercenaries are for. Then you proceeded to meddle. I'll repeat my question. What do you want?"

Ryan noted the lines under Cole's eyes and the weary expression. The last couple of years must have been hard on the freelancer. He crossed his arms. "We have a message for President Barclay. You're going to get us in to see him."

Not likely. "I was told you had a credible security threat. You can pass it on to me, and if it concerns the president, I'll pass it on to him through normal briefings."

Cole didn't seem particularly upset by this declaration. "You know of Alexander Logan, I assume."

"Don't insult me. I've been putting his lackeys away for months."

"And you know how he and I met during the Ceres Incident?"

"I seem to remember that you almost delivered a nuclear bomb into his hands."

"We were one group of many that he deceived. We were also at Gilgamesh."

That one gave Ryan a pause. The colony of Gilgamesh was keeping the details quiet for now, but there had been rumors of outside assistance. Apparently, Cole really knew how to be at the right place at the right time. Or else he was working with Logan. Doubtful considering Cole's personality and beliefs, but it wasn't something he was entirely willing to dismiss.

Cole continued. "We managed to contact Logan afterward. He timed the attack for us to be present and then asked us to pass on a message to President Barclay."

"This is all pretty fishy sounding."

"We have a record of the conversation and can present it as evidence."

Conversations can be staged. Ryan looked at the pair of freelancers. Who was he kidding? Cole was as straight an arrow as they came, making the whole thing even stranger. And at that moment, Ryan realized he believed him. Or at least believed he had a message from Logan. He still had doubts about whether or not it had to be reported directly to the president. But Cole had been involved in the Ceres Incident and had been present for the Gilgamesh attack. Barclay would probably welcome the chance to meet Cole. He made a snap decision.

"Alright."

Cole cocked his head and Abigail visibly started. "I'm sorry," she said. "I just wasn't expecting you to be cooperative."

Ryan shrugged and returned to his desk. He hadn't either, but this was an opportunity to get back into Barclay's better graces after the Hawthorne Brother thing from a few years ago. Even better that Cole and Sharon should be involved. "If you end up wasting our time, you will regret it. I'm making a call. Keep your mouths shut for a minute, please." They shuffled in annoyance, and Ryan smiled to himself. Standard protocol would be to get with the chief of staff, but he wasn't in the mood for the delay and proper processes. He called President Barclay's comm directly, hoping to get lucky.

Jackpot.

"Mr. President, I have a visitor in my office that you may want to see."

Davey moved to the next garden row and, setting down both his buckets, knelt down in the rich brown dirt. Asparagus. Not his favorite vegetable, but he wasn't going to turn down any fresh produce if it was offered. "Okay, what's the procedure on asparagus?"

Elizabeth looked up from the tomatoes she'd been dealing with and joined him. "This will be the last time I harvest them this season. You're looking for nice firm stalks just starting to purple at the tip but not yet opening like this one. It's already gone to seed. Take your knife and cut the entire stalk about two centimeters beneath the soil, like this. Just don't tug the roots out and you'll be fine. Think you have it?"

He cut an asparagus stalk off as she instructed and laid it gently in his produce bucket. "I think so. Thanks." She smiled and went back to her tomatoes. He glanced down the row. The asparagus should only take him a few minutes. Weeds seemed to be mostly under control too. Speaking of which, he grasped a stray offender by the top of the root and gently pulled it out of the soil, shaking the dirt off before throwing it in his second bucket.

This wasn't what he'd had in mind when he'd decided to stay home this afternoon. No sooner had he settled into the rocking chair on the back porch for a nap than Elizabeth had thrown a pair of work gloves at him with a smirk, and that had settled things.

It was a good kind of work, though. Fun even. If Yvonne caught wind, she'd probably expect him to help tend the garden in the hold. Elizabeth's massive garden beside the house put hers to shame.

"How did you learn all this?" he asked as he worked down the row.

"My husband, Albert, taught me a lot. Before we married, I'm not sure if I had ever touched a living plant." She laughed softly. "A lot has changed since then."

"Didn't you think about going back to teaching?" he asked.

"Not even once. This farm is where my husband grew up. Where Matthew was born and raised. Where we made a life. Tilling the earth is a different kind of work and I'm not sure that I love it. But it is fulfilling and I wouldn't trade it for a second chance at teaching literature to college students that couldn't care one iota." She paused. "Besides. Albert is buried here."

There was nothing Davey could say to that, so he kept his mouth shut and went back to his asparagus. In just a few minutes, he had weeded and harvested the row. "Anything else?"

Elizabeth's face appeared from behind one of the tomato plants she'd been putting into the ground. "That'll be good. Thank you, Davey. I appreciate you helping me. I know you were thinking about a nap when I ambushed you."

"There's plenty of time to sleep when living on a ship," he said. "Yvonne thinks there's always work to be done, but she's wrong."

She gave him a look, but let it pass. "Is this guild of Matthew's serious?"

Davey paused, startled by the change of subject. "I don't think I've ever known him to not be serious."

"Hmm. Me neither." She went back to her tomatoes.

He stood for a minute, awkward and unsure of what to do. He could probably go back to the house to wash up his produce, but something in Elizabeth's last question held him in place. "Do you worry about him much?"

"Always. That's been my job for three and a half decades. And now, oh Davey, he's making enemies. The cartels of Europa. The syndicates. This Whitaker scares the daylights out of me. And now these Abrogationists. Of course, I worry." Her voice grew sharper as the list went on before ending with a note of bitterness.

"At least this guild will give us more allies," Davey said slowly, feeling he was on a crumbling cliffside.

"Of that, I'm glad. He was alone for so many years. I was... I was relieved when he took on a crew." Davey saw the glisten of moisture in her eyes. "And now his crew is family. Let's go clean up. Just leave the weed bucket here. I'll have more to do in the morning before the farmhands show up."

He followed her back to the house and through the back door into the kitchen. They emptied their buckets of produce, carrots, asparagus, and fresh lettuce onto the counter. "I'll wash," she said. "If you would, dry for me, please."

They quietly went about their task. Elizabeth broke the silence after several minutes. "Sorry to lay that on you. I really am glad you're with him on the Sparrow. All of you. I'm just afraid he's burning too much fuel. That he'll burn up before he's content to stay in one place. I don't know what put this wanderlust in his heart, but if it isn't satisfied eventually, he'll never have roots. The job of the freelancer is a young man's game."

What would Matthew do when he was done being the captain of the Sparrow? Did freelancers ever retire for that matter? Or would he be like 'Elwa and man his ship till he was old and gray, a grizzled captain wise to all the solar system? "All I know is, I'll be there with him till the end."

She placed a head of lettuce on the counter beside him to dry. "Go ahead and break the leaves off like this and dry them individually. We'll use this one tonight. And that's a bold declaration to make Davey. The solar system is a dangerous place. Neither you nor Matthew may live to see his retirement."

"Is it really getting worse out there?"

She looked thoughtfully out the small window above the sink. "I think so. Would that I had the Shield of Aeneas to read the fates of Rome and know what is to come. Is there victory ahead or is everything vanity?"

He frowned. "Shield of what now?"

She laughed. "The Shield of Aeneas. It's an artifact in the Aeneid, an epic poem about the founding of Rome. It was made by the god Vulcan and engraved with future events as a token and proof of the coming victory."

"That sounds pretty cool."

"The Aeneid is one of my favorites."

Davey pursued his lips. "Do you... Do you have a copy I could borrow? Maybe?" He felt his cheeks warm. It was a stupid question.

Beside him, Elizabeth stood back and gave him a look. "Yes. But you can't start with the Aeneid."

Now he felt really stupid. "Why not?"

"You need to read the Iliad and the Odyssey first."

"Are those about Rome too?"

"No they are much older Greek works, by the poet Homer. Virgil took inspiration and wrote the Aeneid almost as a continuation." She laughed as she turned off the water. "Almost like a work of fan fiction."

Davey remembered the collection of weird unofficial Splendid Sam stories he and Grace had found on the Titan network. Most were pretty terrible, and quite a few he'd forbidden Grace from opening, but they'd managed to find a few gems amongst the garbage. "So do you have a copy of the first one I can borrow?"

"Of course. I'm going to warn you, though. It'll be hard. You'll have to look up a lot of words and names and places. And it's set on Earth, so there's a lot of context you'll need to learn to understand what's going on."

The easy thing would have been to abandon ship. Take the escape pod and get out of there before he got in over his head. But then he remembered his conversation with Yvonne. Maybe it wasn't too late to learn a little bit about the world. "If I run into something I don't get, can I send you a message?"

She put a hand on her hip. "I would love nothing more." She dried her hands. "Come. Let's go find my copy."

Davey followed her out of the kitchen, aware that he'd probably just bitten off more than he could chew. "Hey. Don't tell Matthew. Yet." He wasn't even sure why, but the idea of Matthew watching him struggle through a hard book made him sweat.

"It'll be our secret." She smiled as she pulled a terrifyingly thick book off a shelf. His eyes went wide. That was the book he was borrowing?

The Museum of the First Martians was better without Davey complaining the whole way about how dumb it was. Yvonne was far more interested than he was in the history of the early exploration of Mars, but that didn't really surprise Grace. She'd begun to realize over the last couple years, that while Matthew was smart, especially about people and right and wrong stuff, Yvonne was brilliant. She learned new subjects and skills in a single sitting despite being the oldest member of the crew. It was no wonder she'd picked up mechanics. And piloting. And cooking. And anything else the team needed.

"Can you imagine," Yvonne said, "living in a time when there were new things all the time. New advances and sciences. New horizons and worlds to step foot on."

"That does sound pretty cool," Grace admitted. They'd left the last of the exhibits, the preserved remains of the first ship that brought humans to Mars, and were passing the gift shop. It looked like it was mostly full of junk. She wasn't sure what spaceship-shaped candy had to do with anything. "I think it would be pretty awesome to be the first to step foot on a new moon or planet."

"There are still a few places in our backyard we haven't been," Yvonne said. "During Moses' era, we visited the moons of Uranus but never settled any colonies that far out. There wasn't any need. I've never heard of any expeditions to Neptune or beyond."

"We've got a ship. Let's do it."

Yvonne tsked softly. "As the ship's bookkeeper, I'm going to have to advise against that. The fuel cost would be beyond extreme, and the profit nonexistent."

"Boo. You have no sense of adventure." The automatic front doors of the museum opened and they stepped out into the late afternoon sunlight. "I guess we head back to the plaza to wait for Abigail and Matthew?"

Yvonne shook her head. "We can leave them a message and catch a train home. Maybe we can help Elizabeth cook dinner and learn a thing or two from her."

They walked down the wide stairs from the museum toward the sidewalk. That was when Grace heard him.

"Are we not then an invasive species?" a voice shouted. "A species plucked from its natural environment to disastrous consequences for itself and its new home?"

A young man in a suit stood on the sidewalk, carrying a sign over his shoulder. It read 'Human Abrogation is the Future.'

Grace froze in her tracks and stared at him. "Isn't that illegal?" she asked Yvonne in a voice barely above a whisper as the man droned on.

"In Arizona? No, I think it's okay. As long as he doesn't espouse violence or threaten anyone, he's probably free to say what he wants." She motioned to a pair of police officers standing nearby. "It looks like they're keeping an eye on him."

"But Abrogationists are known terrorists!"

Yvonne shook her head. "Human abrogation is a philosophical stance. Misguided, but its followers have a right to their terrible opinions. Some of them enact their beliefs through violence, despite the fact that the philosophy discourages such actions. If this guy can stand on the sidewalk and spout his ridiculous ideas in full view of the police, then I'm sure he's never hurt anyone." Suddenly she did a double take.

"Umm. You okay there?" Grace frowned and looked back and forth between Yvonne and the protester.

Yvonne's eyes narrowed. "I... I know him."

"What do you mean?"

"It means I'm going to have a word with him." She marched down the sidewalk toward the man. Grace grimaced and hurried to catch up. This had gotten weird on the quick.

The man turned to face them when they were only a few feet away. "Good afternoon! Do you have questions about—"

"I remember you," Yvonne cut him off.

He stopped short. "I'm sorry. I'm not sure I can say the same. Maybe you could refresh my memory."

"Ever spend time in Bright Crater, Ceres?"

He nodded once. "I spent four years there. I take it that's where we met."

She pointed a finger at him. "You used to protest outside my clinic every Monday for nearly three months. You were incredibly frustrating."

Grace saw recognition spread across his face. "Doctor Naude. I remember now. I'm sorry I had forgotten. I hope you know I never meant you or your husband any harm. I hope you're both doing well."

"He's dead, thank you."

Grace winced. If there was one way to turn Yvonne's mood sour, this was it. This guy was playing with fire and he didn't know it. To his credit, he flinched and Grace thought he actually looked remorseful. "I'm sorry. He was always polite to me when we spoke."

"That's because he was a good man that cared about people," Yvonne said. "Unlike followers of your degenerate philosophy."

He took a step back and his expression fell flat. "It's not that we don't care. Human Abrogationists don't wish death or harm on anyone. We believe that responsible people should do what they can to end the colonization of the solar system. We were artificially transplanted by the Great Enabler to the colonies. The current suffering of our race is entirely due to that fact. Humanity's place is Earth. We should return to our radiation-wracked home until we are able to stand on our own two feet."

"I've heard it all before," Yvonne said. "You speak about morals and ethics. But you've stepped outside of every ethical framework to ever exist that wasn't dreamed up in the philosophy department of a morally bankrupt academic institution. What about future generations? Not some hypothetical 'we all go back to die on Earth' future generation, but this one right here?" she gestured at Grace. "Who gave you the right to choose against her generation? Why don't they get to live their lives? They did nothing to deserve your kind trying to steal civilization out from under them." She'd gotten louder and louder as she'd continued. Grace noticed that the police officers nearby had taken interest and edged closer.

"Don't doctors do the same thing?"

Yvonne's face reddened. "Excuse me?"

"Don't you sometimes choose who lives and who dies? You have the concept of triage, where sometimes you have to make hard decisions. You and your husband ran a trauma clinic. Have you never held another's life in your hands and had to choose if they will live to see another day?"

Grace held her breath as every muscle in Yvonne's face stiffened. "That's different than being an executioner like your fellow Abrogationists. Doctors save lives. That's something you'll never do."

This wasn't good. Grace tugged on Yvonne's arm. "Hey. Let's go. This isn't worth the trouble."

"Is it different, though?" he asked. "Are you not an executioner to the one you let die? It's all in perspective. Yes, human Abrogationists choose according to different metrics. But the concept shouldn't be so alien to a doctor."

"To a doctor, all life is sacred!" She was practically in his face now shouting. Grace tugged on her arm again, but Yvonne ignored her. "Even those that don't deserve it. Even filth like you that protest things you don't understand. Even..." Her voice cracked, and she stopped abruptly.

"Ma'am I think you should move on." The police officers were at their side now. "This guy is out here every afternoon. He loves getting under people's skin."

She threw Grace's arm off and turned to march away. The police stepped closer to the protester to talk to him, but he stepped around them and addressed Grace. "Hey kid. Tell her I'm sorry. I don't know what that was about."

"Me neither," Grace mumbled and turned to catch up with Yvonne. She'd seen the shimmer of tears in her eyes as she'd turned away. She had no idea what was going on, but she was going to ask Matthew about it.

President Norman Barclay listened to the story of the two freelancers who stood in his office. One was all swagger. The Shield Maiden of Mars. She'd turned up in news stories and intelligence reports over the years. He was more familiar with her name and reputation than the specifics of her exploits.

The other was a man of particular interest. Matthew Cole's name had been repeated over and over during the last few months. He was an Arizona native, though Norman doubted he had any particular loyalty to his home colony anymore. The media painted him as a hero of the people. Like some kind of cowboy that walked into town, flashed his guns, and suddenly everything was going to be okay.

But the world wasn't that simple, and everyone in the room knew it. Including the half-dozen armed secret service agents that kept a wary eye on Sharon.

Norman sat back in his chair behind his desk tapped his fingers on the arms of his chair. "I have to take this message as a personal threat," he said. "Logan is calling me out personally, and I can't ignore that."

"I understand, sir," Cole said. "Just make sure not to fall into his hands. He's crafty. And we nearly did that at Ceres. If he's calling you out, he's hoping you'll behave in a way that benefits him."

"I see. Hopefully, all of this comes to naught. Our entire intelligence apparatus has been bent toward capturing Logan ever since Ceres."

"I wouldn't get your hopes up." Cole wrinkled his lip, almost looking unsure of himself for a moment. That was interesting. "You're not the only one looking for him. We have a powerful... ally that's been trying to eliminate Logan for a long time. Even he hasn't had much luck."

Thompson shifted at that, and Norman made a note to ask privately what that was about. The minister had more than a few shadowy sources of information. Maybe he knew something about this ally. An enemy of an enemy could also be a friend in a moment of need.

"It's no matter. With the combined forces of the colonies hunting him, the clock is ticking. Logan's previous successes have isolated the Abrogationists from having many political allies. We'll find him. He's tipped his hand in arrogance. And even if we don't, Kyoto and Gilgamesh will have the security to protect their factories. We'll see to that one way or the other."

"Don't underestimate him," Sharon growled. "This isn't a game."

Norman smiled. "Ma'am I've served almost two full terms as president of the colony of Arizona. I'm neither a child nor naive. I thank you for your service to humanity, but I'll take care of things from here." He nodded his head, and the freelancers were ushered from the room by the secret service agents.

Thompson slunk over from his corner and crossed his arms. "Well, sir? What do you think?"

"I believe them. I think Prime Minister Dobashi and I need to have a conversation about updating our status of forces agreement. The Kyoto military won't be sufficient for this threat."

Thompson shrugged. "And now we're outside my area of expertise. I'll continue keeping an eye on the domestic side of things unless you need something else."

"I may, actually. You reacted to Cole's hesitant mention of an ally. What do you know about that?"

"Nothing for sure. But I know a broker of information and..." he hesitated. "Influence, that matches the description. Don't ask me his name. He has a flair for the dramatic and goes by an assortment of monikers. I've worked with him before on various projects. But I wasn't aware that the crew of the Sparrow have as well."

Norman tapped his fingers on his desk. "Would he be an asset to us?"

"Sir, he's the type that would only help someone when it suits his own purposes."

"And our purposes seem to have met. See if he'll work with the Office of Colonial Intelligence."

"Yes, sir. Anything else?"

He waved him off. "You can go." Norman watched as the other man left the office. Despite the previous scandal, it had paid to keep Thompson around. He kept the leash shorter than it used to be, but that was hardly a problem. It took all sorts to keep a government moving, even those that occasionally broke the rules.

Norman closed his eyes to clear his thoughts and picked up his comm. He'd better talk to Prime Minister Dobashi now before this hit official channels. A diplomatic storm was brewing, and it would be better to have it out in private before the press got wind of what was happening.

Dinner at the Cole farm was a hit, as always. Salad, fresh asparagus, deviled eggs, and of course, the promised bacon. Matthew watched as the crew tore into the meal like a pack of starving dogs. At least half of the bacon was gone in seconds, inhaled as though it were the last lungfuls of oxygen from an air canister, though he did notice everyone kept one of their three rashers back, probably to enjoy at the very end. Abigail and Grace laughed at a joke, happy and carefree, and his mother and Davey were in a deep discussion about whether or not asparagus was really worth all the space she had devoted to it in the garden.

Only Yvonne was quiet. Grace had quietly told him about the confrontation with the Abrogationist, relaying as much of the conversation as she could remember.

"She just blew up, Matthew."

"It's alright. Thanks for telling me. I'll check and make sure she's okay."

He hadn't followed through with that promise yet. She'd do as she'd done every time he tried to talk to her about Ceres and blow him off. It was a puzzle he would have to sort out soon. He'd made it a point to respect her privacy and not check the security camera's recording of that day, but he was starting to think that might not have been the wisest course. She might be a free woman, but something had its claws in her.

Dinner ended and the crew went their separate ways after helping clean up. Matthew eventually wandered to the back porch. It was a nice night out, or as nice as cool Martian evenings ever were. He rocked on the bench swing, staring at the stars visible above the Sparrow's dark silhouette.

Eventually, his mother found him. "Room for another?"

"There's a reason I didn't take dad's rocking chair."

She sat beside him, but rather than breaking the peaceful repose of the night with talk, leaned her head against his shoulder. Sometime later, she whispered to him. "I wish you were here more often. All of you."

"I know."

"But I understand. Just promise to come home someday before it's too late."

The quiet chirp of the crickets was the only sound to be heard.

Chapter 5: The Spider's Clutch

Among men's baser instincts is our tendency towards the tribal. Naturally we band into groups for protection and mutual benefit, but our desperate attempts to derive meaning from these groups has always driven us into violence and bloodshed.

And so we formed nations. Though they were necessary inventions for the maintaining of order and civil societies, they also spurred us to war with the sound of patriotic marches. Some of these tribal wars were just. Most were not.

Even Moses knew that he could not do away with the nation state. If there were ever to be a far-off day of gold that humanity was to be united under a single flag, it did not come in his time, nor did he even attempt to weave such a banner. Nations outlived the AI, or else their children did, for though they bore the image of their parents, they were not the same. Their destinies were their own to forge. And yet tribal they have remained. It is, after all, one of the birthrights of our troubled species.

Ulysses Potter
Author of A Political History of the Colonies
Died 50 AM

Abigail stepped off the mag-train into the bright morning sun. Doch Rossiya was only an hour away, so there'd been no reason to burn the Sparrow's fuel when she only planned to be gone for the day. Despite being relatively empty, the station was loaded with security, and she had to wait in a queue before being questioned by the police officer. Ever since they'd spilled the beans last week about the supposed coming Abrogationist attack, things had gotten a little bit tense on Mars.

"Look," she said. "My Russian isn't terrible, but you're either going to have to slow down or use English if you want me to answer your questions."

The uniformed woman frowned harder, if that was possible, and crossed her arms. "What is your business in Doch Rossiya?"

"I'm a freelancer here on the job," she said, presenting her ID.

The officer took the ID and scanned it. "Abigail Sharon. How long do you mean to stay?"

"I'd like to leave before the sun sets."

"Short stay for freelancer work." She tapped a few keys at her computer. "Due to current security concerns, outsiders are not encouraged to visit Doch Rossiya. You have forty-eight hours to conduct your business and depart. I recommend you leave sooner."

Abigail shrugged and took her ID back. "That's not gonna be a problem. I was thinking about hitting up all the tourist traps, but the open hostility has kind of burnt me on the idea. So much for Russian hospitality."

The officer glared ice at her. "Harosheva dnya, Ms. Sharon."

Abigail saluted her and walked past the checkpoint and down the hall to the street exit. On the sidewalk, a sign showed a detailed map of the city. She approached it, edging her way around an older couple, and gave it a good look. It was only a six-klick walk to her destination, and thankfully it was in the opposite direction of her old broker. She hadn't seen or talked to Mistress Medvedev in the last two years, and while she certainly didn't miss the woman, she did feel a little guilty about it. Medvedev had been the one to give her a start in freelancing, even if it was Matthew that had given that career any form of purpose.

The current situation limited her time here. She had every excuse in the world to slip back to Arizona and the Sparrow without dropping by the Mistress' estate. "Next time," she muttered as she set off down the street. "At least to tell her how wrong she'd been about Matthew." But then she probably already knew that herself. Hopefully. She was going to be livid when Abigail tried to recruit one of her freelancers for the guild.

She made good time across town. Walking through the Russian colony was like taking a step back in time. It had been constructed as a monument to that culture's heritage. It was like an eastern European city from centuries previous. Tall neoclassical apartments, their first floors' quaint shops and businesses, lined the streets. The cobblestone sidewalks were broken by occasional trees, neatly pruned to ordered perfection. Those sidewalks were choked with people today. As usual, the locals parted for her in awe, taking big steps back or just gaping, something she usually took for granted. Today, she was thankful for the crowd's consideration of her bulk. Maybe the increased foot traffic was because the roads were clear of civilians. Convoys of military and police vehicles were out in swarms. They really were taking the security threats to heart, which was honestly a bit of a surprise considering Kyoto was a hemisphere away.

Her destination was one of those big roundabouts where five busy roads came and went their separate ways. An imposing statue of Dostoevsky, the greatest of the Russian novelists, stood watch over the lanes of traffic. She navigated half the circle before spotting the bistro on the far side. She checked the time and winced. Milena would be here by now. Professionals like her were never late. She glanced at the faded white tables. They were full, but she couldn't spot her friend, which in and of itself wasn't a surprise. Milena's past as a spook had given her the ability to disappear in plain sight if that was her desire.

"Having trouble finding what you're looking for?"

Abigail turned at the sound of the lightly accented voice. Her face was hidden behind a pair of round sunglasses and her dull copper hair concealed by a trendy hat and scarf. "I knew you were there," Abigail said smoothly.

"It's a good thing that suit automatically disqualifies you from undercover work because you're a terrible liar. Come, let's go somewhere more private to talk."

The woman passed with a swish of her long trench coat, and Abigail fell in behind her without another word as she cut down the alley behind the bistro. They stuck to the alleys for nearly three blocks, making seemingly random turns. Abigail guessed they would have made a strange sight had anyone seen them. An armored titan and a smartly dressed woman of forty-something.

They cut through the back of an abandoned warehouse before climbing through a hidden sliding panel into the stairwell of a tall tenement building. They climbed seven flights up the creaking spiral before finally reaching a locked door. Milena unlocked it and, with one final look around, led Abigail inside.

"Welcome to my nest," she said.

Despite the dilapidated state of the building, the small penthouse was neat and free of even a speck of dust. A small living area, kitchen, and a couple of bedrooms. Nothing fancy. By the far window, telescopic surveillance equipment poked through the blinds, obediently recording everything it saw.

"Who's the current target?" Abigail asked.

"Mafia," Milena said. "An old crime family that previously had ties to the Morgensens. Ever since the shakeup on Ceres, the Martian crime scene has been a mess. The Yakuza's are convinced they can take over Doch Rossiya's underground, but the older families will burn before they see that happen." She took off her trench coat and hat, shaking out her shoulder-length hair. "I'd offer to take your coat, but I know your policy on that matter."

"Thanks. A girl has to keep some secrets."

"Yes. Secrets. Can I get you a cup of coffee? I seem to remember you have a sweet tooth when it comes to your caffeine."

"You know me too well."

Milena moved to the small kitchen. "I used to anyway. It's been what? A couple years now since you've been out from under the Mistress' thumb."

Abigail stooped over the surveillance equipment and glanced at the screen. It showed a small factory yard in crisp detail. According to the readout, it was nearly three kilometers away. "You don't paint Mistress Medvedev in very nice words there. I guess she hasn't changed much."

A snort came from the kitchen. "She grows more severe with each passing season. She's a fierce broker and a champion for those she takes under her wing, but... Well, she has the temper of a sandstorm. And when things don't go as she orders, she has no reservations about turning it on you."

Abigail softly bit the inside of her lip. "Medvedev was always good to me. She helped me land on my feet with this career."

"Of course she did. You were an investment that paid off. Do you think she's so loving to her protégés when they fail to turn a profit?"

Abigail turned away from the window and walked to the kitchen. "If she's so bad, why do you still work with her?"

Milena passed her a steaming cup of coffee. "I'll let you handle the sugar. I already told you. She's a master broker. I'm a surveillance specialist. The average broker wouldn't know what to do with me. Medvedev has connections to every colonial government and law enforcement agency. She convinced them all years ago that I was better than their own people, and I haven't gone more than a week without a job since."

"I see your point." She tried to imagine Benny working with Milena and shook her head. Sometimes he could find the good stuff, but other times she was pretty sure he was just working with the scraps, making do with what meager contacts he had. And now, riding off the coattails of Matthew's fame.

Milena stirred her own coffee cup. "That said, if you talk me into this guild thing, you get to tell Medvedev yourself. She's going to be furious, and I'm not going to deal with that fallout on my own."

Abigail took a sip from her mug and managed to keep her poker face. "My reason for coming to see you was that obvious, huh?"

"Transparent as the vacuum of space. I've been following the media headlines, and I'm not stupid. What I don't get is why you'd ask me. I'm not a public-facing freelancer. I deal with governments. And the ones I work with already know me."

Abigail sighed. "We only wanted people we knew we could trust implicitly in the first batch of recruits. People whose reputation speaks for itself like Gebre'elwa—"

"You talked the old lady into this?" She set her cup down.

"She begged to be on board." And apparently, recruiting her first was going to grease the wheels going forward. They'd lucked out on that. "As I was saying. Reputation or first-hand experience is what we're looking for. My first three jobs were as muscle for you, Milena."

The other woman chuckled. "You never told me those were your first jobs. In hindsight, I should have known you were green when you blew my cover on the Sychov sting."

"I made it up to you," Abigail said, feeling her cheeks warm. "I brought down the whole gang."

"And half the building. We were both lucky there was enough evidence left to convict them. But I still don't see how this will benefit me."

Abigail took a step back. "Maybe it doesn't. But you've always been one of the good guys, and those are the people we want in the guild. We're trying to do some good out there."

The smile on Milena's face crumbled slowly. "You're forgetting that I retired from intelligence after losing my partner to a car bomb meant for me. There's more than a little revenge involved when I put these creeps away."

Abigail had actually forgotten that detail. "I don't think there's a free-lancer out there without a story."

Milena nodded and gestured at her. "Says the woman in one-of-a-kind power armor."

"Like I said, a girl has to keep some secrets."

Behind them, the surveillance equipment chirped. Milena was on her feet at once, coffee and conversation forgotten. "Facial recognition alert," she said from her station at the window.

Despite being curious, Abigail kept her distance, not really sure if Milena would appreciate having someone over her shoulder looking at potentially sensitive information. "How does that even work?"

"I've got an earthtech chip installed that runs all the algorithms. It cost me a fortune but has made it back tenfold. Dammit!"

Abigail waited quietly. She watched Milena pace the short length of the living space twice before going back to her monitor. "Is everything okay?" she risked after an awkward minute of silence.

Milena stepped back and gestured at the screen. "What do you see?"

Taking the invitation, she approached and looked at the display. Same factory yard as before, only now it was a hive of activity. Vehicles being loaded in a hurry. Men running everywhere. "Looks like an operation being scuttled if you ask me," Abigail finally said.

"It is. I've been working on Dmitry Yurchenko's operation for two months, and I'm not about to see it all fall apart."

"Maybe he's on to you?"

Milena shook her head, fists clenched. "Please. I'm better than that.

Something else spooked him."

"I did see a lot of military activity on the roads this afternoon. Could that be related?"

"Officially they're running drills. Unofficially, there's something else going on out there, but none of my contacts will breathe a word about it."

"The customs officer wasn't too keen on my visit and suggested I might not want to stick around." Abigail crossed her arms. "At the time, I had thought she was being rude, but now I'm starting to think she was doing me a favor." She held up a hand and counted on her fingers. "One. Customs drops strong hints to leave. Two. Mass military drills. Three. Local crime lords packing up and heading for the hills."

Milena pursed her lips and grabbed her coat off the rack and fixed her hat back on her head. "They're about to close the borders. You need to get out of here." She slipped a sidearm out of her coat and checked its cartridge.

"I'm not leaving when you're about to do something rash."

"I'm about to lose months of work. Maybe I can at least tag the ship that carries Yurchenko's sorry carcass out of here." She moved to the door, but Abigail blocked her path with her arm.

"You used to contract teams for contact work. Are you going to call one in?"

"I don't have time for that. Move."

She stepped aside. "Fine, but I'm coming with you."

Milena opened the door. "Don't be a fool. This isn't your job. Rossiya won't pay me, let alone you, after the mark bolts."

"It's not about money," Abigail said. "It's about you throwing yourself into danger without backup."

"I see the priest hasn't ground off your stubborn corners yet. If you get stuck here, it's not my fault." Milena was already bounding down the stairs and Abigail hurried to catch up.

"Trust me. Between the two of us, he's the stubborn one."

The roar of jet engines made Matthew glance up from his perch atop the Sparrow as yet another formation of skyhoppers flew overhead. That was at least the dozenth pass today. Drills according to the official state-ment. He wasn't sure he trusted that. Earlier in the week, talks between Kyoto and Arizona had broken down after President Barclay demanded that security of the Kyoto factory be given over to the Highland Treaty Organization, a group of wealthy colonies in the southern hemisphere that included Arizona, Doch Rossiya, and Warszawa, amongst others. Kyoto had reluctantly agreed to allow some foreign troops onto their soil. They blanched at the demand to be relieved of command.

"Let's get this plate in place," he said.

He and Davey wrestled with the heavy steel hull plate to move it back to its proper spot. It had taken damage from a micrometeorite hit a few weeks back, and being ground side for a week was the perfect time to make the repair. Or rather pay someone else to do it. The Spar-row didn't have the equipment to reforge steel. Unfortunately, they still had to perform the backbreaking work of installing the replacement.

With a grunt, they made the final push, and the plate dropped into place. Now a few dozen bolts and some welding work and the Sparrow would be good as new.

"So what's this about?" Davey asked as he wiped the sweat from his brow and sat on a hull outcrop. "The performance up there. I'm guess-ing it's not just for looks."

"It may be just that. Arizona might be making a show of military might to stress the point to Kyoto."

Davey shook his head. "This is a mess, isn't it?"

"It is. And I get the feeling Logan knew just what pot he was stirring. But there's nothing we can do about this right now. Politics and the rivalries of nations is beyond either of us. Let's finish this up." He hefted the power wrench into his hand. "You have the bolts?"

"Yeah, they're—"

Matthew's comm buzzed. "It's Whitaker."

Davey raised an eyebrow. "You gonna take it?"

"I should." He passed him the wrench. "Get those bolts down. I'll let you do the welding this time, but I want to supervise." He turned away and walked toward the aft of the ship. "I'm here, Whitaker."

"About time I heard from you," he said. "I had to come to Mars myself since you've stopped answering my messages."

"We've nothing to talk about. Unless you have information about the last Anemoi piece..."

Whitaker was quiet for a moment. "I'm working on it."

"Then we have no business together."

"Don't be that way, Matthew. We can be useful to one another in more ways than that. Take your Guild of Lanterns. Stroke of brilliance, by the way. If you ever need any assistance with—"

"No." Matthew punctuated the rebuke with utter finality. "You wanted me to be a mover and shaker? To be an equal and opposite force after the same ends? This is my way. Stay out of it."

Whitaker laughed. "I guess I had that coming. Fine. But the offer stands. It's a fun idea if a little quaint. It'll give the folks something to believe in." He cleared his throat. "I'm more disappointed you didn't contact me after you talked to Logan. Ending that zealot's miserable life has become priority number one for me."

So Whitaker had informants within either the Kyoto or Arizona government. There was no other way he could know about that conversation. "I took the information to proper channels. Didn't seem to slow you from finding out."

"Matthew, he's threatening all of our lives. Every man, woman, and child. Let us be allies on this one front. I'm already doing my part to secure the Kyoto factory."

Matthew narrowed his eyes. "What have you done?"

"Just a little push. The subtle application of force. Here's a secret. People aren't likely to be compelled to do things they aren't already inclined toward. You already had half a heart to play the hero, so my job was half done. The same is true here. I probably only changed the timetable."

"You should trust yourself less," Matthew said. "Logan has already shown he's perfectly capable of using competing parties to do his dirty work."

Whitaker sighed. "Alright. I can see you're not in an understanding mood. More's the pity. At least promise me that if Logan contacts you again you'll let me know. I'd rather have his head on a pike than see him unravel everything we're fighting for."

"I'll think about it." He ended the call and felt a stab of regret over his lack of manners. Whitaker was a villain, of that he had no doubt, but he was a fellow human making the best of the world with what he knew. Matthew was confident, however, that Whitaker had left some crucial numbers out of his calculations, and the results would be disastrous. A man who believes the world is a void cannot help but be a part of that void.

Understanding that helped Matthew pity the man.

Behind him, the whine of the wrench droned on. In the distance, more skyhoppers roared. Maybe it was best if they just left Mars. They'd done their duty as good citizens. His mother would be heartbroken, but...

But there wasn't an excuse for that one, was there?

"Do all of you spook types use vans like this?" Abigail asked from where she was folded carefully in the back to avoid breaking anything.

Milena glanced back at her briefly from the driver's seat. "They're useful for hauling equipment. Like you."

"I'm not equipment."

"Fine. Half equipment, half passenger, besides you don't fit up front so into the back you go."

Abigail grumbled under her breath, which she felt was justified, given her status as luggage. "So what's the plan here?"

"There's not one yet. I'm still working on it."

"Great. Just great." Abigail sighed. "Okay, what are the options?"

Milena turned the van around a corner. "Yurchenko's got a ship he keeps stashed at a private landing field on the east side. If he thinks the borders are closing for the long haul, he'll try to get offworld, or at least out of Rossiya. Option one. Get to the ship first and place a tracker on it."

"Then he gets away and out of the jurisdiction of Rossiya. Got anything better?"

"We stall him somehow. Get him tripped up with authorities and he loses his window."

Abigail thought about that one. "Not bad, but there's no telling how long we need to delay. No way to just take him out?"

"I'm not being paid to assassinate him. I'm being paid to help put him away for good." Milena took another corner at speed, and Abigail shifted uncomfortably in the back. "No, we need to stall. If we can get officials involved, that should tar things up enough to accomplish what we need. We'll be at the landing field in two minutes. I've got his vehicles tracked, and it will be nearly ten before they can get there."

"What do you want me to do, block the road?"

Milena hummed a long note. "Now that you mention it, that's not a terrible idea." There was a mischievous lilt to her voice, one that gave Abigail pause.

"I get the feeling I'm not going to like this."

"Oh you may. How do you feel about traffic accidents?"

Milena Drugova checked her tracker one last time. "Two hundred meters out. Are you in position, Abigail?"

"I'm ready. Hope you are."

Milena's van was parked in an alley, behind a dumpster, about two blocks from Abigail's position at the entrance to the landing field. She closed the door of the van and crept to the entrance of the alley. Cautiously she eased around the corner to look down the street. "I've got him. Gray grav car, low profile, six doors. Make it as natural as you can."

"I'm just a pedestrian on her comm, distracted and not looking at where she's going."

"Perfect. He just passed me."

"I see him. I'll talk to you on the other side."

Two blocks away, Abigail stood on the street corner, her armor glinting in the late afternoon sun. As the grav car approached the gated entrance to the field, she walked out into the street right in front of Yurchenko' car. From this distance, it took over a second for the crunch of the impact to reach Milena. If everything went according to plan, Abigail had spun in time to catch the car with her arms and brace against the impact. Milena pulled a small pair of binoculars from her coat. A couple of men had already disembarked from the car. Abigail came out from behind it, arms waving and shouting, putting on a good show.

Milena smiled. Abigail always had liked getting to be the center of attention. Guns were drawn and Abigail took a step back, hands raised. Undoubtedly they recognized her. Time for the second part of the plan. Milena sprinted back down the alley to her van. She started it with a rumble. "Sorry old girl. We've been through a lot of jobs together, but I don't think you're going to like this."

She left the alley going the other direction and raced around the block, coming back at the landing field entrance from a different road. Then she called the police. "Yes, I'd like to report a traffic accident at the entrance to the Pulkova Landing Field. A pedestrian has been hit. No, I can't tell if they are okay I called as soon as—"

She hung up the call mid-sentence. That should be enough to get authorities inbound. She rounded the corner, approaching the scene perpendicular from the direction Yurchenko had come from. Unfortunately for him, Abigail had stopped him with the back half of his vehicle in the intersection. She quieted her breathing and relaxed her body. It wasn't going to be a high-speed collision, but she still didn't fancy a case of whiplash. At fifty meters out, the men with guns saw her coming and started shouting, ostensibly to move the car.

"Too late for that," she muttered. She took a final breath and let her muscles go slack. The thugs dove for cover seconds before she reached them. The impact was a lot louder than she anticipated, and her van was thrown into a spin, tires squealing before it came to an abrupt halt.

She sat back for a moment, half-stunned before doing a brief check. No injuries, but she was going to regret this tomorrow when soreness set in. She opened the door of the van. Luckily, she'd spun so that she was facing the bewildered group. They were still picking themselves off the ground. Better give them a show and something to panic about. Milena undid her restraints and stumbled from the car, made it five staggered steps, and then pitched forward to the pavement, landing in a crumpled heap.

Cursing. Lots and lots of cursing.

"We have to go! Zero hour is in seven minutes!"

"We can't just leave her. Security cameras are recording this."

"A hit and run is the least of my concerns right now. Load up."

"You can't just leave her there!" Abigail mixing things up again.

"Freelancer, you're lucky I haven't given the order to have you shot where you stand."

They definitely knew her then. They'd anticipated that when they came up with this crazy plan.

"Buddy, I don't know who you are or why you have trigger happy lunatics with you, but I eat goons like these for breakfast and pick my teeth with their boss."

Too much bravado. A fight was the last thing they needed. Milena groaned loudly and shifted.

"Well, at least she's not dead."

"No thanks to you," Abigail said.

"What... What the hell are you talking about? The crazy woman ran into us. Enough of this. Load up. We're leaving. Freelancer, if you're so worried about her, you can deal with her."

"I'm not letting you just leave. We'll let the police sort this out."

Milena staggered to her knees and coughed, keeping a hand to her head.

"See she's fine."

"She's injured and I'm—"

Red and blue flashing lights filled the streets, reflecting off the stone of the nearby buildings, and sirens chirped. Milena had to resist the impulse to cheer aloud. Yurchenko's only route out of this now was a gunfight with the police, but his money was too entrenched in Rossiya to risk that. She sat back hard and winced as her tailbone hit the pavement. It was going to be a while before this was over, and she still had a part to play. The sooner she could get out of sight, the sooner she could extricate them from this mess by setting the record straight and revealing her identity to the authorities. As a pair of police cruisers pulled to a stop, she cautiously glanced at Yurchenko. He was crestfallen.

Perfect.

"So it turns out I'm stuck in Doch Rossiya for now," Abigail said.

Yvonne raised an eyebrow and looked at Matthew. They were sitting on Elizabeth's back porch after the day's work and the evening meal. For once she was nearly caught up on maintenance on the Sparrow. The sun had slipped beneath the horizon and the last embers of the sunset lingered in the sky.

"What's going on?" Matthew asked. "You're not in trouble, are you?"

"No, it's not like that. They closed all the borders a couple hours ago. No civilian traffic in or out for at least the next week."

"Lovely." Yvonne said and sighed. If it wasn't one thing, it was something else. At least it was Abigail. She could take care of herself for a few days until they figured this out. "Are you in need of anything?"

"I'm with a friend. And I'll most likely be able to stay with my old broker."

"You sound excited," Matthew said. Yvonne could barely make out his face in the dim light, but she was pretty sure he was smiling.

"Thrilled to my very soul. Hey, Matthew. Do you know what's going on?"

"We've been watching military maneuvers all day. I hope it's just posturing. The Highland Treaty Organization wants Kyoto to give in to their demands. But with Rossiya closing their borders..." He trailed off.

"Hopefully," Yvonne said, "this is nothing more than the classic severity of the Russian psyche." It was a weak excuse, and they all knew it.

"I'll have a talk with customs officials in the morning. My paperwork was only for forty-eight hours, so they'll either have to extend that or get rid of me early."

"Keep us updated," Matthew said. "Stay safe."

"You too."

The sharp chirp of crickets drifted across the fields. Yvonne was reluctant to break the moment of peace, but she could practically hear the hurricane of thought going around in Matthew's head. "You're not worried about her, are you?"

"About Abigail? No. She'll be fine, but I am worried. I was thinking about leaving Mars sooner than we'd planned."

"Elizabeth will not be pleased to hear that."

"It won't happen now anyway," he said. "We better plan on a few days at least. Say, Grace told me you a had a run-in with an Abrogationist protester last week."

The change of subject derailed her train of thought. "It was nothing. A coincidence."

He was quiet for a minute, and she thought that he had dropped the topic entirely when he said, "Grace was worried about you."

She sighed and tried to tamp down the wave of annoyance. "He brought up memories of Tomas. I let it get under my skin. I promise. I'm fine." She believed it when she said it, but a moment later, she wondered if it was a lie.

Matthew must have thought the same thing. "If you ever want to talk about it, or Tomas—"

"Yes," she snapped, "I know you're there to listen."

He took off his hat and gave it a shake. "Actually, I was going to suggest you talk to my mother. I think she's had more life experience in this regard than I ever will. Goodnight, Yvonne." He stood and walked out through the field toward the Sparrow, leaving her alone with a gnawing ache of guilt over her outburst.

It wasn't just about Tomas. That protester. It was as if he'd accused her of murder. She had wielded life and death in her hands, and she had chosen justice. Her choice had been perfectly rational. What any sane human would have done. Kudzu deserved death, probably many times over. And it had been her right to administer that justice. But that had been stolen from her. Something she could never get back. She would never be the one to avenge Tomas' death. Never the one to make it right.

She unfolded her restlessly trembling hands. The past was immutable, and it was all behind her. It was only a matter of making herself believe that was true, along with the rest of the lies she told herself.

Abigail was surprised when Milena readily agreed to join the guild.

"I see no reason not to. We share the common goal of making the solar system a safer place, and the dues per job are paltry. My living is secure. After all, you went out of your way to do me a favor tonight and are now stuck here for it. But..."

There was always a snag.

"You still have to tell Medvedev about it. I'll be there when you take the heat. But you get to take the initial hit."

It was evening by the time they left Milena's apartment for Mistress Medvedev's manor, and the city was lit by streetlamps. The estate was nestled in the heart of a wealthy neighborhood of columned houses. Abigail knew they were nearly there when they passed that familiar statue of Mussorgsky, conducting his eternal symphony of the traffic beneath. The manor was as foreboding as ever, with its silent columns and imposing oak door. Milena parked the badly damaged and rattling van on the street out front. It was better not to dawdle, Abigail thought as she ascended the stairs to knock on the door.

"If we're lucky," she said, turning to Milena, "she's in bed already, and we'll see her in the morning."

"I'm not so sure the woman sleeps like a normal human."

The door opened slowly to reveal Medvedev's stewardess. "Ms. Sharon! I haven't seen you in some time." The young woman opened the door wide. "And Ms. Drugova, the Mistress wishes to speak with you."

"I told you she'd be up," Milena said. "Thank you, Natalya. We'll go see the Mistress together if it's alright."

"I will check with her. But please, come in off the street!"

Abigail followed them into the foyer. Perhaps it was her imagination, but it felt as if the place had aged a decade in the last couple years. There were cobwebs in the corners and paint peeled from the high banisters. Maybe all the travel had given her new eyes. Natalya hurried up the stairs and disappeared into the dark. They waited quietly at the bottom in silence. In less than a minute, the stewardess reappeared and motioned them to follow. They passed up the stairs, down a dark hall, and finally through a set of double doors into the broker's office.

It was always a dark room, owing to the heavy curtains that blocked even scant light from filtering through the windows, but at night it was like a crypt. A single lamp burned on the desk, its light not enough to chase away the oily darkness that pooled in the room's corners. A tall woman with wispy white hair rose to her feet at once. She towered over Milena as she approached. "My daughters. It is so good to see you. And especially you, Abigail. I am glad you have returned to us at last. Is this not a most delightful turn of events, Milena?"

"It's good to visit with old friends, Mistress."

Abigail noted her dodge. She had been skillfully left to mete out the disappointment. "I'm only here to visit, Mistress. My crew still needs me."

Medvedev's long fingers gripped the end of her cane, but otherwise, she didn't react. "I see. I will deal with your abandonment shortly." Abigail had never seen her eyes so cold as she turned to Milena. "And you, daughter, I hope you have news on the Yurchenko operation. Your employers want an update and have been unable to reach you."

"It was a narrow victory, ma'am. He tried to escape Rossiya before the lockdown, but with Abigail's help, we managed to stall him."

She launched into a lengthy explanation of the afternoon's adventure. It gave Abigail more than enough time to stew in her anxieties. First, she had to get out from under Medvedev's ire. Then she'd deal with the guild news.

"I have every reason to believe my cover was kept as well," Milena said. "I haven't worn my hair in its natural color in years. Even if Yurchenko knows who I am, he didn't seem to recognize me."

"Wonderful," Medvedev said. "I shall relay the information. It is good to know that some of my daughters can still be relied upon." She glanced swiftly at Abigail before settling back on Milena. "Your mind has not been poisoned by a man unworthy of your acquaintance."

Abigail bristled, and all of her trepidations fell away at the insult. "I'd appreciate it if you didn't talk about Matthew Cole that way. You've never met him. You don't know what kind of man he is."

Medvedev returned to her desk and lowered herself into her chair. "Please. If that press conference was any indication, he is a shameless charlatan. And that, after all those foolish lies out of Ceres. I simply cannot believe that you would stand behind such falsehoods, Abigail."

Abigail stamped her foot. The sound reverberated through the house. "How dare you! I was there too. We raided a uranium enrichment facility, tracked down the bomb, and flew it into orbit. I was the one that let off the detonator, risking life and limb to dispose of it. We saved thousands of lives!"

"I see he left the most dangerous task to you, my dear."

Abigail took a deep breath. "Never mind. This is a waste of both of our time. I'm sorry you're a bitter old woman. I'm sorry you can't accept that there are decent people out there beyond the grasp of your greedy fingers. But I'm finished with you. I'm grateful for what you did for me in the past, but we're done."

Something like madness settled behind Medvedev's eyes. "Yes, I believe we are. If you ever come again to this place, I shall have you removed with force."

"Believe me. I won't give you that pleasure." She spun on her heels, vaguely aware that she hadn't even accomplished what she'd come here to do. She caught Milena's eyes on the way out the door. Both shared wordless apologies in the space of a heartbeat.

Half an hour later, Milena found her sitting on the front steps of the manor. "I suppose you'd better come back to my place tonight."

"Sorry." Abigail leaned back to look up at the stars. She could only see a few over the glow of the city. Low near the tops of the building, Earth shone a pale blue. It would dip beneath the horizon as the night wore on. She was already in a bad enough mood tonight, and the sight of that planet only made things worse.

"You've got nothing to apologize for." Milena said. "She's had it coming for years. I hear you aren't the only one to have read her her rights on the way out the door."

"Actually I was apologizing for not telling her about the guild. I promised I would."

"I took care of it. She called me a traitor and a dozen other horrible names, but what's she going to do? If what you say is true, and guild members are in high demand, she'll quietly accept it. She won't throw me out. She never gets rid of any of the women that work for her, despite the abuse she hurls at the underperformers. And I'll keep working for her. The old hag is my broker because she's good at what she does, not because she's pleasant to have tea with. The day she loses her golden touch is the day I find a new broker."

Abigail shook her head. "Your patience is inhuman. What happened to her, anyway? Why is she like that? I used to think she was mildly misandristic, but clearly she's a full-blown misanthrope."

Milena stood and gestured to her van. "You don't really want to know. But come on, if you insist, I'll tell you on the way home."

Abigail glanced back at the dark building. No light escaped from any of the windows and she was glad to turn her back on it.

Mistress Tatyana Medvedev sat up long into the night, her work of managing a dozen business empires entirely forgotten. She pushed her papers away with trembling hands.

"How dare she. How dare she."

Abigail had been her pride and joy. Her star freelancer. When she found the twenty-three-year-old woman, lost and without a friend on Mars, she had recognized the potential. Her miraculous armor had been a taboo subject from the beginning, but Tatyana could respect secrets, though her curiosity gnawed at her. She'd taken Abigail in, taught her the profession of freelancing. Even had men train her to fight and think like a warrior. And Abigail had ended up spitting in her face.

Tatyana had always taken it for granted, that someday her wayward tendencies would be slaked. It was madness to think otherwise. And she had been patient. Oh, so very patient as the months had turned into years. There was nothing that vile man could offer her precious Abigail. It had not entered her darkest dreams that one of her daughters could be so ungrateful.

"They always leave," whispered the empty room.

Milena, would, of course, be given more chances. What did it matter if she were a member of some frivolous organization if she were still in Tatyana's tender care? If future chastisement were necessary, it would be dealt with at the appropriate time. Milena would not leave her.

Perhaps she would feel better after a few hours of sleep. Yes. That would help her stomach the betrayal or at least put some distance between herself and the horrible pain. She raised her hand to turn off the lamp but stared at her fingers. Oh, that horrendous shake, the way the tremors took them. She reached for the lamp but knocked it off the desk when she missed the switch. It fell clattering to the ground, the bulb shattering with a pop and flash of light. Then all was darkness. It closed on her, like wraiths in the night, and she laid her head on her desk.

Sometime later, she heard her door open, and a beam of light spilled in from outside. "Mistress? I heard a sound. Are you alright?"

Dear Natalya. She had not left her, not yet anyway. But that day would come. They always leave.

Tatyana stood to her feet. "I was clumsy, child. I fear I won't be able to grasp my cane. Help me to my room."

Her stewardess walked beside her through the dark halls, a hand at her back to keep her steady. Her mind quieted. She was a forgiving woman, and as such, was prone to being taken advantage of. Once, she had tried to force Abigail to see the error of her ways, but she was fixated on that man. And so Tatiyana had deemed patience the kindest of routes. But kindness is not always a virtue.

It was time to be firm with her wayward daughter.

112

Wormwood: Part 1

Tatyana Medvedev was the tallest female student enrolled at the University of Ganymede. At just over two meters, she towered head and shoulders over the other women, let alone most of the men. She could thank her father for the height, or so she'd heard. She only knew the man through vague descriptions from her heartbroken mother. "They always leave," was the lesson her mother had taught her.

During her first term, heads tended to follow Tatyana as she passed through the quads on the way to her next class. She pretended to ignore them, but in truth, noticed every stare and remembered each of them. Such was the curse of near-eidetic memory, that each painful encounter be catalogued in excruciating detail. By the end of her second term, she had memorized the name of every student and faculty member, from the chancellor to the janitors, and off-hand could relay personal information she had heard on half of them.

She kept this little detail from the few acquaintances she made, thinking it would do little to further her social status, but her professors noticed strange patterns on her exams. When analytical thinking was required, she was a bright if not quite brilliant student. But when knowledge and memorization was an asset, Tatyana's marks were perfect.

It wasn't until her second year that she found her life's one true friend. One afternoon, Tatyana was studying for a statistics class on the grounds beneath a gnarled old beech tree when she was approached by a fellow student. Her eyes flicked up at the intruder that cast a shadow on her work. "Yes, do you need something?"

Mara Jane, a fellow Martian, stood before her. "Hi. Tatyana, right? I'm in charge of putting together the student-faculty basketball game this year, and I was wondering if you could be talked into joining the student team."

Because she was tall and obviously all tall people were athletic. Lovely. "I've never played basketball in my life nor do I have any desire to do so," she said.

"Most of us haven't, but school tradition and all."

"I have a test I'm studying for." The message was clear and any socially astute adult should have picked up on her cues. Buzz off.

"Oh? What class is it?"

Tatyana eyed her, not quite able to believe that Mara hadn't gotten the clue. "Statistics."

Mara crept around beside her to look over her shoulder. "Maybe I can help. I've taken several stat classes."

"No thank you, Mara."

The girl paused and eyed her. "I didn't realize you knew my name."

Tatyana sighed. This was beginning to turn into a conversation, something she had been trying to avoid. "I know everyone's name. Now if you'll—"

"You calculated the standard deviation wrong." Tatyana looked at her tablet. Mara leaned over her shoulder and tapped a set of numbers. "Right there. Check your work at this stage and then work it forward. Everything else past that is correct, based on wrong numbers, of course."

How had she even had time to read the problem, let alone work it out in her head? "Thanks. I think."

"Anytime. So you'll help us beat the faculty this year?"

Despite her exceptional memory, Tatyana must have agreed to it, because despite having no memory of agreeing to play in the game, a week later she was on the team that got soundly trounced by the profs.

II.

There was little doubt post-graduation, that Tatyana and Mara, now inseparable friends, would go into business together. One had the memory for retaining and sorting information, the other an inscrutable ability to crunch numbers. Their first endeavor was an operations consulting company run out of Freeport 11 in orbit over Mars. It was nothing short of a runaway success, and soon they had contracts with half the major Martian corporations. By year's end, they had over a dozen employees and a sleek office in the station's commercial district.

Everything was going quite well until a serial killer struck the station. That one of their analysts was among the victims was extraordinarily unlucky. Mara ran the numbers.

She spun her chair around and threw a foam ball at the small basketball goal on the wall of their shared office. Tatyana scowled at her "Can you for once in your life take something seriously for more than five consecutive minutes?"

"What do you expect me to do?" Mara asked. She tossed another ball into the goal. "Nothing we can do will bring Eric back. That's the end of the story." She picked up a third ball. "It's called stress relief. You should try it sometime."

"I refuse to believe that we are helpless. The only helpless are the ones that do nothing." Tatyana muttered. "Losing an analyst and replacing him will be costly enough. The bad publicity of an active killer will drive business away from Freeport 11 before long."

"Real sympathetic there, Tatyana," Mara said. "The police have their detectives on it."

"They've been on it for months."

"And with each kill, they're drawing closer. I hope."

Tatyana had her doubts. A thought came to her mind. She spun back to her computer and ran her fingers across the keyboard. "Perhaps we should consider hiring a private investigator. That would accomplish justice for Eric and solve the business problem."

Mara tapped a pen against the desk. "You want an investigator to come to Freeport 11? You're looking for a freelancer."

Tatyana coughed out a short laugh. "We're looking for a skilled professional, not a mercenary."

"No, really," Mara said. "They all have specializations. We just need to find the right one. This is probably one of the few good ideas you've ever had."

She gave her business partner a critical glare. "You're serious about this?"

"Sure. We can afford it. Worst case scenario, we spend a little money trying to avenge Eric. It's the least we can do and no harm can come from it."

"And in the best case we put a killer away," Tatyana said. "Which wouldn't be bad publicity, either. Very well. Hire a freelancer. I'll leave it to you, though. I don't want this becoming a distraction."

Mara rubbed her hands together. "This'll be fun."

Tatyana went back to her reports from Emcom Mining. Someone had to keep a level head around here and keep the business running. That someone would never be Mara.

III.

The freelancer's name was Liam McCarthy, and he was undoubtedly an attractive man. Tall, well built, and even better dressed. For three weeks, he was in and out of the office, making reports to Mara on his investigation. Tatyana never once bothered to introduce herself as the inquiry wasn't her business. Still, she was curious and kept half an ear open when he was around. It was obvious that Liam deserved his reputation because in just a few days he was making headway. The Freeport 11 police were even cooperating with him in the hopes of bringing the killer down.

At the end of the third week, he introduced himself to her, despite her best efforts at avoiding his doing so. "Liam McCarty. Freelancer, but you already knew that with the eavesdropping you've been doing."

Tatyana averted her eyes. "Yes, you're so observant. I'm sure you're very pleased with yourself. I'm Ms. Jane's partner and I'd be a fool not to pay attention, else her whims might drag us both under."

"Right. The icy Ms. Medvedev. Mara warned me you had a few sharp spines."

"Is that so," she said, making no effort to hide the irritation in her voice. "I'm curious what we're paying you for. I wasn't aware that sitting around the office and harassing your employer was part of your contract."

Liam smiled. "These things take time. But I always get my prey." He winked and left the office without another word.

The next week, Mara and Tatyana received a threatening message.

"Call off your bloodhound, or you'll be the next to die."

Liam's smiles faded at that. "I got cocky," he admitted, "and the killer knows I'm on to him. You two need to move somewhere safe till this is over."

"Nonsense," Tatyana said. "I have obligations to fulfill. Clients that expect my full attention on their projects. Pray tell me how I am to remain ahead of my workload out of the office?"

Mara quietly put a hand on her arm. "Please. Can you for once in your life not be stubborn? We can stay with my folks in Arizona for a few days."

Tatyana threw her off. "I will not be intimidated."

Her partner left that evening on the last shuttle out. Liam continued to stop by the office supposedly to make reports, but Tatyana knew he was actually there to check on her safety. It both irked and pleased her. "I can take care of myself," she said and slammed the door in his face. But she did not mind that he kept an eye on things.

A few days later, she went on her nightly walk through Freeport 11's public park. A narrow strip of greenery roughly thirty meters wide and two hundred meters long at the center of the station, it had a beautiful view of Mars through its transparent canopy. She had a faint notion that it was quieter than normal, and a warning buzzed through the back of her mind. But Tatyana Medvedev did not give in to fear, and she kept her steady pace.

Suddenly, the sound of a scuffle broke out behind her. She turned to see Liam tackle a man to the ground and a moment later wrestle him into binders. The man thrashed and screeched like an animal, but Liam held him firm and gagged him.

"There now," he said. "I believe Freeport 11 will be safer after this. Though I wish you hadn't decided to play live bait for a serial killer."

Tatyana looked at the face of the killer, the man that had stalked Freeport 11 and killed one of her most favored employees. Through sheer force of will, she resisted the impulse to shiver. "You seem to have had things in hand," she finally said to Liam.

Liam jerked the man to his feet. "I didn't think you had that much faith in me."

She'd walked into that one. "Just enough, it seems. You are to be commended for a job well done."

He winked on his way by. "Maybe you can tell me about it over dinner."

"I will do no such thing," she said, but she did give him a small smile and a nod. After all, he had saved her life.

IV.

As the years passed, the business grew beyond consulting. They began to make acquisitions and expanded into other fields, forming their very own empire. By the time they hit their thirties, Tatyana Medvedev and Mara Jane were among the wealthiest women in the solar system. They left Freeport 11's commercial district and returned to Tatyana's home colony of Doch Rossiya.

Liam always dropped by whenever he was in town, much to Tatyana's annoyance and secret pleasure.

"Well look who it is, fresh off the job," Mara said. "Our favorite freelancer."

"Mighty sweet of you," he said, leaning against the door jamb of their office "It just so happens that the two of you are my favorite clients."

Tatyana didn't look up from her work. "Flattery is for the simple and weak of mind. If you are here for a social call, you will be sorely disappointed. We are, as always, busy."

"Be polite," Mara said. "An evening off for an old friend wouldn't be so bad. I've already cleared the schedule."

"Awfully convenient," Liam said.

Tatyana looked back and forth between them and sighed. "If I am the victim of a conspiracy, then let us get it over with."

"I have reservations to treat you both at a nice steakhouse," he said. Tatyana raised an eyebrow at him. Real ranch-raised meat was outside the budget of most freelancers. He shrugged. "Business has been good."

"Oh dear," Mara said, clapping a hand dramatically over her mouth. "I'm a vegetarian. I guess I'll have to pass."

The plan was suddenly laid bare to Tatyana. "Since when are you a vegetarian?"

The other woman shrugged and gave an impish grin. "Yesterday? But you two go on. No use wasting a good reservation."

Tatyana straightened her back and nearly refused outright on principle. But Liam was as attractive a man as they came, and he had been rather persistent these last several years. And besides, he had once saved her life. Perhaps it wouldn't be an unpleasant evening to give in just this once. "Very well. I have been tricked and betrayed, but I accept being outsmarted for the time being." She stood from her desk and offered her arm to Liam. "Come. Let's get this over with."

V.

Tatyana hated the feeling of being shackled to another human being. Besides Mara, of course. Their partnership had been long and fruitful. The woman was reliable like clockwork, even in her eccentricities, and had never once let Tatyana down in any meaningful way, despite her regular accusations. Such was the nature of their friendship. But in every other relationship, she could look down the spotless annals of her memory and relive a thousand small disappointments. Being unable to forget such griefs became a greater burden as the years extended behind her.

Liam would let her down someday and probably sooner rather than later. It was inevitable, and yet Tatyana couldn't tell the man no. When he rolled into town every few months like a dust storm, she was caught in his wake. And she knew it would be impossible to nail his boots to the ground. But there were perhaps other ways. Ways that took her time and effort to implement.

"When were you going to tell me you had started brokering for freelancers?" he asked one day as she welcomed him into the imposing new manor she had purchased.

"When it was your business," she countered. "I only take on crews helmed by women."

"Kind of a niche market, don't you think?"

"Money is hardly the end goal."

"How many of Jupiter's moons do you own? At least three by now, I imagine."

She scoffed. "Don't be ridiculous."

"So you wouldn't make an exception and be my broker?"

"I broker for women. What's the matter with Orson?"

Liam scratched the back of his head. "He dropped me without an explanation a month ago. It was the weirdest thing after all the years we've worked together."

"Oh my. Liam, I'm sorry." She feigned surprise at the revelation. After all, she had paid Orson a healthy bribe to do that very thing. "Maybe we can work something out, though you may find I'm a cruel mistress to work for." She smiled. With a shorter leash, perhaps there was hope for their relationship after all.

VI.

Tatyana was as good a broker as she was a businesswoman, and in truth, she enjoyed it more than any of the other industries they had fingers in. Utilizing her extensive library of contacts, her freelancers never had want of jobs. She knew them, her daughters as she called them, perfectly, and could expertly guide their careers to success.

Liam was another story. She did her best to keep him on Mars, and near Rossiya, when she could. If he noticed, he never said anything. She had long ago worked her way into his finances. He would never be in need and would never have to take a harder look at the jobs he took. It was a small price to pay to keep him in her arms, and it worked for many years.

It was Mara who brought ruin upon all of them.

The years and diverging interests had kept them apart more and more. Such was natural. Perhaps that was what had taken its toll. Or perhaps Mara had always been a snake lying in waiting.

When she showed up at Tatyana's manor, she seemed unsure of herself and reticent. Peculiar behavior for her.

"Well, what is it?" Tatyana asked. "I have a full schedule, as I'm sure you have."

"Liam came to me," Mara said, and Tatyana froze, hearing the subtle footsteps of doom. "He was having trouble with making sense of his finances, and we all know that's my thing. So I audited his accounts. As a friend. As it turned out, there were irregularities, which I'm confident you know about."

"Do not be coy, Mara. Say what you will."

"I did some checking, even got in contact with his old broker." She slowly shook her head. "Why? Why did you ruin Liam's career?"

"You wouldn't understand." Tatyana stared at her hands. "You won't tell him, will you?"

"I already did. He gave me a message to pass on to you." She handed Tatyana a small scrap of paper. Tatyana unfolded it with shaking hands to read the familiar handwriting: 'Go to hell.'

She crumpled the paper. "I see. He was always going to leave, I suppose. But you. You've been my friend for all these years."

Mara shook her head in bewilderment. "You brought this on yourself."

"Leave me. We are partners, but that shall be more difficult if I cannot stand the sight of you."

Mara left without another word. As for Tatyana, she was left with only her memories, memories of each and every moment spent with Liam, and the knowledge that if she had only been more clever or covered her tracks better, he wouldn't have left her.

VII.

The long and profitable partnership between Tatyana Medvedev and Mara Jane ended five years later. Their friendship had long cooled to icy professionalism. After Mara made her intentions clear, it took over a year to disentangle her from her numerous responsibilities.

When it was finally done, she came to the estate to say her final farewells.

"It's a pity after all these years," Tatyana said. It was empty sentiment, but it filled the dead air between them.

Mara nodded briefly. "I suppose you could say that."

"What are your plans now?"

"I'm getting married, actually. And moving to Amalthea."

This took Tatyana aback and she struggled to find words for a minute. "I wasn't aware that you were seeing anyone. I suppose congratulations are in order."

"Thank you. Yes, it took me until my forties to realize that I should seek some small happiness for myself." Mara smiled and turned to go.

"Do I know the lucky groom to be?"

She didn't turn back around. "It's Liam, actually. Goodbye, Tatyana."

She was left with a thousand unanswered questions, none of which had answers that would provide her with a shred of peace. "Ungrateful. Selfish," she murmured to herself over and over. "A conspiracy to deprive me of the only people I have ever loved."

Tatyana threw herself into her work. There were freelancers to mother, and now she was the sole head of the business empire. And when the news came some months later of a suspicious depressurization accident that killed nearly forty people on Amalthea. She paid it no heed.

But she slept little from that day forward.

Chapter 6: The Eye of War

—◁◫▷—

The Highland Treaty Organization started as little more than a public relations stunt between the colonies of Arizona and Doch Rossiya. Named after the southern highlands of Mars that is home to both colonies, it was founded in 2 AM to give an assurance of peace to the rest of the planet. The centuries-long feud between the United States and Russia is well documented, and as Earth fell to war, the colonies looked at each other in fear, praying that the rest of the solar system would be spared from old rivalries.

Arizonan President Williams and Rossiyan President Federov signed the treaty to much fanfare. But to the surprise of all, the partnership became more than just a symbol that ancient griefs had been laid to rest. The alliance put both colonies in strong political positioning to lead Mars into its first few fragile years without Moses. As the years rolled on, new members were added with full status. Most were smaller colonies that joined on the promise that they would be defended if attacked, though a few more influential colonies, such as Warszawa and Stockholm, eventually joined as well.

There has never been any doubt though who the real power brokers of Mars were, and as the first major international crisis of the post-Moses era reared its ugly head, Arizona, Doch Rossiya, and their treaty were at the forefront of that conflict.

Barbara Clancey
Churchill, Member of Parliament
Died 111 AM

Ex Commissioner-General Yuuto Kagurazaka rose before the light of dawn from a fitful sleep of uneasy dreams. So as not to wake his wife, he crept out of bed and padded softly down the hall to the kitchen to start a pot of tea. Outside the window, the dark sky was moderated by the first gray of dawn. As his tea steeped, he picked up his tablet to read through the never-ending articles on the negotiations between the Highland Treaty Organization and Kyoto.

Just yesterday, Churchill had entered the conversation, placing their political clout behind Kyoto, claiming that the colony was competent to lead its own security. He wondered if they did so simply to diffuse the political decision. In truth, despite his deep ties to his home colony, Yuuto had spent the week wondering if perhaps it might be best if the more defense minded colonies handled security at the factory. It had been over three centuries since the Japanese people had given up their martial heritage.

But now it was pride that ruled the conversation. Pride that Kyoto could take care of their all-important factory. Pride that the HiTO thought they could do better. He poured himself a cup of tea and set aside the news. He was only a retired police commissioner and his expertise had never been foreign affairs. The future would come in his despite and not at his behest.

He turned off the house's alarm and pushed the back door open, releasing it gently to keep it from waking the rest of the household. He pulled his robe tighter around him to ward off the morning cold. The coming dawn made headway against the stars as one by one they slowly faded from view. Jupiter was high in the sky, a faraway point of light. He walked through the garden to the pergola, sat in a chair facing east to watch the rising of the sun. There was color to a Martian sunrise, and it had beauty enough, but Yuuto had often wondered how it compared to an Earth sunrise. Pictures and paintings rarely do any justice to the true nature of a thing, especially something as ephemeral and sublime as a sunrise.

No sooner had he settled, than a sound from the south caught his attention. Aircraft. A formation of skyhoppers screamed overhead, and he stumbled out from under the pergola to get a better look. Dozens of them of all sizes, not one of them a model used by Kyoto's security force, and the guttural roar was deafening. Higher in the sky, engines burned like stars as an invasion force of ships, most likely carrying troops and armored vehicles, deorbited toward the Kyoto Factory Exclusion Zone.

Yuuto sighed and felt a weariness in his bones that he shouldn't have felt so early in the day. The HiTO had made good on their promises and threats: the factory would be safe, even if that was accomplished through hostile occupation by a foreign force. He returned to the house, suddenly feeling an overwhelming helplessness as the surface of the world spun too quickly and left him behind.

Elizabeth heard the news about the invasion shortly after she awoke. Her morning routine involved listening to the radio over a bowl of oatmeal in the quiet hours around dawn. This morning she sliced a few blueberries in half and dropped them into her bowl before sitting at the table. She leaned back and flipped on the old radio on the shelf behind her.

"—ernight a coalition of Highland Treaty Organization forces led by Arizona and Doch Rossiya have occupied the Kyoto Factory Exclusion Zone. While we're waiting on official confirmation, eyewitnesses report that military forces from the HiTO have deployed to the northern hemisphere under cover of night."

She dropped her spoon into her bowl and jumped to her feet in surprise. The colonies had escaped Earth's fate and been peaceful for almost a century. Why now? Why would they sacrifice that trust? She

125

turned off the radio in frustration and marched out the back door of the house. In the east, the sun was peeking over the distant red ridges, and it shone dully on the hull of the Sparrow. She crossed between the fields and walked up the ramp to the airlock.

"Oh, what is that blasted code?" She entered a number sequence on the keypad, and it flashed an angry crimson. Vaguely she remembered Matthew warning her not to be wrong three times or else the ship's security systems would engage. She pushed a lock of gray hair back behind her ear and tried again. Much to her relief, the pad turned green and the door opened. She shut it behind her and tiptoed down the halls to Matthew's cabin. For a brief moment, she hesitated. He had enough stress in his life, and perhaps another hour of sleep wouldn't hurt. But she knew he would want to know as soon as possible. She rapped her knuckles on the door.

A minute later, he slid it open, hair disheveled. "Oh. Good morning." He looked down the hall to the common room. "What's wrong?"

She motioned toward the cockpit. Matthew sighed and led the way. Elizabeth settled into the copilot's chair and hesitated just long enough that he gently prompted her. "Well?"

"Turn on the radio. Anything local will be carrying it."

A look of unease crossed his face as he reached forward to the console. There was a pop as the speakers turned on and the sound of static. Matthew scanned for frequencies and stopped when the noise turned into a human voice.

"I thought you'd want to know as soon as possible," she said, watching his face as he listened to the announcement. His sandy hair was ruffled and the scruff on his face longer than normal. But it was the lines by his eyes that she took note of, the way they seemed deeper. They creased as his frown deepened. Lines of worry etched into her son's face by hardship. She looked away, unable to bear the sight any longer.

They listened in silence for ten minutes to the broadcast. Eventually, when it became clear there was no new information until the Arizona government made an official statement, Matthew turned the volume down. He ran a hand through his messy hair.

"This isn't your fault, you know," Elizabeth said. "For them to have moved so quickly, they must have already had plans drawn up."

"I was the messenger boy."

She scoffed. "And that matters how? Had Logan sent his message

126

straight to Barclay, this would have been the end result. You don't have to carry the weight of the world on your shoulders."

His countenance broke and he looked at her. "I didn't mean it like that."

Her heart softened. "I know. But there's nothing you could have done here. You're not a politician. The movers of our age don't all heed your voice." She reached across and took his hand. Despite his hard years as a freelancer, her years on the farm had given her the thicker callouses. "People may believe in you because you are a good man, but you are just one man."

He took a deep breath and let it out slowly. "You'd have me walk away from this, despite Logan's effort to involve me?"

"I fail to see what you can do against nations," she said. "Spend your strength elsewhere. Finish your business on Mars and move on."

"First time you've ever tried to run me off," he said with a half-hearted smirk.

"I'm used to being alone," was her less than mirthful reply.

He stood. "I need to get the others up—"

The comm chimed and he reached over and hit it. "Morning, Cole. Ryan Thompson. No, I'm not happy to talk to you either." Elizabeth frowned. The Minister of Law that Matthew had had so many problems with.

"I know your voice," Matthew said.

"Good. Turns out the boys over in intelligence want to have a word with you about Alexander Logan."

Matthew paused briefly. "If I come in willingly, are you going to let me leave on the same terms?"

Thompson sighed. "Cole. We aren't going to arrest you. You're a damn hero to the public. Consider it a full debriefing. The better picture intelligence can put together on Logan, the better chance we can bring him in or snuff him out."

Matthew let out a long slow breath. "Okay. But I don't want anything to do with it after this. And I need something in return. One of my crew members is stranded in Doch Rossiya. Help me get her home and I'm all yours."

"The border isn't really my department, but I'm sure I can work something out. When can you make it?"

"I'll be on the first train into town."

"Come to my office. We'll go from there." The call clicked off.

Elizabeth crossed her arms. "I thought you and Davey had a job in Warszawa?"

He frowned. "We did, but Thompson just clipped my wings. Plus, if it gets Abigail home it'll be worth it."

"I can take care of it," Davey said from the hall.

Matthew spun in his chair. Elizabeth hadn't heard the young man's approach either. "Eavesdropping?" Matthew asked. "You're up early."

Davey shrugged and leaned against the door frame. "We had a job, and I still do. Let me take care of it."

"I don't know if that's a good idea," Matthew said turning away.

Davey pushed his way into the cockpit. "I can handle it. And if something comes up, you're just a call away for advice."

Matthew frowned and looked away from him as if looking for an excuse, anything to tell Davey no. His eyes fell on Elizabeth. She only favored him with a small smile, recognizing in him the fear that all parents have as their children grow up. "You know, I didn't really want to let you leave for Ganymede, either."

He closed his eyes. "Alright. Take your sister and call me often."

Davey pumped a fist and his eyes sparkled with excitement. "She's not up yet."

"Then you'd better wake her because you have a train to catch. I'll send you the job info. But I have to admit, I'll be a little disappointed to miss this one."

Elizabeth eyed him suspiciously. "Why's that?"

He smiled. "I was looking forward to meeting up with an old friend."

Later that afternoon, after a three-hour mag-train ride, Davey and Grace stood on a corner in Warszawa. "You sure this is the place?" Grace asked.

Davey looked back at the nearest street sign and then nodded. It matched their directions close enough. "Unless I'm going crazy." He looked at the garage in front of them. They weren't in a bad part of Warszawa by any means, but the fresh, clean paint on the building made it stick out from the rest of the street. Must be a new business. They walked past the open garage door. A blue grav car was up on a lift and two mechanics were poking around beneath it.

"Seems like a strange place to hire freelancers," Grace whispered as they stepped past the opening.

"Maybe. Matthew said that Mr. Luna has hired him before, though." He pulled the main door open and stepped back to allow Grace entrance.

"Such a gentleman," she said with an exaggerated curtsey.

The interior had all the drab appeal of ten thousand other waiting rooms. A screen in the corner turned to the news with the latest on the invasion of Kyoto, old car magazines scattered on a small table between the chairs, and even a vending machine that offered an unhealthy variety of overpriced sweet and salty snacks. A pair of customers looked at them as they entered and then immediately lost interest.

"Can I help you?" asked a short man in oil-stained coveralls from behind the counter.

"Yeah, we're looking for Mr. Luna," Davey said.

The man pointed at the name sewn onto his breast pocket. Vicente Luna. "That's me, amigo. What can I do for you?"

Davey took a breath and extended his hand. "Davey Long. Crew member on the Sparrow, Matthew Cole's ship."

Vicente's eyes lit up and a smile filled his face. "It's good to meet you. Señor Cole didn't have a crew the last time we met. I'm glad he's not alone on his ship anymore. He seemed kind of sad and lonely."

Davey thought it was best to ignore that part and gestured toward Grace. "My sister and I have been working on the Sparrow for about two years. Unfortunately, the Arizonan government requested Matthew's presence today, so he couldn't catch the train to Warszawa with us. He sent us in his place to see if we could help you."

Vicente was obviously a little taken aback, but he recovered quickly. "He must have a lot of faith in you kids," he said, in an obvious attempt at being polite.

"Hey," Grace said. "Davey's nineteen. And I'm fourteen. We're not kids."

"What my sister is trying to say," Davey said, putting a firm hand on her arm, "is that we're capable members of Matthew's crew, and we're good at what we do." He put on his best confident face and desperately hoped he bought it.

The mechanic didn't quite seem to be on board yet, but he shrugged.

"If it can't be helped. I had hoped to get a chance to see Señor Cole again. He smuggled me off of Europa for my daughter's wedding and I owe him my life."

Well, that sounded like Matthew. He must not have been an entirely crusty old codger before everyone showed up. "Maybe he'll be free in a few days," Davey said. He realized his mistake and hastily added, "After we've finished the job, of course."

To Vicente's credit, he seemed to be relaxing. "Come back to my office. We'll talk about why you're here."

He led them through a door into a dingy room badly in need of a secretary. Beneath a dead clock, a half-open filing cabinet stood against the wall with paperwork spilling out. The desk wasn't any better, and Vicente rushed to tidy it up before nodding his head at the pair of chairs. "I don't normally have guests," he explained.

Davey wasn't going to judge. If he had an office, it might not be any better. "So let's go over the details. I know we're supposed to help with an investigation into a carjacking ring."

Vicente nodded. He gestured at a bowl of mints and then took one for himself. Grace obliged, but Davey politely declined. "Big carjacking ring," Vicente corrected. "Well organized. It's been going for months. Police have caught jackers, but never traced them back to their shop."

"What's this got to do with you?" Grace asked. "If you're willing to hire freelancers, you've gotta have a stake."

He looked nervous. "When a car is stolen, it's rarely left in one piece."

"Too easy to identify?" Davey asked.

Vicente nodded. "It's broken down and sold for parts. Well, most of it. If it's a grav car, the grav plate most likely ends up on Ceres and is used to make black market thumpers." He scratched his head. "Either way, some of my competitors have been offering steep discounts lately, and I'm losing customers."

"I see," Davey said. "The carjackers are messing up the parts market and running you out of business." Talk about collateral damage.

"Sí, amigo. I just got this place up and running with an investment from my son-in-law's family. I can't let it fail. Not after starting over."

"I don't think we're going to be able to take down an entire gang," Davey said. "Maybe with Abigail we could, but not with just the two of us."

Vicente shook his head. "I just need evidence. I'm willing to donate an old car to be stolen. You'll leave it out in the jacker's favorite part of town, and then you'll track it back to their chop shop to get hard evidence for the police."

"Sounds too easy," Grace said, narrowing her eyes. "Why haven't the police used bait already?"

"Maybe they didn't have a car," Davey said. "Doesn't matter really, does it?"

"What if it does?" she challenged.

"Then we'll do what they couldn't." He turned back to Vicente.

The man had that nervous smile again. "Are you sure you can handle this? Maybe I should just wait on Señor Cole."

Davey felt the blood rushing to his face in embarrassment. Stupid. Stupid. Stupid. Matthew trusted him with this one and he was acting like a child. Aloud he said, "We're professionals. Grace, do you have the trackers? Let's go rig up the car Mr. Luna is donating to the cause." She was already digging one out of her backpack. He put as much confidence into his smile as he could manage. This was his first solo job if you ignored the fact that Grace was along. He was going to complete this one way or the other or go down trying.

Grace stifled a yawn. It was nearly three in the morning and they'd been watching the car from a nearby rooftop since sunset. "And now I know why Abigail says that stakeout's suck," she said. She grabbed a package of pretzels from her pack and tore it open. A steady stream of snacks was just about the only thing keeping her awake.

Davey hadn't moved from his post with the binoculars at the edge of the roof in at least an hour. "Tell me about it," he muttered. But he still didn't budge.

"Want me to take a watch?" she asked, hoping he would turn her down on the offer.

"I'm good."

Success. "You know," she said carefully. "You don't have to kill yourself over there. The car has a tracker. If they pick it up tonight, which I'm starting to doubt, we can just follow it. We don't even have to be here."

"But then we would miss out on valuable information. What kind of vehicle are they driving? How many of them are there?"

Grace shrugged and popped another pretzel into her mouth and pulled her blanket up around her neck. "Is it alright if I take a snooze then? You can wake me if something exciting happens or when you get over yourself and let me take a shift."

"Whatever."

Grace fluttered her eyes with exaggerated sleepiness and made a big show of stretching as she leaned back against the air-recycling unit. Above, the stars shone with pale light in the Martian sky. She yawned again, this time not fighting it and let her eyes drift shut.

"Grace. I've got something."

Not even ten seconds. She pried her eyelids open. They felt like steel bulkheads. She threw the blanket off and crawled over to the edge of the roof. Half a block away in front of a boarded-up coffee shop sat the car Vicente had donated. Grace had questioned whether the thieves would be interested in an old piece of junk like that, but the mechanic had scoffed at her skepticism and insisted it was a sought after classic. She didn't quite see the point in getting sentimental about a rusted-out hulk, but then the men she knew consistently chose weird things to get emotional about.

A large truck with a flatbed trailer had pulled up beside said classic, and a team of black-dressed men jumped out to work on the car. Grace and Davey kept their heads low in case someone happened to look in their direction. "Tracker still working?" he asked, voice barely a whisper.

She waved a small device at him. "I've got a good signal." She looked back at where the car was already being winched up onto the flatbed. "Dang. They're good."

"Just one left working on the car." He squinted and leaned forward. "What's that box thing he has? I can't see well enough from here."

"Signal jammer," she said confidently.

"What? How can you tell?"

She sighed and showed him the receiver. "I've lost the signal. It's just gone. Completely. Which explains why the police have been stumped."

Davey swore and jumped to his feet. "Come on! We've gotta get down there. Maybe we can bug the truck itself." He ran toward the fire escape they'd climbed up.

"Cool it. I've got this." Grace said. She'd already dug another tracker out of her pack. She ran up to the edge of the building, looking for any way to catch her fall. There. She ignored Davey's wild protests, took a breath, and jumped. It was a three-story fall, barely time to pick up speed, but she reached out with her bracelet and grabbed a streetlight, turning her vertical momentum into a horizontal swing. She hit the ground at a run and, with only a slight stumble, sprinted down the dark street.

The brake lights on the truck turned off and it started pulling forward. Grace gritted her teeth and grabbed the next streetlight, flinging herself further down the street, using the building on her left, to steady her breakneck pursuit. She was close. Maybe if she could land on the bed, she could place the second tracker. She grabbed a third and final streetlight and pulled with all her might, throwing caution to the wind.

Her wild arc brought her flying toward the truck right as it began to accelerate. If she could get a hold of it, she could stick the landing. She grasped it for the briefest of moments and then felt it rip away as it moved out of range. Grace barely had time to push off the ground to keep herself from striking the pavement like a meteor. She hit at an angle and rolled end over end before landing on her back, bruised and bleeding.

For a minute, she lay stunned, before peeling herself off the asphalt and limping out of the road to the sidewalk. Davey found her a few minutes later, picking gravel out of the skid marks on her arms. "Just... Don't say it," she said through gritted teeth.

He closed his mouth and unslung his backpack to look for first aid.

"Told you the job was too easy," she mumbled.

He still didn't say anything, and Grace thought that she probably had the best brother in the solar system.

"We lost the car, the tracker, everything."

Matthew winced as he listened to the tale. He took a sip from his morning coffee and set it back on the console. "What do you do now?"

The comm was quiet for a minute before Davey responded. "I'm not sure. Vicente gave us a key to his garage and let us camp out on the floor of the back room. I don't think he's going to be happy when he gets to work today only to find out we botched it."

"No, I imagine not," Matthew agreed. Outside the Sparrow's canopy, the sun was just rising over the hills and flooding the Arizona plain with light.

"Did I mess up? Would you have done anything different?"

He heard the plea in Davey's voice. Tell me I did okay, it said. Matthew wanted to tell him that yes, he would have done the exact same thing. But the truth wasn't that simple. "Maybe," he said. "Without having been there, I can't say. Maybe I would have seen something different than you, or else I might have made the same mistake. But I'm not there and I can't be there for several days."

"You can't?" The kid sounded miserable.

"Arizona wants my life story, apparently. And the Russians want Abigail's. They won't let her come home unless we cooperate."

"What good is that going to do?" Davey asked. "You told them everything you know about Logan, right?"

"Twice. And you know how reticent Abigail is about talking about her past. From what I am hearing, they're rather displeased." Matthew sighed. "I'm sorry, but this is going to take a few days to sort out. You two are on your own."

Davey was quiet again. "I don't know if I can do this."

"Maybe not," Matthew said. "But you agreed to that job, so for now, you're committed. Give it some thought, and we can talk about it this evening. You two are clever. You know what you're doing. I trust you'll figure something out."

Silence again. "Alright. I'll talk to you soon."

Matthew stared out the window. Worst-case scenario, he and Abigail could sweep through Warszawa just before they left Mars. He really didn't want to leave Vicente out in the cold, but he still had hopes the kids could pull this off.

He felt a twinge of regret when he thought about Abigail. There wasn't anything he could do to bring her home. He knew she was this close to cold-shirting it across the Martian landscape in her suit to get back to Arizona, but that would put her in bad stead with the Russians and probably the Arizonans too, something they were better off avoiding. But there was no way they were going to get from her what they were hoping. Odds were good they wanted to know how to get their own shiny versions of her suit. If Matthew's suspicions were right, she couldn't help them even if she wanted to. He knew she'd be okay, but right now, she was swimming in an ocean of red tape. An ocean that probably only spoke in angry Russian.

He drained the last of his coffee and put her out of mind for the time being. He had enough problems of his own to deal with.

To Davey's relief, Vicente didn't say much about the loss of the car. He had a pained look in his eye, but Davey just reassured him that they had other avenues of investigation.

Grace was moving slow today. She'd been pretty banged up by her reckless stunt. He felt like yelling at her but knew that wouldn't get them anywhere. The mess of her right forearm would probably leave some scarring. That was the worst part for him. He didn't want his baby sister covered in marks from fights. It made him feel like a failure.

They hid in the garage's backroom, away from Vicente as they ate their breakfast of vending machine donuts. "Well. What now?" Grace asked.

Davey paced the short length of the room. "I don't know yet. We don't have another car for bait, so let's figure out what we learned from the first run."

"These guys are good," she said around a full mouth. "They hit fast, hard, and don't leave a mark. That car was apparently more desirable than I thought it was. We should have set up closer to the bait."

"None of that is useful."

She shrugged. "Okay then. What did you learn?"

He closed his eyes and stopped pacing. "They're not afraid of the police. They bagged a car that had only been abandoned for a few hours, which meant they weren't worried about a trap. They think they own the town."

"Maybe they do," Grace said.

"Maybe, but if they're cocky, they might make a mistake. They've got buyers to appease, so they're making nightly raids. Probably scouts out looking for targets." He started pacing again. "Maybe that's the tactic. Start at the buyers and try to work back to the carjackers."

Grace snapped her fingers. "The garages that are getting cheaper deals."

"Exactly. We get a list from Vicente and camp them out."

"And then we plant trackers on any delivery truck that shows up."

Davey frowned. "Do you have enough for that?"

There was no missing the smug look on her face. "We all know how Abigail swears by these things. I brought a whole case. There's like forty of them in there."

He scratched his head. It was true that Abigail was a bit obsessed with them. But if it meant they had enough for the current job, he wasn't going to complain. They were working an uphill battle at this point. "I'll go get the list from Vicente. You find us a good map of Warszawa on the network. We're going to have to record a lot of data to look for patterns."

He left the room feeling more confident than he had the previous day. After all, they were professionals. It was going to be hard work, and maybe they would fail. But if he was going to fail, he was going to fail with his head held high.

The next three days kept Davey and Grace busy. During the day, they split up, casing rival garages and tagging any delivery trucks that arrived. Thankfully, mechanics seemed to constantly need parts delivered, so they had nearly a dozen vehicles tracked by the end of the week.

What they learned was far more complicated than they had banked on. Davey found a print map of the city and mounted it to the back of a piece of glass. Taking the data from the trackers, they began marking routes and stops with markers.

"This is a lot to take in," Grace said.

"You're telling me," he agreed. Most trucks stopped more than once per trip, adding new businesses to the map until it was an interconnected web of colored lines and notes. "Okay what's at 3821 Wzgórze Street." He'd massacred that name for sure.

Grace looked back down at her tablet. "Umm. The directory says it's Pulkowski Automotive. They're... yeah, another distributor. Legitimate business."

Davey's shoulder slumped. "All we've mapped is Warszawa's supply network for car parts." He gestured at the network of lines. "And in painful detail. There's got to be something here."

"We can send it to Matthew," Grace suggested.

"I will, I will. But I want to figure this out for myself."

She gave him a funny look but mercifully said nothing as she set aside her tablet. She grabbed her chopsticks and took another mouthful of noodles from the ramen shop they'd found a couple blocks away. "What if it's one of the distributors that runs the chop shop?"

He turned that over in his mind. "I guess it's not impossible. Seems like a risky business decision, though. Maybe they're buying from them instead. Let's see... Here. This distributor—"

"Red Auto," Grace said.

"Right, Red Auto. They deliver to every one of the garages that are getting the cheap parts. And Vicente doesn't use them. So we can at least check them out. Maybe you're right and they're the bad guys, or maybe they're just the middleman."

"That would still make them bad guys."

He sighed. "Thanks for the obvious."

"I'm here to help. So it's another highly entertaining stakeout then?"

"Unless you have a better idea. Still got trackers?"

She patted the case on the table beside her. "Plenty."

Davey frowned. "How much does each one cost?"

"Beats me," she said with a laugh. "I swiped the case from Abigail's room."

He looked back over at the map and counted the trackers now spread all over the city, and his heart settled in his stomach. No way they were getting even half of them back. "She's gonna kill us," he said.

"No." Grace patted him on the arm. "She's going to kill you."

With the kids in Warszawa, Abigail in Rossiya, and Matthew downtown, the Sparrow was a quiet place. There was no one to distract Yvonne from her work. She'd spent the last two days communicating between Julia on Venus, the other Lantern crews, and their brokers working out the final few hiccups in the guild charter. Julia's lawyers and Elwa's husband were going to take a last look over it before distributing a final copy. Hopefully, that would happen by the end of the week. When they left Mars to fill their ranks with more recruits, she didn't want any more snags in the process.

She hit send on her final message of the day to Julia and set aside her tablet. She looked around the common room and, despite her previous appreciation of the quiet, now it felt like an oppressive weight. She looked at the clock. Nearly four in the afternoon already. By this time, Elizabeth was usually done with commercial work and had moved on to her personal garden.

Yvonne left the Sparrow and walked across the Cole farm, waving an acknowledgement at a couple of the farmhands as they worked on one of the combines. Considering the number of pieces strewn across the ground, she doubted they'd be finishing tonight. When she reached the house, she rounded the corner to the garden. "Elizabeth?" There was no answer from the rows of vegetables. Perhaps she'd already gone in for the day.

"I'm up front!"

Elizabeth leaned around the front corner of the house and waved at her. When Yvonne joined her, she found the older woman trimming the shrubs along the front porch. "Sorry you had to come looking for me." She gestured at the row of plants. "I've got so much other work around here that I let these turn into misshapen things."

Yvonne reached down to the nearest branches. The delicate silver-gray leaves were silky to the touch. Almost at once, she smelled the heady aroma, almost like sage. "What are they?" she asked. "They smell wonderful."

"Artemisia absinthium. Or rather, this is descended from that species and adapted to Mars."

Yvonne glanced at her.

"You may know it as wormwood," Elizabeth said, trimming another branch. "Smells lovely, but it's bitter on the tongue. It has a few medicinal uses but is mostly famous for being a key ingredient of the green liquor absinthe."

Yvonne touched the leaves again. "Why do you have it?" Absinthe struck a chord in her memory. Perhaps something from medical history, but she couldn't place it.

"It looked nice at the plant nursery. There. The wormwood has been tamed." She stooped to start collecting the cut branches, and Yvonne did the same. "It's funny, you know, that we even have this plant."

"What do you mean?"

"Why would we have bothered to bring a mostly worthless plant with us to the colonies, but forget so many more important ones? Take strawberries, for instance. Have you ever had a strawberry?"

"I don't believe I have."

Elizabeth straightened. "No one alive has. Because as far as anyone knows, there's not a single extant strawberry plant in the colonies. And yet we have bitter wormwood."

"That's not the only thing we brought that should have been left behind," Yvonne said, darkly.

"And I'm sure strawberries are the least of what's been forgotten. We can take these cuttings to the burn barrel out back." Yvonne followed her around the side of the house and back behind the garden, where they both dumped their armfuls. "Thanks," Elizabeth said, brushing her hands off over the barrel. "How's the Guild coming along?"

Yvonne looked back toward the Sparrow. "I think we finally have everything ready to go. We're waiting on everyone to get one more look at the last round of revisions. Matthew's going to read over it one more time tonight."

"And what do you think of the charter?"

"I've only been in the freelancer business for a couple of years. I'm hardly qualified to have an opinion."

Elizabeth grunted. "My son doesn't seem to think so."

"Your son has many talents but having a good business sense is not one of them."

They returned to the house and entered through the back. The screen door slammed with a bang that always made Yvonne jump, no matter how many times she heard it. "Sorry," Elizabeth said. "I should replace those old springs. Everything around here is getting old, myself included." She turned the radio on as she entered the kitchen.

Yvonne wasn't surprised that news reports droned on endlessly about the occupation of the Kyoto factory. "Speaking of something that should have been left on Earth." She sat at a barstool and watched as Elizabeth dove into the pantry.

"We haven't had a war since Earth, and now rather than unite against a common enemy, we're at each other's throats and dividing into factions." She set a container of dried rice on the counter and stopped. "Wait. What are they talking about?"

Yvonne refocused her attention on the radio.

"—sident Barclay revealed the existence of a joint Highland Treaty Organization project known as the Phobos Platform. Inspired by the Vatican's once-secret defense system known as the Four Horsemen, the Phobos Platform has been under construction for many months. Built inside Mars' low altitude moon, The Phobos Platform will be an array of thumpers on its Mars facing side. They will have the ability to strike at any threat across almost the entire Martian surface. The platform is expected to be online by the end of the month. Phobos, a familiar sight that crosses our skies twice in a day, will soon be known as a symbol of peace and security. When asked about how the platform is being paid for, President Barclay deferred to Minister of Defense—"

Yvonne shook her head. "Now I'm left to wonder if the invasion of Kyoto was planned long ago."

"Politicians are opportunists at heart," Elizabeth said, "and will seldom let a crisis come to naught. If it wasn't already planned, it was certainly well-timed." She filled a stockpot with water. "And just for the record, I voted for Barclay's opponent."

Yvonne turned her attention back to the radio. A century of relative peace, gone in the space of a week. "The HiTO is pointing a gun at the head of an entire planet," she said. "I hope their security up there is good."

"I hope your security up there is good," Matthew said as he barged into Ryan Thompson's office.

For his part, Thompson only looked tired. "What are you even doing here? You're done. Ms. Sharon is coming home tomorrow afternoon."

Matthew sat in the chair across from the desk and tossed his campero onto it. "Unfortunately, you're the closest thing to a friendly face in these parts. And that's saying something."

"You're too kind."

"I am. And I meant what I said. You guys better have good security up there on your fancy new weapon."

Thompson spread his arms wide. "Cole. I'm the Minister of Law. Domestic threats are my domain. I've got nothing to do with that budget

140

sink."

So there was disagreement on the Phobos Platform inside the Arizona government. Interesting. "Nonetheless, yours is the only office of rank that I can walk into without getting arrested." Thompson intertwined his fingers and a muscle on his neck twitched, but he didn't say anything. "You haven't answered my question yet."

"I assume it will be well-defended. Military installations tend to be."

"I don't think you're getting me," Matthew said. "Your enemy is a terrorist that recently turned an atomic bomb against its creator. If you think Logan isn't salivating over the gun you have pointed at his prime target, you're not thinking straight."

That got through to him. For the briefest moment, Thompson's facade cracked as lines of worry creased his forehead. Then it was back to business. "I'll mention it to the president."

"You should tell him the whole project is a disaster waiting to happen." He grabbed his hat off the table.

"I have to keep my job too, you know, if I'm going to be your errand boy. Your part in this is done, Cole. I'm well acquainted with your tendency to meddle, but after today you're done here."

"We'll see about that," he said. He left the room as dramatically as possible, making sure to throw the door wide open and leave it like that. He honestly wasn't even sure what he meant with that parting shot because he did really intend to wash his hands of the developing political and military debacle. Maybe he was kidding himself. Either way, he imagined Logan thought involving him from the outset was a hilarious joke. The jerk. If Matthew could bill the terrorist for lost sleep, he could go ahead and retire.

On his way out, Thompson's secretary smiled and waved at him. Matthew tipped his hat politely to her. He was pretty sure that his visits were one of the most entertaining parts of her job.

Grace kicked the dumpster they'd spent the better part of the day lurking behind. "Another waste of time."

"Easy there, sis," Davey said. "If someone heard you, it would be awkward having to explain what we're doing here." He was still pouring over the tracking data they'd collected throughout the day. Whenever trucks had pulled up to unload, he'd creep out and slip a tracker into their undercarriage. He had to admit, though, that the handful of deliveries Red Auto received hadn't made things any clearer. Most returned to warehouses scattered across either the industrial district or near the train yard.

It was a little tricky determining warehouse ownership from public records, but by the end of the day, they had figured out that most of them were probably legit. The chance of a legitimate business having a side gig hung over them like a specter. The next step would be to investigate every one of those warehouses, and the distributors too, something Davey wasn't looking forward to doing.

"Let's go," Grace said, a hand on his shoulder. "It's late. Red Auto is closed for the day. We can come back tomorrow if you want. Nothing says that they get deliveries from the carjackers every day." Her stomach rumbled loudly. "And yeah. There's that too."

"A little bit longer," he said. "Maybe they deliver after closing.

Not twenty minutes later, a truck pulled up. Davey turned to give his sister a spectacular told-you-so look. She probably couldn't see it in the dark, but he felt better for giving it. They watched in silence as the bay doors opened and a much smaller group of men came out to unload the goods. "Only some of the employees in the know," he said. "The truck's make and model matches the one that took Vicente's car, aside from the flatbed. I think this is the most promising lead we've had all week."

Grace gave that disgruntled sigh that meant she knew her big brother was right. "I'll take care of this one."

He shook his head "What? No way! If these are the jackers, then there's no way I'm letting you do it."

"They're sure to be watching more closely if this is a hot shipment," she said. "I'm quicker than you. And besides, I'm much more likely to be able to talk my way out of it if they see me, and if they shoot, I'm bulletproof. I have no idea why everyone needs constant reminders of the obvious."

He took a good long look at her, or rather what little of her he could see in the dim light of the alley. She was competent. He knew that. But then that wasn't the point. She shouldn't have to be so competent. Not even fifteen yet, and she never blanched going into a fight. It wasn't fair, but then fair wasn't the hand that they had been dealt. "Alright. This one's on you. Be careful."

She flashed him a quick smile and slipped across the street towards the warehouse. She kept to shadows, and more than once, he lost sight of her in the night, before catching some glint of movement. In a few minutes, she had reached the suspect truck, though she kept out of sight behind a giant cable spool.

"Watch to see if there is a pattern to their movements," Davey said as if she could hear him.

When the workers' backs were turned, she flitted like a shadow across the opening and disappeared under the bed of the truck. Davey fist pumped. Okay. Mission accomplished, now she just had to get out of there. The workers continued to go about their business, and Grace didn't have an opening for several minutes. And when she did get an opportunity, it didn't end up working out all that well.

The driver got out of the cab and they ran right into each other.

Davey reflexively put his hand on the holster at his hip. He couldn't hear what was going on, but the driver had called a couple other men over. He glanced across the street and decided to close the gap so he could at least be on hand if things got out of control. Then his comm buzzed. He pulled it out of his pocket and frowned when he saw that Grace was calling him.

"Not a safe part of town for a girl like yourself," a rough voice said.

"I got... I got separated from my brother," Grace said, with a touch of pathetic helplessness. "I want to go home!"

"Now, now. Calm down, miss," a third voice said. "You can just come right on into the building, and after we finish with this shipment, we can call the police. They'll come right over and sort this out."

"But my brother..." Grace whimpered. Davey, despite his fear, smiled at the show she was putting on.

"The police will find him too. Let's get you inside."

And that was that. Grace was on his own and they would have to figure out how to meet back up later. He watched for the next ten minutes as the men, now that the distraction Grace had provided was over, went back to work. Finally, the truck left and he pulled out his tablet to watch its progress across town. No doubt with their luck, it was going to head to yet another legitimate warehouse in the nearby industrial district.

Davey raised an eyebrow when the blip on the screen turned and

143

left town entirely. By the time it finally reached its destination, it ended up at a complex near the edge of Warszawa's environmental shield. Whatever the buildings were, the current directories had no mention of them. If he was going to find the chop shop, this was his best shot. He grabbed both of their packs, since Grace had left hers behind and boarded the old rickety grav bike that Vicente had loaned them for the week. After a few laborious coughs, it started and Davey set off into the night.

It was nearly two in the morning by the time he crept up to the series of buildings. He'd parked his bike a hill over and crawled through the scrubby bush to approach without being seen. From a rise a hundred meters out, he pulled out his binoculars and turned on the night vision.

Whatever the complex used to be, it had long been abandoned. Most of it had fallen into disrepair over the decades. Only the largest central building appeared to still be relatively intact. If this was an illicit operation, they would almost certainly have guards on patrol. He flipped the night vision over to thermal imaging.

Bingo. One at the gate and a few patrolling the grounds. Few enough that he could evade them. He stashed his binoculars and took a camera and snapped a few pictures of the buildings. They would be grainy in the poor light, but he would get more. He was here for evidence, and he wasn't leaving without it. He closed the gap to the chain-link fence and used a pair of cutters to slice his way through. The nearest building was a half-collapsed pile of rubble. He clung to the shadows of its one standing wall and watched as an inattentive guard lazily passed him. These guys were about to get their whole organization cut out from under them because they weren't paying attention.

Davey took the next gap in the patrol to cross to the main building. Light shone out of a few high windows, but sadly none were low enough for him to pry open. Which left him few options. Try and find an unlocked door and risk running into trouble or see if there was roof access. He worked his way on down the building, fine with either so long as they got him out of the open.

He got no further than twenty meters before a guard rounded a corner. The deadly cone of light from his flashlight flicked dangerously

144

close to Davey before he slid between two pipes affixed to the side of the building. He held his breath, muscles frozen, as the guard came within two meters of where he stood. If the man turned his head a few degrees to the right, he'd be staring at Davey, and he doubted the shadows would do much to protect him at that range. Maybe he should draw his gun, just in case. His hand crept to his holster.

The man continued without so much as a twitch in Davey's direction. He let out a slow breath and made to slip out from the pipes. On a whim, he looked upward. The pipes continued all the way to the roof before turning a ninety-degree corner and disappearing. With a little effort, he could shimmy up between them. He worked himself up a few feet to test the theory. No sweat.

Or so he thought. It took longer than he imagined it would, and by the time he pulled himself over the ledge and onto the roof, his muscles were twitching. "That was dumb. That was real dumb," he whispered. Grace would have berated him for that, but then who was she to talk. She could just magically pull herself up to the roof. After a minute of rest, he rolled over to get his bearings. Skylights not twenty meters away. Perfect to get a view into the building, and at night, he wouldn't cast shadows. He crept over to the paned windows and hazarded a glance.

He was so relieved at the sight of the chop shop beneath that he nearly teared up. Before his very eyes, a cherry red car was being torn apart with ruthless efficiency by half a dozen men. He fumbled to get his camera out of his backpack and started snapping pictures. Surely this would be enough to get the police in here to clear them out. He smiled. He wasn't going back to the Sparrow with his tail tucked between his legs after all.

Headlights on the horizon grabbed his attention, and he instinctively flattened himself to the roof. A small motorcade, at least three cars and a truck on approach. Maybe they had another shipment going out? Or more likely a buyer coming to them, given the escort. He palmed the camera and crept over to the edge to watch what happened next.

The vehicles were met at the gate by a contingent of armed guards. Davey was glad he'd gone for the roof after all. It was getting too crowded down at ground level with all the fresh faces. After a few minutes, the vehicles continued up to the main building. Light spilled onto the yard as a garage door beneath him opened. A long pair of shadows attached to two men emerged.

Two of the cars opened up, and armed guards wearing business suits piled out. "White Void," Davey whispered under his breath. No way they'd send this much firepower for car parts. They were here for grav plates. This was an arms deal. He took a few more pictures, careful to keep as low a profile as possible. Still, something about that appraisal bothered him. He'd been around enough syndicate goons to get a feel for the way they carried themself. There was something different here. A certain aura of authority that even the most organized criminals lacked.

His theory would prove itself true or false soon enough. That center vehicle would have the white suit that signified the leader of every group from the syndicate. But when the door opened and only more men in black suits got out, Davey got worried. If they weren't White Void, then who were these guys? A local mafia of some sort?

A few members of each side met in the middle. Davey cursed that there was no way to hear what they were saying. He was missing something important. It was obvious an exchange was taking place when a forklift came out of the building with a steel container. Those would be the grav plates, maybe already removed from their housings. The lead man for the newcomers gave the other side a suitcase. They retreated a few steps and opened it up. They seemed pleased at the contents and rejoined the rest. Davey took even more pictures, hoping that he caught everything important. He wasn't sure how well the faces would come out, given the lighting, but maybe the police would be able to get what they needed to track these people down.

He was looking at his camera, trying to adjust the settings in the dark, when all hell broke loose. The newcomers opened fire in perfect unison, cutting down the chop shop crew. Davey flattened himself even further. The truck opened up and men with heavy weapons pointed at the building. He recognized a thumper.

There was no time. He was a dead man if he didn't move right now. He pushed himself away from the edge and scrambled to his feet right as the shockwaves began to tear apart the building beneath him. Somehow he ran, praying that the roof would hold long enough for him to—

How would he get down?

Didn't matter. Nothing to do but run. The building groaned and shuddered as its structural supports were blasted to pieces. Part of the roof to his left gave way as a load bearing beam warped under the stress, ripping girders and concrete with it. He shifted to the right and put everything he had into running as his vacuum damaged lung screamed with the effort. All at once, he ran out of roof. In the fraction of a second available to him, he saw a tall line of shrubs along the rear fence.

He jumped.

It was half an eternity before he crashed into the thorny bushes. The branches tore at his skin and ripped through his clothes. His ears filled with horrible snapping noises as the plant gave way before him. And then it was still. But it wasn't quiet. The building collapsed in a groan like thunder, and he was choked with the dust.

But he was alive. Injured maybe, or even probably. He pulled himself out of the bush and was surprised when he still had a full meter to the ground. If the shrub row was that big, then the drop had been even further than he'd thought it was. There was still the occasional pop of gunfire, but it sounded like the suits were nearly done shutting the operation down. His camera lay nearby on the ground but didn't appear to be damaged. Whether he'd dropped it mid-jump or sometime after the crash landing, he couldn't tell. He palmed it as he limped toward a narrow gap in the fence.

He hobbled as fast as he could across the open ground, looking for some sort of cover to hide in and figure out what to do next. When he pitched forward into a shallow ditch, he laid there unmoving, listening to the last of the fighting. He hoped Grace was okay. Probably stuck overnight at a police station. She'd be fine, though. She was a tough kid. And was going to have a better night than him. It would be hours before it would be safe for him to try and sneak to his bike. He closed his eyes and settled in for the long haul.

The next morning he collected a very irate Grace from a local police department. She cooled off the moment she saw how banged up he was. "We both got the short end on this job, didn't we?" she said as they walked back into Vicente's garage.

He grumbled a little, but his mind was elsewhere. He couldn't get the men in suits out of his mind. What motive did they have to shut down the chop shop? They were obviously the buyers of the grav plates. Why would they shut off the supply? A suspicion had started to settle into his gut like a lead weight. They were covering their tracks. Whoever had been buying the grav plates had a reputation to keep.

"Hey are you even listening to me?" Grace said.

He shook his head. "Sorry, I'm just thinking. I need to call Matthew."

Matthew came to the same conclusion that he did. "They're government men," he said.

"That was my theory too," Davey said. "Which brings me to the next pair of problems. What happens if I take this to the police? They might throw the evidence away if it's someone local. And do we still get paid if the carjackers got shut down through sheer chance."

"Hmm." The comm line went silent for a minute. "As to getting paid, Mr. Luna and Benny will have to hash that out. It depends on the wording of the contract. And the evidence? Take it to the media. Find a couple of news agencies in town and give them copies. That way, no matter what happens, even if the locals are crooked, the truth will be published."

Davey nodded thoughtfully. That was good. He wasn't sure he would have thought of that one. "Thanks, I'll take care of it. This whole thing reeks. I hate conspiracies."

"You and me both," Matthew said. "While we're on the subject, will you send those pictures to someone else for me?"

"Sure. I don't see why not."

"You remember that comm number I told you to never call unless it was an emergency?"

"You want me to send them to Whitaker?"

"Ask if he can identify the suits. He's got eyes everywhere, and we may as well put them to use. Just remember who you're talking to and that he can't be trusted. I'm going to have to cut this short. I'm getting a message from Benny. Stay in touch."

"I will. See you soon."

Grace raised an eyebrow. "So you're really going to talk to Whitaker?"

Davey shrugged. "I don't see why not." He placed the call and waited to see if it would connect or if he would be forced to leave a message. Honestly, he didn't know if he was hoping for one or the other.

"Well, well," came the familiar voice. "How did the solo mission go, kiddo?"

Davey frowned. Whitaker shouldn't have known about them. Grace made a motion with her finger telling him to continue. Right. Don't let him get under your skin. "Terrible, as always. The party got crashed by some unidentified government agents."

Whitaker chuckled. "I'm shocked. But as exciting as that sounds, I doubt you called purely for the social stimulation. Unless the apple has fallen a lot further from the tree than I realized."

"Umm... right." He wasn't really sure what to follow that up with, so he started over. "I'm going to send you a couple pictures. Do you think you can try to identify any of their faces for me?"

"It can't hurt for me to take a look."

Davey looked at Grace as she fiddled with the tablet for a moment and then nodded.

"Okay they're coming in now. Let's see." Whitaker went silent for a minute. "You know I thought you were sending me a puzzle I'd get to work on for a few days. I'm a little disappointed. Upfront, that's Damon Stein. He works for Arizona's Department of Defense on loan from the Office of Colonial Intelligence. He's been a busy man these last few months running errands for his boss, the minister."

'Wait, hold on," Davey said. "You're telling me that Arizona has been buying black-market grav plates?"

"No that's what you just told me," Whitaker said. "But it tracks with current events. I've been wondering how they were able to afford all the grav plates that the Phobos Platform needed for its weapons array. And now that it's time to announce it to the public, they're closing loose ends. Fascinating."

Davey and Grace had only half kept an ear to the news this week, but like everyone else, they'd been trying to keep up with information about the Phobos Platform.

"Oh, and kids," Whitaker said in his most patronizing voice. "I would think twice before you show those pictures to anyone else. You don't want to end up a loose end yourself."

And with that, he was gone. Davey met Grace's eyes. She was thinking the same thing he was. Why did this kind of thing always happen to them?

Chapter 7: Heartbeat

Give it a few decades and everyone's memory gets hazy. It's been what, twenty years? And everyone has already forgotten that for most of us life hasn't even changed all that much. It's not like Moses had this great influence over everything. Not in our daily lives anyway. Certainly not in mine.

Sure, you no longer saw one of his frigates pull into orbit when he had some big project or another. It was something you'd look up and go, "Oh I guess something fancy is being built," and go on with your life.

When he left, things just kept on turning, at least here on Mars. I don't speak for Earth. I guess it's rough that Moses left some things undone. Would have been nice if he'd have gotten the air breathable, so we didn't have to live under shields, but what are we going to do about it?

Go cry about it and write a few more fancy philosophy books. Shouldn't have left the keys to a damn AI, huh? Lesson learned too late. Glad I'll be long gone before it actually does turn into a mess. And good riddance.

Franklin Harvey
Construction Foreman
Died 32 AM

"I'm going to have to cut this short," Matthew said as the console pinged a notification. "I'm getting a message from Benny. Stay in touch."

"I will. See you soon," Davey said.

Matthew pulled up the message on the main monitor. Considering they were both on Mars it was unusual for Benny to send a message instead of just calling.

Someone is trying to kill me. Please help.

Davey and Grace's drama was erased from his mind in the space of a heartbeat. The two short sentences were followed by an address in Flagstaff. Hopefully, whoever was after Benny wasn't in a hurry because it would take thirty minutes to get there. He sent a reply consisting only of the words 'On my way' and jumped to his feet. Yvonne barely had time to leap out of the way as he ran out of the cockpit to his cabin.

"Watch where you're going," she said. "Normally it's the kids I have to chide for running around like they've lost their minds. And sometimes Abigail."

"Benny's in trouble," he shouted as his door opened. He put on his holster and loaded his revolver before grabbing a handful of speedloaders and slipping them into the pockets beneath his poncho. If this could have waited another hour, Abigail would be off the train, and he'd feel a lot better about going into an unknown situation. But no, Benny just had to get into trouble when he had no backup, not even Grace or Davey.

He opened the door to his cabin and nearly ran into Yvonne a second time. "I'm coming too," she said.

"I don't know what we're going to find," he said. "Not a good idea."

"And if he's been hurt, you'll wish I was there."

"How about you wait here and send Abigail my way as soon as she gets back."

"Or we can leave her a message, and I can be there just in case."

It wasn't the time to have an argument. "Fine. If it gets dangerous, you're staying out of the way."

"Obviously."

Matthew ran down to the hangar to prep his bike. By the time he had pulled it out and onto the lift, Yvonne was working her way down the ladder.

"I tried calling Abigail," she said, "but she didn't answer. I left her a comm message and a note upstairs."

"Hopefully this is nothing."

They mounted the bike as Matthew hit the control to lower the lift. "Have you ever met Benny in person?" she asked.

"I've not even seen a photo of him. He likes his privacy. Standard policy with most brokers from what I can tell, especially the ones that handle shady jobs. The less likely a job can be traced back to them, the safer they are. But that gets harder when you have a high-profile client." He scratched the back of his head. That was the thought that had been nagging at him. The one that stabbed him with guilt. Benny was a decent enough guy. He didn't deserve to have his life ruined just because one of his freelancers meddled with the powers that ran the solar system.

"You don't know that this is your fault," Yvonne said from behind him.

He didn't reply. The lift bottomed out and he flared the engines and took off down the lane between the fields. When he hit the road in front of the farmhouse, he opened up the throttle. Yvonne was wrong. It was his fault. He could feel it in his bones.

The address was a two-story apartment building on the rough side of Flagstaff.

"You'd think he'd live somewhere with a few less roaches," Yvonne said, giving the building a critical eye. Given that Matthew struggled with finances, she wasn't surprised to learn that his broker wasn't exactly wealthy, but this fell short of even her most conservative expectations.

"This is the address he gave." He dismounted from the bike and she accepted his offered hand. Bikes always left her sore. Why couldn't they have a nice small utility vehicle for the whole crew to use? "I'm going to call him." He dug out his comm and waited for a moment. No answer. "Well, that's not helpful. We don't know which—" The comm buzzed as a message came in. Matthew frowned at its screen. "Unit Twenty-Six."

"Second floor it is," Yvonne said. "Lead the way."

Matthew nodded and his hand briefly wandered to his holster before he seemed to decide against it. He locked down the bike and they took the sidewalk to the front entrance. The building was in terrible disrepair.

At the very least, it needed a thorough power washing to scrub the years of grime off the concrete faces. Matthew opened the front door and stepped into the foyer, glancing down the hallways before heading for the staircase.

Yvonne stayed close. She wished that Benny had told them more about what they were walking into. If there was an immediate danger, she assumed he would have warned them, but it was still enough to disquiet her mind with a low buzz of anxiety. They reached the second story, and Matthew took off down the hall. To Yvonne's relief, it was empty, unsurprising considering it was the middle of the day.

"Unit Twenty-Six," Matthew repeated as he reached the door. He lifted a hand to knock but hesitated.

"What are you waiting for?" Yvonne hissed.

He banged on the door. Almost at once, it cracked open and the face of a long-haired teenage boy peeked out. Yvonne frowned. She wouldn't have guessed that Benny had kids from what she knew of him. And if he was in danger, what was he doing letting a kid answer the door?

"I'm looking for Benny?" Matthew said.

The kid stepped back with downcast eyes and gestured for them to enter. They cautiously entered the apartment. The kid locked the door and then stepped past them down the entryway into the cramped living room. "Mom! They're here."

Yvonne's eyes took in the room at a glance. While it was clean and neat, the owners were clearly impoverished. The furniture, consisting of only two recliners, had clearly traded hands many times, if its threadbare condition was any evidence. The walls were bare of adornment. A single computer with an ancient monitor was shoved into a small wall nook. An attached kitchen was equally spartan, with only a tiny table and two folding chairs. Two chairs. That meant that Benny was—

A tired-looking woman with a small oxygen compressor at her hip entered the room. Matthew extended a hand and took off his hat. "I'm Matthew Cole, ma'am. I'm looking for Benny."

She smiled. "It's good to finally meet you, Mr. Cole. I'm Candace Greene, and Benny is my son."

Okay, Benny wasn't the woman. Benny was the kid. Yvonne nearly laughed aloud.

The teen shoved both his hands in his pockets and blew a strand of hair out of his face. "Yeah, it's me. Get it over with. Go ahead and laugh."

Matthew's face screwed itself up into the most dumbfounded look that Yvonne had ever seen. "You can't be... How old are you? Sixteen?"

"Seventeen," Benny said, as indignant as any young man whose age has ever been underestimated.

"That means you were... What thirteen or fourteen when you became my broker?"

Benny looked away and nodded.

Candace jumped to her son's defense. "He was thirteen. I'd lost my job because of my illness and... He found a way to make some money for us. You were his first freelancer." Her nose wrinkled in a smile. "We had to start somewhere. Mr. Cole, you had a reputation among the Brokers Alliance, and no one else would take you."

Yvonne snorted. She covered her mouth when everyone looked at her. "Sorry, that just, well, that sounds like Matthew." She patted him affectionately on the shoulder. "He can be hard to work with." She turned to Candace. "I'm guessing you're the business partner we've heard Benny reference."

Candace nodded. "My son is smarter than I am, but he doesn't have as many years handling surly men." She shrugged her shoulder apologetically at Matthew.

The moment of levity seemed to give Benny a second wind of courage. "I'm good at what I do," he said. "Now, anyway."

Matthew let out a long slow sigh. "You are. And I'm thankful that you took me on. I guess I didn't realize I was that much of a liability." He extended a hand. "I'm glad to meet you, Benny."

He turned red as he shook Matthew's hand. "You too."

"What about this death threat?" Matthew said. "What's going on?"

Candace picked a handwritten note up from the table. "This was on our front door this morning." Yvonne craned her head to get a look at it.

Drop the Sparrow crew or your business partner dies.

"Not very subtle," Matthew said. "And they deliberately tipped their hand as to how much they know about you."

Benny nodded. "I've only ever referred to mom as my business partner to you guys. Which means my network traffic is being intercepted? I've got more control over the encryption method if I bypass the comms and send it straight over the network. Hence the short message you got. No way they'll be able to crack that anytime soon."

"Do you have any ideas who this could be?" Yvonne asked.

"Not a clue," Benny said with a shrug. "Given Matthew's newfound celebrity status, it could be anyone."

"You shouldn't have called me here," Matthew said. "You're putting yourself and your mother in even more danger. You should have complied with their demand."

Benny looked at his mother. Candace smiled and gestured around the apartment. "Mr. Cole, we can't afford to drop you. And you can't afford for us to drop you either. Not right now. We thought maybe you could take us somewhere safer. Help us disappear and Benny can keep supplying you with jobs."

Matthew looked crestfallen. "You shouldn't have to leave your life because of me. I'm sorry."

Benny raised an eyebrow and crossed his arms. "We're not exactly giving up much."

Yvonne put a hand on Matthew's arm. "Antioch could handle a couple more residents." She saw the look of relief in Candace's eyes. That was what she had been hoping for.

"It's not that simple," Matthew said. "I know you didn't have a safe way of contacting me, but they almost certainly have this building under observation. We can't just walk out of here with you and your luggage in tow."

That broke Benny's confidence, and he looked back at his feet. His shaggy hair fell over his eyes. "Yeah. Well, you're here now, and I know you won't leave us out cold. You always make things work in the end."

Matthew took off his hat and set it on the table. "Give me a minute to think." He paced the length of the short room like one of Warlord Dan's caged animals.

"Abigail should be back soon," Yvonne suggested. "We can wait on her for backup."

"But what happens when we leave?" Matthew asked. "Do they follow us back to the Sparrow? Do they open fire? There are too many unknowns."

155

"Disguises?" Benny suggested.

Matthew shook his head. "Disguises only work well when someone doesn't know they're looking specifically for you. We were probably seen on the way in." He stepped over to the window and cautiously pulled the curtain back to peek out. "If we only knew where they were and how many, we could take the fight to them." He let go of the heavy fabric and turned his back to the window. "Maybe if we—"

The window shattered and Matthew fell forward with a cry of pain as the sharp crack of gunfire rang out. "Get away from the window!" he roared through gritted teeth as he pulled himself along the floor. "Around the corner." He slumped down and coughed.

"Benny, help me. Now," Yvonne said. An eerie calm settled over her. Together they each took Matthew by an arm as they half dragged him to safety and away from the deadly window. Her eyes roved quickly over Matthew. Entry wound behind his right shoulder. Exit wound lower on chest based on the expanding bloodstain. Punctured lung.

"Lay him down gently," she commanded. "On his left side." The dim hall was cramped with the four of them huddled together. Out of the corner of her eye, she saw Candace breathing erratically. She didn't need another patient right now. "Candace, I need clean cloth," Yvonne said. "Anything cotton will do. And I'll need more after that, so get ready to follow orders." The woman raised her eyes to meet Yvonne's and nodded then crawled toward the rooms in the back.

"My gun," Matthew wheezed. "They might push our position."

"Stop talking," Yvonne ordered. "Benny help me get his poncho off."

The teen pulled a small knife out of his pocket. "Will this help?"

"Perfect." She cut through the fabric and tugged it away before working on his shirt.

"Take my gun," Matthew said again. "Just in case."

Yvonne's breath hitched. She reached for the holster and took the revolver. "Do you know how to use this thing?" she asked Benny.

He shrugged. "I've been to a range once or twice."

"I've trained you, Yvonne," Matthew whispered.

"Stop. Talking." Yvonne said as she finished cutting the front of his shirt open to reveal the exit wound. She breathed a sigh of relief at its relatively small size. "I'm a doctor, not a killer. Don't ask me to shoot someone, even if they deserve it." The sentence nearly made her sick to her stomach the moment she said it. She shook her head. "Benny. Take the gun. Watch the door."

"What about the window?"

She pointed at the floor. "See that mark? The bullet went straight through him and hit the floor right there. They're higher than us. Keep to the wall and they won't have the angle."

"I'm sorry, Matthew," he said pitifully. But he obeyed. Candace returned with handfuls of clean t-shirts. Yvonne took one in each hand and, squatting over Matthew, applied as much pressure as she could muster to both the entrance and exit wound. "This will slow the bleeding, but we'll have to stop it."

Candace bit her lip. "What do I do?"

"It's probably a fool's hope to think you have chest seals in your first aid supplies?"

"I don't even know what that is."

"Then I need sterile plastic and tape. The strongest you have."

"Wh... What about a plastic bag?"

"What kind?"

"The sealable kind for sandwiches. And I keep engine tape around for fixing things."

"Those will suffice. Hurry. You should be able to enter the kitchen if you keep to the wall." As Candace scurried away, Yvonne leaned down to check on Matthew. The shirts were soaking through, but not at an alarming rate. "Looks like it's your lucky day," she said. "Whoever decided to shoot you must have thought you wear body armor on the job. The shell remained intact and punched clean through you. Most likely armor piercing. If that had been a hollow point..." She shuddered.

Matthew groaned but didn't say anything. At least she'd got that into his stubborn head. "You know," she said quietly. "I thought this was going to happen a lot sooner when I first came aboard. But I do wish you hadn't broken your streak." It was a silly and crass thing to say, but it helped keep the emotions at bay. That was one thing she couldn't afford right now. She'd kept her feelings in check the last time too. Maybe that meant something was wrong with her. At least this time, she wouldn't be forced to watch as someone she cared about died.

Candace returned, supplies in hand. "Perfect," Yvonne said. "Do you have someplace I can wash my hands?" Candace pointed at a door. "I need you to apply pressure with fresh shirts like I am until I get back. Can you do that? Don't touch the wound." Candace took her place.

Yvonne assessed her. "More pressure. As hard as you can." She ran into the restroom and, flipping on the light, soaped her hands, doing her absolute best to sterilize them.

By the time she returned, Candace's hands were shaking. "Just a little longer," Yvonne said. "I'm going to improvise an occlusive dressing."

"What's that?" Benny asked from across the room.

"Matthew has a punctured lung. It's creating new air pathways. I need to seal the wounds to keep air from leaking in or out and stop the bleeding. The plastic will form the seal to make it airtight, and the tape will keep it in place and apply pressure. Candace, on three I need you to move your hand away from his chest. Exit wounds are always more serious, so we need to deal with it first. Matthew, are you still with me? I need you to breathe out. Okay. One, two, three!"

Her hands moved fast, almost without thought as she sealed the wound. She would have preferred to work with medical-grade supplies, but this would do the trick until she could properly dress it. She inspected her handiwork. "Okay, we need to repeat the process with the entry wound. Matthew, breathe out again for me."

Soon it was over. Candace disposed of the bloodied rags, and Yvonne leaned over to check Matthew's pulse and breathing. Both were acceptable considering circumstances. "How are you feeling?" she asked gently.

"It all hurts," he whispered. "I'm cold too."

"We'll find you a blanket." Candace nodded and went to one of the bedrooms.

Matthew's comm buzzed and Yvonne nearly wept for joy as she answered it. "Abigail, get my surgical kit. We need you now!"

Abigail ran through the Sparrow at a blind panic. She knew Yvonne's surgical kit was in one of the upper cabinets in the common room, she just didn't know which. She started opening them at random. In her haste, she crushed one of the latches between her fingers, effectively sealing it shut. She stared at it for the space of three heartbeats before tearing the door off its hinges and tossing it aside. As luck would have it, it was the right cabinet. At least she would have an excuse when this was over.

If Matthew didn't die.

The thought twisted her insides in ways she couldn't explain. She grabbed the kit and rushed for the hold. A few minutes later, her over-sized bike was thundering away from the farm toward Flagstaff. The ride gave her time to think, which was the last thing she needed right now. Dark thoughts threatened to crush her, fears over the future, and all the ways this could go so terribly wrong. It was over if Matthew died. He was the heart and life of the crew and if something happened to him... Funny how you could go into danger so often and it never felt real until you lost and someone got hurt. Then it was all you could think about.

After an eternity of driving, she stopped her bike two blocks from her destination. She grabbed her comm. "Yvonne, I'm here. Got an update for me?"

"We're okay. Whoever shot Matthew seems content to wait. Or else they think he's a dead man trapped in here."

"Is he?" Abigail asked carefully.

"He will need more medical care than I can provide in an apartment but he's no longer in immediate danger. Abigail, they may open fire."

"That's the least of my concerns right now," she said, tucking the kit under her arm.

"Matthew was hit with an armor-piercing bullet."

"Meant for fiber armor and low-grade plates most likely," she corrected, "not vehicle grade steel alloy. I'll be there soon." Still, she pulled her shield off her back and deployed it. It wouldn't hurt to be careful. She could cover two blocks in a manner of seconds when she wasn't being slowed down by anyone else. Get in. Get Yvonne the supplies she needed. Figure out how to get all of them out of there.

She shifted her shield to her left hand, the side fire would most likely come from, and took off at a sprint down the sidewalk. Her passing rattled nearby windows, and pedestrians scattered out of her path. She reached the run-down apartment building and slowed up to look around. There were too many nearby buildings where a sniper could be hiding, waiting for them to try and evacuate. This was going to be a problem. As she turned to enter the apartment, a shot rang out, and a bullet struck the armor in the middle of her back. She spun, shield raised, but the marksman decided against wasting any more ammo and revealing their location. Cautiously, she backed into the entrance and shut the door behind her.

Abigail felt the crumbling stairs groan beneath her suit's weight and wondered just how old the building was. Walking down the hall, she knocked on the appropriate door. "Special delivery."

Benny took a big step back as he let Abigail Sharon into the room. He knew what to expect, but she was terrifyingly huge in person. She shut the door behind her and looked down at him.

"Benny," she said.

He swallowed. "Abigail," he replied as bravely as he could.

She pushed past him. "I'll make fun of you for hiding your age after this is over. You're not off the hook."

"Down here, Abigail," Yvonne said. "Watch the window."

"I can solve that problem," she said and blocked the entire window with her shield. There was a sharp metallic ping and crack of a gunshot. Benny flinched, squeezing an eye shut. He'd already seen one person shot today and had no desire to see another. For her part, Abigail didn't bat an eyelash. "See? It works like a charm. Now, let's get you guys out of that cramped hall."

Feeling ignored, Benny went back to watching the door. The gun felt like a lead weight in his hand. Honestly, why did he still have it now that Abigail was here? She could stand guard and actually do some good. Instead, she was fussing over Matthew like... Well, he wasn't sure exactly, but she wasn't making any attempt at masking her concern as Yvonne went to work.

For his part, the guilt was getting unbearable. It was his fault Matthew had been shot. He mentally kicked himself. Now everyone was in danger. He listened to the quiet voices of the women as they talked in hushed voices before working up the nerve to interrupt. "So... How is he doing?"

Yvonne answered without looking up. "I'm suturing the wounds closed. Then I'll have to make an incision and insert a drain to remove fluid and air from the chest cavity."

"How long is that going to take?"

"Time enough for someone else to figure out how to get us out of here," she answered shortly.

Abigail brushed Matthew's hair back. "Hang in there," she said and stood to her feet. "All exits will be watched. I guess we could call in the police, but that's putting more people in danger, and there are too many private buildings where those shots could have come from for them to check."

"Can you bring the Sparrow?" Benny asked. "We've got roof access."

Abigail shook her head. "One pilot is down and the other is trapped here. Unless someone you know has an armored vehicle we can back up to the building, we'll be leaving on foot."

The room dropped into an oppressive silence at that thought. Benny went back to watching the door and wracked his brain. Did he have any other contacts that could be here quickly with transport? After several minutes of rejecting idea after idea, he snapped his fingers as the answer came to him. "I've got it. The old tunnel we used to play in."

His mom narrowed her eyes. "You told me you never went down there."

"I was like ten. I lied. A lot."

"Tell me about this tunnel," Abigail demanded.

"A group of us found it years ago while playing in the halls. Beneath the staircase, there was an old boarded-off room with a ladder leading down to a tunnel network. We tore through the boards."

"This is promising," she said. "What kind of tunnels are we talking about? Maintenance? Sewer?"

Mom shook her head. "A century ago, Flagstaff started a tunnel system to bury the trains underground."

"A subway system," Abigail said. "This is perfect. Why was it abandoned?"

"I think Moses was doing the digging, so when he disappeared, the project just stopped. The kids pried open the room and found something no one had seen in decades. They'd been playing down there for a week before we found out and closed it off again, permanently this time."

"Abigail can remedy that," Benny said.

"Sounds like our best shot," Abigail said. "Can we move Matthew safely?"

Yvonne set aside a tool she'd been working with. "It's less than ideal, but so is waiting here for them to come finish us off. You'll have to carry him. Gently. He'll be out for a little longer." She placed a mask over his face and clipped a portable compressor to his belt. Benny grimaced.

Mom wasn't the only one on oxygen now. Yvonne packed up her surgical kit, and his mom shouldered the backpack they'd put together, little more than a couple changes of clothes and the drives from his computer. They were traveling light.

Abigail came over to Benny and laid a heavy armored hand on his shoulder. It felt like a load of bricks. "Take me to the tunnel entrance. We'll make sure the path is clear, and then I'll come back for Matthew and the others." They moved Matthew out of view from the window, and she retrieved her shield. She turned to Yvonne. "Be ready."

He took a deep breath and hoisted the revolver. Abigail opened the door and crept out into the hall, head darting both ways. "We're clear. Come on."

What was he doing? He wasn't sure he could hit a target at one meter. This was what Matthew was for. This was why he was a broker. Directing other people to do stupid crap was a lot safer than doing it yourself. Now Matthew was injured and his mom was in danger. Everything was flipped on its head.

Abigail led him down the staircase and checked the halls in either direction again. He jumped when the front entrance opened, but it was another tenant that he recognized. They saw Abigail and immediately spun on their heels and left. Smart move.

"Where's this entrance?"

"Right here behind the stairs."

"It's just a wall."

"They plastered over it to make sure no one else spotted it and got curious. How are we going to—"

She rammed her fist through the wall and started pulling away great chunks of plaster. He rushed forward to help her. In a minute's time, they had exposed a hole large enough that even Abigail could slip through. Beyond the half-destroyed wall was a small dark closet, and he saw the locked hatch that covered the ladder leading down to the tunnel. Abigail leaned in and pinched the lock off with two fingers. "Stay here," she ordered. "I'll be back as soon as I can with the others."

For two minutes, Benny jumped at every sound. He even pointed the gun at Mrs. Warhol when she came down the stairs. If she'd turned around, the old woman probably would have screamed. It was weird thinking he would never see her again. Never see anything in this town again. Maybe that wasn't a bad thing, though. He'd have to start making more contacts in the Jupiter neighborhood, but that was a challenge he'd enjoy.

The sound of Abigail coming down the stairs was unmistakable. She rounded the corner, Matthew wrapped in a blanket and cradled in her arms. Soon the whole group was crowded around the hole in the wall. Yvonne crawled through it first. "Candace, follow me. Then Abigail and Matthew. Benny, bring up the rear."

She pulled back the hatch and disappeared down the shaft. His mom took a deep breath and followed her, giving one last nervous look at Benny.

"Are you gonna be able to climb down there while carrying him?" he asked Abigail.

"It's going to be a trick, but I'll make it work." When the other two had had plenty of time to make headway down the ladder, she disappeared as well. Benny slid into the small closet and watched as the bobbing lights of Abigail's suit descended into the darkness. How had they ever done this as kids? He took a deep breath and swung his legs over the hole and climbed down into the abyss.

Yvonne fought to control her breathing. It was pitch black. The ladder was rusted and slick. And her knee, of all times her knee was complaining. All of this was made worse by the awkward surgical kit slung over her shoulder. She didn't know how long the ladder was, and she was glad Benny had never told them because the only thing keeping the panic away was the belief that the next rung might be the last. She'd descended at least a few dozen meters by this point. It couldn't be that much further, right? A subway would have to be deep, deep enough to burrow beneath buildings and for the bedrock above to still support them.

"Almost there," she whispered to herself. Not because she believed it, but because she wanted it to be true. "Almost there."

At last it was true. Her foot planted onto solid ground and she stepped away from the ladder, stumbling in a limp as her knee decided it was finished. She fumbled with shaking hands for the flashlight in her pack. She swept its beam around her. Just a dark concrete tunnel that stretched further in either direction than her tiny light could illuminate.

Hopefully, there was a way out of here because getting trapped in forgotten tunnels beneath Flagstaff sounded like a bad way to die. The panic receded, and she shined the light at the bottom for the others to see the approach.

Candace finished her descent and sidled close to Yvonne and her tiny source of light. "I can't believe the kids used to come down here."

"No, kidding," Yvonne uttered. "Why does that ladder even exist?"

"As best as the city could tell from old records," Candace said, "there were emergency escapes dug every few hundred meters. The apartment complex was built a few years after the project was abandoned and simply constructed over the existing escape. The kids just stumbled upon the entrance."

Abigail finished her descent, her suit lighting up the tunnel, driving away some of the oppressive atmosphere. "Alright, we're down," she said to Matthew. "Sorry about the bumpy ride. You still okay?"

He mumbled something that no one understood.

"Lay him down. I need to check his vitals." Abigail obeyed and stretched Matthew along a rubble-free length of concrete. "Matthew," Yvonne said, "since this isn't exactly a safe medical setting, I barely dosed you with light anesthesia to work on you. It's wearing off, and as you wake up, you're going to be in for a world of hurt. I've put a fentanyl patch on your arm. It should help, but until we get you to safety, there's only so much I can do for you."

He seemed to register some understanding of this as she checked his pulse and blood pressure, followed by unspooling an oximeter to check his blood oxygen. She checked the small suction drain that emerged from his chest. It hadn't filled with as much blood as she feared. She unscrewed the small bulb, dumped its contents, and reattached it, not knowing when she'd be able to do so again. So far, so good, but she hated to think of the sutures being jostled by Abigail carrying him.

She had no idea how combat medics dealt with this kind of thing and kept their sanity.

Matthew muttered something low under his breath, and Yvonne, despite the danger, chuckled.

"What did he say?" Benny asked as he stepped off the ladder.

"He asked if he could have his hat." She gave his hand a gentle squeeze. "I've got it with me in my pack right now. We didn't forget it."

"If it's safe to keep moving with him," Abigail said, "we need to start out. They'll come looking for us eventually. And when they do, they'll find the wall we broke down."

"Then let's get out of here," Benny said.

Yvonne flicked her flashlight in either direction. "Which way?"

Benny pointed. "That way. The other direction is blocked after a couple hundred meters."

Yvonne stood and backed away from Matthew as Abigail stooped to lift him into her arms. Yvonne had never seen her move with such fine control before, and it helped relieve a few of her fears. Matthew was in good hands between the two of them. "Benny," she said. "Take the flashlight and lead the way with Abigail."

He took the light from her and set off down the direction he'd indicated. "We never explored to the end. There's at least a few kilometers of tunnel, mostly in a straight shot, but I do remember there being a couple of spurs."

"We won't need to get that far," Abigail said. "We should try to find another emergency exit and make for the surface."

They settled into silence for several minutes. Periodically, the tunnel was partially obstructed by fallen debris or old equipment, including strange broken-down robots that must have once been under Moses' control. Had they not been rusting for a century, they would have been of interest to the University. Abigail would stand back and shine her lights on these and other obstructions to make sure no one hurt themselves in the dark. Ahead of her, lights bounced down the never-ending tunnel. Yvonne found the whole experience disorienting and hypnotic. Every couple hundred meters, they found an escape shaft. The first one had been filled with cement. The second was collapsed with debris. The third Benny climbed up to find it sealed at the top.

"We're never getting out of here," Candace said quietly as they continued their march through the dark. Yvonne would have liked to dispel the woman's fears, but the possibility did exist that there wasn't another exit they could take. If they got lost down here, Matthew's condition would deteriorate rapidly. She doubted her quick surgical fix had been perfectly sterile, and the chance for infection was high, if not extreme. She wasn't about to watch him die down here in the dark.

She stared at the back of Abigail's head, silhouetted by her lights. Odds were, she wouldn't stick around to watch that happen either. She'd most likely brandish her shield and wade back into battle and maybe get herself killed long before Matthew was in any more danger than he already was.

"Here's the junction I mentioned," Benny said. He shined his light down an identical side tunnel.

"What do you think?" Abigail asked. "Take the new path or keep on the current one?"

No one answered, and on impulse, Yvonne looked back the way they'd come. "I think we had better come to a decision and keep moving. These tunnels aren't quite as empty as they used to be."

Behind them, hundreds of meters away came the faintest of light. Their enemies were on their tail.

Candace whimpered. Abigail just sighed. "They'll move fast without wounded slowing them down. No offense," she added with a quick glance at Matthew. If he answered, Yvonne didn't hear it.

She tried not to imagine the pain he would be in if they made it out of this. With all the jostling, it would be a miracle if the suture held. "If we can see their light," Yvonne said, "they can see ours. Let's kill the light and then take the side tunnel. Once we're a couple dozen meters in, we'll turn it back on for a few minutes and try and get as much distance as possible."

"Then we have to lie in wait and hope they pass us," Abigail said. "Alright hands on the wall, everyone. Shuffle your feet. It's going to be pitch black." When everyone was ready, she turned off her lights, leaving only the tiny pool of Benny's flashlight. With a barely audible click, they were plunged into inky darkness, the kind that felt like it would smother any light that challenged it. "Forward," she said. "We're on a schedule here."

They stumbled along in deepest night, and, for the first time, Yvonne felt her nerves wearing thin. Darkness ahead and enemies behind. Matthew slowly dying and her own thoughts choking out her breath one shallow pull at a time.

Suddenly Abigail flicked her lights back on. "That should be far enough. We have at least a few minutes until they reach the junction. Move. Faster. Sorry, Matthew." Their hike turned into a desperate flight. Abigail was able to keep a walking pace, but the rest were jogging. Yvonne no longer even knew what the plan was.

All at once, Abigail skidded to a stop, and Matthew cried out in pain. "Sorry!" It was almost a squeal. "I'm sorry. I just... There."

166

She pointed at a small alcove in the wall. They'd passed several similar pockets on their journey, and Yvonne hadn't given them a second thought. It clicked all at once. "We'll hide and hope they pass us by."

"That's crazy," Benny said. "No way."

"We're running out of time," Abigail said. "They'll be at the junction any second. Unless they turn their head at just the right time, they'll pass right by. And that's assuming they even take this path. Get in."

Candace crawled back into the alcove. "And if they do see us?"

"Then they'll have me to contend with. Benny, hold the corner until you see their lights at the crossroad."

They packed into the darkest recess and turned out the lights again. Yvonne kicked herself, wishing she'd checked Matthew's vitals again. It was too late now. She was debating asking for the flashlight when Benny hissed, "Lights in the junction."

Yvonne felt her heartbeat hammer. Please take the other path. Please take the other path.

"I can't really count, but there's a bunch of men. They... They just split. A group is coming this way."

She heard Benny shuffle back into the alcove with them. The subtle metallic ring of Abigail deploying her shield. Candace's rapid breath beside her. The woman was going to hyperventilate. Yvonne fumbled and found her hand and gave it a firm squeeze. "We're here," she whispered. "Slow breaths. Nice and even." Candace fought it and slowly brought herself under control.

Then there was a distant glow as lights approached from the direction they'd come from. No one moved a muscle. Slowly the diffuse cones of light sharpened into four beams.

They came into line of sight. Four armed men, guns at the ready as they marched down the tunnels. If one of them turned their head even a fraction, it would be over. Best case scenario, Abigail charged out. The noise would draw the rest for sure. They kept walking, each step taking an agonizingly long time. Now they would have to turn around to see them.

Then they were past. And still, no one dared to move. They hadn't planned this far ahead.

After several minutes, Benny whispered, "I'll check the corner again." Fabric rustled as he moved out of the alcove. "I can see their lights. It looks like they've stopped. Maybe it's a dead end."

"That's a best-case scenario," Abigail said. "Because it means they'll come back this way and write this passage off as investigated."

"Wait, two of the lights are coming back this way."

"Shift to the other side!" Yvonne said. "Hurry."

They all moved in the dark, taking care not to disturb Matthew more than they had to. Then came the next agonizing wait. They heard the voices almost before they saw the light.

"Yeah that's right. There's a half-blocked exit down this path. It lets out at a train yard. I don't know. I'm not familiar with this part of town. If they came through here, they're already home free. I left Miller and Jamus outside to guard it just in case." Two men came into view. One had his gun slung over his shoulder and his comm out. "We're on our way to rejoin you. If you meet that Shield Maiden down here, you're gonna want all the help you can get."

Yvonne grimaced. That wasn't going to help Abigail's ego any. They waited another five minutes before anyone dared to breathe. "Okay," Abigail said. "One more push in the dark. No lights. If we stay on the wall, we should reach their exit. I'll lead out." Yvonne heard her pick up Matthew again.

"Tell me this is some kind of nightmare," he mumbled.

"We're almost out," Abigail reassured him. "We're going to have to keep quiet a little bit longer and we'll be free."

He didn't respond, which was just as well. But Yvonne had been glad to hear his voice. They pressed on in silence, and the minutes and distance blurred together. She brought up the rear, occasionally bumping into Candace in front of her when the cadence of their footfalls fell out of rhythm.

When she saw the faintest of glows ahead of them, she thought she imagined it, that it was a trick of a light-starved brain trying to make sense of absolute darkness. She squinted her eyes. It was real. By the sighs of relief, she knew the others had seen it too. The tunnel ahead was filled with debris, but it was backlit by a distant light. They rounded the detritus. Someone had long ago carved a pathway through the cave-in. Natural outside light spilled into the darkness.

"Wait here," Abigail said. She set Matthew down for the last time and took her shield in hand. "I've got a couple of would-be assassins to set straight." She disappeared around the corner. They heard a quick shout and then a pair of heavy thumps. Abigail reappeared moments later. "Let's go. Watch the eyes, though. It's going to hurt."

She was right. As the five of them stepped out into the trainyard and around Abigail's victims, the afternoon sun beat down painfully. Yvonne squinted up at the sky, never so happy to see it as she was now. She snapped herself out of it. They weren't in the clear yet. "Set Matthew down. I need to check on him before we go any further. And call Elizabeth. We'll need her to come pick us up."

Chapter 8: This Mortal Coil

───────────◁◻▷───────────

It's difficult to separate the historical Josiah Carver from the one of popular legend. His close association with Moses is well documented, but the folk tales make them out to be brothers, the eccentric and charming socialite and his AI sidekick. Maybe Carver was the sidekick.

I remember one such story about Carver rescuing a kidnapped child. He walked into the mafia boss's lair as Moses shut down security, diverted guards, and magically unlocked doors in front of him. No one saw him coming or going, at least until he was outside the compound. The story goes that the gangsters opened fire on Carver and the child, but their bullets never reached him, instead breaking apart on an invisible shield. Then he just disappeared.

There's no way to judge the veracity of this tale or the others. Carver loved being in the public eye, but he also loved running circles around the press and officials. Unfortunately for him, his residence was on Earth, and Moses' disappearance wasn't kind to our ancestral home.

But I get the feeling Carver would have approved of his growing legend. By all accounts, his ego was greater than one lifetime would allow.

Spenser Slate
Professor of Folklore Studies,
University of Ganymede
Died 80 AM

---◁◍▷---

Elizabeth Cole held it together. Somehow. If she lost control of her old farm truck, then she would have failed Matthew in his utmost hour of need. To hear that your only son has been shot is an abrupt derailment of life. Even worse that it wasn't a random act, but the fulfillment of long-simmering fears.

She made the last turn onto a deserted side street a few blocks south of the old trainyard and pulled over in front of a boarded-up fuel station. She caught movement out of the corner of her eye and turned. Abigail came out of the garage and looked around cautiously, and Elizabeth opened the door and waved to her. The other woman disappeared back into the dark station before emerging with a bundle in her arms. Elizabeth ran to him, eyes already prickling with tears.

"He's okay," Abigail said. "For now. But we have to get out of here."

Abigail lowered Matthew down to where she could see him better. Her son's eyes were squinted shut against the light. She cupped his face with her palm and wiped the wet off her cheek as she fought back the sudden wave of emotion.

He opened one eye and tried a weak smile before closing it again.

"Not to break this up, but we need to go," Yvonne said as she stepped out of the building. A woman and her son followed closely behind her, presumably Candace and Benny.

Elizabeth nodded determinedly and turned away from Matthew, though it took a herculean effort. "Then let's load up." They carefully strapped Matthew into the cramped back seat. He grumbled and looked to be in more than a little pain, but the task was accomplished without incident. Yvonne climbed into the cab. Abigail and the newcomers would have to ride in the bed. Unfortunately for them, Elizabeth had recently moved a load of fertilizer. Hopefully, it wasn't too rank back there.

When they were finally situated, she started the truck and pulled back out onto the street. "To the hospital?" she asked.

Yvonne didn't immediately answer, and Elizabeth's heart sank. They were going to run. Couldn't they have a normal life for once? Just once.

"Whoever the assailants are, they've already set one trap for Matthew," Yvonne finally said. "And make no mistake. He was the target. I don't trust any hospital security team to keep him safe."

"Spell it out for me. What are you going to do?" Elizabeth said, mouth dry.

"We leave Mars. One of the Martian freeports should be safe enough. We'll let him recover for a few days and then move on."

Elizabeth turned onto a larger street with more traffic. She resisted the impulse to turn around and check on Matthew. Yvonne had it in hand and would see to him.

"Which, unfortunately, brings us to you," Yvonne said.

Elizabeth knew where this was going. "No. I'm not leaving."

"I don't think you get a choice in the matter. And I'm sorry."

"What do I have to do with any of this?" she asked. It was a stalling tactic. She was well aware.

"Whoever's after Matthew has already shown that they're willing to use the people in his life as bait. It's a miracle they went for Benny first instead of you."

Elizabeth passed a slow-moving tanker truck. "There's a cousin I can stay with."

Yvonne shook her head. "With how well informed these guys were, that's not an option. You would only be putting more people in danger. I'm sorry. I really am. But if you disagree, you can take it up with Abigail. With Matthew out, security decisions are technically her call, not mine."

She was being ripped away from her farm and her life in the space of a heartbeat. Would it be safe for her workers to continue the work until harvest? She hoped so because she wasn't about to let it all go to waste or let them lose their jobs. Even for Matthew. Everything he had done, everything he had become, had finally caught up to him. And it was destroying both of their lives.

She choked back the old feeling of bitterness and nodded once, resigning herself to the inevitable. "I'll need to pack a bag."

⎯⎯⎯⎯⎯⎯⎯⎯⎯⎯⎯⎯⎯⎯⎯ ◁◊▷ ⎯⎯⎯⎯⎯⎯⎯

As they approached the farm, Abigail went on full alert. She stood up from her perch in the bed of the truck and peered out over the cab. The grounds looked quiet as far as she could tell. It was late enough in the afternoon that the farmhands had already left.

"What are you doing," Benny asked as they slowed down to turn into the lane.

"Making sure our friends didn't out-think us and beat us here," she said. "Do you fancy a bullet between the ears? Because I don't."

He grunted an agreement. "You know, I always imagined the Sparrow to be smaller."

"And I always imagined you were a grownup," she replied. She vaulted over the side of the truck and hit the ground running. She easily passed the truck and ran up to the porch. She snagged the hidden key from beneath a loose stone and unlocked the front door. It was dark inside, save for the light coming through the curtains, and utterly silent. She wasn't going to take a chance here. She checked every room in the house before heading back outside.

"It's clear," she said to the group as they climbed out of the truck. "Elizabeth, you've got ten minutes to pack." The woman gave her a rather displeased look as she stepped off the running board. Abigail tried not to let it bother her, but she really did love the old woman and it stung to be on the receiving end of her frustration. It wasn't like any of this was her fault. She opened the back door of the truck and leaned in.

"We going for another ride?" Matthew asked.

"I see the drugs are wearing off," Abigail said. She leaned in to unstrap him, but he pushed her hand away and tried to do it himself. "You know you're going to have to ditch that independent streak."

His hands fumbled with the restraints, and he gave up. "Sorry."

She didn't say anything else but carefully unstrapped him and lifted him out of the back seat.

"Aaugh. Yup. Drugs wearing off," he said between clenched teeth.

"You'll have to talk to the doctor about that. We'll get you fixed up

173

better on the Sparrow." Ahead of her, Yvonne led Candace and Benny through the fields. "You know you really scared us this time." He didn't answer and they passed the trip to the Sparrow in silence. Yvonne had the ramp down and the port airlock open by the time they caught up.

"Where do you want me to take the patient?" she asked.

"Take him to his cabin. I've got to get preflight started and call Davey and Grace. They need to be ready for pickup. Then I'll come to check on Matthew."

Well, at least she had something to do. Abigail ducked through the airlock entry. She was just useful when something needed hitting. "This is the common room," she grunted at Benny. "Set your stuff down here and don't mess with anything."

"I'm not going to touch—"

"Save it." She continued on through the hall and opened Matthew's door. "Hope you've picked up your laundry." He snorted in reply and Abigail took that as a win. "Alright, I'm going to set you down right here on your bed." She propped him up with pillows then stepped back, feeling a sudden surge of awkwardness. "Anything else I can do for you?"

"I'm thirsty," he said, settling back.

"Sorry, can't do. Yvonne said nothing to eat or drink yet. So, I guess I can't help you then. I'm sorry. She'll be by in a minute to check on you." She rubbed the back of her neck. "Sorry." She cocked her head and leaned in. His breaths were slow and deep. She frowned. He must still have plenty of drugs in his system, after all, for him to drift off mid conversation. A dozen thoughts chased each other in circles for a long moment before she turned away.

Yvonne was just leaving the cockpit when she opened the door. "Preflight is started, and I called the kids to let them know we're on the way."

Abigail frowned. "Did you tell them about Matthew?"

She shook her head and elbowed past Abigail. "That can wait. No need to cause panic. We've all had enough of that for the day."

Abigail's comm buzzed. "Elizabeth, I wonder what she needs." Yvonne left Matthew's door open as she entered, probably so she could eavesdrop. "Yes?"

"A vehicle just pulled up to the house." The woman's voice was calm, but there was a tension in her tone, like a cord stretched too tight.

Yvonne's head turned, and she met Abigail's eye. "I hoped we would have a little more time."

"Me too," Abigail said. "Stay put, Elizabeth. I'll be right there."

Elizabeth locked her bedroom door and had a sudden flashback to the last time her farm was attacked. They'd been after Yvonne that time. She looked at her half-packed bag, thinking of how many things she wasn't going to be able to bring with her. On an impulse, she zipped it closed. This would have to do.

She opened her closet and got out Albert's old rifle and loaded it. This was far too much like two years ago. She moved to the window and eased around the edge to get a view of the farm. All appeared quiet. A field away, the Sparrow sat, humming the deep throb she'd come to associate with its take-off. Its ramp was still down, but the door was shut fast.

She opened the window, and, as she propped the rifle on the sill, breathed in the familiar Martian air, the sharp tang of dust with a hint of sulfur. How many days would pass before she would come back to her homeworld? A week? An entire season. The Sparrow's airlock opened and Abigail strode out, shield brandished.

Gunfire instantly rang out across the farm. Abigail tucked behind her shield and charged down the ramp and disappeared into the field. Elizabeth looked for the source of the shots but to no luck. They sounded like they had come from just beneath her. Perhaps they were using the house for cover.

She fumbled with her comm. "Abigail, I've locked myself in my room and—"

"I see you up there. Keep your head down. I'm on my way."

Elizabeth kept the call open. She didn't ask how they were supposed to get to the Sparrow under fire, but she doubted Abigail had come to a conclusion on that end either. In the field beneath, she could make out glints of the woman's armor as she barreled through the wheat toward the house.

The sound of the front door getting kicked in froze her blood on the spot. "Abigail, someone is in the house." She took cover behind her bed and pointed the rifle at her door.

"I'm coming," she hissed back. "They're flanking out wide around the house. Probably trying to encircle me in the field and get to the Sparrow. Whatever you do, don't reveal that you're inside until the last possible moment."

Elizabeth concentrated on the door. They were probably just being cautious. The Sparrow was their target, and with it warming up, they'd have to move fast. Maybe they would reach the locked bedroom door and move on. The stairs creaked. "Running out of time, Abigail."

More gunfire outside. "Busy, but on my way."

The door handle rattled.

Elizabeth aimed down the sights.

Crack. A kick landed against the door. A second. On the third kick, the door jamb gave way.

She took in the sight of the man in an instant. Face covered by a balaclava. Dark gray combat fatigues. Gun raised. His eyes widened when he saw her. She squeezed the trigger and put a bullet in center mass. She reached for the lever to chamber another round as two men rushed into the room. It was too late. They pulled the gun from her grasp and held her with strong arms. She shrieked and thrashed to break their grip, but it was no use.

An indescribable sound erupted from just outside the window and the men froze. Like a car plowing into a building, suddenly, the wall and window were ripped away as Abigail tore through. The men tried to swing their guns to meet her, but she backhanded one with her shield, sending him crashing into a dresser with bone-crushing force. The other she grabbed with her left hand and flung out through the hole in the wall. He'd hit the ground somewhere well beyond the house, given his trajectory. "They know we're here now," Abigail said. She hefted her shield and ran to the door to block anyone else from entering the room.

Elizabeth could only stare at the hole Abigail had torn through her bedroom. It was shocking to see the ease with which she'd done so. An irrational part of her brain was furious and later, she might even cry about it, but right now—

The high-pitched whine of the Sparrow turned into a deafening roar. "Are they leaving?" she shouted.

"Never," Abigail said. "If I had to guess, Yvonne is coming to get us."

Elizabeth crept to what used to be her window and peered out, leery of showing her face. The Sparrow lifted off the ground with its landing thrusters and swung around to face the farmhouse. Then the chin gun opened fire.

The ear-shattering buzzing was the loudest sound Elizabeth had ever heard, and she covered her head and dove for cover.

"No time for that!" Abigail said, pulling her back to her feet. "She's coming in!" Elizabeth could only make out what she said over the ringing in her ears by watching her lips.

The Sparrow drifted slowly toward the farmhouse and she saw the ventral lift lowering. "How are we going to get there?"

"I'm going to jump. You're going to fly." Before Elizabeth knew what was happening, she was hoisted into the air. Abigail ran out onto what was left of the roof and threw her across the fifteen-foot gap. She hit the surface of the lift and rolled end over end before catching herself. She was going to be a bruised mess come morning. There was an impact and a loud clang. She turned and saw Abigail grasping the edge of the lift, half hanging over the farmyard. Elizabeth moved forward to help but then hit the deck as gunfire sparked off Abigail's armor. She swung her legs over the edge and shouted into her comm. "We're on. Raise the lift. Go!"

The Sparrow raised its nose and slid backward away from the house and toward the ridge. The nose gun fired one last time, and Elizabeth watched in awe as a pair of black grav cars were raked with cannon fire and shredded to useless scrap. Then the lift pulled them up into the hold and they were away. Her head spun. She laid down flat on the metal surface and tried not to tear up as she left behind the home she'd shared with Albert.

"Thanks for the ride," Davey said, offering his hand to Vicente. "And I'm sorry this didn't work out like we wanted."

Vicente shrugged. "The problem got solved." He'd agreed to pay half and negotiate on the remainder later. Considering the circumstances, Davey thought that was more than fair. His hand drifted to his pocket where he kept the drive of photos. Matthew had said to take them to the press. Whitaker said to never show them to anyone. Davey decided it wouldn't hurt to sit on that decision for now.

"There they are," Grace said.

Davey squinted into the westering sun as the Sparrow made its approach. Vicente had driven them to the outskirts of Warszawa after they'd gotten the call from Yvonne. The mechanic had hoped he'd have a chance to see Matthew but given the urgency with which they were leaving Mars, Davey doubted it would be a long reunion.

The Sparrow set down with a crunch on the rocky ground, and the side ramp lowered at once. Davey was surprised when Abigail showed her face and not Matthew. Grace skipped ahead to meet her, but he held back. He knew that Abigail would never be excited to see him, but she was usually a little happier about seeing Grace. Something was wrong.

"How big of a hurry are we in?" he asked.

Abigail bit her lip. "Matthew's been injured. We have to go."

Grace stopped in her tracks at the bottom of the ramp. "Wait. Like serious injured?"

"Serious."

Davey felt a fist tighten around his heart. He turned to Vicente. "I'm afraid that reunion got put on hold."

The poor man looked at a loss for words. "Let me know how he is," he said sadly.

"I will. I promise." He jogged up the ramp to catch up with his sister. This wasn't the homecoming he had imagined from his first successful job. Abigail ribbing him. Maybe a few kind words from Yvonne. A nod of the head and a smile from Matthew. He closed the airlock behind him and entered the common room. An unknown woman and teen stared at him. He stared back.

"Passengers?" He asked Abigail.

"Benny and his mother."

Benny's face turned bright red and he shook his hair out of his eyes. Davey laughed despite knowing he shouldn't. "Sorry. I was just expecting a grownup."

"Yeah well, you're just as short as I was expecting."

Davey closed the distance and had him by the collar of his shirt before Abigail could pull him off. "Whoa. Not right now. We've got bigger problems." She gave Benny a light shove. "Behave, or I'll lock you in a closet."

Grace kicked Benny in the shins as she passed. "Not cool."

Benny's mom looked mortified at the whole exchange. "Sorry," he mumbled.

"Yeah, whatever, me too," Davey said. He pushed past him to the cockpit.

Yvonne was just lifting the Sparrow off the ground. "Good to see you. You've missed a rough day."

"Apparently," he said, sitting in the co-pilot's seat. "Is Matthew okay?"

"For now. Elizabeth is with him, but you can see him later if you'd like."

Okay, it had to be bad if she were aboard. "So, what happened?"

"Someone is trying to kill Matthew," she said. She pointed the Sparrow toward the sky, and the familiar thrum of the engines rumbled through the deck. "So we're leaving Mars. I can't provide definitive medical care. One of the older freeports should be able to. Right now, I'm leaning toward Freeport 2. It's in a distant orbit around Mars and we should be able to be there in a couple hours."

He heard a door behind him and turned his head. Grace had entered Matthew's room. Apparently, she got visiting rights before he did. That figured. He turned his attention back to the cockpit.

"Looks like you had an adventure too," Yvonne said, giving him an appraisal out of the corner of her eye.

"I'll be fine," he mumbled. "Just a building blown out from under me with a thumper."

Yvonne chuckled and then sighed. "You two may not be related by blood, but the way you get into trouble, I'd still say you're a chip off of Matthew's block."

Davey wasn't sure how to take that, and the hand squeezing his heart gripped a little tighter. A light on the console distracted him from the thought. "What's that?"

"Intercept warning."

"Meaning?"

"It means a ship on the scopes has changed course to intercept with us."

He sucked in a breath. "Do I need to—"

"Yes."

He leaped to his feet and sprinted out of the cockpit, down the hall, and through the common room. Benny and his mother both jumped

179

out of his way as he plowed on toward the turret. As he sat in the familiar seat and powered up the targeting controls, he let out a quiet breath. It felt better to be on this side of the thumper this time.

Yvonne looked at the display showing their course vs. the incoming ship. She made a slight adjustment to their heading, dipping the Sparrow's nose a couple of degrees toward the horizon and watched as the computer updated predicted paths. This put them further from frameshift but gave the other ship less time inside firing range. At least until they adjusted their own heading.

Benny stumbled into the cockpit. "What's going on?"

"Someone is still trying to kill us, and it seems they have a ship."

He stood unmoving in the doorway mouth agape.

She recognized that expression. "Sorry, your first-time off planet is going to be a rough ride. This isn't the safest bird to fly on."

"It's beautiful," he said.

Yvonne looked down at the rust-red world, patched by occasional cities and spots of green life. "It is," she agreed.

Abigail and Grace crowded into the cockpit, the latter worming her way into the co-pilot's chair. She fiddled with the scopes. "Three minutes to contact. I'm guessing they don't want coffee."

"Not likely," Abigail said. "Freeport 2 is out. What's plan B?"

Yvonne had been trying not to think about that. "It'll have to be the Jupiter neighborhood," she said after a long pause. Venus and Ceres are farther with their current alignments."

"There are other places in the asteroid belt that might be closer," Benny suggested.

"I would consider going to Vesta, but right now, that's farther as well. The Freeports I know of in that orbit are lawless warzones. I can do better than any doctor we find there." She shook her head. "We'll go to Jupiter."

Davey's voice crackled over the speakers. "So what's the plan here? Am I shooting at something?"

"Probably," Yvonne said. "Single target coming from a higher altitude orbit. Two minutes to contact."

"Fifteen-hundred-klick range," Grace said. "They just shifted course.

180

New contact time in one thirty."

Benny started to say something but only stammered before shutting his mouth. "I know," Abigail said. "The space stuff is the worst. You spend your time waiting for something you'll never see to blow you apart."

"Then do something useful," Yvonne bit out. "Take Benny and make sure everyone on board has oxygen masks in case we lose pressurization." As soon as they left, the cockpit started feeling better, less like a cage, and more like a place to work.

"Target has launched two torpedoes," Grace said. "Marking them for you, Davey."

"I see them... What the...? Why are they moving like that? Some sort of death spiral?"

Yvonne leaned over to look at Grace's display. "They're called corkscrews. And that spiral is to throw your aim off."

"I can tell," Davey said. "They're entering range. Aiming for the first one."

"Twenty seconds to impact," Grace said. "Fast little thruster nozzles, aren't they?"

"I can see that!"

Yvonne and Grace watched on the rear camera as he tried to track the spiral of the first corkscrew. "Try leading your shots more," Grace offered.

"He knows," Yvonne whispered.

"I know!" Davey shouted.

"Six seconds."

Yvonne gripped the controls.

The first corkscrew blossomed into fire.

"Eight seconds to second impact," Grace said.

"I can't... Yvonne!"

She fired maneuvering thrusters and spun them ninety degrees, keeping the main engines at full burn. In theory, a corkscrew gave up maneuverability for its spiral. Just how much was the subject of the current experiment.

"Three, two, one." Grace gripped the chair.

"Sweet mother of Moses, that was close!" Davey shouted. "Less than ten meters. I saw it right outside the turret."

"Then why didn't you shoot it?" Yvonne asked, killing the engines

181

and spinning the Sparrow to give him a shot at the torpedo, trying desperately to correct its overshoot.

"This is hard," he said, sullen. To his credit, he landed the fourth shot, disposing of the threat once and for all.

Yvonne put them back on course. "The ship is almost in range," she said. "Davey, start firing in its direction and let's hope it gets the memo."

He opened fire. The space-time shockwaves faded before reaching the approaching adversary, but that must have been enough for them. "They just fired retro-rockets," Grace said. "They're disengaging."

"They probably don't have a thumper of their own," Yvonne said. "They can't risk approaching into cannon range now that they know we have a good gunner."

"Damn right, we do," Davey muttered.

Grace tsked, "Just because Matthew's in for repairs doesn't mean he's okay with you cursing over comms."

That was the sobering reminder, the inexorable tug of gravity pulling their feet back to the real world. It took Yvonne another few minutes to frameshift them away from Mars, drop out, and then set a course for Jupiter. She joined the others in the common room. Elizabeth still hadn't emerged from Matthew's quarters. Yvonne would need to check in on him soon. She had a feeling she would be redoing his sutures the way they'd dragged him around all afternoon.

"Alright, everyone," she said, getting their attention. Five pairs of eyes pointed her way. "We're three days out from Jupiter. The good news is we're safely away. The bad news is, we're not stocked for eight people. It's going to be thin rice and bean soups, but no one is going to starve. I'm going to offer Elizabeth the extra room. Candace, Benny, you're welcome to sleep in the common room. We have extra bedding from the last time we had extras onboard. If you want more privacy, you can take the hold, but it won't be as comfortable. Your choice." No one looked pleased, but she wasn't half done yet. "I wasn't expecting to be spaceborne yet, so we'll have a long maintenance list tomorrow." That set Abigail and Grace grumbling at the least.

She heard a sound behind her. Elizabeth walked into the common room as if in a daze.

Davey was by her side in an instant and took her gently by the arm. "Is Matthew alright? Are you okay?"

"He's fine," she said. "It's not that. It's... I talked to one of my workers

182

shortly after leaving Arizona, and he visited the farm with the police." She trailed off and looked away, obviously fighting off tears. "They torched the house and fields. It's gone. The house my husband grew up in. The house where Matthew was born."

There was no stopping the torrent of tears now as she slumped against Davey. Grace ran to her and embraced them both in a hug. Yvonne just turned away, retreating to Matthew's room, a dark fire burning in her heart.

There was no justice in the universe. Moses wasn't the only one that had abandoned them. God himself had turned his back on their miserable race.

"You're not in too much pain?" Abigail asked, pushing a strand of her hair back behind her ear. She sat in her wheelchair by Matthew's bed, too tired to stay awake, but too stressed for sleep. Yvonne had awakened the patient to get his vitals, and Abigail had jumped at the chance to talk to him until she was chased away again. They'd made the collective decision not to tell him about the farm yet. Better to leave that tragedy for another day.

"No more than the last two times you asked," he said. His voice was thinner than usual and she didn't like it. "It's only going to get worse for a day or two." He shifted back against the pillow propping him up and winced.

She did her best to ignore his discomfort, but she itched to fix it. Somehow. "Why's that?" she asked instead.

"Serious injuries always hurt more a couple days in," he said.

"Oh. I guess I haven't had a lot of injuries in my career so far." She picked at a thread on her sleeve.

Matthew started to laugh, at least until his face screwed up with pain.

"Sorry!" she said, rolling forward a little.

"It's fine, I promise. A little laughter won't kill me."

"What won't kill you?" Yvonne asked, entering the room.

Abigail rolled her chair away from his bed. "I made him laugh. It was an accident."

Yvonne hummed an unintelligible response as she hung an IV bag on the tower beside him. Abigail looked away as she fiddled with the lines. She could handle broken bones and gunshot wounds, but needles gave her the creeps.

"What's on the menu?" Matthew asked.

"An antibiotic," Yvonne said. "Just in case. I'll be back to check on you in a few hours."

"Can't just let me sleep, huh?"

She shook her head. "I'll be losing sleep too, so at least you have that to comfort you."

Abigail rotated her chair toward the door. "I guess that's my cue." She faced Matthew one last time. "People are in the habit of getting shot around here, and I'd appreciate it if they wouldn't."

He smiled, but Yvonne stiffened. "What are you talking about?"

Abigail raised an eyebrow. "Ceres. You know."

"I don't know—"

"Matthew took a grazing shot at Bennet Tower, remember?"

Yvonne's face drained of color. "Of course. Goodnight." She practically ran from the room.

Abigail stared at her retreat. "What was that about?"

Matthew shifted again and she turned back to him. "Whatever it is has been eating at her for months. Something happened on Ceres. And no, she won't talk about it. I've tried."

"Well don't worry about it," Abigail said. "Get some sleep before the doctor comes back to prod you some more."

"You too," he said and closed his eyes.

She rolled out of his room and reached for the door to her own cabin before pausing. On an impulse, she went to the cockpit instead and closed the door behind her. The room was a pain for her to get around, suited or wheelchaired. She managed to wedge in between the chairs, and if she leaned forward over the console, she could just reach the displays.

She tabbed through several screens before pulling up the security archives. She moved back through the files until she got to Ceres. Hmm. Where to start? Yvonne had only left the Sparrow twice, both times related to the opera job, and Abigail couldn't see any link between that night and the previous conversation. Her bounty had kept her pretty well isolated from the outside world.

Now that was a bit of a mystery. Yvonne had been evasive about the details of the bounty's lifting, and Matthew hadn't even believed it until he'd looked it up on the syndicate boards himself. That had been three days after the Prodigal's detonation. She pulled up all the cams for that day and played it in reverse at high speed.

This was stupid. What was she even expecting to see? People came and went from the Sparrow in a blur of movement. There probably wasn't even anything to see in the first place. Yvonne may have had a private comm conversation. In fact, that was probably it. Whatever drama had occurred would remain a secret until the woman would just fess up and be out with it. She was about to clear the display when the screen showed an error message.

"File missing," she read aloud. She backed up to a date-by-date view of the archives. The entire day was gone. The day they'd stolen back the Prodigal and saved Ceres. She stared at the screen in disbelief. Whatever had happened, Yvonne had gone to the trouble to make sure no one would find out.

Abigail shut down the display and turned out the lights. "We'll see about that," she muttered.

The next morning, long before the others were up, Yvonne woke Matthew to check his wounds and vitals.

"Couldn't have waited another hour, huh?" he asked.

"No. Hold still."

He grunted as she peeled back the bandaging and inspected it. Only a few spots of dried blood. Her eyes fell on the wound itself. The sutures, the ones she had redone after they had nearly been tugged out by the action yesterday, were holding nicely. However...

She ran a gloved finger lightly over the faint red streaks emanating from the area. They were warm to the touch. She replaced the bandage with a fresh one. "I'll be right back," she said.

"Something wrong?"

"It's nothing to worry about yet."

She left his room and returned to her own. Her small case of pharmaceuticals was open on the floor beside her bed. She dug out two small vials and returned to Matthew.

"It appears," she said, as she began to work on the IV tower, "that your exit wound is infected. There's some reddening of the skin in the area. You aren't feverish, so it's likely localized for now. I'm going to hit you with all three antibiotics in my pharmacy and hope to put a stop to it."

He frowned. "And if that doesn't work?"

"It most likely will," she said, putting on a mask of confidence. It wasn't that she thought she was lying. She believed it too. It was more that he didn't need to worry about it right now. "My medical stores are rather limited by necessity, so I've been very picky about my selection of drugs. These three antibiotics are quite capable of dealing with a broad spectrum of bacterial infections."

"Great," he said. "Well as long as you let me eat today, I think I'll live. I'm starving."

She smiled as she started the new IV drip, trying to put the infection out of her mind for now. "I think that can be arranged."

"Dinner's ready!" Grace called.

Davey set the thick book he'd borrowed from Elizabeth by his bed and went to the common room. In the couple of weeks since he'd borrowed it, he'd struggled through the opening pages. Hard stuff. The whole crew, minus Matthew, plus the added three passengers, were already congregating. "What's cooking?" he asked.

"Rice and bean soup," Grace said, shoving a bowl into his hands. "Just like yesterday. Just like it will be tomorrow."

"I was hoping you'd figured out a way to get creative with it."

"Yeah let me go through the cupboards and find something else. Oh wait. There's nothing else."

Davey took the bowl and went to the table, but then decided against it. There were too many of them to sit together anyway. May as well let the women have it. He slid down against a wall a meter or so from Benny. He took the first mouthful of the soup. It wasn't actually bad, despite his earlier complaints. Sometimes simple food could satisfy in a way that the fancy stuff could only dream of.

Once everyone had their bowl, Yvonne cleared her throat. "I need to talk to everyone now that we're all together."

Davey looked up. She looked calm as ever, but Elizabeth was pale and haggard. He frowned.

"Matthew's infection has progressed rapidly since this morning," Yvonne continued. "It hasn't responded to any of the antibiotics I have on board, and he has begun to run a fever." She paused. "We're still two days out from Ganymede. Matthew's life is now in serious danger, and there's nothing I can do about it."

The room went deathly silent, save for a clatter as a couple people set down their spoons.

"Elizabeth and I spoke with him a few minutes ago about the possibility of returning to Mars. Such a trip would only take a single day and give Matthew a better shot at survival. However... He has refused, as that would likely put the entire ship in danger."

"Screw that," Abigail growled. "We can handle a little danger."

"It's his ship. He's the captain," Yvonne said. "He's made the decision for the good of everyone, not himself."

"What are his chances?" Candace asked quietly. Davey knew she and Benny felt some responsibility for this mess. It was foolish, because Matthew had probably been the target all along, and if they hadn't found him then, they would have another time. But then he knew the feeling. He'd been wondering what would have been different if he and Grace hadn't botched the first stakeout and had finished their job soon enough to be home when Benny called.

"I don't know," Yvonne said. "Either he lives or he dies, and I won't know until you do."

Davey set his bowl aside. "And there's nowhere closer? Not even one of those freeports?"

"I've checked," Yvonne said. "From our current position, we could be at Freeport 30 in a day, but the latest information says that it's a barely habitable, gang-infested wasteland. That report is almost two years old."

Right. So it was worse by now. That was definitely out.

"And there's no way we can go any faster?" Candace asked.

"I've set the frameshift to as high a speed as I can without risking repeated dropouts."

"Can't you just keep restarting it?" Abigail asked.

"You risk extreme damage to the whole system like that," Yvonne said. "We're going as fast as we can. I promise."

Benny waved his hand to get everyone's attention. "We could go faster if we frame-skipped."

"Frame-what?" Grace asked.

"Frame-skipping," he repeated. "Doesn't anyone else follow the racing circuits out of Venus?" He looked at Davey as if he of all people should know.

"Don't look at me." Davey responded with a shrug.

"What's frame-skipping," Elizabeth interrupted. "And is it a practical solution for us?"

"It's a technique the racers use to push the boundaries of what frameshifting is capable of. See, we all know you can only go so fast with a frameshift. The faster you go, the shorter the bubble lasts, and you get kicked out to normal speed. The strain of maintaining the high-speed bubble builds up massive heat in the system too. Burns everything out. Frame-skipping is using a team to water cool the heatsinks to keep the temperatures manageable."

"Which lets you risk higher speeds," Yvonne said. Davey could see her wheels were already turning.

"So how fast are we going?" Benny asked.

"One point five two percent the speed of light. We'll get about twelve hours before we get kicked."

"We could probably hit one point nine eight," he said. "The pros can reach a solid two-point oh four for up to a day, but we won't get anywhere near that."

Yvonne closed her eyes. "That would knock twelve hours off the trip."

"Is that enough?" Elizabeth asked. Davey heard the desperation in her voice. It was hard for him to imagine that Matthew was really in that much danger. He could take a bullet through the chest, but something as simple as an infection could take anyone.

"It might be or it might not," Yvonne said. "The faster we get Matthew to Ganymede, the more likely he lives." Her eyes snapped open and locked onto Benny. "How much do you know about this? Enough to actually pull it off?"

"Please," Benny said. "I've been following the Rudaski Racing team since I was twelve and—" He broke off when he saw the looks everyone was giving him.

Davey eyed him. "Yes or no works better right now."

"Then, yes."

Yvonne stood to her feet, dinner forgotten. "Follow me to the hold.

You're going to tell me everything you know about frame-skipping. Everyone else get ready. This might be a long couple of days."

An hour later, they had their plan. If all went well, they would be at Ganymede in about thirty-six hours. Yvonne and Grace would handle the cockpit. Grace would be learning to fly the Sparrow as they went so that when Yvonne needed to rest or attend to Matthew, she would be able to take over. It made Davey a little uncomfortable to think about her flying the whole ship, but this was about the simplest it could be. The Sparrow would enter frameshift at one point nine eight percent the speed of light. When they were inevitably kicked out, less than four minutes later, the pilot would reaffirm their current heading, and as soon as the frameshift device had recharged, they would set out again.

Thirty-six hours of four-minute marathons.

In the hold, Abigail, Davey, and Benny would form a bucket team. Unfortunately, they didn't have enough hosing to run water all the way to forward engineering from the main water tank, so they would be filling buckets of water at the entrance and running them to the exposed heat sinks of the frameshift device. They'd sealed off as much of the machinery as they could with tarps so that runoff would flow down to the floor. Elizabeth and Candace had squeegees and mops to refill another pair of buckets to ensure the room didn't fill with water as the hours wore on.

"Standby for the first frameshift," Yvonne said over the intercom.

Elizabeth fidgeted nervously with her squeegee. "God, give us endurance. May it save my son's life."

"Amen to that," Davey muttered. He was finding an even deeper respect for the woman. How she kept going without cracking under pressure was nuts. She'd lost her house, her farm, and now her son was in danger of dying.

The intercom crackled to life. "Frameshifting in three, two, one." There was the familiar moment of disorientation as the Sparrow suddenly lurched to ludicrous speeds.

Abigail hefted her pre-filled bucket. "I guess I'll go first." Benny and Davey followed her into engineering. She approached the exposed heat sink like it was going to explode. "So is it hot already?"

"Warm," Benny said. "Give it another thirty seconds."

"None of this makes any sense," Davey said. "Like I get that we weren't prepared with enough hosing to just soak the thing, but racing teams really do bucket brigades? Why aren't they better prepared."

"Because it's against the rules," Benny said.

"I've never understood organized sports," Abigail said. "They always have to do things the hard way. Like the whole dribbling thing in basketball."

"I know," Davey said, setting his bucket down and gesturing widely. "Like, just run down the court. Who thought that bouncing—"

"Time for the first bucket," Benny interrupted.

Abigail lifted her bucket and carefully poured its contents across the heatsink. Water hissed down the ribbed fins of the meter-wide module. Most of the water ran down to the floor. "That's it?" she asked.

"Refill and repeat," Benny said. "Davey you're next."

Over the next two minutes, it became clear that the heatsink was getting hotter and hotter despite their efforts. The humidity rose rapidly, and Candace and Elizabeth tried to stay out of the way as they fought to keep the water from pooling on the floor. One of the first lessons Davey learned was to pour the water from as close as he could to keep the splash of scalding droplets to a minumum. Which meant also trying to keep his body as far away from what was starting to amount to an exposed cooking element.

"Thirty seconds to probable dropout," Yvonne said over the intercom.

"So how do we know if we're doing this right?" Elizabeth asked. "If we're keeping the system cool enough?" The edges of the heatsink had started to glow, and it was enough to make everyone a little jumpy.

"We don't," Benny shouted from outside forward engineering. He poked his head back in with a freshly filled bucket of water. "We'll give it an hour, and Yvonne can run a diagnostic from the cockpit. It'll take a few minutes, but if we're damaging the lattices, it'll let us know." There was the brief jolt as the frameshift dropped. "Now we get about forty seconds to rest," he said.

"What have you gotten us into," Davey said, stretching his arms. This would be fine for an hour or two. But for over a day?"

Yvonne must have left the intercom channel open. "We're buying precious hours to save Matthew's life. We'll take some breaks and set the Sparrow at a more sensible speed when we must."

He took a look at the strange crew gathered in the belly of the ship. Abigail ran on battery power, so she'd be good for a long time, and Elizabeth was as tough as a woman her age could be. He thought Benny would run on stubborn pride long past his own strength, but he was worried about Candace. He wasn't sure why she was on oxygen, but he didn't think that could possibly help.

Nothing for it. Matthew was dying of an infection that neither his body nor Yvonne's medicine could fight off. They were all in. "We'll go as long as we can," Davey said and meant it.

"Good," Yvonne said. "Because we frameshift in five seconds."

Twelve hours in, Yvonne called a two-hour break.

Elizabeth ignored her protesting arms and pulled herself up the ladder. She made a beeline for Matthew's room. Yvonne had already beat her there. "How is he?" she asked.

Yvonne put aside the thermometer. "The fever is higher and the drain in his chest is now beginning to fill with pus."

"I'm not dead yet," Matthew said. He didn't open his eyes, and his voice was distant.

"No," Yvonne agreed. "But you are very, very sick." She stood to her feet. "And I don't know that I can do anything for you." She left the room without another word.

Elizabeth covered her mouth with her hand and sat by the bed. She was too exhausted to cry. Instead, she took his hand and squeezed it. "Hang in there, Matthew. We're trying so hard. Even Benny and Candace. She has to take a lot of breaks, but she's doing what she can. We all are and..."

"Lot of trouble," he said. "Over just me."

"Your crew loves you, Matthew. Those kids, you've become their father. They need you, especially Davey, and they'll do anything for you."

"It wasn't what I imagined when we found them stowed away." He shifted his shoulders uncomfortably and winced. "Now I can't imagine anything different."

"I'm proud of you," Elizabeth said. "You're a good man."

191

"There is none righteous, no not one."

She rolled her eyes. "You're my son, not my priest. I'll call you good if I want," she said and smiled in spite of herself.

"Go rest," he said. "Get a couple hours of sleep."

"Only if you promise to do the same."

He opened one eye and cracked a sad half-grin. "I'll see what I can do."

The second leg of the frame-skipping marathon was brutal on the entire crew. Lack of sleep and physical exertion was getting to everyone, even with Grace taking shifts with the bucket gang. Abigail did her best to pick up the slack as the others' flagging strength began to fail, but there was only so much she could do. Eventually, they had to lower their speed by point oh three to reduce the heat load.

When they called a second break, nearly everyone passed out in minutes from sheer exhaustion. Yvonne took a pair of caffeine pills and downed a cup of coffee before marching to Matthew's room.

He refused to rouse from the fitful slumber into which he'd fallen.

"I've messaged ahead to both the Vatican and University," she said quietly. "Ultimately, we decided to take you to the Vatican hospital. They're waiting on you and have a full team standing by to board the Sparrow the second we hit the ground." She unbuttoned his shirt and stared at the sickly redness that had spread across his chest. "Every antibiotic in the colonies. Ready to go."

"But I don't know if you have that long. And I'm..." She choked up. "I'm sorry."

She gave him a shot of a topical anesthetic just in case he woke up. Doubtful. Then she took a pair of medical scissors and one by one began to cut the stitches.

"I don't know what else to do. I don't even know if this will help."

Scalpel in hand, she slowly cut through the wound and fully reopened it. The smell worsened and she was careful to only breathe through her mouth. Using her tools, she began to cut away some of the infected tissue at the edges of the wound.

"This is the last of my saline. There's nothing left for the IV after this."

She irrigated the wound with the precious fluid. Maybe this would slow the infection and buy Matthew a few more hours. She was rolling dice at this point and running out of surface to roll on. After ensuring that there was no residual fluid in his chest cavity, she lightly bandaged the wound. No more sutures. It would be open for the doctors at the Vatican.

Despite the heavy dose of caffeine, being up for almost two full days had taken its toll on her. She slumped into a sitting position beside his bed, her chin dipping until it rested against her chest.

"I'm sorry," she said, "for everything."

A few hours later, they started one last frame-skipping session. It would be a short one as they were nearing Jupiter. They were ahead of the original schedule but not as fast as they had hoped. The time spent recuperating had eaten into their efficiency. Now, they would go until they could go no longer. Matthew's pulse was faint, his breathing shallow.

Elizabeth and the kids had said their goodbyes.

But Abigail refused. Stubborn tears burned her eyes as she fell into her rhythm. For every bucket Benny and Davey poured, she did three. Her armor carried her on, untiring, their resting periods enough to keep its batteries charged.

But it wasn't enough, was it?

What good was a suit of power armor if it couldn't save the people she cared about? No matter how hard and long she worked, it wasn't going to be fast enough. Matthew was going to die. He was going to die alone because they were all too busy trying to save him to actually be there when he went through death's door.

She was aware of the tears slowly dripping down her face, probably leaving ugly dirty trails.

She passed Davey in the engineering compartment, and his eyes lit on her face. "Hey," he said. "It's okay. It's..." He laid a hand on her arm, but she shook him off and he fell down in the brackish centimeter-deep water.

"I'm sorry," she said, pulling him to his feet. "I just..."

"It's fine. I know."

An hour later, they arrived at Ganymede.

The rest of the hold crew lacked the strength to take the ladder, but Abigail was up it in a shot. "How is he?" she demanded as she entered the cockpit.

"Hanging by a single thread," Grace whispered. She sat in the co-pilot's seat, her knees hugged to her chest.

"Vatican Tower Control, this is SPW 5840," Yvonne said. "I'm coming in hot. Please respond."

"We see you, SPW 5840. Proceed to pad twelve. Emergency personnel are on hand. You've got ten thousand people praying for your safe arrival."

Abigail stumbled to Matthew's room and opened it. He was pale as death, and she thought the room stank of it. She gently took his hand. He wasn't going to be alone anymore, and she wasn't leaving his side until they made her. Soon the engines burned to slow their breakneck descent, and when they hit the ground with a heavier than usual thud, she still didn't move.

Only when half a dozen strangers loaded with medical equipment barged into the room and insisted she remove herself, did she let go of his hand. Twenty minutes later, they were moving him by gurney to the hospital. Abigail followed, the only crew member left standing, the only one able to be there for their captain.

It was a lonely and terrible hour in the waiting room. She dozed and dreamed of restless searches for something she had forgotten. She knew it was the most important thing, but it kept just beyond her knowledge, just beyond her ability to reach.

"Abigail, dear. Be at peace," came a gentle voice, one she knew. She opened her eyes to warm brown hands on her arm. Bishop Elias had come from Antioch. The weight of it all fell on her at last, and she broke and wept freely as the old man wrapped his arms around her.

Chapter 9: Splintered Bonds

I will never cease to be amazed at both the astounding resilience and utter fragility of the human body. We are capable of amazing feats of endurance, capable of being driven to the point of death and yet survive. But even the strongest may be felled by disease or simple injury. Despite the greatest of our advances in science, some die when they should live.

We have never outrun the tragedy of mortality that haunts us, nor shall we ever. Not even Moses could help us there. How could he, when it seems even he was mortal?

The fairness of these things is never in question. If there are rules to this game, we did not make them and are subjugated to their tyranny.

Yet those same rules give us breath and allow us to live our lives. They allow the babe to both cry in pain and be nurtured in love. The cold and cruel universe harbors our spark of life in this quiet corner of the Milky Way against all likelihoods. This terrifying fact is one that we must accept in a manner not that different from faith, else it drive us to nihilism.

Mark Mallick
Pediatrician, Freeport 3
Died 132 AM

He lived. Barely.

It was three days before the hospital would allow more than one of them into the intensive care unit where Matthew wandered through dreams beneath the veil of consciousness. Two days further before he began to stir beyond minimal alertness. One quiet afternoon nearly two weeks after they arrived on Ganymede, when he was finally moved to a normal room, Abigail took the kids with her to visit him. Yvonne and Elizabeth had spent the morning there, and Candace and Benny planned to go say hi to him sometime after dinner.

They were taking visiting rights very seriously in their determination not to leave Matthew alone.

As they walked through the halls, Abigail wrinkled her nose in disgust at the hospital's bland white walls. "You'd think they'd make this place a little cheerier. A little bit of color would go a long way."

"Imagine if you hated the color of your hospital room," Grace said. "Like if it was mustard yellow."

"Why would you paint a hospital mustard?" Davey asked, frowning.

"I don't know. It was just an example."

The pair of armed Swiss Guardsmen parted when they reached Matthew's door. "And I'm sorry I brought it up," Abigail said as she knocked. There was no answer, so she carefully pushed the door open. Matthew was out cold, campero over his face and snoring lightly. Grace snickered and closed the door behind them. "Don't wake him," Abigail whispered. "We'll wait."

Davey had come prepared with the massive book he'd been lugging around. Abigail wasn't quite sure what had possessed him to dig into the Iliad and the Odyssey of all things, but he'd been making a steady dent this week. Grace hadn't brought anything, but she turned on the screen, muted it, and flipped it to the channel the hospital had endlessly playing old movies. Not very good ones. They were probably just the cheapest stuff they could show that wouldn't offend the sensibilities of the legions of devout Catholics around here.

Abigail leaned against the wall and yawned. She still hadn't caught up on the last bit of sleep from their desperate flight to Ganymede. She glanced at Matthew and tried to unwind the knots of anxiety her stomach was in these days. It had been so close. The very brink of death

196

from what the doctors had said. A few more minutes and he'd have been beyond their help. Life without Matthew, the Sparrow. It had nearly all come undone. And she was so stupid and emotional when the old bishop found her alone in the waiting room. Thank God, no one else had been around to see that. Grace had been giving her a hard enough time lately as it was.

Matthew sneezed under his hat and then groaned in pain and almost came up out of the bed with clenched teeth.

"You okay?" Grace said, at his side in a moment.

He leaned back and set the hat aside. "That hurt. A lot. Remind me to never sneeze again."

"How are you feeling?" Abigail asked.

"The same as every other time someone asks me," he said through gritted teeth. "I'm having the time of my life."

Injured Matthew was even grumpier than usual. Maybe it was the pain medication making him so sarcastic. "We know," Abigail said softly.

He looked back and forth between her and Grace and ran a hand through his messy hair. "I'm sorry. I'm not used to people sneaking up on me in my sleep."

Davey tapped the IV pole with his foot. "This might have something to do with that."

Matthew rubbed his face. Abigail had never seen him looking so miserable. It was probably just now beginning to dawn on him how long the recovery was going to be. "Can we do anything to make you more comfortable?" she asked.

"Either rewind time to give me a do-over or fast forward it." He sighed. "Sorry, I'm being ungrateful. My mother told me what you all did for me and I certainly won't ever be able to repay you. It was crazy to try frame-skipping just because Benny had read about his favorite racing team doing it." He trailed off and looked away. "But thank you."

Abigail opened her mouth to respond, but Davey beat her to it. "No way. This doesn't even get close to making us even. I think I speak for everyone when I say you've turned our lives around. Mine anyway. Uh... So rest up. We need you back."

Abigail clapped Davey on the back. "I didn't know you did sappy so well. It suits you better than surly." His face turned deep crimson and they all laughed. At least until Matthew winced and gripped his sides.

They sobered up quickly. "No one say anything funny," she chided.

"Then bore me with business," Matthew said. "Did you find our bikes?"

In their hurry to get off Mars, there had been no hope of retrieving either Matthew's bike or Abigail's. She'd spent nearly an entire day sending messages to various government offices in Arizona, trying to get any information.

"That's probably not going to be a very happy subject," Grace warned.

He grunted. "Seems appropriate. Let me have it."

Abigail twiddled her thumbs. "After a few inquiries, we found my bike. It got towed for illegal parking. I paid the ticket, but it's still in impound, probably stacking up more fees. I'm trying to figure out who I can ask to go pick it up for me." She'd been relieved. Her oversized bike had been a custom job and wasn't something they could afford to replace.

"Despite money not growing on trees," he said. "That's not too bad. I'm guessing you're about to follow up with worse news."

"Your bike is gone. Probably stolen. No one has seen it. Probably never will."

She watched his face closely. Outside of his lip twitching twice, he made no response for fully half a minute. Finally, he half shrugged. "Davey, I'll be borrowing Vanquisher the next time I need to go out."

Davey's mouth dropped open. "Hey now. Let's talk about this before—"

"Tell you what. You pay to keep that tank full, and we'll let you ride it." Grace said. "Deal?"

"Not a chance," Matthew said. "I warned you two when you bought it that you'd regret how much fuel it would drink." He looked at the clock on the wall. "Say. Grace, pass the remote." She frowned as he flipped through the hospital's meager selection of channels.

"Are you looking for something," Abigail asked, puzzled at the out of character behavior.

"Only my childhood."

She turned to the screen. "Qash Quiz Qlub? What is this? Some kind of old game show? That's a terrible name."

"Local show out of Arizona. Watched it growing up. Well, my dad and I did. My mother thought it was a waste of time. I figured out a couple days ago that the hospital plays episodes in the afternoon. I bet I can beat all three of you combined."

She raised an eyebrow, not one to back down from competition. "If that's what you want. You're on."

"He's going to roast us," Davey warned, pinching the bridge of his nose, and despite knowing that he was probably right, Abigail wasn't going to be deterred.

It wasn't even close. Even on painkillers, Matthew's encyclopedic knowledge was enough to give them a thrashing. So much so that she began to wonder if he actually remembered the answers from his childhood. Still, she wouldn't have traded the afternoon for anything. She couldn't remember the last time the crew had had so much fun together.

A week later, when Bishop Elias returned to Antioch, he took Candace and Benny with him. Benny was itching to get set up and back to his career. He'd been struggling to find peace and quiet to work uninterrupted in the visiting dignitary suite the Vatican had set the crew up in and had been slipping back to the empty Sparrow every morning since they had arrived.

"When Matthew is able," Elias had said, "come and spend some time at Antioch. You have friends and loved ones anxious to see you."

"I'm sure we'll swing by," Yvonne said, her mind already trying to plot three steps ahead. It was going to be more complicated than just taking some time off, regardless of what everyone else wanted. "I think the Vatican docs will want to keep him for a good while. He'll have some rehabilitation too."

"Yes, I was afraid of that," he said. "Still, I am thankful to the maker of all good things that Matthew survived. And in such a near-miraculous fashion. Abigail tells me that the Sparrow's frameshift device has been 'cooked to a crisp' as she put it."

"We'll have to go easy on it," she agreed. "The lattices are brittle as toffee. Another burnout would crack them and we'd be stranded." And if that had happened on their trip to Ganymede, Matthew would have died. No question.

After he left, Yvonne called a meeting with the crew. Elizabeth was with Matthew, so it was just Davey, Grace, and Abigail. It was peaceful again after all the extra faces. The others waited patiently in their suite's sitting area as she paced, deciding best how to begin.

"The calendar hasn't stopped," she said finally. "We're eating into our cash reserves, even while grounded. And we're behind schedule on recruitment for the guild."

"We have to head back out," Davey said. "I was afraid of that."

"We can't just leave Matthew here alone," Abigail said.

Yvonne crossed her arms. "I wouldn't think being left in the care of his own mother qualified as alone, but if you disagree, speak your piece."

Abigail rubbed the back of her head. "Right, well, what do you propose then?"

"We'll make short cargo runs around the Jupiter neighborhood and contact the crews Matthew has already pegged for recruitment. If we stay close, we can stop by if we're needed."

"Do you think they'll buy into it without Matthew?" Grace asked.

"We'll find out. Some may need additional encouragement when he's mobile. Abigail is well enough known by this point that she may provide all the assurance they need."

Abigail grumbled something, and Grace shook her head. "You weren't going to get to stay here, you know. Look, Yvonne. Let me stay to help keep Elizabeth company. I'll just be taking up space on these kinds of jobs. And if whoever it is that wants Matthew dead figures out where he's hiding, I'll be there to smash them."

Yvonne resumed her pacing. There probably wouldn't be any harm in Grace remaining behind, plus they'd be in and out over the next several weeks so they could always swing through and pick her up. "Okay. I doubt there will be any danger here with the Swiss Guard keeping so close an eye on him, but I can see the sense in you staying behind. For now." She ignored Abigail as she wrinkled her nose in disappointment. She was pretty attached to Matthew these days, but it wasn't like the duo would be out shaking up the solar system anytime soon, regardless.

"I'm sure you've talked to Matthew about this already," Davey said.

"This morning, yes. And Benny should have us a cargo run by tomorrow. Most of the crews we're recruiting in this phase are ground-based, and without ships, they'll be easy to meet up with. We won't be chasing them down."

Abigail shook her head. "I still can't believe you're charging headfirst into guild recruitment so soon."

Yvonne frowned. "We have prior commitments and the means to fulfill them. If you disagree, you can take it up with Matthew."

"I don't think he's in the best condition to be making decisions right now."

Yvonne sucked in a breath and planted her feet. "Which is why I made them and then confirmed them with Matthew."

Abigail took a step toward her. She towered over Yvonne. "You'll forgive me if I have some doubts about your judgment these days."

The temperature in the room dropped about ten degrees. "Excuse me?"

"Maybe you should tell us about that deleted file."

Through sheer force of will, Yvonne didn't physically react. "What are you talking about?"

"You know damn well." She had taken another step forward.

Davey appeared between them. "Cut it out. Both of you." Yvonne glared daggers at him, but he didn't flinch. "Abigail, back off. Yvonne, what is she talking about?"

"I told you, I don't..." She threw her hands up in exasperation. "I don't have time for this. I have to make sure the Sparrow is ready for flight." She stormed out of the sitting room and down the staircase, feeling the steady drumming of her heart. She wouldn't tell them. It wasn't their business. It had been her right to pull that trigger, and no one was going to tell her otherwise.

Only now she would never escape the questions.

For Matthew, the days in the hospital dragged on intolerably, one much the same as the rest. Especially after the Sparrow took off for Callisto and he was left with just his mother and Grace. They soon fell into a routine. His mother, being an early riser from years on the farm, would spend the mornings with him. Grace, never giving up a chance to sleep in, showed up around lunch and stuck around long into the evening.

For Matthew, his recovery was far too slow. It started with agonizingly painful walks through hospital halls, IV tower in tow. While Grace and his mother seemed to get excited over the tiniest improvement, he was less than impressed. Worst of all was that infernal contraption they made him breathe through to gauge his lung capacity. Apparently small children, or at the very least teenage girls, had tougher lungs than he did right now. To his absolute horror, Grace procured one of the devices herself.

"A little competition won't hurt you, will it?" she said.

"You're getting me confused with Abigail."

"And you're losing."

He scowled and put the tube in his mouth to try again. She still beat him.

It was strange knowing that the Sparrow was away on business taking jobs without him. The daily updates from Yvonne were brief and to the point. "Rasheed has agreed to join the Lanterns. Delivery went according to plan." Sometimes he got near hourly updates from Abigail, mostly short and clearly aimed at keeping him entertained while recovering, but occasionally there were long diatribes about how Yvonne would barely look at her, let alone speak to her. He'd heard about their tense standoff a week ago. Everyone had reported back on it, except Yvonne. Matthew never thought he'd see the day when Davey would be the peacemaker, but he and Yvonne had apparently switched places.

And for the first time, Matthew was at a loss about what to do for his crew member. Figuratively, he'd worn a lot of different hats since they'd come on board. Captain, partner, friend, father figure. But what hat could he wear for Yvonne? She'd hardened a spiny shell around herself. And he'd come to the conclusion that, in all likelihood, he wouldn't be the one to crack it.

All he could do was pray.

One evening, after a typically unsatisfying hospital dinner of overcooked particle meat, dry mashed potatoes, and mushy green beans, he and Grace sat up talking. "Did I tell you that I met the pope this morning?" he asked. "He came here with half the Swiss Guard in escort."

She flicked a lock of hair out of her eyes from where she sat on the corner of the bed. "We all met him last week."

"Huh," he said. "No one told me about that."

"We weren't sure if you were going to be upset or jealous."

He laughed. At least that was starting to hurt less. "I may have been a little disappointed. But he is just a man. An important one, but a man none-the-less."

"Do you know what he said about you?" Grace asked. That gave him pause. Pope Willems had been polite and thoughtful but had neither said much nor stayed long once they had finished their business. She continued. "He said that you might just be the most important man alive, what with Ceres and now the Guild."

Matthew's mouth went dry as the arid Martian wastes. "He doesn't know what he's talking about."

"That's what I said."

He stared at her in horror. "You didn't. Please tell me you didn't."

She winked. "Abigail's right. It's way too easy to freak you out."

"He's right, you know," a third voice said from across the room. Whitaker. "Though by those metrics, I'd surely rank as well."

Grace just about fell off the bed, but recovered and had her arm extended, most likely ready to thrash the man into oblivion if he so much as looked at them wrong. "You know," Matthew said. "If you'd knocked, I would have said to come in. I hope you haven't hurt my guards outside the door."

"They're fine, fit, and doing their job."

In hindsight, Matthew realized the door was still closed. Whitaker's little disappearing trick could either move him through solid matter or he'd been in the room for some time already. "Well, you're here. And you always want something. So go ahead. A relic of Moses? You should know I'm a little indisposed right now."

Whitaker's lip curled. "Your guess is as good as mine as to where the last Anemoi piece lies hidden. No, truth be told I was in the area and wanted to see how you were doing."

Grace snorted and Matthew just raised an eyebrow.

"Why is it so hard to believe that I'm actually invested in your well-being?" Whitaker asked.

"Maybe because you sold my colony into slavery, left me in the wastes of Io for dead, and have been a thorn in my crew's side for two years now. Doesn't seem an unreasonable position to take in my eye."

"You know that saying of yours. Iron sharpens iron, does it not? You're a stronger man for my meddling ways."

"What about the others that have suffered?" Matthew said.

"And here surfaces our age-old argument on the degree to which utilitarianism is moral. Let's not bore Grace on grounds we've already staked out."

"Too late," she said, giving him her well-honed death glare.

"If looks could kill," he said before turning his attention back to Matthew. "I'm sorry about what happened to you. I have some theories about who was behind the attack and I'm having my contacts on Mars look into it. Rest assured, they won't get another shot at you."

Normally Matthew would refuse any help from Whitaker, and yet... And yet how was he supposed to protect his crew from an assassin? "I'd appreciate that," he said, crossing his arms. "Would those be the same contacts you used to help convince President Barclay to invade Kyoto?"

"One and the same, actually, though again you overstate my influence. Barclay was more than prepared to secure the Kyoto factory without my aid, but I'm privy to how the board is stacked to grease the wheels a little. Our mutual friend Logan could strike at any time, and he'll have a much harder time of it now."

"And I suppose the Phobos Platform was your idea as well?"

Whitaker hesitated for the briefest moment. It was one of the few times Matthew had ever seen his characteristic overconfidence evaporate into thin air. Maybe it really all was just a performance. "No," he said. "I'm less keen on that one, though I've been aware of the project for some time."

Matthew shook his head. "And the thought hasn't crossed your mind that instead of calming the waters, you'd just help drive the colonies closer to war? That there's a giant gun pointed at most of Mars, including the factory that's essential to the survival of humanity."

"It's not online yet," Whitaker said sharply. "And there's more at stake than you realize. If half of Mars is allied against Kyoto, then the other half is talking quietly about supporting them. The factory needed protecting and I won't apologize for ensuring that happened. But if the invasion tarried too long, then Kyoto would have had allies leap to their defense and brought war to the red planet."

"That may still happen."

"It might," Whitaker conceded. "But at least it's not assured this way."

"You're too rash in your prognostications."

"You have to be if you don't want to spend your life second guessing every decision. About Phobos, if I can't get the project scuttled, then I'll at least be sure it's as well defended as the factory itself. I promise."

"Not another Ceres," Matthew warned.

"Agreed." Whitaker tipped his hat to them. "And I'll see what I can do about that assassin. With that, I'll bid you a goodnight." As expected, he was gone in an instant.

Matthew turned to the door. It remained shut. "Grace, do me a favor and run around the room with your arms extended." She looked at him like he'd grown a second head. "Just trust me."

She shrugged and obeyed. It was a small room and in less than three seconds, it happened. Whitaker appeared, arms in front of him to keep Grace from bowling over him. She squeaked and jumped back, eyes wide.

Whitaker tipped his hat to Matthew. "Clever. You outplayed me that time." He placed a hand on the door and pulled it open, disappearing in the same motion.

Two startled swiss guardsmen ran into the room. "Was someone just in here?" Are you alright?"

Matthew smiled and leaned back in the uncomfortable hospital bed, hands behind his head, turning over what he'd just learned. "Everything is just fine."

Milena Drugova rubbed her hands together. She sat in the back of a grav car driven by a chauffeur who had yet to say a word. Pretty typical for a government job on the hush. She wasn't sure it was all that good an idea for a Rossiyan citizen to work for Kyoto's government, given the current political climate. There was a century old treaty and a factory dividing them at the moment.

"Since we've left the city, I imagine we're almost there," she said, attempting to engage the driver. "There's not anywhere else to go in Kyoto."

He glanced at her in the mirror and then looked back at the road.

She turned to stare out the window at the passing Martian scenery of red rock and scrubby plant life. It looked the same pretty much anywhere, at least to her eye. She'd always heard that Earth's geologic and biological diversity was such that every place looked different. Pictures existed, of course, but that wasn't the same thing. Earth was a paradise from an alternate reality as far as the colonies were concerned.

The grav car turned down a sideroad. No, it was a driveway up to a manor of some sort. The driver parked and walked around to open her door. "Thanks," she muttered. She wrapped her calf-length coat tighter around herself.

"This way," the driver said, the first words he'd spoken in the hour she'd been with him. She followed him through a side garden to a rather well-groomed sitting area beneath a pergola. An aging Japanese man stood to greet her. Did they shake hands in Kyoto? She'd never spent much time out of the Southern Highlands. No, they probably bowed, but she wasn't about to stumble over cultural norms to which she wasn't privy. Instead, she inclined her head respectfully.

The man smiled and returned the gesture perfectly. "Ms. Drugova. I trust the trip here was pleasant?"

"Enough. I'll admit I'm surprised you arranged the seat for me. These days, it's not easy to get into Kyoto, or out of Rossiya for that matter."

"There are those of us on both sides that wish to see friendly discourse continue. It's just a matter of knowing who you must speak with."

So the colonial governments still talked, even when they were at each other's throats. Or else members on both sides were breaking the law. "And to whom do I owe the pleasure of speaking?"

"Retired Commissioner-General Yuuto Kagurazaka. Please. Have a seat."

She sat in the indicated chair. "How can I be of service, Mr. Kagurazaka?" He passed her a tablet. Her eyes scanned down the document. Surveillance of an Arizonan government agent. This was going to potentially make enemies if things went south. "I trust there's a reason you're hiring a freelancer rather than using Kyotan Intelligence assets for this job."

He smiled. "You give the Kyotan government deniability if you're caught. As do I since I am happily retired."

An older woman approached with a tray and set tea out for them both. From the warm smile Kagurazaka gave her, she was clearly his wife. Milena politely took a cup of tea and thanked her. She sipped at it and then set it on the table. "And it doesn't concern you that I'm a citizen of a Highland Treaty Organization member colony?"

Kagurazaka shook his head. "You were hired not only for your skill set but also for your associations. Ms. Abigail Sharon is a trusted friend, and I have a good deal of hope for this Guild of Lanterns that Matthew

Cole has put together."

"I see." The guild had already landed her a job then. Her rather specific niche sometimes meant weeks in between work. She'd barely finished the Yurchenko job when this one came through. The guild would indeed be good for business after all. "Why is the government of Kyoto interested in agent Stein," she asked, "besides the occupation of Kyoto? I don't mind dipping my toes into political waters, Mr. Kagurazaka, but I'm not sure the guild's purpose is to pick sides in intercolonial disputes."

"Then it should ease your conscience to know that the agent in question is hardly an upstanding character. There has been more than one... incident with which he is suspected to have been the cause. The assassination of Prime Minister Rinne, for one."

That had been a big deal. Rinne had been the chief opponent to the Finns joining the Highland Treaty Organization. After his death, the colony had quickly capitulated to Russian pressure. It had gone without saying that it was a politically motivated crime, but it had been done so carefully that it had been impossible to peg the responsible actor. Apparently, in knowledgeable circles the perpetrator wasn't quite so mysterious.

"I see," Milena said. She looked at the tablet again, scanning more of the details. "You want to know who he is associated with."

"Intelligence thinks there may be crooked ties."

"Any hints as to who that would be?"

Mr. Kagurazaka only smiled politely. "All of them. Mr. Stein is well connected with the undesirable elements in the solar system."

Milena grimaced. Given her intelligence background, she knew the type well. Or rather knew of the type. Give some people information and a modicum of authority, and no leash is short enough to keep them on your side. Vipers. She imagined that in coarser circumstances, they were the type that became serial killers.

"I'll get what you need."

"Excellent. Keep your distance. I don't expect he would give you quarter should he become aware of your surveillance. And, Ms. Drugova, I'm a retired police officer, and have no stomach for spy games. I bring the guilty to justice through the law, not knives in the dark. I'm not interested in a body, yours or his."

"You'll find no complaints here," she said. "I'm a surveillance specialist, not an assassin." She finished her tea and stood to her feet. "How soon can you get me back into Arizona?"

"Before the sun rises tomorrow."

In the month that they'd been gone from Ganymede, Davey had nearly been driven insane at least six dozen times by Abigail and Yvonne. That is, until he came to the firm conclusion that, for once, it wasn't Abigail's fault. No matter how he wracked his brain, he couldn't get his head around what Yvonne's problem was. It was either stony silence or sharp jabs these days, and it didn't take him long before he was either avoiding the cockpit or actually seeking out Abigail when he was bored.

At least he was getting a lot of reading done. He'd worked his way through the Iliad, slowly at first, but with increasing confidence as he went on. Daily messages to and from Elizabeth had helped explain which characters were related, what a particular god reigned over, or the significance of some obscure Earth reference. He knew he was missing a lot of the complexity, but he understood the gist of the war and who the main characters were. And what a pointless conflict it was. Sure, on the surface it was over a stolen wife, Helen, but in truth, it seemed like just a play for the gods of Greece to meddle in the affairs of men.

That most wars appeared as such to the average citizen didn't escape him. He'd been closely following the news from Mars with new eyes. While the colony of Kyoto seemed to be steadfastly enduring the occupation, it was obvious that public sentiment across the red planet wasn't too keen on the conflict. Maybe they could dimly see the importance of that factory, but that the gods would threaten war over it was beyond what they could swallow.

After reading through the news, he pulled up the pictures he had taken in Warszawa, particularly the ones where the Arizonan agent, Damon Stein, as Whitaker had identified him, were clearly visible. He hated that he had sat on the pictures. Something rotten was happening on Mars, or had happened, to speed up the construction of the Phobos Platform. He had the proof, and they were going to get away with it. Abigail and Matthew had decided that handing the photos over to the press would most likely further destabilize Mars' fragile political situation.

They were probably right. But it felt like lying.

He felt the rumble of the engines through the deck. They had a job between crew recruitments, and this time it was a real job. One of the Theban colonies had hired Abigail and him to take down a local drug lord. Given the scale of the operation, she promised it would be done in under a week. He tossed aside his tablet and checked through his pack one more time before throwing it over his shoulder and opening the door to his cabin.

He turned toward the cockpit, but seeing the excuse that Abigail's door was open, he happily diverted. Yvonne was just going to be a grouch anyway.

"Are you ready to go?" he asked.

She was rummaging through her piles of equipment and found the case she was looking for. "Almost, just need to grab a few more things."

Too late, he recognized the case. Her trackers. "Oh. Hey. About those..."

She opened the case and stiffened when she saw that nearly half of them were missing. "What in... Where did..." Her eyes narrowed and then rose to meet Davey's. "What do you know about this?" she demanded.

Of course Grace wasn't here to take the heat. Maybe he'd rather hang out with Yvonne after all.

When two months had passed, the Vatican doctors finally allowed Matthew out of their sight. He'd long graduated from the hospital room to the suite with Elizabeth and Grace, but bi-weekly checkups, as well as rehabilitation in the afternoons, had kept them from leaving the Vatican entirely. Now that that was over, they made him promise not to leave Ganymede for at least another month.

When the shuttle crossed the short distance across Ganymede's frozen plains and landed at Antioch, Grace was the first person to bound off. As usual, Bishop Elias and her grandfather, Arthur Morgensen, were there with the ground cart, though she also noticed a contingent of Swiss Guard. The Vatican had recently decided it best to keep the fledgling colony well-defended, considering its founder had recently suffered an assassination attempt. There was no telling what they might do to get to Matthew.

She wrapped her arms around her grandfather. "You haven't been worrying, have you?"

"I've missed you," he said. "And of course I have."

"Oh, we're fine," she said, turning to watch as Elizabeth and Matthew came down the ramp. "Well... He is now, anyway."

"He'll finish his recovery swiftly," Elias said, "He's still young."

Grace had thoughts about Matthew's age that she kept to herself. They would be pretty rude in front of two people much older than he was, even if they were true.

Elias set aside his cane and wrapped Matthew in a hug. "I have never prayed harder, nor thanked God for answering those prayers as much as in the last months," he said. Grace looked away, feeling like she was intruding. But it didn't stop her from overhearing.

"And for that I'm grateful," Matthew said voice low. "I'm not sure I've ever felt so lost."

Grace didn't catch the reply, but it struck her that the bishop was to Matthew what he was to the rest of the crew. It never occurred to her that even Matthew needed backup.

After the greetings were finished, they loaded their luggage into the ground car and set off down the road between the fields toward the colony. "So how have things been lately?" Grace asked her grandfather, mostly to pass the time. She heard from him regularly and wasn't lacking in news of his personal life.

"Oh, mostly the same. Antioch is an ambitious operation, and there have been lots of ways I've been able to improve both function and efficiency."

Grace kept only half an ear on what he said. Her grandfather was really a nerd when it came to numbers, and she was glad he was putting it to good use. But that didn't mean it was stimulating conversation talking about the price of grain, constructing housing for new residents, or negotiating with businesses that wanted into the colony. The colony itself grew by several dozen buildings every time they visited. The streets were laid out to make room for that expansion, and Grace suspected a day would come that she wouldn't even recognize the place. Even now they passed a new row of freshly built houses that looked empty. She wondered where Candace and Benny lived.

They pulled up in front of the town square. Dinner was being provided in the community center so they could catch up with old friends, some from Villa María and some they'd made since then. Grace mostly wanted to see the old gang from Ceres. Especially—

Her grandfather put a hand on her shoulder. "Grace, I should probably warn you about something before you find out the hard way."

"Oh, what's that?"

"It's about Jason."

She fought back the sudden flush. Why did everyone have to give her a hard time about him? "I don't really know what you're—"

The front door of the community center opened, and most of the kids from Ceres piled out, crowding around her and Matthew. She spied Jason at the back.

He was holding hands with Eva.

Oh.

She plastered a fake smile on her face and pretended like nothing was wrong. Because nothing was wrong, besides the silent whimper threatening to make her heart stop. Mishka wrapped herself around Grace, and Raj gave her a friendly wave.

"Why are you crying?" Mishka asked.

Grace wiped the rogue tear away. "I'm just so glad to see you guys," she lied with a smile.

"Hey! It's starting," Davey shouted from the common room.

Yvonne let out a long sigh and closed down the monitor. She wasn't sure that she was looking forward to this. If he'd been around, she would have told Matthew this was a terrible idea. Frankly, she was surprised that he didn't think it was a terrible idea. The sedentary lifestyle must have driven him to boredom.

She walked down the hall to the common room. Abigail and Davey were both already huddled around the radio. He looked her way and smiled, but Abigail didn't look up. Yvonne ignored the quiet sting in her heart. She'd toughed it out for the first couple of months, but the long quiet days aboard the Sparrow were starting to get to her.

The radio was already on, and Davey turned up the volume.

"This is the Colonial News Bureau broadcasting out of Titan. Thank you for joining us tonight for Faces of Humanity. I'm your host, Glenn Sherrin. This week I sat down with our most requested guest. You've asked and we made it happen. Allow me to introduce you to Freelancer Matthew Cole."

"I can't believe he agreed to this," Abigail muttered." Yvonne could only nod gravely.

"How are you doing tonight, Mr. Cole?"
"I'm good, thank you, Mr. Sherrin."
"Please, call me Glenn."
"Then Matthew will do as well."
"Now Matthew, we're all aware that you're the leader of the newly founded Guild of Lanterns, and I want to talk about how that's going this evening, but first I must ask after your health. You've recently been recovering from an injury, have you not?"
"An occupational hazard, I'm afraid. It's hard to be a freelancer and not make a few enemies."
"Maybe you can tell us about some of those. The Vatican put out a press release about the incident, and they're calling it the 'Miracle Voyage of the Sparrow.' It's an amazing tale and I'd like to encourage our audience to read it. Is there anything you'd like to say about that, Matthew?"
"My crew went above and beyond to save my life. I owe each of them many times over, but that's what crews do. We're a family. Closer than that sometimes."

"Awww..." Abigail said. "He's talking about us." Her face fell. "I hope he doesn't say anything embarrassing.

"So tell me more about these crew members. Let's start with the Shield Maiden of Mars."

Abigail's face froze in panic, and Yvonne couldn't help but chuckle. Thankfully, Matthew kept the personal details to a minimum. That didn't stop him from making jokes however, but even so, they each came off as the best version of themselves. In her case it was a lie. The noble doctor simply didn't exist.

The interview meandered through a range of topics over its half-hour duration, and overall, Yvonne had to admit that he did well. He spoke candidly about his past as a priest, Villa María, Antioch, Ceres, and the Guild. When the broadcast neared its end, the host threw a final curveball question.

"Seeing as you're a fellow Martian like myself, I have to ask your opinion on the current situation with the Highland Treaty Organization's occupation of Kyoto."

"And here it comes," Yvonne said. "A question that's liable to get him in trouble."

"I'll admit I'm rather loath to get into politics. It's not my area of expertise. But I do think it's dangerous to let ourselves get swept into regional conflicts at a time like this. There's a dangerous ideology out there right now. Human Abrogation is an aberrant morality. Rather than trying to make the universe a better place for future generations, it tries to undermine them. We who believe in humanity must utterly reject it, or we'll destroy each other. Fighting amongst ourselves distracts from the real threat."

"Then I'll take it you're not a fan of the Phobos Platform that came online this week."

"You could say that, but then that would be an understatement. The Phobos Platform has taken a once familiar sight in the Martian sky and turned it into a threat. I grew up seeing Phobos passing overhead twice a day. Now, future generations will fear it. But I'm afraid what's done is done. President Barclay and the other leaders of the HiTO now have a terrible responsibility upon their souls. I had a friend relay a message to him, and I'll repeat it again here in the hopes that he hears this broadcast. Make sure that moon is well defended."

"I'm sure he'll get the message loud and clear. Mr. Cole. Thank you again for taking the time to sit down with us."

"Thank you for coming all the way from Titan. It was a pleasure."

"And with that, we conclude this week's Faces of Humanity. I'd like

213

to thank the cast and crew that made this possible, including—"

Davey flipped off the radio. "Huh. That wasn't terrible."

"I won't have to sit on him when we get back to Antioch," Abigail said, shrugging.

Yvonne stood. "Even if the public eats this interview up, the tide of opinion won't change what's happening on Mars. I just hope Matthew doesn't come to regret calling out Barclay."

Elizabeth tried to take each day one at a time. The loss of the farm and Matthew's near-death experience was more than she could cope with, so she focused entirely on the latter. And despite the aching hurt, Albert's farm was just a place. Mere material possession only. And her memories were more potent than the grief of loss, or they would be some day.

Right now, she would just focus on Matthew, though he needed the attention less and less with every passing day. He'd managed to gain back most of the weight he'd lost and was working on a plan to get back into shape. Which meant that she had very little to do around the guest house that Bishop Elias had kindly loaned them. At least until she was asked to teach a few classes at the school.

"I haven't taught in twenty years," she said, desperately looking for an excuse. "And I worked with adults. College students, not children."

The old man smiled, the skin around his eyes wrinkling. "I wouldn't have thought a Cole would be afraid of a few teenagers. It's a pity because I think they would love you. And if Matthew's love of the written word comes from you, then I know you'll do wonderfully."

She agreed, of course. Mostly because she felt she owed something to this man that had been so influential in their lives. She spent a few days preparing and then, on the first day of class, arrived with notes in hand on a lecture about the power of storytelling. The community center doubled as the school right now since there were only about seventy children and more than enough space to hold them on the three days that class was in session.

The room was absolutely silent when Elizabeth entered, and twenty teenagers of varying age turned to look at her, including Grace. She'd

214

been voluntarily attending classes with her friends from Ceres, whether it was to socialize or actually learn anything, Elizabeth hadn't figured out yet. Grace gave her a thumbs up.

Elizabeth set her tablet down on the podium. "Good afternoon," she said, feeling like she'd stepped out of an airlock without a pressure suit. "I'm Mrs. Cole, and Bishop Elias has asked if I would give a few lectures during my stay here at Antioch."

Blank stares.

She looked hard at her tablet. On a whim she closed her notes and instead pulled up her favorite short story. Flannery O'Connor's *A Good Man is Hard to Find* had never once failed to stir an audience in the three centuries since it had been written, and it wasn't about to start now. As she read the story of the Grandmother and her son Bailey's family, the class slowly became more and more enraptured. When the Misfit arrived after their car accident, every eye was wide. As the family was slowly murdered, there was a murmur of movement through the class. And when Grandmother herself was finally killed, one of the older teens let out an expletive before turning red and apologizing.

"What was the point of that story?" asked a girl.

"Did you enjoy it?" Elizabeth asked.

"Well, yes, but it was horrible."

"Then what was O'Connor trying to say? Because I have never read a more true story." She was met with silence and Elizabeth smiled. Maybe she had missed this after all, but she knew she was going to have to feed this group. She doubted they'd ever been challenged to think deeply about a work of fiction. "Grandmother believes herself to be a good person. But is she?"

"She's not as bad as the misfit," came the first reply.

"But she was pretty terrible," another said. "She treated her family something awful."

"She seemed okay. At the end, anyway."

She let the class talk it out, a small smile creeping across her face. When it began to dwindle, she said, "It's a complex story. And of course, it leads back to the idea of grace. No, not you, Grace, but your namesake. At the best, we get good things that we don't deserve. We're all imperfect, and it's a fatal mistake to think you are anything but sinful. Grandmother lived all her life prattling about good things, thinking that she was just that, and only in that last moment with the Misfit does she realize that she's something else entirely. Human. Broken. Sinful. That's why it's so hard to find a good man." She paused for effect. "There are none."

When she dismissed the class, half of them, Grace's friends, swarmed around her and asked what story they'd read next. "Oh, I'll find something. I haven't decided yet." She smiled as she scooped up her tablet and walked out of the room with the last of the students. She had missed this. So very much.

<hr/>

Julia's eyes lifted from her monitor to the open window. Her office in Discordia, a spire above the Imperial Palace, gave a near three-hundred-and-sixty-degree view of the cloud formations that endlessly swirled around the city. Discordia, floating free on the wind experienced sunrise and sunset as it drifted through the Venusian atmosphere. There was just the first hint of reddening to the towering structures. Natural days there lasted over a hundred standard days, but the turbulent winds pushed the city along far faster, the skies above changing from day to night in just a few days' time.

With effort, she brought her attention back to the matters at hand. Matthew's blockbuster interview had only increased the demand for guild crews. The line of freelancers wanting into the elite club was backed up. Matthew's injury had slowed down the current process, and after a couple of months, Yvonne and Abigail had only begun to make a dent in catching up.

She made a snap decision and began to type.

Yvonne,

I propose a different route. There's only so much the crew of the Sparrow can do. Allow me to aid in the recruitment process. We had initially planned on there being only three shipboard crews, the Sparrow, the Queen of Sheba, and the Red Dragon for the guild's first phase. I propose that we can double it to six crews. If it's acceptable with you and Matthew, I can go through resumes and invite appropriate captains to Venus to discuss the guild. I'll begin at once if you give me the go-ahead.

I'm glad to hear that Matthew's recovery continues. Tell him I said

216

hello and that my father and I look forward to his next visit.
   Julia of Venus

She proofread the message twice and tapped the send button. Having finished that, she switched back to the reports her father had asked her to go through. She slumped back in her chair as her eyes scanned the numbers. They were nothing new, just the end of a century-long trend, and that trend only had one possible destination.

The complete collapse of the Venusian economy.

"Are you up here, Julia?"

"I'm here, Daddy." She turned as his head poked up from the spiral staircase that led into her tower.

"I appreciate the spectacular view the tower affords," he said, coming up behind her and placing warm hands on her shoulders, "but I wonder how you tolerate the stairs."

"The exercise is good for me, especially when you keep me chained to a desk all day."

"You have the best head for numbers in the family," he said. "I've got no one else I can trust this with." He paused. "It's bad isn't it?"

"It's exactly what you would expect from a pair of floating colonies. We have no resources," she gestured at the clouds, "besides sulfur, which is easily acquired elsewhere. Our economy has always been based around service industries and with the Martian colonies at the brink of war..." She shook her head. "There aren't any more tourists."

"Then we're doomed?"

"Not immediately, no," she said. "We'll be fine for years, most likely, and we'll be able to hide that we're struggling for some time yet. And of course the current trend could moderate somewhat if the Martian situation settles down."

"Things never go back to the way they were," he said, letting out a long quiet breath. "We'll press the schedule and finish the Contingency. Divert funds to ensure it's completed before we're bankrupt."

She turned and gave her father a hard stare. "You'll accelerate our demise."

"If it gives humanity a chance?" He let the question hang. "Maybe the Sparrow will come through with their artifact search. Maybe our efforts are for nothing and they'll find Moses out there somewhere."

It was a foolish endeavor. There were better things the Sparrow could spend its time pursuing than hunting for so-called miracles. Like all things romantic, her father was enamored with the idea and had laughed when Matthew revealed that he held in his possession the very artifact that had, in fact, been stolen from the palace's collection. Her father had turned around and officially gifted the item in question to Matthew, who had, in turn, secretly left it back in her father's care. The whole thing was a silly waste of time.

"Speaking of the Sparrow," she said in an effort not to chase stray meteors. "Did you see Barclay's response to Matthew's interview?"

Her father rubbed his hands together. "Oh, I bet this will be good."

"Not quite as dismissive as I would have thought. I don't think he was quite willing to brush off the famous Matthew Cole. One moment. I saved the clip. Here."

"It's a little discouraging that Arizona's most famous son has been taking political potshots at me, but I've tried to take him at his word. We all know Mr. Cole is as good and trustworthy as one can find in these barbaric days. I can assure both him and everyone else on Mars that the Phobos Platform is the most well-guarded installation in the Solar System, and if Mr. Cole wishes to see for himself, he can. Matthew Cole, consider this an open invitation. At your leisure, come and inspect the defenses yourself. The brave men and women of the Highland Treaty Organization will give you the full tour of Phobos. Then perhaps we can have another sit down. I fear Matthew Cole and I have passed each other on the tracks without really meeting in the middle."

Her father chuckled. "Matthew really pushed a few buttons there, didn't he? Remind me to give Barclay a hard time the next I see him."

Julia rolled her eyes. "Dad... Please don't make this worse."

"I'm kidding," he said. He clapped his hands on her shoulders again. "Will you make it to dinner tonight?"

She looked at the array of economic numbers on her screen. It wasn't a problem to be solved overnight. Or more likely, not at all. Maybe it was best if the royal family started living a little more frugally. She pasted a smile on her face. "Sure, Dad. I'll be there."

The Sparrow made the long trip out to Saturn only once in the nearly three months since they had set out. It was at the very end, their last trip before returning to Ganymede, and everyone was ready for the crew to be whole again.

Most of all, Yvonne. She'd never felt more alone in her entire life. Not even in the months after Tomas died. Abigail continued to stonewall her on all but business, and Davey... Well, she was fond of him, but there was no way she was going to survive much longer if he was her only meaningful social interaction. At least Matthew wouldn't hold things against her. He didn't hold anything against anyone. It was just one last trip, and then things could go back to normal.

Titan had been a disaster. The crew rejected the offer to join the guild, which admittedly was a bullet dodged, and Abigail and Davey botched their job horribly. So badly that Benny was still trying to negotiate their way out of being financially liable to the client. When they left the surface of the moon, not even Davey and Abigail were speaking to one another. A dark corner of Yvonne's brain was secretly quite pleased that she wasn't alone in her misery.

As she pulled the Sparrow out of Titan's soupy atmosphere and into orbit, the comm buzzed. For a moment, she considered ignoring it. They didn't have any more business here, and this would just delay their departure.

Davey hit the comm switch. "This is the Sparrow."

"I can see that," a familiar voice deadpanned. "I was starting to think you didn't have time for an old woman."

Gebre'elwa. Yvonne glanced at the scopes and saw the massive shape of the Queen of Sheba three and half thousand klicks above her in orbit. "Sorry, 'Elwa. Been a rough few months. We're on the backside of a wasted trip."

"Oh, I've had my share of those. Tell you what. We're waiting on a refinery to get their act in gear and send over their tankers, but it's going to take a few hours. Swing by the Queen and I'll have my chef whip up something nice."

"I appreciate that offer, but we're ready to get back to the rest of our crew."

"I'll throw in some good wine," 'Elwa suggested conspiratorially.

"Say yes," Davey whispered. "Matthew would turn down the wine."

"You're only nineteen," Yvonne replied.

"Which is plenty old enough," he said. "In some colonies."

"That settles it then," 'Elwa interrupted. "I'll see you soon." She cut the channel and Yvonne stared at the scopes. It really wouldn't hurt and 'Elwa was a friend. Davey let out a cheer when she altered their course.

Dinner was squash stuffed with braised pork shoulder and parmesan-crusted polenta. The meat may have even been real, not lab-grown. Yvonne was afraid to ask, because she couldn't bear the feeling of being further in debt to the woman's hospitality. As for the wine, Yvonne and Abigail made Davey strictly promise that he would never speak of this to Matthew.

"I'm not going to tell him," Davey said, taking another sip of the dry red. "But I'm not going to lie. So if Matthew ever asks, I'll spill."

Abigail shook her head and took another bite of her polenta. "What are the odds he's going to ask 'Davey did 'Elwa give you wine?' It's not going to happen."

"I don't know. Grace and I have a theory that he can read minds." Yvonne just raised an eyebrow at him. "He was a priest," he finished lamely.

'Elwa and her husband, Mateo, laughed. "You know," she said. "There were stories about Matthew before his history with the church was made public."

Abigail sat up straighter. "What kind of stories?"

"None of the other freelancers quite knew what to make of Matthew Cole. A quiet man who was insufferably honorable, had a tendency to be just shy of polite, never drank a drop of alcohol when most in our profession practically bathe in the stuff. He was most certainly talked about. An enigma among freelancers. I never ran into him, so that was all I knew of him."

"He'll be rejoining us when we get back to Ganymede," Yvonne said softly.

"How is he doing?"

"It's been a long recovery, but he's ready to be back out here."

"I bet we wouldn't have screwed up that job if Matthew had been around," Davey muttered. Abigail looked as if she was going to disagree and then deflated. Yvonne just continued her meal in silence. Unsurprisingly, no one wanted to talk about the disaster the three of them had become lately. Or rather that Yvonne had become. Try as she might, she couldn't pretend the fault lay elsewhere.

Soon enough, the meal was over and before she could escape back to the peace and safety of the Sparrow, 'Elwa had her by the elbow and was pulling her aside. Yvonne watched as the other two disappeared down the corridor.

"Something has made you decidedly unhappy."

She shrugged the other woman's arm off. "We're just ready for things to get back to normal."

"I'm sure that's all there is to it," 'Elwa said, and it was clear she believed nothing of the sort.

And yet Yvonne couldn't turn away to leave, despite every good sense telling her to do so. For the first time in three months, she had a willing set of ears. A pair that had sought her out.

"I've been thinking about... My husband lately," she lied. It wasn't entirely untrue. Anything related to Kudzu ultimately led back to Tomas. He would have hated her for pulling that trigger, but then he was always clear-eyed about the harder questions in the universe. Right and wrong weren't a mystery to be wondered at for him.

"It's been three years if I remember," 'Elwa said. She turned back toward the other hall and called for her husband. "Mateo, go to the Sparrow and let Ms. Sharon know that I need to speak with Yvonne. She'll be along in an hour or so."

He nodded and passed them by with a polite nod and smile to Yvonne. She was aware that the other woman was leading her back toward her parlor and away from the Sparrow and she sighed. What was she doing? This woman had nothing to offer her.

"Closure is a funny thing," 'Elwa said. "Let me tell you about my first husband."

Being home was wonderful, though Abigail had started to struggle to define what home really was. It wasn't the Sparrow. Not quite. She'd been aboard it for the last three months, and while the place was the same, things were missing. People were missing. Well. Really just one person. Sure, Grace was important, but Matthew was the beating heart that made it work.

She tried not to think about what that meant. Because it was complicated and he was a priest or rather had been a priest. It was better if she didn't turn into some sort of blubbering maiden. That sounded, frankly, mortifyingly embarrassing.

Still, she missed her partner because they were just that. Partners.

The day the Sparrow landed on Ganymede, they stayed up long into the night, talking, catching up on all that had been missed. Abigail left her suit in her room, wheeled into the bridge, and transfered herself to the co-pilot seat.

"So Grace has really been attending class for the last month?" she asked. "Seems hard to believe. She's always been less interested than even Davey in your boring attempts at educating them."

Matthew ignored the jab. "On the pretense of hanging out with her friends, yes. But I think she's been enjoying it. Even with Jason and Eva around."

"Pity about that," Abigail said quietly. She was pretty sure Grace was already asleep, but it never hurt to be careful. She had poured her little heart out to Abigail in message after message over the last month. "Teenage crushes are confusing things."

"And usually short-lived," Matthew said. "She'll get over this and be wiser for it. With the Sparrow only stopping by Ganymede once every few months, it was inevitable that his attention would move elsewhere."

"Maybe so," Abigail agreed. She bit her lip. "So how are you, Matthew. I mean how are you really? Are you fit and ready to be back on the job?"

"Physically, I am, though it will be a while until I'm ready to run a marathon."

"You're still looking a little scrawny," she said. He raised an eyebrow, and she responded with a shrug. "Just saying."

"And then, of course, there's the hurt pride that you guys have gotten along just fine without me. Which is good," he said quickly. "I'm glad you were able to get some jobs done and continue with the recruitment, but you do have me wondering what I do around here." He gave her a half-smile, and she knew he was mostly joking. Still, it rubbed her the wrong way.

"You wouldn't have botched that job on Titan."

"I told you it happens to everyone."

"This one wouldn't have happened to you," she insisted. "And I don't know if it's the random sermons or other bits of wisdom you sprinkle in, but this place just isn't home without you. We're lucky to get two words in with each other without a fight."

"I was hoping you and Davey had been exaggerating," he said quietly.

"Not one word," Yvonne said from behind them.

Abigail half fell out of her seat as she turned to stare at the woman. She stood stock-still in the doorway to the cockpit. Abigail couldn't help the miasmatic feeling of guilt rising in her throat. "Look. I'm sorry—"

"Save it," Yvonne said.

Matthew just gave her a curious look. What did he see? Abigail turned her attention back to Yvonne, trying to see through his eyes. He would pity her for being... lonely? Ashamed? What was it about that recording that had driven her away from them? There was a hollow look in her eyes and Abigail at last recognized it.

Despair.

Yvonne tossed a data chip at Matthew. "There's your missing recording. Shut the door before you watch it. And I will never speak about this again. To anyone." Without another word, she fled back down the hall and closed herself into her room.

Matthew turned and held Abigail's gaze for a long quiet moment before he obeyed and shut the door. He slid the chip into the computer and pulled up the file. He fast-forwarded until there was something to see on the outer cams.

They watched in silence as Lexter Miyoshi died at the bottom of the Sparrow's ramp. As Yvonne boldly faced down the White Void enforcers. Unfortunately, they couldn't quite make out the conversation, but it was obvious when the tables turned and Kudzu was held against his will. Abigail's breath hitched in her throat when the short, pasty-looking man passed her a gun.

And then it didn't fire and Yvonne threw the weapon at him and clawed at his face. Abigail covered her mouth with her hand. She wanted to avert her eyes, but it wasn't over yet. The pasty man brutally executed Kudzu, and she finally did turn away.

All their questions. All her strange behavior. It was no wonder Yvonne had come away from Ceres a different person. And she'd born her secrets in grim silence. Her own harsh treatment of Yvonne came back to haunt her in full force.

Slowly she turned to Matthew. He would know what to do. He always did.

But he only stared out the front canopy, eyes tired and filled with grief.

Wormwood: Part 2

"Come on, mom. Give me a chance. You promised."

Gebre'elwa reluctantly took her hands off the controls and sat back, flashing an entirely fake smile at her eldest son, Tamru. She folded those hands neatly in her lap over her dress.

Her husband, Kofi, chuckled over the comm. "Dear. You did promise him."

She sighed loud enough so that Kofi would hear. "I feel I have been the subject of a conspiracy between you two. Perhaps I'm not quite ready to have my baby flying."

"I'm twenty and not even the baby of the family," Tamru said, his hands flying over the bank of controls. "And you were behind the yoke by the time you were sixteen."

"It was a different world then," she said. "The space lanes were a lot safer. And I am worried. You're not going to alleviate my fear by telling me not to worry. That's not worked on a single woman in history. Just... Be careful and make me proud."

He rolled his eyes at her and then turned back to his instruments. "Checking sequence-rigging to the Jade Adder right now." 'Elwa craned her neck to get a look out of the canopy. Off to her right, the Adder floated in perfect formation, their computers linked and control delegated to the Qolxad, flown by her son. The sequence-rigging would allow them to stay together through frameshift on the long trip out to Saturn, otherwise, they'd most likely drift out of communications range. It had been an annoying technical hurdle to overcome, but hopefully, one that would end up saving them time down the road.

The Adder was a big step for the family business. A second ship meant they were able to carry twice as much cargo, and while for now, they intended to stick together, it also gave them the option to cover more ground. Movement from the Adder caught her attention. Kofi leaned forward to wave out of the window at her. In spite of herself, she smiled. "Yes, dear, I can see you over there." He chuckled over the comm but left it at that. "How's the Model 42 handle?" she asked.

"It was good before Tamru wrenched control from me. Smaller and sleeker than the Qolxad."

Tamru cleared his throat. "I'm ready for the sequence-rigged frameshift."

"Don't tell me," she said. "You're the captain."

"Right," he muttered and opened a comm to both ships. "Standby for frameshift," he announced to the nearly two dozen crew members.

There was the characteristic moment of disorientation as they were translated to a new high-speed reference frame, and then they were on their way. 'Elwa leaned forward again to get a good look at the Adder. It was still beside them in perfect formation. Looks like the rigging was on point.

"Good job, kiddo," she said. "We'll make a pilot out of you yet."

He shrugged. "That was the easy part. Landing will be the bigger challenge."

"Depends on what the weather's like on Titan when we get there. You'll be fine. The moon's upper atmosphere can be nasty, but it's usually nice and calm at the surface. You've got a few days before you have to deal with that." She crossed her arms. "What's on the itinerary in the meantime?" He looked at her in confusion. "I'm not in charge, captain. You'd better be thinking about duties to hand out to the crew because I'm not going to do it for you."

"I know who is cleaning the toilets."

She narrowed her eyes. "And then you'll find your mother is a vengeful woman."

Their laugh was interrupted when the frameshift suddenly failed, and they reverted to their previous speed. 'Elwa's hands flew to the scopes. "Asteroid four hundred klicks ahead. And the tug that dragged it into our path."

"We've got company," Kofi said quietly from the comm. "You don't suppose it's—"

"Who else would it be?" she bit out. She switched the comms to an open frequency. "Meriadoc, I assume you're out there?"

A heavily armed patrol craft breached the asteroid's horizon on an intercept course. "Captain Meriadoc," he corrected. "It's good to see you, Gabby. It's been, what, nearly a year?"

"Fourteen months," she corrected. "I was hoping for longer." She glanced at the main display. Tamru had already altered their course to both retain their speed and reach the edge of the asteroid's gravity. As soon as they were to the boundary, the sequence-rigged ships would frameshift out.

"Well, you remember the drill," Meriadoc said. "Dump an appropriate offering of cargo and you get off peacefully. Or we make it a chase. Given our current positions, this would be an exciting one."

Sometimes she accepted the deal. The Qolxad had twenty containers attached to its belly and it wouldn't be difficult to detach one as an offering for the pirate. But their current cargo was far too valuable. And with the recent purchase of the Adder, things were tight at the moment.

"You'll have to catch us this time," she said into the comm. "Sorry to disappoint."

Meriadoc laughed. "Why would I be disappointed in a bit of sport? See you soon, Gabby."

She cut the open comm. "You get all that, Kofi?"

"Yes, ma'am. Turning over the helm to Rolf. I'll be a lot more comfortable in the tail gun."

'Elwa allowed herself a smile. "Take care of our old friend permanently this time, won't you, dear?"

"I'll see what I can do."

Tamru scratched at his head nervously. "Anytime you want to take the helm back would be good."

"You're fine," she said. "For now. Keep our course straight for our exit until they're in firing range. Then start evasive maneuvers. Rolf?"

"Right here, 'Elwa," the pilot of the Adder returned.

"We're going to disengage the sequence-rigging. Stay close. We'll reengage if we can for our escape, but if not, you're on your own."

"Understood."

"Mom, are you sure..." Tamru asked carefully.

She waved him off. The situation favored them, so this would be a good experience for Tamru. Meriadoc's gunners would get in a few shots, and then they'd be away. He wasn't getting anything this time, and judging by the asteroid's position, it would soon be out of the ever-shifting lane of traffic between Jupiter and Saturn. She wouldn't mind the pirate wasting his time and fuel for a fruitless catch.

"They're in range," Tamru said, quietly. Louder, he spoke into the comm. "Return fire. Make them regret pulling us out of frameshift."

'Elwa breathed a soft exhale of relief. The angles were even better than she'd realized. Meriadoc's gunners weren't going to have time to get a clean shot before they were safely away. The Qolxad and Adder bobbed and weaved, and the thumper fire from the patrol craft vainly tried to track their movements at nearly a hundred kilometers.

"Ten seconds to safety," she called. "Re-engage the sequence-rigging."

"Done," Tamru said after hitting a few buttons on the screen.

Beside them, the Adder began to mirror their movements. And then they were away. They'd have to reset their heading, but they were beyond the reach of Meriadoc and his killers. She placed a hand on Tamru's arm. "You did well."

He wiped the sweat from his forehead. "Yeah. Sure. First time you let me fly a run and we almost get murdered. Thanks, Mom."

She just chuckled. "Rolf? You guys okay over there?"

No answer.

"Rolf?"

"My lady I..."

She gripped the arms of her seat. "What happened, Rolf?" The man hesitated and in her heart of hearts, 'Elwa already knew what he was going to say. The foul taste of bile rose in her throat.

"Kofi's turret was hit. I'm... I'm sorry."

II.

It was a hazard of the occupation. They'd talked about it for years, but they'd gotten off so well that the dangers felt inconsequential. What a lie to swallow.

Kofi was gone in an instant. The entire rear turret of the Adder had been sheared off by a thumper blast. In all likelihood, he'd felt no pain,

228

just been snuffed out of existence as the gravity shockwave tore him apart. What was left of him would orbit the sun in a small field of debris until the end of time itself. Which meant that when they finally arrived back at the Ethiopian colony of Zerai-Deres on Callisto, there was nothing to cremate.

'Elwa had a beautiful orange and teal urn made anyway. And when the days of mourning and public funeral were over, it sat on a mantle in her office at the family compound. Her ships weren't safe enough for such a precious possession. Not anymore.

For the first time in her career, 'Elwa wasn't on those ships. Tamru was given command of the Qolxad, while she stayed with her other two children on Calypso. She threw herself into her work, mostly to drown out the grief, scheduling shipments and jobs for the two ships as they hopped around the solar system.

Her daughter Zuri found her sequestered in her office four months after Kofi died. "Mom. Get some fresh air."

'Elwa looked up from the reports she was pouring over. "I've work to do."

Zuri crossed her arms. "Don't pull that crap with me. You're not even this busy when you're on the Qolxad."

'Elwa set her bifocals aside and looked at her daughter. When had she become an adult? She stood in the door to her office, looking like a window into her own past. But it wasn't a perfect mirror. Zuri had some of Kofi in the way her nose hooked. "If I slow down," she said slowly, "I'll start thinking. And that will lead to regret. There's a thousand things that could have transpired differently and if any of them had happened—"

"It's not your fault Dad died."

She paused and then decided lying was the easiest solution. "I know. But I can stop it from happening to someone else."

Zuri stepped around the desk, and 'Elwa hastily cleared her work away. "Mom," her daughter said threateningly. "Show me."

She should have ignored her and sent her from the room. Instead, she pulled up the files. Zuri leaned over her shoulder and peered at the screen. "What am I looking at?" she asked. "Dates, coordinates of... attacks? You're looking for Meriadoc." It was a simple accusation.

"Yes. As I said, I can stop anyone else from suffering as we have. God knows I've run into the pirate more than I want to admit. I should have done this years ago and then—"

"Mom. It wasn't your fault."

She didn't try to lie this time. "Leave me to my work."

Zuri shook her head and walked to the door. "Revenge rots the soul."

"I'm not going to kill him," 'Elwa said. "There are over a dozen bounties on his head. I'll capture him and make a fortune, ensuring no other families lose their father. It will never end if I don't stop it. No one else needs to..." And then her voice cracked, and she slumped back as the tears began again. How she hated them. Zuri was by her side in an instant, arms wrapped around her, and together they wept for Kofi, the best husband and father they could have asked for.

III.

If finding the solar system's most elusive pirate was going to be easy, someone would have done it long ago. Captain Meriadoc's career had spanned almost four decades. 'Elwa had heard rumor of the rogue before she had been taught to fly by her own father and had a run-in with him only a few years into her career.

Everyone who frequented the lanes between the planets had a story about Meriadoc, or at least knew a story. 'Elwa collected them greedily for her research, desperately searching for a clue as to the pirate's whereabouts. The stories all had a similar thread.

Meriadoc, captain of the Mordant Jewel, thought of himself as a gentleman. He would never open fire if he was offered cargo and he never went back on his word. There were tales of him even letting ships go after a good fight or a witty banter of words. His tactics were always the same. Tug an asteroid into a space lane to collapse a passing ship's frameshift, collect the cargo, and then disappear to who knows where. And that was the real question. Where did the Mordant Jewel fly out of? Ships needed maintenance and fuel. They weren't self-sufficient.

The obvious answer was one of the Freeports. The independently owned stations were scattered across the solar system. Some were owned by businesses or individuals, homes to a few thousand proud citizens. Others were owned by criminals or split by various factions. A few had gone dark and silent over the years, failed societies that had wasted away before ultimately disappearing forever.

'Elwa spent the next three years personally visiting every Freeport she could. Her empire was growing and it was easy to find excuses. Even the most dangerous Freeport rolled out the royal welcome for her, though there were many that Tamru insisted on doing business with on her behalf. In all that time, they never found any hint of the Mordant Jewel's passing.

"It's not one of the Freeport's," Tamru said. "You're going to have to give this up."

'Elwa sighed and rubbed her head. "I know. But it feels like... like failing."

"You tried. We all did. And it's all right to not always win. I don't think Dad would have wanted you wasting the rest of your life on a fruitless quest for revenge."

She rounded on him. "How dare you pull that on me!"

He didn't even flinch. "Someone has to say it and without dad here..." He shrugged. "It falls to me."

She gestured at the door. "Just... Leave me alone." To her surprise and secret disappointment, he left. She hated that he was right. She'd burned three years on this search already, and she was no closer to a solution than she had been at the start. What a fool she'd been to think she could accomplish what no bounty hunter had been able to in the last few decades.

On a whim, she pulled up her monitor to the public bounty boards and placed a reward of twenty thousand for anyone who could provide a tip that led her to Meriadoc. What was a little more incentive when there was already so much? Then she went back to her research. Despite what her children thought, this wasn't an endeavor to give up on. She would she spend the rest of her life in pursuit of the elusive goal if need be.

She would end Meriadoc's reign of terror, one way or the other.

IV.

Nearly a year later, she got an anonymous tip from the bounty boards. She called Tamru to her office. "It's a short message," she said, pulling it up. It read 'The information you requested' and was followed by a set of orbital parameters and an offset value she didn't understand.

"That's Mars," Tamru said. "Or rather the orbit itself is. I would guess that the offset means our target is trailing behind the planet."

"A station maybe," 'Elwa said.

"Something old and forgotten," he agreed. "Or cobbled together and never on any books."

She gave him a triumphant look. "Shall we check it out?"

"We'll do it," he said. "But remember this is a business opportunity. It's not about revenge. Captain Meriadoc is worth more alive than dead."

"I've told you it never was about revenge. But then you never did want to listen to your mother."

A few days later, the Qolxad and the Jade Adder dropped out of their sequence-rigged frameshift at the target destination. "Coming around on the target," Tamru said. 'Elwa's hands itched to be at the yoke, but she had given that up to her son and would not take it back. Instead, she peered at the scopes. Ahead of them a medium sized asteroid, perhaps five hundred meters across, floated dark in space, but that was a facade. It radiated heat, as sure a sign as any of human settlement.

"Separate from sequence-rigging," she said. "Adder, come around topside. Let's make sure we have our angles covered."

Rolf acknowledged, and out of the corner of her eye, she saw the Adder rotate and perform a short burn.

As they closed to less than a hundred kilometers, the scopes gave a better sense of what they were looking at. "There's a large hangar," she reported, "perhaps half the volume of the asteroid. It appears to be occupied. And there are also at least four gun turrets, though considering their placement, I expect at least two more."

"Do I order gunners to take them out?" Tamru asked.

"Negative. Not yet. No shooting until we ascertain if this is our quarry." She paused. "Forget that. I've identified the ship in the hangar. It's the Mordant Jewel. Have the gunners disable the station's weapon emplacements. Adder, park outside that hangar, just don't give anyone a clear shot at you in case they have other heavy weapons. As long as the Jewel is trapped, the fight is already over."

"Yes, ma'am."

The Qolxad burned retro rockets and whipped around the back of the asteroid. Like precise clockwork, the station's defenses were targeted and destroyed. 'Elwa nodded with pride. Her people knew their job. "Come around on the bottom, Tamru. Their power plant is exposed. We'll park and wait for Meriadoc to show face. If things get ugly, we can shut off his whole station."

It took only a few minutes before they were hailed. "Well, Gabby," Captain Meriadoc said. "This was a rude way to awaken an old man in the middle of the night."

She allowed herself a tight smile. "And you've misplaced your streak of arrogance. It's over. I've won."

"Maybe, but we'll get to that in a minute. I've been going out of my way to avoid your ships, you know."

"And I've been trying to find you. Funny how the game has changed."

"It took you long enough to track me down." The comm went silent for a moment. "I'm sorry about Kofi. There wasn't any profit in his death."

She bit her cheeks in anger. "Unfortunately for you, there's profit for me in your capture. So let's stake out the rules of the game. You surrender and I win a king's ransom, or you play stubborn, and I have to settle for blowing that station out from under you."

He tsked softly. "There's a third option and I choose it with no shame. I wait you out. You see there's a few hundred good folk on my station. The wives and children of my men. They have lives too, you know. You wouldn't dare kill them just to get to me. Then the game gets interesting. Who gets backup first? Do you get enough to storm the station, or do I get enough to chase you off?"

"I choose option four," 'Elwa said and cut the call. She keyed the comm for an open channel transmission. "This is Gebre'elwa aboard the Qolxad. Captain Meriadoc is using you and your families as hostages. His reign of terror ends today one way or the other. Allow me to make an offer to all who live on the station. Overthrow your captain and deliver him to me, and I will grant you one-third of his bounty price to divide equally among you all. Then I will take stewardship of this station. Your lives will be your own. You may perhaps find employment with me, or you may seek your fortunes elsewhere. You have ten hours."

She turned to Tamru. "Broadcast that on repeat. I think it will only be a matter of time now."

Six hours later, they got the call. Meriadoc, along with most of his lieutenants, was in custody awaiting transfer to the Qolxad. The crew of the Mordant Jewel had mutinied against their leader at last. Some wanted the reward. Some wanted a better life. 'Elwa only cared that the deed was done.

"Do you wish to speak to him?" Tamru asked.

'Elwa could see that he was nervous. What did he think, that she would scream and rage at him or perhaps kill him herself? The Martian governments would do that for her. There was no need for her to ever lay eyes on that miserable man. She shook her head gently and wiped away a tear. "No, I don't believe I will."

V.

In the end, most of the station's inhabitants stayed. 'Elwa took it over as a service station for her ships and made it her base of operations. The bounty money was quietly saved away for a later date. There was a super freighter with her name on it, and she already knew what she was going to name it.

When the noise and excitement died down a few days later, Tamru found her in her new office, staring out at the stars. Meriadoc had insisted on all viewports being covered to keep light from leaking, but 'Elwa had reversed that policy immediately.

"You know I'm not quite sure what I expected to feel," she said as he sat on the couch. "I've spent years waiting for this. And now it has come and gone in a whimper."

"I thought you were going to kill him," he said.

She cracked a wry smile. "Your mother told you she wasn't in it for revenge. Justice will suffice, and he'll meet the hangman soon enough. And yet..."

"And yet, what were you looking for?"

She had spent thousands of hours searching for the pirate. It had been something of an obsession, coursing through her veins like poison. And she had certainly hated Meriadoc with all her soul. But that was ash now, insubstantial remains of a fire long spent. In the distance, Mars was a pale red disc, its ice caps just barely discernible at this range. She stared at it for a long moment before turning back to Tamru. "I don't think I even knew what I was looking for until it was over," she said. "Closure. I wanted closure."

He folded his hands together. "And did you get that? Can you finally lay dad to rest after all these years?"

She pondered his question for several minutes before forming the beginning of an answer. "I don't think closure works that way," she said sadly. "Who can say where lies the end of grief? A lost loved one never returns." She shook her head. "There is no closure. Only a slow diminishing until what was once fiery pain is but an echo. And maybe that's not so terrible a thing. In ten years, I'll think of your father and be grieved, but it will be less than the day before. I think I can live with that. It's enough hope to keep going. And if all our hopes are true and there is a reunion beyond the walls of night..." She turned back to the window as her eyes filled with tears. Tamru joined her and put an arm around her shoulders, drawing her close. "Then at long last," she said, "there will be closure."

Chapter 10: Summer's End

———————◁◫▷———————

Take a visit to most colonies and you'll see a familiar sight. The bones of a world lost, from a seemingly ancient past or else a never achieved future. You know what I mean. You've seen them yourself. Pieces of infrastructure and grand public buildings, engineering feats that humanity never rose far enough to achieve on our own.

The floating cities of Venus. The Opera House of Churchill. The Resorts of Enceladus. The grav plate factories of Gilgamesh and Kyoto. The Well of Ceres. The Silent Hall of Dione. Each is a wonder beyond our imagining.

But Moses was selective in the way he bestowed his gifts. For the most part, he allowed us to settle and found colonies after our own fashion. We built cities as we did on earth, though beneath the care of Moses' protective technologies. But even then, the Mosaic frigates would descend, and legions of robots would construct something that would change a colony forever.

Some of the wonders have been lost in the last century. Two of the cities of Venus have sunk beneath the clouds. The Orbital Tether of Titan fell forty years ago, leaving devastation across its murky surface. There is no restoration for such miraculous creations as there is no resuscitation for humanity.

In ten thousand years, when our solar system is cold and uninhabited, there will remain monuments of two sorts. Those of men and those of Moses. If our ruins are ever visited by intelligent species, they will be very puzzled at the mixed archeological record we have left behind. Great works whose very foundations are laid with adamant beside concrete hovels, crumbling to dust.

Leah Foster
Department of Culture, Churchill
Died 103

⟨⦚⟩

Milena Drugova checked the feed from her camera and trackers. They were all still operational this time and she breathed a long sigh of relief.

She'd never stalked a target quite like Damon Stein. For starters, there were no good angles to surveil his apartment, something that was probably deliberate. She'd had to find public places to conceal her cameras to watch the entrances. Within a week, one of them mysteriously disappeared. She'd replaced it, being far more devious about her method of occulting it. And then there was the matter of his vehicle. No sooner had her camera gone out, than the tracker on his grav car disappeared. The next day, he had a new vehicle.

He was on to her, and they played a dangerous game. He may have been an expert in assassination and sabotage, but she was the foremost surveillance expert in the colonies, and that meant eluding detection herself.

She'd spent weeks carefully charting out his life and activities. Within the first month, she had him talking to White Void, two different Yakuza groups, and government officials from at least three HiTO members. Stein seemed to have contacts with nearly every organized group in the solar system. She dutifully logged these and forwarded them to Mr. Kagurazaka in Kyoto.

Unfortunately, Stein had slipped her dragnet yesterday and hadn't shown himself since. Which meant he might have skipped town. Without her seeing his exit vehicle, there was little chance of tracking his movements beyond Arizona. It wouldn't be the first time he'd pulled this sort of stunt. No matter. He wouldn't be gone for long and she'd pick his trail up again when he made an appearance. Ensuring the facial recognition alarms were set across her network, she closed the monitor and looked around her tiny living space.

This time she'd found a room on an abandoned floor of an office building. Previously boarded off, she'd cleverly loosened the door, while leaving its sealed appearance. It didn't give her a platform for any useful cameras, but it was situated on a network hub that she was quietly stealing bandwidth from. Unfortunately, her headquarters was only about three by three meters, barely room for her cot, equipment, mini-fridge, and coffee pot. She sighed. It was the next best thing to staying in the five-star Gennadiya in Doch Rossiya. Well, almost.

She scooted over to her fridge and dug out a self-heating meal. To-night's choices were... Actually there weren't any choices. Just the fake-baked chicken, powdered mashed potatoes, and gooey creamed corn. There was a reason it had been left an orphan as she ate everything else. She pulled the tab out and set it aside. A chemical reaction in the pack-age began to sizzle and heat the meal to a barely warm enough temper-ature.

A proximity alarm beeped on her system, and she leaped to her feet. That wasn't the facial recognition. It was the sensor she'd placed in this building to warn her of approaching hostiles. It was pinging one target. She grabbed her gun and moved into position beside the door. Perfect silence. No. There was the slightest scrape outside.

If it was Stein, she was dead. If he'd left town only to loop back and take her out when she dropped her guard, it was a move well played. Hopefully, it was just a vagrant looking for a place to spend the night.

Someone cleared their throat outside the door. "We both know you're in there. Go ahead and open up."

Hmm. It wasn't Stein at least. She didn't answer.

"Can't anything ever be easy," he said. "Look. We're on the same side. Probably."

Probably?

"I don't know who hired you to watch Stein, but he's recently been put on my list too."

Maybe working for Stein and trying to get her to lower her guard. Still no good.

"My name's Ryan Thompson. I'm the Arizona Minister of Law. Your name is Milena Drugova, and you're in this colony illegally."

She frowned. She'd never met Thompson, but she certainly knew of him. Given the number of jobs she took for law enforcement, that was unavoidable.

"Here's what I'm going to do," he said. "I'm dropping my gun." There was a leaden thud outside the door. "I'm taking five steps from the door." She heard the muffled scrape of dress shoes. "My back is to the door. My hands are behind my head." His voice was a little muffled as he turned away. That one was harder to tell. "If you open that door and anything is amiss, I expect you to gun me down where I stand. Sound fair?"

She kicked the door open before he'd finished the last word, pistol pointed at the back of his head. He'd been telling the truth. She kicked his gun into her room. "Turn around," she ordered.

"See," he said as he slowly rotated. "Everything is on the up and up. I just want to talk."

"Get started," she hissed. In her mind, she was already trying to figure out how to salvage her equipment and make an escape. Running into an Arizonan high government official while spying on one of their intelligence agents hadn't been on the itinerary.

"First, I want to know who you're working for. That's going to make a big difference as to what happens in the next few minutes."

"You're not in any position to threaten me," she said.

"Nor you me," he said, almost lazily. "I've got plenty of men outside. I've been waiting for Stein to leave town, so I didn't blow your cover to have this talk. You're in Matthew Cole's little guild, so I assume you're working for one of the good guys. Which one?"

It would be easy to lie, but he knew enough about her already. Maybe he already knew the answer and this was a test. "Ex-Commissioner General Kagurazaka."

Thompson nodded. "An old friend and colleague."

That checked out. They were both chief law enforcement officers of their respective colonies or had been until Kagurazaka retired. "What do you want?" she prodded.

"Everything you have on Stein," he said calmly.

"He's your own agent. Ask him yourself."

"Come now, Ms. Drugova. We both know he's crooked as sin. And you're the best at what you do. So let's make a trade. I'll give you eve-rything I have on him, and you give me what you've learned. Now, in good faith, I'm going to give you a photograph. It's in my coat, so I'd appreciate it if you didn't shoot me when I reach for it." She tensed as he took his left hand from his head and did as he promised. He laid the picture on the ground between them. "Go on."

She took a cautious step forward, never once letting the gun lower, and squatted to get a look at the picture. It was Stein in what looked like some kind of standoff.

"This took place three months ago in Warszawa," he said. "A mem-ber of Matthew Cole's crew took this as Stein was shutting down an operation he funded. Vehicle jacking gang. Stein was purchasing the grav plates on the cheap for the Ministry of Defense."

"The Phobos Platform," she said.

"Precisely. Now. I want you to understand something," Thompson said. "I'm domestic law enforcement. Intercolonial disputes are above my pay grade and outside my jurisdiction." He gave her a hard look. "But if members of the administration are operating outside the law, that is my responsibility."

Milena raised a curious eyebrow. "The little whispers on the wind tell me you're not much of a saint yourself."

"Says the woman coming out of Russian intelligence. Classic. There's such a thing as scale. If members of the HiTO are running roughshod around the law to help build weapons of mass destruction, President Barclay is going to hear about it."

"And if he's in on it?"

"Good question. I'm more inclined to think the Ministry of Defense is the problem, but I'm open to the possibilities. Presidents are no strangers to scandal, and if the capstone of my career is sinking my own boss, I won't care. As long as he deserves it. Now I'll give you one more freebie about Stein. After that, you're going to have to reciprocate."

She nodded, and even half lowered the gun in good faith. "I'm lis-tening."

"I've got every reason to believe it was Stein that put a bullet through Matthew Cole a few months back."

That had made the news, even before Yvonne Naude had updated all the guild members on their desperate flight to Ganymede. She hadn't met Cole yet, but Abigail seemed to think the world of him, despite doing everything in her power not to talk about him. It would have been sweet really, how oblivious she was, if it hadn't been a little eye rolling. If Stein had hurt Abigail's friend, then Milena owed it to the woman to make sure he paid.

She regarded Thompson for another long moment before finally deciding to holster her weapon. Maybe, he could make that payback happen. "I'll have to report this conversation to my employer."

"I'll inform Mr. Kagurazaka myself."

"And this is a one-time trade of information," she said. "If you want anything after today, you'll have to pay for it."

He chuckled. "Freelancers. They all want to be seen as heroes, but only on the backs of the almighty dollar."

"Says the man paid by taxpayers," she said. "Let's get this over with. I trust you only a little more than Stein."

He nodded. "Then maybe, just maybe, you'll live long enough for us to take him down."

"All aboard!" Abigail shouted down from the airlock of the Sparrow.

Grace grumbled as she dragged her bag up the ramp, not even bothering to pick it up. The vinyl duffle made a muffled buzzing sound on the ridged steel incline. "We're all coming. Keep your screws in, alright?"

Abigail crossed her arms. "What do you mean all?"

Grace motioned behind her with a flick of her head, then blew a stray lock of hair out of her face. "Did you know Momma Cole would be joining us for a while?"

Down on the tarmac, Matthew was helping Elizabeth get her bag out of Bishop Elias' ground car. "That's news to me," she said.

"Late change of plans, I think," Grace said, dropping the straps of her bag by the airlock. "I'm kind of surprised Matthew is okay with it, honestly."

"Maybe she doesn't want to let him out of her sight," Abigail suggested. She'd never known her mother, but she'd heard they could be clingy. Though that really didn't line up with what she knew of Elizabeth. "Or maybe it's the other way around."

Grace turned and looked back at the pair. Elizabeth was giving the bishop a quick hug. "I bet you're right," she said. "The whole time you guys were gone, he was worried that someone would attack the Sparrow to get at him. He worries about everyone these days."

"That dummy," Abigail muttered. "He should worry about himself."

"He's got doctors for that. And they say he's a terrible patient," Grace said and dragged her bag into the ship.

Abigail chuckled, imagining Matthew arguing with half the hospital staff. "I hear you're joining us," she said as Elizabeth approached.

"For a time," she said.

"Good. Because I can't answer any of Davey's questions about that giant book you gave him. When you don't answer his messages fast enough, I'm next in line."

They laughed. "Consider yourself relieved from duty," Elizabeth said.

Abigail reached out a hand to stop Matthew. "Can I have a word?"

He nodded. Elizabeth took her luggage from him. "I can show myself to my cabin, thanks."

She left them and they watched in silence as the Bishop's ground car passed through security and disappeared. "So Mom is along for the ride, huh?"

"For now," he said.

She rolled her eyes at the repeated sentiment. "I'm not complaining, but what's the deal? Are you worried about her safety here? The Swiss Guard is a permanent feature in Antioch now."

"It's not about safety," he said quietly.

"I'm listening."

"She's here for Yvonne. As a friend."

Apparently she'd misjudged things. "Wait you showed her—"

"Keep it down," he hissed. "No. And the kids don't know about it either. Maybe they don't ever have to know. I told my mother that Yvonne was in the middle of a crisis over her late husband, and she insisted on coming herself."

"You do remember Yvonne promised to never speak about it again."

He turned to the airlock. "If that dam should burst, she's going to need someone and I don't think it's going to be you or me." Abigail sighed as he boarded the Sparrow and then followed in his steps. It was true. She'd barely had a civil conversation that wasn't about business with Yvonne in three months. At least Matthew would be here when the warheads started flying.

In the common room, Grace and Davey were already getting settled. "Hey, where's our job?" he asked. "Where are we headed?"

Grace snapped her fingers. "It's the one that makes me think of Mexican food. We haven't been there yet."

Abigail stopped abruptly. "I don't even know what you're talking about."

"Enchiladas," Grace said with a smirk.

"Enceladus?" Davey asked.

Matthew nodded. "Enceladus. Hope you guys like snow."

A few days later, the Sparrow dropped into orbit around Enceladus, the sixth-largest moon of Saturn. Only five hundred kilometers across, it sparkled a brilliant white in the light of the distant sun. It was the brightest, most reflective object in the solar system, due to the whole world being covered with nearly pure water ice. But that didn't mean it was featureless. Shades of white and palest blue formed ridges and canyons across the surface, while only a few fresh craters marked the pristine face. It was like a coruscating crystal floating in the void of space, a sight unlike any other in the solar system.

Now that there were six on board the Sparrow, there was no way that everyone could cram into the cockpit at once, and given that Matthew was the only one who had ever been to Enceladus before, they all wanted a chance to see it. Rather than tempt Yvonne's wrath, he sent those that were comfortable topside.

Matthew was the last out of the hatch, joining Grace, Davey, and Abigail.

"Are you making it?" Abigail asked, offering a hand to pull him up onto the hull.

"If I can't take a simple ladder, I'm in no condition to return to work," he said. But he still accepted the help.

Grace and Davey stood a few feet away, boots magnetized and stuck to the hull. "What's going on down at the pole?" she asked.

Matthew stepped around Abigail to get a better look. Near the south pole of the moon, a faint curtain of mist billowed from the surface to drift out into space. It was a bit like a white aurora emanating from the planet. "Cryovolcanism," he said. "Ice eruptions. Beneath the surface of Enceladus is a liquid ocean. Water that makes it close to the surface erupts in the form of ice along stress ridges. The fine spray forms a curtain. Some of it will fall back to the surface, almost like snow. The rest will ultimately end up in orbit around Saturn and add to one of its fainter rings."

"Is it always erupting like that?" Davey asked.

"No," Matthew said. "Often enough, but we're still lucky to see it today."

"We should come here more often," Grace said. "The view is killer."

Abigail hummed softly. "We're not rich enough to come here all the time."

Grace turned to face her. "What's that supposed to mean?"

As the Sparrow orbited around the moon, the night side crept around the horizon. Its surface was almost completely dark. "There aren't any normal colonies on Enceladus," Matthew said. "Not with masses of people. The belief is that Moses wasn't too fond of destroying such a beautiful place by covering it with cities. Instead, there are a half dozen resort and sightseeing colonies scattered around the moon. It used to be a big tourist destination. Still is, I guess, but like everything else, it's not the same. The resorts use fancy casinos to attract high-rollers and keep the doors open. A night on Enceladus costs at least a kidney."

"So what kind of job would a resort have for us?" Davey asked.

"Not one you have to worry about," Matthew said. "Abigail and I will take care of it."

Davey turned away from the moon, and Matthew could see the indignant expression through his faceplate. "I'm part of the team."

Matthew clomped forward a few feet and put a hand on his shoulder. "Yes. And you've been carrying the weight for the last few months. I'm thankful for that. And proud of you. Which is why you get to take a couple days off. Grace has been chomping at the bit for you guys to get some brother-sister time. And this one is really only suited for Abigail and me, anyway." He watched as Davey chewed on that. His eyes had brightened when Matthew had praised him, but he still seemed like he was deciding whether or not he was going to be put out.

"Oh, come on," Grace said. "We'll have some fun." She paused for a moment and then continued with a mischievous lilt in her voice. "Let's give them their alone time."

"What in the...?" Abigail stuttered.

Matthew reached instinctively for his hat, before remembering it wasn't there. "Very funny. And subtle as a solar flare." He changed the subject as quickly as he could without making it look like that was his goal. "Get in your last look at Enceladus. It's time to deorbit."

The Sparrow had landing permits for a private yard at the Sarandib Grand Resort near the equator. Yvonne set the ship down with a gentle bump. The yard would support a ship twice the size with ease, making for a stress-free landing. "And just what are the rest of us supposed to do while you and Abigail are being productive members of the crew?" she asked.

Matthew flipped a row of switches, initiating the final shutdown. "Chores in the morning. Afternoons are your own business," he said. "But I recommend checking out the resort. Part of the deal on the job was an all-access pass. Includes the buffet."

Yvonne gave him a hard stare. "Please tell me Benny didn't negotiate this to give us a vacation."

"I doubt it, but you would have to ask him yourself. It's pretty well known to freelance crews that Enceladus jobs have perks. For most, that means losing everything they earn in the casinos."

"Sounds like a win-win for the resort. I imagine you'll be giving a lecture on vices to the kids."

Matthew gave her a half-smile. "You think I'm so predictable. I think they're mature enough to make their own decisions." He left the cockpit without another word.

Yvonne lingered for a few minutes, starting the Sparrow on a self-diagnostic. She'd get the results later and compile a chores list for their time on the surface. With Elizabeth around, the household tasks that Yvonne and Grace normally split had divided another way. They really would have a lot of free time, especially if that buffet was anything like she hoped. A few days free from the endless deadline of mealtime would be a welcome break.

But then idleness would also bring time to think and thinking allowed her traitorous conscience to level accusation after accusation.

When she'd given Matthew that data chip, she'd expected him to be furious. To throw her off the ship in a fit of anger. Instead, he'd quietly gone along with her request to never talk about it again. He'd watched her try to murder someone, and somehow he kept on as if nothing was wrong. But she saw the look in his eye. Condescending pity. Matthew could keep his preaching to himself as far as she was concerned.

She was yanked from her thoughts when snow splattered across the front canopy. She stood and peered frowning. Where had that come from? There wasn't anything above—" Another handful of snow hit just in front of her face. She sat back down and pulled up the external cameras. Davey and Grace were making balls of the white powder. She hit the external intercom. "Very funny, you two. Do you know what would be a better target than the Sparrow? Each other."

Grace halted mid-throw and looked at her brother.

He wasn't able to duck in time before she smacked him in the face with her snowball. Yvonne smiled to herself as she sat back to watch the ensuing battle.

"I thought we'd agreed on no more undercover jobs," Abigail hissed under her breath.

"You weren't very specific about the terms of that agreement," Matthew replied easily. "I'm not sure my own mother would recognize me right now."

Abigail grunted and sat back in her wheelchair as Matthew pushed her through the front entrance of the Casino. It was the first time she'd been in public without her suit since she'd first stepped foot on Mars. It was humiliating, and she felt like everyone was staring. Worse, she was wearing a dress.

"It'll be okay," Matthew said, giving her a quick pat on the shoulder. "You agreed to this a week ago."

"Are you sure it was me? Maybe I have a twin sister."

"Then she's your equal in sarcasm, and my life just got a lot more complicated. Don't worry, we're just here to do some gambling."

Her annoyance broke and she laughed aloud, taking a look around the gaudy lights of the casino floor. There was a low buzz of noise, but she thought it felt a little empty for supposedly being the biggest casino in the colonies. "So everyone else gets a short vacation while you and I are forced to do what is furthest from our nature."

"The perfect disguises," he said.

She glanced over her shoulder at him. He really did cut a strange sight. Heavy body armor over a black combat suit and a ballistic face mask. He was playing the part of personal bodyguard to a wealthy heiress with enough money to get a masked man through casino security. In truth, it was the casino that had hired them. They were here to play the mark, winning an improbable amount of money through games rigged in their favor, before finally turning the tables on the bad guys.

"Easy for you to say," she finally said. "You don't have to wear a wig and a dress. I am not a blonde, and no heels in existence would make these calves look good."

They passed by a row of flashing slot machines, each ludicrously themed, most alluding to Earth's legendary times. She scowled at a scantily clad warrior woman, thinking that her armor wouldn't protect her from a stiff wind, let alone a blade. Ridiculous, but then if it drew the eye, it was probably doing its job.

Matthew coughed. "You look very nice, Abigail. Nothing to worry about."

She about choked. "You're the hired help, remember? No hitting on your employer's fabulously wealthy daughter."

"I wasn't... Never mind."

She kicked herself for being an idiot. The compliment was making her head kind of fuzzy, even though she knew he didn't mean it. The red evening gown was long and covered her atrophied legs entirely, but she wasn't what men would consider an attractive woman. Or at the absolute best, she was half an attractive woman. She did keep her upper body in shape to move around outside her suit, but that was hardly all there was to it, right? She hadn't really thought about it much since she was a teenager. In recent years, she'd craved and demanded respect more than adoration. Besides, men were more interested in tarts like that warrior on the slot machine.

"Thanks, though," she mumbled. "Tell you what, wheel me over to a blackjack table. Let's win some money, and then I'll buy you a drink for trying to butter a girl up." Matthew started to say something, but she cut him off. "Oh be quiet. I'll have a nice glass of ridiculously expensive wine. I'm rich, remember? But I'm sure a fancy place like this has at least one bottle of cherry soda hanging around for the help."

"This moon is something else," Elizabeth said, looking over the railing across the frozen landscape. "Beautiful. But so very alien."

Yvonne looked over her shoulder toward the garish casino lights spilling out onto the balcony. "It's like being on two worlds at once. One overwhelmingly cheap and shallow and the other, a pristine wilderness." She joined Elizabeth and looked down, amazed at how high up they were.

The Sarandib Grand Resort, an angular structure of glass and steel, was suspended on massive arches a couple hundred meters above the surface of Enceladus. No doubt, this had been designed and built by Moses himself. The colonies certainly didn't have the engineering capabilities to build anything on this scale. Far beneath them a group of skiers threaded down a course of flat land lit by floodlights. Grav plates could make a mountain slope out of a plain if need be, and before starting the regularly reshaped slopes, skiers could select the incline difficulty. If Yvonne was twenty-five years younger, she might have considered giving it a shot. Sadly, her knees precluded any such athletic activity these days. Tomas would have been out there in a heartbeat, but their modus operandi of setting up shop where doctors were in critical shortage had certainly never brought them to Enceladus. The resort had a first-rate clinic with a surgery center for the inevitable injuries that came in from the snowfields.

A soft snow began to fall out of the darkness. It was dropped from a massive zeppelin floating high overhead, since little of Enceladus's natural snow would make it through the environmental shield keeping their air in. There was apparently a schedule you could look up for when the snow would fall. Yvonne pulled her coat closer around her. The resort sure went to a lot of effort to give guests an experience they couldn't get anywhere else. Well, except for Earth. With the ice age it was currently locked in, you could most certainly find snowfall, so long as you didn't mind a nice dose of radiation as well.

"I can't say I feel at home here," Elizabeth said, finally breaking the comfortable silence, "but I'm glad to have seen it once. For all I've read about the weather, there's so much of it that now resides only in imagination. To see something I've read described so many times in Shakespeare, Dickens, Lewis, and others..."

Yvonne regarded the other woman quietly. She'd borne the loss of her home with quiet endurance. Yvonne didn't think she'd managed half as well when she lost everything, first Tomas and then being chased from Ceres by a madman. But then she suspected that Elizabeth was made of stronger stuff than she was. Physically and morally. "How do you do it?" she whispered. "Keep going after all you've lost?"

Elizabeth smiled tightly but remained staring at the softly falling flakes. "Well, it hasn't been easy, if that's what you're insinuating."

Yvonne scoffed. "Never."

"When is the world not malevolent? Either you come to terms with that and endure, or you don't and succumb." She paused. "But that was a fight I fought long ago. Maybe I'll tell you about it sometime."

She didn't think she could bear to hear how Elizabeth had overcome when she had failed. The whole Cole family was as pious as they came, and Yvonne didn't fancy any sermons from her any more than from her son. She was suspicious about why Elizabeth was along to begin with. She had the distinct impression that Matthew had brought her along as a babysitter, and not for the kids. It rubbed her the wrong way, but at least Elizabeth would speak to her. Yvonne wasn't sure the last time Abigail had even made eye contact.

They went back to staring at the gentle fall of snow and passed the evening in silence.

Matthew hated the job almost before it really got started. "This contract was for everyone else," he said, mostly as a reminder to himself. "Not for me."

"What's that?" Abigail whispered, turning to face him from her poker game.

He shook his head and she went back to her cards, pretending to study them intently. Casino operators were feeding her information through an earpiece. This was one of the games that she was scheduled to win big on. It was a bizarre night. Matthew had stoically escorted her around the Casino to the various games and machines. Most of the time she played fairly, which predictably led to big losses. The house always wins, after all. But on occasion, at pre-planned moments, she won big enough to obliterate her shortfalls. She'd stop Matthew and point at a slot machine. "This one," she'd say, and he knew that her earpiece had informed her that particular machine was rigged in her favor. Or a blackjack dealer would count cards to give her easy wins.

He tried to shrug it all off. It was all a farce. They weren't keeping the winnings, and they weren't eating the losses. But it did start to bother him when they reached the poker tables. They were supposed to draw attention, which would require them hitting more social games. Unfortunately that meant there'd be losers. Sarandib Grand Resort had promised him that anyone Abigail personally took money from would be reimbursed after the job was complete, he just hoped they were keeping a close eye on the numbers and not going to cheat anyone.

It was a world of vice, and the ex-priest in him was getting twitchy.

At least Abigail was having fun. Once she'd warmed up to the role of rich heiress, she had decided to ham it up.

"Hey," she called out to the barrel-chested man across from her with the giant white cowboy hat. "I could have run a marathon by now." Everyone at the table stared at her wheelchair, but the big man was intimidated into making his play. He pushed in his handful of chips. Matthew tried not to wince. He wasn't well versed in poker, but he was fairly confident Abigail was breaking a lot of casino etiquette with her banter. She was drawing attention, which was the whole goal of this operation, but it still made him feel like he was on the wrong side.

Besides the mostly harmless man that Abigail had just bullied, there was a man from Europa covered in tattoos identifying the slave cartel of which he was a member, and another in a white suit that Matthew was certain was White Void. If you knew anything about the solar system, and those wealthy enough to come to Enceladus most certainly did, you knew that white suits meant only one thing. Either it was worn by a brazen idiot or a high-level syndicate enforcer.

The white-suit won that particular hand. Abigail leaned over and patted his arm. "You seem to know what you're doing."

He jerked away. "Do not lay another hand on me, ma'am."

She recoiled as if burned. "I would have thought you would be the type to appreciate the attention of a lady, but perhaps that's so uncommon an experience for you that you don't know how to behave when it happens."

He sneered at her. "The attentions of half a woman are hardly worth noticing."

Abigail's mouth turned up in a smile, one that Matthew had seen a thousand times. "If you think I'm wounded by the scorn of a tenth of a man, you're flattering yourself."

The cartel man laughed and nearly spat out his drink. "Leave her be, Scissors. She's just trying to get into your head. How do you think she's been cleaning us out?" Abigail blinked at them innocently.

The man with the white hat motioned to the dealer, clearly irritated with the unnecessary drama. "Let's get on with this."

Abigail won, of course, with the coaching in her ear. How could she lose when they were cheating? But Matthew felt a little less guilty knowing that two of the people losing were criminals. The fellow Martian was short about fifty thousand because of the casino's own meddling. He would get it back, or Matthew would lodge a complaint against the Casino and go public on this one.

Shortly after midnight, Abigail called it quits, and Matthew wordlessly pushed her out of the gaming halls to the tram-station. The attendant made sure they were safely loaded into the hanging car and sent them on their way to the heiress' suite.

"I can't wait to get out of this dress," she moaned. "I haven't worn one of these things since I was a teenager." She gripped the wheels of her chair and moved closer to the window. He stepped up beside her. The tram took them out over the snowy fields to one of the other crossing arches. The resort's rooms hung independent and free beneath the graceful steel curves to give them each a spectacular view of the surrounding landscape. Matthew would have rather gone back to the Sparrow, but that wasn't part of the gig.

Someone was preying on women who were winning big at the casino. There had been three incidents. One blackmail, one kidnapping, and one outright robbery. Each had happened after several days of success on the floor, and all of the events started when their supposedly secure rooms were invaded.

"I don't really like using you as bait," Matthew said.

"Hold up. You were the one telling me it would be okay earlier, and now you've got complaints?"

Matthew grunted and closed his mouth. Okay, maybe that was a little bit of a heel turn.

She poked him in the side, and he turned on her with a frown. "You okay?" she asked.

Their tram pulled up to the suite and the door opened into an ante-chamber that would make the palace on Venus blush in shame. Seeing the opulence just soured his mood further. He tore off his face mask and started to take off the armor, dropping them in a corner by the door to his room.

Abigail wheeled forward and stopped in front of him, arms crossed. "You ignored my question. Are you okay?"

"I'll be fine," he said, and he was pretty sure he was telling the truth. He knew he couldn't put the strange disquiet he felt into words. Not yet, anyway. He gestured to her room. "Go get suited. We've got a long night of sitting up waiting for you to get attacked."

Grace and Davey spent the first full afternoon on Enceladus out in the snow, learning to ski. Davey tried to convince her it was a worthless endeavor, because when would they ever get the chance to use that skill again?

She just stared at him and wondered where her brother had gone. "You're starting to sound like Matthew," she told him. "All work, no play. Except for your boring books. I'll probably be better at it than you anyway."

She was wrong. Maybe it was because he was short and had a low center of gravity, but he was a natural, zipping across the snowfields like he'd been born here. She hated having to eat her words, and every time he helped her dig herself out of the snow after a fall, he gave the grand-est, most insufferable smirk he had in his arsenal. It bothered her until she found the courage to admit defeat.

The craziest part of the snowfields was the way gravity changed. You'd pull up to the beginning of a perfectly flat slope and approach a console and select a difficulty. And then gravity would change directions in a gut-wrenching fashion. Davey wasn't as phased by the way the world suddenly changed from flat to mountain slope.

"You should have seen what I was up against on Ceres," he said. "Driving across the roof of a city is way worse."

By the end of the day, they were both tired, and Grace was already talking about how late she was planning on sleeping in. Once they had cleaned up, Davey had to drag her out of the Sparrow and back to the tram that led to the main resort. She was silent on the trip over the fields, face pressed to the window. A hundred meters below them, she could make out some of the slopes they'd hit earlier. In some places, large treaded vehicles scoured the powdered surfaces flat again, erasing the marks of the day's skiers.

They grazed the buffet for the second night in a row. The food was great, if not quite amazing. Grace was pretty confident that Elizabeth's cooking was better, but she did appreciate the bounty of choices available. Tonight she stacked her plate high with Mexican food, including a pair of enchiladas drizzled in a green sauce, in honor of Enceladus. Unfortunately, the green sauce had cilantro. She ate it anyway, never willing to waste a morsel of food. But the real glory of a buffet was seconds and thirds if you wanted. She was going to pack on a few kilos before this was over at the rate things were going, but at the moment she didn't care.

They spent the rest of the evening exploring the nooks and crannies of the resort. It was habit. Instinct. Whenever they had moved to a new neighborhood in Blight, they would scour every street, looking for possible sources of food, bolt holes, shortcuts. If you didn't know the lay of the land like you'd been there your entire life, you didn't stand a chance.

Which was how they found an out of the way bank of slot-machines in an abandoned lounge. For such a big and supposedly popular resort, there sure were a lot of empty venues. Grace walked over to the closest machine and jabbed a thumb at it. "Hey, do you think Matthew would get on to me if he knew I was this close to a machine of destruction and sin?"

"Probably," Davey said, joining her. She saw the spinning lights reflect off his eyes.

"Give it your best shot," she said.

He eyed her. "I have no idea what you're talking about."

"Do your best Matthew impression. Full priest mode. He's been training you to be a shorter version of himself for two years now. You know you have it in you."

He stared at her, mouth agape. He tried to start talking twice, and each time shut his mouth before he got out a single word. Finally, he frowned. "I think I'm offended."

"Nah. The solar system could use a second Matthew. Go on. Try."

He looked back at the machine and sighed. "Look, I don't have the speech thing down. But Matthew sometimes likes to demonstrate with object lessons so..." He dug out his wallet and found a five-dollar coin. "You owe me for this, by the way."

"Sure," she said, gesturing for him to continue.

"Umm. Matthew would talk a lot about honest work and how valuable it is, and then he'd also explain about how casinos aren't here to give you money and maybe something about stacked odds. And to prove it..." He put the coin into the machine and pulled the lever. The lights changed, and some wheels began to spin.

"I think you have to hit that flashing button," Grace suggested.

"Right." He hit the button, and the wheels slowly turned to a stop. A bunch more lights flashed, and an annoying chime rang out. The machine printed out a ticket.

"Umm, is it supposed to do that?" Grace asked.

Davey tore off the ticket to look at it, and she saw the color drain from his face. "I think I just won two-hundred dollars."

Grace snorted once. And then she bent double from laughter. "Worst demonstration. Ever!"

"Crap, crap, crap," he muttered. "Matthew is going to kill me."

"So just throw the ticket away," she said, wiping the tears from her eyes.

"He'll know. He always knows!"

Grace patted him on the back. "Oh, man. This is your problem. I haven't laughed this hard in months. Good lecture."

He still looked stricken. "Maybe if I buy groceries with it, he won't be mad."

"Keep telling yourself that," Grace said, patting him on the arm. "Come on. Let's go get your payout."

He groaned as they left the abandoned lounge. The lights automatically dimmed behind them. "How is it that every time I get in trouble, you're involved?" he said through gritted teeth.

"Hey," she said, giving him an elbow. "Even if I'm a bad influence, you're still the common factor in all your screw-ups."

He let out a long, despondent sigh. "And you just made a better Matthew speech than I did."

254

Milena Drugova took a sip of her black coffee. The diner she sat in was nearly deserted at this time of the afternoon, but that was for the best. She wasn't here to be social. Idly she turned to look out the window. Beyond the busy sidewalk and traffic was the largest park in Flagstaff. Between the rolling grass-carpeted hills sat a lake that sparkled in the afternoon sunlight. It would have been a lovely place for a walk had she not been here for business.

She'd barely gotten word of the meeting in time to set up a camera in a nearby tree last night. Unfortunately, she wasn't able to wire it, meaning she'd have to stay within its transmitter range. If the coffee hadn't been so good, that would have been a more annoying proposition. On her tablet, a man walked into the camera's field of view where a bench overlooked the lake. It wasn't Stein, nor was it any of the contacts she'd previously seen. He wore a satin vest under a long duster and a cowboy hat. Nothing out of the ordinary for Arizona, but the tailoring looked on the expensive side of trendy. He turned away from the camera, so she couldn't get a good look at this face. With luck, she'd get a view on his way out.

Milena double-checked the audio feed to her earpiece. There wasn't anything to hear at the moment other than the gentle lap of water and the distant sounds of a playground full of children, but the feed was loud and clear. She took another swig of her coffee and settled in to wait as the man did the same.

Ten minutes later, he was joined by Stein himself. She pushed her coffee away and upped the volume. To her relief, the microphone was able to pick up the voices well enough to hear them over the ambient noise. Still, she adjusted the EQs to make their voices stand out from the background.

"What's so important that it can't wait," Stein asked in his deep baritone.

"I'll be off Mars for a few days," the stranger said in a clipped British accent. Churchill wasn't a HiTO colony. Stein's connections were continuing to get more complex. "I have an appointment to keep that can't wait."

"You still owe me for Gilgamesh."

255

Milena frowned at her table. Gilgamesh was the location of the Ganymede grav plate factory. Either this was a coincidence, or she had just stumbled onto something crucial.

"And you'll be paid for the work you did. Soon. The loss of the grav plate shipment was an unfortunate set back to my finances. But your payment is still a priority."

Stein only shook his head. "That's not how I operate. This is your fault for playing games with Cole. There was no reason he had to be present for that operation. I'm not paying for the consequences."

"On the contrary," the stranger said. "His presence was required and will soon pay dividends. You nearly ruined everything with your ill-fated attempt to kill him. Thankfully, he survived and the Sparrow is far from your reach."

Milena pursed her lips. Thompson had been right about Stein being the assassin.

"You're not my only client. I can't help that there are conflicts if you aren't specific enough in your contracts. I've held to my terms. You're the one who has failed to execute."

"That will be rectified soon enough. Once I have what I want, I'll have more than enough leverage to settle our accounts."

"You'd better," Stein said. "One last chance, or I'll collect my own way." He cracked his knuckles in an overly dramatic fashion that had Milena rolling her eyes. "Now," he said, "Why the meeting? It wasn't just to make excuses."

"No," the stranger said. "It was to give you a warning."

Stein scoffed. "You're threatening me now?"

"As if I could harm you. Others can, though, and that's what concerns me. If anyone were to learn of our business relationship, I suspect your career would suffer considerable harm. And you still have yet to deliver certain codes you've promised."

"Don't flatter yourself. I've done business with worse than you."

"I doubt the Arizonan government would agree with that assessment," the stranger said, an amused lilt to his voice. "Very well. I'll keep my warning to myself." He passed a data chip to Stein. "You'll have the codes by the time the operation commences?"

"I'll play my part. And then you'll have my payment, or I'll cancel our arrangement."

He didn't make subtle threats, Milena thought.

"Of course. You won't hear from me before then."

Stein stood and left without another word, leaving the stranger alone on the bench. Milena reached for her now cold cup of coffee. This was going to be quite a report to send back to Mr. Kagurazaka. And Thompson. He'd promised payment for further information, and this was about as good as he was going to get. Confirmation that Stein was behind the attempted assassination and that he was working with what appeared to be an Abrogationist, if the Gilgamesh comment was to be believed.

After about a ten-minute wait, the stranger stood to leave. "Turn your head," she muttered. "Just a fraction to the right and—" As if he heard her, he turned and walked up to the tree that concealed her camera. Then he looked right at the lens and tipped his hat to her. There was no mistaking that face. After the Ceres Incident, it had been broadcast all over the colonies. Alexander Logan.

She tucked her tablet into her coat, and jumped back from her booth, springing out the diner's door. This was way outside the purview of the job, but if she could somehow apprehend him... Her camera was only a couple hundred meters away. Maybe she could reach it in time. She dodged through traffic, ignoring the blaring horns and hurled obscenities. When she hit the grass, she briefly stumbled, as her shoes weren't meant for running cross country, but she kept going, heart hammering in her ears.

It was too late. She reached her tree and spun in circles, trying to lay eyes on the famed terrorist. He was gone.

He'd known the conversation was being watched. He'd wanted her to see him, and he was sending a message. But to who? Kagurazaka? Thompson? Maybe it was Cole himself. She'd landed in the middle of a tangled web, and on every web, there's a spider. The problem was, she wasn't sure where it was or how to avoid it.

Abigail and Matthew's schedule remained the same for several days. Evenings were spent in the casino. Abigail quickly discovered that she didn't even need a new persona. The Shield Maiden's boisterous confidence worked to intimidate just as well from a wheelchair. No one saw it coming. In some ways, it was a revelatory experience for her, the implications of which she would have to think about. She'd always made certain assumptions about how people viewed her disability. Perhaps some of them were true, but when she came in bludgeoning them with banter, she gave them an education.

So she had her fun in the evenings, but she could feel Matthew radiating misery. Gambling and alcohol were the name of the game in the casino, and she knew he would never be keen on either. She did her best to ignore him while they were on the floor, though. There was nothing she could do about it, and she had to play her part.

Every evening after midnight, they packed up and retreated to the suite, where they sat up in the dark, waiting for something to happen. It was the usual stakeout that she hated. By the time mid-morning rolled around, they would give up and get a few hours of sleep before starting the process over.

By the fourth night, she was sick of it. When two in the morning came, she was resuited and leaned against the wall in her palatial bedroom. She could barely see Matthew where he had sunk down into a club chair in the corner. "Are you going to make it?" she asked, keeping her voice down out of instinct. Despite the fact that she'd given up on the scheme, they were still on the job.

"I'm fine."

"Said no one ever, who was actually fine," she replied. "Come on. I've been looking forward to being back on the job with you, but you've been a wet blanket all week."

She heard him sigh in the dark. "Maybe this one just isn't for me."

"Someone is preying on women, you know."

"I didn't mean it like that, Abigail."

"Well, then what did you mean?"

He was quiet for a long minute before responding. "I spent the last three months itching to be back out in the Sparrow. Long hours of exercise trying to regain some form of physical fitness. Even spent time at the firing range. But now that I'm here..." He paused, and Abigail wished she could see the expression on his face. "I've almost died hundreds of times doing this job. And I've never regretted it. I've done a lot of good. Most of it since you guys came on board. But since the injury, I just wonder if it's worth it anymore."

"Isn't it a little early for a mid-life crisis?" she asked. As soon as the words escaped her mouth, she regretted the attempt at levity. "Sorry I shouldn't—"

258

"Don't be. I turned thirty-six a couple weeks back. I'm not quite... young anymore. Never will be again. I spend my time chasing terrorists and mafioso around the solar system. Even my father, drunken boor that he was for most of his life, had put down some roots by thirty."

Abigail decided not to remind him that that was the mark she'd just passed. She felt the weight of his words and knew where he was coming from. The Shield Maiden of Mars couldn't exist forever and someday her life would inevitably change, whether she kicked and screamed or not. Had Matthew's already shifted when that sniper put a bullet through him? It was a terrifying thought because the Sparrow was all she had. And she refused to accept it. At least not yet.

"Matthew, you're doing important things," she stammered, unsure how to describe what she was getting at. "Your leadership saved Villa María and Ceres and hundreds of others along the way. And think what good the Guild will do. You're giving those crews a new purpose. A better one. No one else can do what you're doing."

His silhouette leaned back in his chair to stare at the ceiling. "Maybe not," he said. "But the universe would go on without me being a free-lancer. No one person is that essential."

Abigail wasn't sure she agreed with his assessment, but she let it slide. "What about the Anemoi and Whitaker?"

"I would love nothing more than to hand both of our quarters over to him and never see him again."

She frowned. "And if they do lead somewhere? Are you going to let Whitaker control that discovery?"

"And this is why I didn't want to talk about this," Matthew said. "Because you know that the answer is no. You know I have to keep doing this. And that I will."

"You want to know what I think?" she asked.

"You're going to tell me either way."

"And you're going to listen because I'm the best friend you've got."

He snorted but sat up a little straighter. She imagined he had a smirk on his face. That one that bubbled up unwillingly when she tried to cheer him up with a joke.

"I think you're a little down from your injury. Maybe even depressed. Hell, Matthew, you almost died. Everyone, even Elizabeth, said their goodbyes to you that last morning. It's okay to be off your game. And..." She thought about how to phrase this next one. "And maybe you're right, and this kind of life isn't for you much longer. But we all need you. At least for a little while. There's only one Matthew Cole."

They fell silent, and the only sound was the water feature from the suite's antechamber. Abigail wondered if she was being selfish, preserving her own way of life while trying to twist Matthew into doing something he no longer wanted to do. She nearly opened her mouth to apologize, but he beat her to it.

"I'm sorry. I'm just thinking out loud—"

There was a soft click as the lock on the main door turned. They both snapped to attention, and Matthew drew his gun. She could barely see his brief nod as he flattened himself to the wall beside the door the assailant would soon enter. She did the same on the other side, though honestly, even in the dark, the odds of missing her hulking form were laughable. She strained her ears to hear the door opening, and then a soft footstep. Stupid water feature. The bubbling hid their numbers, though she'd guess the answer was at least two, probably three.

A masked man in jet black stepped through the entryway they'd conveniently left open, and like a moron, he moved right for the lump in the bed. Abigail bit her cheeks to keep from laughing. They'd propped pillows under the covers and put the wig she'd been wearing on the pillow, and he took the bait.

The second man was more cautious and turned his head both ways to check his corners. He missed Matthew in the dark, but he stumbled in panic when his eyes landed on Abigail. She gave him a smile. "What's up?" Then she grabbed him by the scruff of his collar and threw him across the room at his buddy by the bed. They landed in a tangled heap on the floor, probably with a broken bone or two.

Matthew spun around the corner and crouched. "Don't move!" he shouted. Abigail heard a brief shuffle and Matthew fired his gun once. "I gave you an order. That means you too—" He leaped forward. "Runner, Abigail."

"On it," she said, gently pushing him to the side and stepping over the injured intruder. Her eyes focused just in time to see the main entrance to the suite close. She reached it in two bounds and mashed the open plate. Nothing happened. The lift had already begun to pull away, and the door had engaged safety features. She ripped the door out of the wall and tossed it aside. The blast of cold air on her face was immediate and intense. Getting a grip on the steel frame, she leaned outward.

The tram was only about three meters away, not having had time to accelerate down the lines. She leaped and caught the side, causing it to swing violently. Briefly, she looked down and then decided that was a bad idea. Taking care to make sure her grip was sound, she shimmied around to the door. A figure in black scurried to the far side of the tram as she pried the door open and let herself into the tiny capsule. It felt a lot bigger in her wheelchair, that was for sure. "I'd tell you to pick on someone your size," she said as she pushed him to the ground. "But, in your case, that would actually be good advice."

Internally she breathed a sigh of relief. There would be some wrap-up work, and probably a lot of questions to answer about the damage she'd just done to the facilities, but this job was on the backside. The sooner they got off of this moon, the better.

Yvonne stifled a yawn as she put the finishing touches on her report. One of the newer Guild crews, the Jameson Brothers, had made an excellent suggestion a month back. They thought it would be good to write up short reports after jobs and submit them to the guild, not only for accountability but also to share information and tactics. Some of the younger crews were eager to learn from the old vets. The proposition would have to be formally voted on now that the charter had been adopted, but she expected it to pass when Julia's lawyer finished the legal copy for the amendment.

No one was looking forward to the extra paperwork or the effort to redact the reports to protect their clients' and crew's privacy, but it was a good idea, and Yvonne decided that she would go ahead and start to set the example.

It had been two days since Matthew and Abigail had crashed the casino ring. It had unsurprisingly been an inside job. Who else would have been able to cut through security like a plasma torch through steel? Matthew was right. There was always a mole. Every single time. There was always someone looking to take advantage of their situation. But then she was a doctor that had pulled a trigger to kill a man, so no amount of evil would ever surprise her again.

The sound of a throat clearing interrupted her, and she turned to see

Abigail framing the door. She turned back to the report, chest constricting. "Yes? What do you need?" Because there would be a reason. Abigail never approached her without reason these days.

"I wanted to apologize."

Funny. There can't be anything to apologize for when you haven't even had contact with a person. Yvonne kept typing. "It's fine. Whatever it is."

"Is it?" Abigail asked. "Look. These last couple months... I can't imagine what it was like to be in your shoes. To have someone take everything away from you and then be put in that situation. I didn't understand, and I'm sorry for shutting you out."

With a sigh, Yvonne shut down her monitor but didn't turn to face her friend. She could still call her that, right, even if they hadn't been talking? "It wasn't just you. I haven't made the effort either. Why the sudden change of heart?"

The seconds ticked away. "I guess I got a reminder that nothing lasts forever."

"Matthew change your mind?"

"Not intentionally, no. Look. I'm sorry. I can't pretend to know what's going on or how to help, but I don't want to be mad at you anymore."

"Me neither," Yvonne whispered. "I'm sorry too."

And that was the end of it. Abigail turned and left Yvonne to her swirling nebula of thoughts. It refused to collapse into anything useful, no bright star to give her a heading to chart a course. Matthew and Abigail already knew that she was a fraud, and it seemed like they had come to terms with it somehow. If only she could do the same.

The console lit up with a message, and she flicked her monitor back on. It was from Arizona Minister of Law, Ryan Thompson. Wonderful. Matthew was going to be thrilled to hear from his favorite bureaucrat. She opened the message.

Unless it's life or death, drop what you're doing and return to Mars. I have evidence pointing to the attempted assassin. Further, it seems he has a partnership with Logan. Don't bring the Sparrow. We think they're tracking it.

She inhaled sharply. "Matthew!" she shouted. "You need to see this!"

Chapter 11: Machinations

---◄◊►---

Evil men have always been drawn to the siren call of the halls of power. The governments of men have ever been subject to this infection. And it is not limited to the highest position. If they cannot become king, then they will settle for prime minister. If they cannot become the prime minister, then a senator, or a mayor, or a faceless bureaucrat may wield the sword as effectively as any. Even a pencil-pusher can be a tyrant.

Moses proved an effective impediment, but not a cure. Overnight, he was able to fulfill the office job of nearly every government worker in the world. From tax processing, to licensure, to welfare, he streamlined every governmental function while still allowing each nation the autonomy to rule themselves as they saw fit.

It became nearly impossible to hide corruption from Moses. Any that he uncovered was revealed to the world, allowing the appropriate authorities to deal with it in accordance with law. The only method of evading the AI was to cease using computer systems entirely and never speak of delicate matters in front of any microphone connected to a network. It was difficult, but evil will always find a way.

When Moses disappeared their path was once again clear. No sooner had the AI vanished, than the

263

snakes began to work their way back into the colonial governments. As the wisest of men once said, there is nothing new under the sun.

Chaim Ben-Artzi
Collector of Books of Antiquities
Died 132 AM

The best thing about Elizabeth being on board the Sparrow was that she insisted on doing the cooking. Grace dipped a healthy portion of stew from the pot and smiled as she got a good whiff of the hearty aroma. Definitely better than anything she or Yvonne could scrounge up, even on their best days, and with all the same ingredients too. She couldn't figure out what magic the older woman was working. She grabbed a spoon out of the drawer and joined Davey and Abigail at the table.

"We shouldn't get used to this," Abigail said, taking a mouthful. She froze and her eyes drifted over to Grace. "No offense."

"None taken," she replied honestly.

"You'd better be learning everything you can from her," Davey said. "No telling how long she sticks around."

"I'll see what I can do," Grace said. "Personally I think it's either in the genes or it isn't. Sadly I'm afraid I only got half of it. I can cook edible food, unlike either of you, but it's not going to change your life."

Abigail scoffed but didn't bother to disagree. Matthew emerged from the cockpit, followed by Yvonne and Elizabeth. "I see you were patient while we wrapped up business," he said.

Davey swallowed a mouthful and set his spoon aside. "In our defense, Elizabeth told us to start. But sure. Go ahead and try to make us feel bad."

Matthew eyed him before turning away and picking up a bowl. "Fine then. Don't stop on my account."

"No," Davey said, putting on his grumpy face. "I'm waiting and we're going to have a nice dinner all together."

"Unfortunately it'll be the last for a while," Yvonne said, setting her bowl down beside his.

Grace frowned and glanced between Matthew and the other adults.

264

After three months of being separated and one measly job, one that she didn't even get to help on, they were splitting up again? "Care to inform the rest of us?" She slid aside to make more room for Elizabeth as Matthew squeezed in. The table was a little tight for all six of them.

Matthew poked at his stew but set his spoon aside. "Abigail and I are going back to Mars," he said.

"Yeah, and we're coming with you," Davey said. Oh, he was going to be mad about this. Grace could already see exactly where this was headed.

"Hear him out," Elizabeth said gently.

Grace looked at her, not bothering to hide the scowl she knew was fixed on her features. "You're in on this too?"

"It was my decision," Matthew said sharply. "But it's not arbitrary. This is for everyone's good."

Davey crossed his arms. "We're listening."

"Someone out there wants me dead," Matthew said. "And until we put a stop to them, they're a danger to you all as well. They've already chased Benny and Candace from Mars as well as my own mother." His eyes shifted briefly to Elizabeth. "I'm not going to get anyone I care about killed. Being a freelancer is dangerous enough as it is. Our old friend Ryan Thompson says he has intel on the killer for us, so Abigail and I will go back to Mars and deal with this. Once and for all."

"And you trust Thompson?" Grace asked. She'd only seen him once, the time Matthew had dragged the whole crew into his office to set the man off balance. Matthew had made it pretty clear that he'd regarded him as an enemy at the time.

"On something like this? Yes," he said. "We got off to a rough start, and I don't think he'll ever be glad to see me stroll into his office, but I think we have an understanding. If he says that he has information for me, then I trust it. Unfortunately, he also suspects the Sparrow is being tracked, and if that's the case, we can't take it back to Mars."

"Sounds like the Sparrow is a real safe place for the rest of us," Davey said.

Matthew shook his head. "If our mystery assassin was going to come after the Sparrow, they would have months ago. Maybe they're confined to Mars, or maybe it was a hired hitman, and their contract didn't demand they chase me halfway across the solar system."

Elizabeth scrutinized her son. "What does that mean?"

Matthew rubbed the back of his neck. "Well. I've not exactly ever taken up that kind of contract, but I've been around long enough to know that the terms can vary, and they might not specify the added expense of leaving the planet. Regardless, the Sparrow has been left alone, and we can reasonably hope it will remain that way. And if it's not, Davey and Grace, you'll be here to protect it."

"Benny is going to scrounge us up a few shipping jobs," Yvonne said. "He'll keep us moving, and hopefully, the assassin won't realize that Matthew and Abigail took public transportation back to Mars."

Grace frowned at that. "So Elizabeth isn't going with you?"

"Not yet," Elizabeth said. "The farm is gone, it's well past planting season, and I'd just be a liability until this is dealt with. I'm afraid you're stuck with me."

"As long as you're cooking," she said, "you're welcome to stay as long as you like. Or forever."

Elizabeth hummed softly at that but didn't say anything. With plans made, everyone went back to eating as if the conversation had never happened. Grace stared at her bowl, appetite completely out the airlock. So that really was it. They were splitting up after one crummy job. She grabbed her spoon and forced herself to eat. Things used to be simpler. Back before Ceres. Before Villa María even. When it was just the five of them and the Sparrow. No guild or government officials, and the only miracles were the ones on her wrists. She kicked herself for sounding so much like a boring adult. When had she gotten old enough to even have good old days in her past?

"When are you guys leaving?" she finally asked.

"As soon as we can," Matthew said. "We have to catch a shuttle to Freeport 36, and then it'll be a commercial flight to Mars. Yvonne is in charge. If there's a security threat on the ground, Davey, you take the lead."

Not an hour later, Grace watched Matthew and Abigail march down the ramp into the snow and disappear. She stared after them for a few minutes before closing the ramp. "Bad things happen when we split up," she muttered under her breath.

The trip to Mars was as delightful as Abigail expected. She tried rolling over in the pitiful little shelf that passed for a bed, knowing it was a lost cause. The last time she'd taken a commercial liner was before she'd met Matthew, a trip to Ceres to have Ivan do repairs. After a few fitful attempts at sleep, she groaned, pushed aside the privacy curtain, and pulled herself to the edge of the bed, being careful not to hit her head on the bunk above her. She grasped the edge of her kneeling exosuit and, with some difficulty, swung her legs through the open back.

It took her some time to get situated and close up her armor. She stood, careful not to bump the walls of what amounted to little more than a closet. Since traveling between planets took days, most passengers were assigned sleeping periods in tiny bunkrooms. Given that Abigail had a secret to protect, Matthew had paid for a private one. He had generously opted to use the public bunkroom. She looked at the clock. It was still an hour until their sleep period was over, after which a steward would come clean the room for the next shift of sleepers, though she doubted there would be anyone even scheduled for this room.

The commercial liner was at least half empty. The canteen always had plenty of room, the walking track felt half deserted, and the general seating area lacked the usual buzz of conversation. Which was fine with Abigail since it made getting around the tight corridors easier than normal in her bulky suit. She found her locker and grabbed her bag, making her way to the washrooms. Thankfully, the line for a private one was short.

Twenty minutes later, feeling much cleaner and with more manageable hair, she made her way to the canteen to find Matthew already nursing a cup of coffee. "You're up early," he said as she sat across from him.

She began tearing open sugar packets to dump into her coffee. "A slab of granite would be more comfortable to sleep on. You?"

"Had a snorer a few bunks over."

"Ugh. Sorry about that. The sooner we get to port, the better."

He glanced at his watch. "You'll have to wait about thirteen hours. If we're on schedule."

"Which I doubt."

Unfortunately, she was right. Fifteen hours later, they were required to strap into their seats as the liner entered Martian space in preparation for deorbiting. She caused some minor fuss for the attendants, since there wasn't any possible way for her to strap into one of the tiny chairs. Ultimately, they settled for her sitting in the aisle by Matthew, something he thought was hilarious.

"Laugh it up, Gaucho," she grumbled.

"I said nothing and will refrain from doing anything of the sort." She could see the way the corners of his mouth creased ever so slightly upward. Jerk. "We should be in Martian network range," he said, picking up his tablet. "I'm going to grab the most recent newspaper out of Arizona. I feel like I've been out of the loop since, well, my injury."

"Last I heard, the occupation continues but life goes on. Kyoto isn't happy, but what are they going to do about it? On the plus side, it doesn't look like Logan's going to be able to hit the factory with that much firepower around it."

"I wonder about that," he said. She watched as he thumbed through articles, doing little more than scanning headlines and glancing at photos. "The editorials are giving Barclay a rough time these days," he said. "It's still a year from the next election, but I wager this will be a hot topic of debate."

"Do you vote still?" she asked, raising an eyebrow.

"Not every election. It's a hassle to get a ballot, but I'll make the effort this time. Barclay has made my bad list."

There was a rumble through the decks as the retrorockets fired. The captain's voice droned for a few minutes about the upcoming landing, but Abigail tuned her out. When it was finally over, Matthew passed her the tablet. She read the article title aloud. "Guild of Lanterns Heroes Defend Diner from Armed Gang. Hey, it's the Ongkara Crew. Those guys were great."

Matthew frowned. "I feel I missed a lot. They operate out of Thebe if I recall?"

She nodded. "A group of cousins. The locals already adored them, but now it looks like the rest of the solar system is going to hear about them too." She passed him his tablet back. "And for some reason, you don't look too happy about that."

"Oh, you know me," he said. "I'm a glory hound."

She coughed a short laugh in her throat. "Then maybe you shouldn't have volunteered to be a figurehead whose sole purpose is to give the colonies a shining symbol of hope."

"Don't remind me. I wasn't actually counting on this little gambit to

268

be successful."

Abigail shook her head, wondering if Matthew was actually that dense or was just playing at it. Most likely an unconscious mixture of the two. Less than an hour later, they walked off the passenger liner into the main terminal of the Arizona spaceport, each with a small bag in tow. Unfortunately, it was around noon local time, which meant this was going to be one long day. Spaceport security eyed Abigail cautiously, but a quick flash of her ID as a freelancer settled things. Nothing out of the ordinary.

As they stepped out onto the street, she glanced upward. It always felt good coming back to Mars. While it would never be home, it was as close as she could ever get. Far above, Phobos trailed across the pale sky. Despite being little more than a captured asteroid at roughly twelve kilometers across, its precariously low orbit made it easily visible as it circled Mars at high speed. Now, it was a heavily guarded Highland Treaty Organization military site. Her gaze lingered on the moon for a moment before turning away. They had business to attend to, and thankfully it didn't involve the mad schemes of nations and their quest for power.

By midafternoon, they'd reclaimed her bike, stashed away in a dusty old storage facility on the far side of town. "At least you get yours back," Matthew grumbled. "I had that bike for nearly ten years."

"At least you're alive," she countered as she mounted the bike.

Matthew rubbed at his chest where the bullet had pierced him and climbed on behind her. She'd noticed him doing that anytime the subject was breached, and she wondered if he was even aware of it. "Okay, I'll grant that," he said. "Let's go see our favorite politician."

The meeting was to take place that evening, on an abandoned floor of a crumbling old office building a few blocks off of downtown. They arrived a few minutes early and cautiously crept up the stairs. "I still think it's weird to meet a government official somewhere so unofficial," Abigail whispered as they reached their floor.

Matthew shrugged. "Thompson has gone off the books with us before. I suspect this is going to be the same." He pushed the door open and entered the boarded-up remnants of an office. What little furniture was left was draped with tarps. It looked like the office had more spiders hard at work than employees if the cobwebbed corners were anything to go by. "Well," he called out. "Are you here?"

To Abigail's utter surprise, her friend Milena Drugova stepped from around a corner, looking as trendy as ever with a hand planted firmly on her hip. "It's my lucky day," she said. "Looks like I finally get to meet the famous Matthew Cole. I've heard so much about you. Mostly from Abigail."

Abigail's mouth went dry. Matthew chuckled and adjusted his hat. "I hope it's good things she's told you. And who, may I ask, are you?"

She offered him a hand. "Milena Drugova. Surveillance specialist and part of the Guild of Lanterns."

Matthew shook her hand. "I should have guessed. Sadly, I only know your general resume, as Abigail seems to have been more chatty with you than about you."

He gave Abigail a lopsided smile, which made her want to dive out the nearest window. "Very funny," she said, turning back to Milena, "What exactly are you doing here? We were expecting someone else. Are you working for Thompson?"

Her friend gave her a wry smile. "It's a bit more complicated, I'm afraid."

"And we're hoping you'll be able to help sort it out," came a new voice from behind them. Ryan Thompson stepped into the room, and Abigail thought he looked even more irritated with the world than usual.

Matthew looked between the two of them. "I don't think you care about my well-being enough to track down my would-be killer, Thompson, not without there being something in it for you as well. So tell me. What kind of mess are we getting ourselves into?"

Thompson gave them a weak and tired smile, and it was genuine enough that it made worry itch at the back of Abigail's mind. "Hopefully," he said slowly, "one that you and the Shield Maiden are going to help get us all out of."

Matthew scratched his chin after it was all laid out. "Let's walk through the sequence one more time. Three months ago, Damon Stein was at the Gilgamesh grav plate factory, in some capacity."

Milena nodded from where she sat by a window, arms crossed. They'd scrounged a couple chairs, but Abigail would crush them, and Matthew was a pacer anyway. Thompson had accepted a seat and sipped thoughtfully at a coffee. Matthew was beginning to regret turning down the offer of a cup of his own.

"He wasn't at our production line," he said, pushing the thought of caffeine aside. "We were thorough. And he wasn't at the one that the Abrogationists successfully hit, because he would have been on that freighter when Gebre'elwa's interceptors took it down."

"You said the factory's air defenses were disabled," Abigail said. "Maybe he was involved in infiltration and sabotage."

"Sabotage and assassination are his specialties," Thompson said quietly. "Since I've been digging into Stein's past, I've discovered his resume is a little more extensive in that regard than the administration realizes."

"But is he an Abrogationist?" Milena asked, "Has the Arizonan government been infiltrated, because if it has..." She glanced at the ceiling, and they got her drift. There was a moon in orbit that would make an awfully tempting target for a terrorist within the system.

"No, I don't think so," Thompson said. "Not counting his actual work for the Arizonan government, it's hard to find a pattern for his personal contracts. You've seen it yourself. He has business ties with nearly every organization in the solar system."

"Are we going to operate on the hope that he's just a mercenary then?" Abigail asked. "A well connected one with a dangerous set of skills?"

"For now," Thompson said.

"A few weeks after Gilgamesh," Matthew said, "he shows up in Warszawa and shuts down what appears to have been a long-running scheme to source grav plates. As near as I can tell, it's a complete coincidence that Davey was there to see that."

"One that nearly got him killed," Abigail agreed.

"I'm not a big fan of writing things off to chance," Thompson said. "That's how you miss connections and get nasty surprises that come back to bite you. You sure there's no way that client could be connected to either Stein or Logan?"

Matthew stopped midstride. "Not a chance. I've worked with him before. Even saved him from slavery on Europa. Vicente Luna is as harmless a man as they come. I think the bigger question here isn't how my crew became entangled, but what you're going to do about the implications that your administration was involved in a very illegal carjacking ring."

Thompson sipped his coffee. "I can't do anything until we have Stein. If I so much as breathe a word about the Warszawa ring, I'll either end up in a body bag or, at best, out of a job. If I'm going to mire the administration with a scandal of that size, I'll need proof in hand."

Matthew nodded and went back to pacing. It bothered him that Thompson had seen the pictures that Davey had taken that night. Outside of the crew, Whitaker was the only one that had laid eyes on them. That definitely confirmed a theory that Matthew had been entertaining about who Whitaker's contact in the Arizonan government was.

"The day after the car-jacking ring was shut down," Abigail continued, "Stein puts a bullet through Matthew."

"I have secondary evidence on that," Thompson said, "based on movements of a team under Stein's command and forensics at what was most likely the sniper nest."

"And I can provide corroboration," Milena said, "based on the conversation between Stein and Logan."

"But the problem," Matthew said. "Is that we have no idea who hired him."

"Logan wasn't happy about it," she agreed. She narrowed her eyes at Matthew. "Just what is his relationship to you?"

Matthew opened his mouth to answer, but Abigail beat him to it. "Complicated. Matthew attracts psychopaths that like games. He duped us at Ceres. And we almost didn't recover from it."

He clenched his fists at the memory. "And then goaded us at Gilgamesh, having us pass on the threat to the Kyoto factory to the Martian governments."

Milena actually laughed at that, her fingers worrying the hem of her coat. "Trouble comes to you, doesn't it?"

"You've no idea," Abigail said.

Thompson grunted and turned back to Matthew. Do you know who might have paid Stein to go after you? If so, we can work the other end."

"How long do you have?" Abigail asked. "Matthew's a saint. We've managed to make enemies of crime syndicates, slave cartels, even a few governments. The shorter list is who doesn't want him dead."

Matthew gave her a brief look, but then slumped his shoulders. "No leads. No suspicions."

272

"Helpful," Thompson said, "as always. And finally, we have Ms. Drugova's testimony on the conversation between Stein and Logan. Not only does it tie several of these events together, but it also brings up one last disturbing detail."

"He knew I was watching," Milena said, gripping the arms of her chair. "Further he wanted me to know that he knew I was watching, and he wanted me to positively identify him."

The room went silent, save for the sound of Matthew's footfalls across the creaking floor. This really was the crux of the matter. The game that Logan was playing. He frowned. Or maybe this time it wasn't a game. "I think that was the whole point of the conversation," he said slowly.

"That's the conclusion I've drawn as well," Milena agreed.

Thompson tried to take a sip of coffee but frowned at the empty cup. He set it aside. "Explain."

"The only thing he really said to Stein was a warning to watch his back, that it would be dangerous for him if it were known that Logan was one of his clients."

"I see," Abigail said. "And then he turns to the camera and more or less gives you a wink."

The light from the window began to dim as twilight set in. Abigail gave a yawn, and though Matthew agreed with the sentiment, he had the self-control to resist its infectious influence. "Milena, I'll take you up on that caffeine offer now, if you don't mind."

"And I'll have a second," Thompson said. Milena disappeared into the side room she'd emerged from, what she had called her nest. Abigail followed her, though she remained hovering outside the door.

Matthew just continued to pace, though he stopped when Thompson caught his eye. But then the lawman looked away. Well, if he wouldn't bite, Matthew would. "Why not just arrest him yourself? We both know I'm not on your list of favorite citizens to work with."

"Because there are some things I have to do by the book. To arrest Stein, I'd have to get a warrant issued. He'd get wind of it and bolt, never to be seen in Arizona again. He's got ties to an Abrogationist, one that's already dropped hints about the connection being blown. He's going to be skittish." Thompson made eye contact again. "I may not like you, Cole, but I do trust you. I'd be a fool not to at this point. I'll help you capture the man that tried to kill you, and then I'll issue a warrant for his arrest. You get to be the hero. You and your guild prosper, and

I get a star witness to figure out what's going on in the Office of Colonial Intelligence and the Defense Department."

Matthew held his gaze. "Is the man that once helped prop up a gang of outlaws in the name of a supposed greater good really going to clean house in his boss's administration?"

"I'm not going to try to justify my decisions. Not to you. But I think it's appropriate to keep in mind a matter of scale. Allowing a small-time outlaw to fill up space so White Void didn't move in is a different matter entirely than widespread government corruption facilitating the construction of a weapon of mass destruction threatening an entire planet."

Milena reentered the room with a pair of mugs in hand. "Am I interrupting something entertaining?"

"Not in the slightest," Matthew said, accepting the coffee. "Thanks."

Abigail resumed her place by the window. "Let's cut to what we're all thinking," she said. "Logan wants us to do him a favor and take Stein out."

Milena nodded. "That's the conclusion that I've drawn as well. He owes Stein money for his part at Gilgamesh. He can't pay because you guys foiled the theft of those grav plates. He tips his hand to me, knowing I'm in the guild and will report back to Matthew that Stein was the attempted Assassin."

"That's all well and good," Matthew said. "But then why not leak the information that doesn't implicate himself as the source."

Thompson drained the last of his coffee, apparently needing the caffeine more than even Matthew did. "Because Logan is a damned lunatic. He'll have us second-guessing our own motives and which hand is which if we let him. I want Stein, and when I get him, I'll break every bone in his body one at a time if it gets me Logan and anyone in the administration that has even a whiff of what they've been up to."

Matthew cleared his throat. "The Guild of Lanterns doesn't condone torture."

"Neither does the Colony of Arizona," Thompson said, "but if it saves lives..." He shrugged. "So how do we do this? Freelancers are supposed to be good at planning impossible missions. I'm just a bureaucrat along for the ride, waiting for prisoner transfer."

The window was dark. They had been here for over an hour, and there was no indication that they were even close to finished. Matthew's eye trailed over the other three in the room. Abigail gave a curt nod. "I

274

might have a few ideas," he said with a tired smile. "And you might just be issuing that warrant after all."

Damon Stein knew from a young age that something was very wrong with him. His first clue was when he watched a beloved family pet get run over, and he only felt a passing curiosity in the event. Oh, he faked being affected, because otherwise his parents might have been concerned. His suspicions were proven true as a teenager when a bully from school followed him home one afternoon. After enduring a heaping of mockery, Damon killed him without a second thought and disposed of the body. He even attended the funeral, feigning sadness that an acquaintance had met a tragic end.

It's not that he particularly enjoyed causing pain or suffering. He was rather indifferent to it either way. Life was full of pain, no matter how hard you tried to avoid it. But getting away with causing it and never being discovered, that was one of life's real joys. His other discovery was that most people were imbeciles, making it easy to evade detection. A good actor can fool anyone, friends, family, and even enemies.

He attended the University of Ganymede and easily earned a degree in criminal justice, before spending a brief stint in Arizona's military and finally diverting into intelligence work. And there he found his true calling. For ten years, he got away with countless atrocities in the name of his home colony, though he went above and beyond his job description. Bombings, kidnappings, assassinations. Damon Stein could do anything for any client.

It was that overconfidence, as he now grudgingly recognized it, that led him to the Gilgamesh job. The Abrogationists were the worst of the worst, at least in the eyes of the colonials. Chasing the slow death of civilization itself was an unpardonable sin that made Damon look like a saint. Working for them would damn his soul. So he wholeheartedly threw himself into it for the challenge.

And somehow or another, that was what made it all go to pieces. He was more than aware that he had a stalker watching his every move. He'd disabled more than one camera and knew that that was only the tip of the iceberg. Whoever it was, kept well out of sight. No one in the Arizona government was that good, and his own contacts spread throughout the administration would have heard about it by now anyway. Someone of equal skill was on his trail. He just had to endure another month. Logan had one more job. The big one. The Phobos platform. After that, Damon would disappear a fabulously rich man, at least until the itch to create havoc struck him again.

And then Logan had demanded a meeting, having little to say. Damon knew good and well what that meant, that Logan had no intent to pay what he already owed and was scuttling the Phobos operation. The meeting had linked their association to whoever was watching Damon, and it was only a matter of time before the cards came crashing down. He'd spent the days since then cleaning house, preparing to burn every bridge, destroying all evidence of his storied career. He'd disappear into the night like a wraith.

And all of this made his life more exciting than it had been in years. For the first time, there was a new thrill. Fear. Fear that just this once, he had overstepped, made a mistake, or made enemies that were smarter than he was. That was part of why he waited to make his move, savoring the tension. He could walk into the sunset with zero risk, or he could play the game a little longer relishing in the excitement, and maybe, just maybe, squeeze payment out of Logan before he killed him.

The final round came on one of the rare afternoons that Damon spent in the Office of Colonial Intelligence's main building on the backside of the capital complex. Paperwork was the bane of any government employee's existence. Over the years, he'd perfected the ability to get it done from anywhere but the home office, but sometimes even his skills couldn't overcome the monolith that was the bureaucracy.

He was elbows deep in said duty in his third level basement office when the message crossed his screen.

Warrant issued for arrest of Damon Stein. Thompson himself wrote the affidavit. Twenty minutes tops.

Damon sat back and rubbed his short goatee. Perhaps his stalker had ties to the government after all. He closed his work in a flash, then fired up a program that would wipe the drives clean. If they were issuing a warrant, they had everything they needed to put him away, but there was no sense in doing their job for them. He unlocked a drawer and pulled out a special holster designed for two pistols. He automatically checked both to make sure they were loaded and one of them to ensure its power cell retained its charge. Clipping it around his waist under his suit jacket, he checked the time. Nearly four in the afternoon. Perfect.

He stepped out into the hall and calmly walked toward the elevator, then changed his mind and moved toward the stairs.

"Agent Stein," a familiar voice said as he passed an open office. He paused only because ignoring Max would be more suspicious. Max joined him in the hall, straightening his tie. "I wanted to talk to you."

"Make it fast," Damon said, motioning toward the staircase with his head. "I'm on my way out."

Max fell into step beside him. "Funny thing about that. A little birdie from the Ministry of Law just sent me a tip. It was about you."

Damon fell into comfortable patterns of faking surprise. "Really? I haven't done any work with them in ages. What's this about?" They hit the stairs.

Max followed him up the staircase. "Didn't say. Not sure he knew. Look, Damon. Let's go check with the director. He can probably head this off and get it sorted out before it turns into a scandal."

They hit the flight between floors. Damon stopped and turned to face Max. "I appreciate the offer, but I'll have to take care of this one myself." In a single motion, he drew the earthtech magnetic pistol from his holster and put a silent slug between Max's eyes. He was dead before he hit the floor. Damon stepped over him and continued up the stairs. With any luck, it would be some time before the body was found.

A few minutes later, he stepped out into the ruddy afternoon sun. There was a chill wind in the air as he walked down the sidewalk going over his limited options. He needed to get out of the downtown area before the entire capital complex was breathing down his neck. From there he could chart a course forward. The one thing he couldn't do was look like he was fleeing. No doubt, the stalker had the OIC under surveillance. The moment he deviated from course, he'd lose the element of surprise. On the average office day, he would walk to the parking deck and leave from there. Most likely, his current vehicle was being tracked, so that wouldn't get him very far. He made an abrupt turn and jogged up the stairs to the train station at the last possible second. The timing had to be perfect on this. If Max had delayed him for too long, this wasn't going to work.

An attendant tried to stop him at the turnstile. "I'm sorry, sir, the four

PM is about to pull out."

He waved his OIC badge and walked right past the dumbfounded employee. The boarding platform was already empty, but he picked up his pace and slipped into the only car with open doors just as it closed.

The car was empty. He narrowed his eyes, half expecting some enemy to leap out of a nonexistent hiding place. In attempting to elude one trap, he'd walked into the real one. He grabbed his comm and called the squad leader of his most trusted team.

"We're burning bridges," he said. "I need a pickup. I'm on the four PM westbound. Expect hostiles."

"Understood. We'll be airborne as soon as we can."

Damon's eyes switched back and forth between the front and back doors of the train. Odds were good his enemies weren't just planning on picking him up at the next stop. The question was from which direction would they advance on him. And who would it be. Thompson may have issued the warrant, but Damon doubted that desk jockey was creative enough to pull off a setup like this. Not only had the warrant been issued, it had been issued knowing it would be leaked, and that he would try to slip onto this exact train. The timing had been perfect.

The rear door of the train burst open, and the Shield Maiden waltzed in, a smug grin plastered across her face. "Looky here," she said. "I've just caught Arizona's own little madman."

So it was the freelancers. Cole evading his prescribed death had been a nuisance, but his crew's reputation was well earned. Damon drew his gun and fired at the same time Sharon brandished her shield to harmlessly absorb the shot. "Is that all you've got?" she said, advancing steadily across the train.

It wasn't, but he turned and ran, hitting the emergency release on the car's front exit and barreling through it. Outside, the city was a blur as the train raced down the elevated downtown tracks. Too fast, he noticed distantly. The train wasn't sticking to schedule but leaving the city in a hurry, most likely to remove a potential danger to the citizenry. He stepped across the narrow gap between cars and slipped into the next one.

It was half full of people, men and women staring out windows or on electronic devices. They looked at him with curiosity for a few moments but then went back to their previous diversions. No doubt, many, if not all of them, were undercover officers, ready to spring the trap when the

Shield Maiden showed up to catch him in a pincer. There were still a few seconds to even the odds. He reached into his coat pocket and pulled out a silver disc. It began to hum when he activated it, steadily increasing in pitch.

"Come on," he muttered under his breath. "Finish charging."

The door behind him slammed open as Sharon advanced with almost as much force as the train itself. He leaped aside and threw the disc at her. It magnetized, and with a clink, fixed itself to her chest, delivering an EMP. Even as she crashed to the aisle, he drew his pistol and turned on the rest of the train cabin.

Every other soul had drawn on him except one. A man in a cowboy hat stood and lifted its brim. "Trying to kill me is one thing, but attacking poor Abigail like that is unforgivable." It was Cole. He'd lost the recognizable hat and poncho for Arizona styles, making him surprisingly hard to spot in the crowd, but it was undoubtedly the gaucho. "If I were you, I'd lower that weapon. You're good at what you do. But not good enough to take out a whole car of officers."

He was right. Opening fire would just get him killed. And there was always a way out. Sometimes it just required patience. He dropped his gun and raised his hands, willing to stall until his men arrived. "Well played, Cole. I see you've recovered from your injuries."

"I appreciate the concern," he said as he stooped for the fallen weapon. Then he took the earthtech pistol and began to pat him down. "Your sincerity is suspect, but it's a start."

"We both know it wasn't personal," Damon said as two officers wrestled his hands behind his back to cuff them.

Behind him, the Shield Maiden cursed. "None of that 'it's just business' nonsense. You're nothing more than a psychopath who gets his kicks out of chaos. Matthew, a little help here?"

Damon rolled his eyes but admired her savvy observation. Outside, the tall buildings had given way to suburbs. It wouldn't be long now.

His comm buzzed from an incoming call. In fact, his escape was already here.

He squeezed his eyes shut as the exterior windows of the train blew inward. There was a deafening series of blasts and, even through closed lids, the flash from the stun grenades burned after images into his retinas. He opened his eyes to a chaotic scene, one that seemed frozen in time. He could still see, which was better than the rest of the occupants, but no one would be hearing anything for quite some time. He stamped his right heel hard into the floor, extending the hidden blade in the sole. The officers behind him never had time to recover before he delivered a swift kick to each of their abdomens. They stumbled back, hands fumbling for the unexpected stab wounds.

A pair of men in harnesses slipped through the window, each taking one of Damon's arms before they were all yanked out of the car. He felt glass from the window frame cut through his coat and down his back, but that was a small price to pay for an exceedingly narrow escape. As they were hoisted into the air, his eyes fell down at the receding train. It was a well-crafted trap, and Damon was willing to admit that he had gotten lucky in the timing of his team's arrival. The freelancers' presence meant the pesky shadow that had been watching him was most likely the Rossiyan freelancer Milena Drugova. She was both the top of her skill set and part of Cole's little club. Idly, he wondered if she knew that it was her witch of a broker that had hired him to kill Cole.

And then his boots were hitting the ramp of the skyhopper. He straightened his back as his men set him down. He gave them each a nod and headed for the cockpit. "Get us out of here," he told the pilot. "Fallback point alpha."

Slowly his heart rate began to recede. The escape had delivered more excitement than he had hoped. His career may be entering a new stage, but there were new thrills to earn. Perhaps getting away with killing in the open would be more entertaining than killing from the shadows. Still, there were loose ends to tie up before he moved on from Mars. Between dealing with the freelancers, Thompson, and Logan, he was going to be very busy disposing of potential threats.

Abigail had to swallow her pride. Much as she wanted Matthew to chase the officers from the room so she could open up her suit to reset it, it was an unreasonable thing to ask of him. Whatever Stein had thrown at her had shut her off cold, and there was that insane design flaw that required her armor to be open and unoccupied before it would reboot. Unfortunately, there were two seriously wounded men in the car currently receiving first aid for stab wounds, as well as the minor glass injuries on nearly everyone else. There wasn't going to be any clearing the room.

It had been going so well too. They had isolated Stein from any possible aid, and yet he'd magically had a team of commandos show up and whisk him away. He knew that they'd be coming for him. She shifted her neck around, uncomfortable the way she was laying on her side. They'd played a game of trying to outguess a shrewd enemy, and he'd guessed one step ahead, or at the very least figured it out in time to juke their takedown.

Matthew knelt by her. "You okay?" he asked. Blood ran down from his hairline, and her eyes traced the bright red drop.

"Are you honestly going to ask me that when you're the one bleeding?"

He wiped his forehead and looked at the smear of blood on his hand. "Sorry. Glass, I think. I'll be fine. Hopefully, they'll be fine too," he added quietly with a look behind him at the injured.

"Hey," she said. "I have to reboot, but I'm not going to do anything until that device is off of me."

He stepped around to her front. "Do you know where—"

"Front side. About halfway down, I think."

"I've got it," he said, prying the disc off. "Earthtech?"

"Without a doubt" She hit the internal release for her armor and let the back plates separate before starting to wiggle herself out from the strange position. "A lot more subtle than that pulser White Void has."

"And a lot riskier." He offered her a hand, which she accepted gratefully. "You may be able to conceal it on your person, but if you miss your throw, you're gonna have some buyer's remorse."

He brushed the glass off one of the car's hard benches and helped her up into it. "Let's keep it," she said. "It may be reusable."

Matthew pocketed it with a nod. Absently, she noticed that Matthew was between her and Thompson's officers, blocking their view of her. It was a sweet gesture because she felt half-naked in the tank top and athletic shorts. The feeling only got worse when Thompson himself entered the car and headed their way. She refused to make eye contact, even though she could feel his eyes on her, making judgments. Her disability was going to go on her permanent record in Arizona for sure this time.

Her suit chimed as it finished its reboot and Matthew was already reaching down for it. She frowned. "Hey put it in—"

"Follow mode," he finished for her. "I know. You've shown me

281

how." He took her suit by the hand and gently lifted it to its feet. In follow mode, it was like a giant posable doll. It was the only way for someone else to easily move her suit, considering no one else in the colonies had an implant in their neck to control the thing.

Matthew offered her his hand, but she just reached for the suit herself, feeling the heat on her face. Something about Thompson being around made her less keen on accepting Matthew's help.

"I've had an APB issued for Stein," Thompson said, "and we're sending it on to every colony in the solar system. Standing order is to wait on backup. I don't want anyone else getting killed."

Matthew spun on him. "Anyone else? The two he stabbed—"

"Will live. Probably. We've got emergency services meeting us at the next stop." Thompson shook his head. "Stein killed a fellow agent in the stairwell on the way out of the office."

Abigail closed the suit and breathed a quiet sigh of relief as her awareness shifted from her own body to her armor. "So what now?" she asked.

"We're checking with the Department of Defense on radar records to track that skyhopper. That was one of their stealth models, so that may be a tricky affair."

"And if that fails?" Matthew asked.

Thompson crossed his arms. "We'll move on to satellite imaging, but that will take time. We'll get him. Between corruption in the Department of Defense and the Abrogationists, he's too valuable to let get away. And when we find him, I want you two on point."

For their history, he sure was willing to throw critical missions their way. "You know," she said, "we normally get paid for work." Matthew gave her a quick side glance, but she just shrugged. "Just voicing Yvonne's opinion since she can't be here."

"We can settle on that part later if it's appropriate," Matthew assured him.

Thompson nodded and left. He may be tolerating them, but it looked like he wasn't up for unnecessary conversation. She leaned down to look out the window. Hopefully, the next stop was coming soon, for the sake of the injured. "Speaking of Yvonne, have you heard from them? They should be to Ceres by now."

Matthew didn't answer immediately, and she looked at him questioningly. Finally, he sighed. "This morning, she sent word that they'd arrived and were heading into town for business." He paused briefly. "I replied with a follow-up question, but..."

"You haven't heard back."

"It's been nearly six hours."

"Time difference, maybe?"

He shook his head. "They're only an hour off from us right now."

"Hmm," Abigail said, mostly because she didn't have anything better to say. There wasn't much they could do about it either way. They'd find out what was going on when they heard from them. Matthew was going to worry until then, no matter what she said. Still, as the only one around, it was her duty to make him stop. "Hey," she said. "I'm sure it's fine." He gave her a look that said he didn't believe her, but then she didn't think her assurance held much water either. The Sparrow was separated from its two primary guardians. Grace and Davey were alright in a scuffle, and Yvonne was a slick pilot, but it felt wrong knowing they were millions of kilometers away.

"You're right," she said, feeling the lump in her throat. "It's probably not fine."

Chapter 12: Merely Human

The story of human civilization revolves around a single sentence, the most important ever put to paper. This one collection of words added a new idea to our collective consciousness, one that has haunted us ever since.

'So God created man in his own image, in the image of God created he him.'

The idea has changed everything, and we have wrestled with ourselves, our nations, the universe, and perhaps even God himself over this foundational precept. If each and every human bears an image of the divine, then they have intrinsic and inalienable value from which they cannot be divorced. If this is only a mere collection of words, then they hold no power, and the concept of human dignity is but an illusion.

Are not all of our wars, our struggles, our hatreds, and prejudices linked to our resentment of this idea? For how would we be transformed if we could truly believe that we are each an echo, an imperfect reflection of someone beyond our collective ability to fathom?

Davignon Brault
Neurosurgeon, Churchill, Mars
Died 44 AM

Davey knocked on Elizabeth's door, book tucked under his arm.

"Come in," she answered. He stepped into her cabin and held out her book to her. "Finished already?" she asked with a smile.

"Already," he scoffed. "It's been three months. You were right. It wasn't a quick read. Or easy. I had to have a dictionary open half the time."

Elizabeth sat on her bed and folded her hands in her lap. "And what do you say of the epics of the ancient world?"

He rubbed at the back of his head. "I think I'd have to read them a few more times to get everything. Honestly, it took me a long time to even get into the feel of things, but I think I was enjoying it by the end. And I think I understand your comment on the shield of Aeneas now, about how it filled him with hope. We don't have that. Maybe during Moses' time there was confidence, but look where that left us." Another thought crossed his mind as he remembered more of the Aeneid. "Now, it's like Juno is about to open the Gates of War."

Elizabeth smiled sadly. "She may already have. You know, the Greeks named her Hera, and her grandson was Phobos. Phobos is mostly mentioned in the service of his father, the god of war."

"I remember seeing that name mentioned in the Iliad," Davey said. Given the current political situation on Mars, it had been impossible to miss.

She nodded. "Phobos represents the terror of war. The threat his father brings on mankind."

He chewed on that thought. "That's convenient. I wonder if they were thinking about that when they built the platform."

Elizabeth made a humming noise. "I suspect someone along the way may have noticed. So now the god who brings the terror of war stands high above the surface of the red planet. Waiting only for his father, Mars, to give the command. If the Gates of War are not yet open, then they might soon be." She reached out and took the book from him.

"Thank you," he said. "I learned a lot and... I think I liked most of it."

She hugged the book to herself and her eyes teared up. Davey felt a surge of panic. Had he said something wrong? "Are you okay?" he asked, hating the sound of his own voice in that moment.

"I lost my entire collection of books when they burned the farm," she said simply. "Decades of collecting and they're all gone."

His breath hitched in his chest. He knew how much Matthew loved his small library. He couldn't even imagine what it would be like to lose something so valuable. And now he had the smallest inkling about the power that such volumes could contain. They weren't just stories, but ideas and thoughts come to life. The gods of Greece and Rome had never lived, yet they held a power to stir the imagination. Even now a century after the last statues in their honor had been blasted to dust.

Phobos would never again just be a moon to Davey, but a vengeful deity bent on the fear of death.

"I'm sorry," he said. "I never realized..."

Elizabeth was on her feet and drew him into a hug before he could protest. "Don't apologize. Your curiosity saved one of my favorite books."

"Well. I'm glad I borrowed it then. Thanks."

She stepped away, still clutching the volume. "Should we pick another book? I'm afraid you'll have to get a digital copy this time."

"Another book? I mean I hadn't really thought that, but yeah, I guess." He paused. "Sure. So what's the next one?" It wouldn't hurt.

"I was thinking Shakespeare this time. If power-mad men are threatening to open the Gates of War, perhaps we should go with a tale about soul-destroying ambition. How about Macbeth?"

He'd heard of Shakespeare, of course, but not Macbeth. "This one won't take me three months, will it?"

"You'll be able to finish in just a few days. I'll send you a copy."

"I guess I'll get started tonight." He'd never been to school, but apparently homework was still a thing. He got the feeling that Elizabeth would let him bow out but would secretly be disappointed, and he didn't think he could bear that. What was it with the Cole family that made them so hard to let down? And who was he kidding? He'd enjoyed it. "Maybe I'll get a ways in before we get to Ceres tomorrow."

"Read the first act," she suggested, "to get accustomed to the style, and maybe we can talk about it at breakfast. I can answer questions about the history and setting then as well."

"Just so long as there isn't a test at the end," he shrugged and let the door slide shut. When he passed by Grace's open door, he heard a single word.

"Nerd."

He laughed and leaned in to make a rude face at her.

Yvonne started the coffee pot on her way to the hold. Despite Matthew's absence, his rigid way of conducting business on the Sparrow was still observed. When carrying cargo that required refrigeration, always check their temperature first thing in the morning. If something had gone wrong overnight, there might still be a chance to salvage things if you catch it at the earliest possible moment. She stepped off the ladder and crossed the open hold to the single shipping container.

"Of course, if the unit ever broke, I don't know what I would do to fix it," she mumbled as she pulled up the screen. Negative twenty. Still frozen hard as a rock, though she wondered if the buyers would even know if she simply refroze the container. They were carrying ice from Enceladus. The material, though, nothing more than water with a mixture of minerals, was a heavily regulated export. Not because it was rare. The moon was covered with the stuff. But forced rarity created luxury commodities, and the wealthy of the solar system would pay to have their drink chilled with ice from Saturn's moon.

"Morons," she said, turning her attention to her garden. She walked the aisles of plants, hands brushing the leaves. They'd never looked better and having a farmer on board wasn't hurting at all. Yvonne probably should have been offended that Elizabeth had taken over two of her duties, cooking, and gardening, but with her extended lease on the acting-captain gig, she wasn't going to complain. She imagined a life in which she hadn't been a doctor, but the captain of a ship like 'Elwa. Yvonne and Tomas would have wandered the colonies. But then there was no safety in that freedom either. Tomas may have met a fate like Kofi had.

No, there were no assurances in any life, in any stage of history.

She pushed aside the fantasy. She wouldn't trade the life she'd had for another, though like anyone, she would edit a few moments, take back a foolish comment or adjust a poor financial decision to a wiser one. And then, of course, there was one moment in particular. She had thought enough about it to know that in a perfect world, she wouldn't have done what she did. But then she couldn't imagine ever doing anything different.

In the end, she was only one vengeful woman and had been an executioner cheated, and in a thousand lifetimes, she would have made the same decision in every last one of them. She had thought that reaching this conclusion would bring her some level of peace. Instead it brought her an uneasy disquiet.

She hadn't had enough coffee yet to be having these thoughts. With a sigh, she climbed the ladder back up to the main deck just in time to claim a mug at the earliest possible moment after it was ready.

Davey slid into the copilot's chair and looked down at Ceres as they orbited far above. They hadn't been here since, well, the incident.

"It's not the most welcoming sight anymore, is it?" Yvonne asked.

He looked at the stark gray surface broken by the lights of cities and shrugged. "We were bound to come back eventually. It's just a place."

"One with a lot of history."

He nodded in concession and silently granted that she had more here than he did. "Are we still waiting on Benny?"

"Until he tells me where this hunk of ice goes, we're just wasting time."

It was an odd job. Normally when they picked up cargo, the ending destination was already decided, but in this case, the seller was still trying to negotiate a buyer. It felt like a big business risk to Davey, but he supposed the client would know better than he did. Ceres had millions of people, and one of them would probably be stupid enough to buy a cargo container of overpriced ice.

The console pinged an incoming message. "And speak of the devil," he said.

Yvonne leaned forward and pulled the message up on the main display. Davey shifted to get a better look and read silently. By the time he finished, he was frowning. His eyes shifted over to Yvonne. Rather than looking annoyed or angry like he had anticipated, she was thoughtful. "At least he apologized," she said.

He sighed. "I guess it isn't his fault. Still, sending us to Bright Crater..."

The last time Yvonne had been there, she and Abigail got caught at an opera house between two syndicates. And before that, it was the place her husband died. She had every right to be annoyed at going there, and given how on edge she'd been the last few months, Davey was expecting an eruption.

"It's just a place," she said, but he knew that there was a lot she was leaving unsaid. "I'll record a quick confirmation." She pulled up the comm. "Thanks, Benny. We're already in orbit and ready to make the delivery. I appreciate your concern for my feelings. It's sweet, but I assure you that I'm an adult and capable of handling it."

Davey wasn't sure if she was being passive-aggressive or just honest. He supposed if the broker was used to dealing with Matthew, he'd be more than capable of dealing with Yvonne.

"We'll send confirmation once we're done," she continued. "Go ahead and dig up our next job while you're at it. Talk to you soon." With a few taps, she sent the message on its way before pulling up navigation and setting Bright Crater as their destination. "We've got about five minutes until our deorbit window. Do you want to do the honors?"

Davey chewed at his lip. "I guess. I'll take us down, but you have to land us. This will probably be a private hangar instead of an open landing field."

"You'll do just fine," she said.

He stared at the navigation chart for a long minute before grunting, "Sure. Why not?"

Ever since Matthew's injury, Yvonne had been teaching him to fly the Sparrow. It would pay to have someone else with hours behind the helm just in case something happened to her or there was an accident. Grace had gotten a few hours behind the yoke while frame-skipping, but he'd had good practice while the crew was separated. It made sense to learn, but actually doing it always shot his nerves. Partially because of how easy it would be to screw up, especially on a tricky landing, but also because they hadn't told Matthew yet. Yvonne thought he would be pleased. Maybe even proud. Davey wasn't nearly as confident. The Sparrow wasn't replaceable, and it wasn't like teaching someone to drive a grav bike.

Learning to fly had involved a few long and very involved lessons on orbital physics. He was horrified at the outset. "I learned in my fifties," Yvonne said curtly. "You'll be fine." And he had been. In the end, he'd even agreed that there was something beautiful about the delicate ballet of putting an object in perpetual freefall around a source of gravity. The computers handled all the numbers, thank God, or else he would have been totally lost, but he did have to learn the vocabulary and understand the basics of what was happening and why.

That part was actually fun, but he wasn't going to admit it to Yvonne. He didn't need the inevitable gloating.

"Coming up on our window," Yvonne said.

"Right." He took the flight yoke and began to rotate the Sparrow. "Adjusting heading to retrograde." The Sparrow was small enough to only have one set of main engines. That meant whenever you wanted to slow down, you had to use the maneuvering thrusters to spin and face the way you had come from and burn the engines. Somewhat larger ships had forward-facing thrusters built in to solve that problem, and the biggest, like some of the colonial military frigates or Gebre'elwa's super freighter, had a set of forward-facing main engines. Some of them didn't even have a true forward or aft.

Not the case with the Sparrow. They had to ride into a planet or moon's gravity pointed at the stars.

"Thirty seconds to burn," Yvonne said. "It'll be a nice and easy one. No more than twenty percent of throttle. Keep an eye on the charts, and you'll be fine."

Right. Ceres had low gravity, so the orbital speed they had to shed was low. When the clock ticked to zero, he eased the throttle forward, feeling the steady rumble through the deck. The Sparrow began to decelerate, and as they no longer maintained the velocity to stay in orbit, Ceres' gravity drew them down to the surface. While he guided the ship, Yvonne called ahead to secure specific landing instructions. "You lucked out," she said when she pulled up the coordinates to the hangar. "Top entry hangar rather than side entry."

Davey noted that they had ever so slightly drifted off course and made the appropriate adjustments that the computer suggested. By the time they approached Bright Crater, the Sparrow had followed a graceful arc down to the surface and had killed its orbital speed. He pulled the ship out of its retrograde heading and directed it toward the hangar. The rest of the landing went without incident, save for a slightly harder than normal thump when they touched down. He winced, but Yvonne didn't seem concerned. He couldn't figure out how she and Matthew set down a few thousand tons of metal so gently.

"Whoa. When did you start flying?"

Davey groaned as Grace pushed her way into the cockpit. "When you were sitting around on Ganymede."

She crossed her arms and gave him an unenthusiastic look. "I think it should be a rule that if someone new is piloting that a notice be posted. If I'm going to die, I want to know in advance."

He opened his mouth to retort, but Yvonne beat him to it. "Very cute. Go see if Elizabeth wants to help you move the shipment onto the lift. Davey and I will finish and then head out to meet with the contact."

Grace made a parting shot about narrowly escaping fiery death and then disappeared.

He helped Yvonne as best he could with the shutdown sequence. He only half-understood what he was doing, despite knowing the procedure. Spaceships were big, complicated machines with a lot of moving parts and systems to let them do their job. Keeping one flying was way outside his pay grade.

He snuck a glance at Yvonne out of the corner of his eye. She looked fine, but he could see the tension in her forehead. He knew that Bright Crater was on the bottom of her list of places to visit, regardless of her claims. "You okay?" he finally asked.

"Yes. Why wouldn't I be?"

"Oh, I don't know. Maybe the obvious reason."

She sighed and stood up. "I appreciate your concern, but I really am okay."

"Are you?" She tried to leave, but he stopped her with a hand on her arm. "I'm not blind, you know. I know it's been hard. I just..." He struggled for words. "We're a family, sort of, and I know there's nothing I can do, but I wish there was."

She smiled. The genuine sort that Davey didn't think he had seen cross her face in months. She stepped into the hall. "Meet me at the port airlock," she said over her shoulder.

He watched her go and then ran to his room to arm himself. They were on the ground, which meant Matthew expected him to be on top of things. He may not have been able to help Yvonne with whatever she was dealing with, but he could at least keep her safe.

"You weren't kidding," Elizabeth said as she pushed the massive cargo container across the hold using the grav pallet. "This is fun." She'd operated plenty of heavy machinery on the farm, but most of that was mechanized. This one let you handle hefty cargo like it was nothing with just your bare hands.

Grace was all smiles. "Push it another foot toward me. There we go."

Elizabeth let go of the handle and walked over to the garden while they waited on Yvonne and Davey. Always being on the go, yet taking your home with you, was a strange and new feeling for her. In the past, she'd only rarely been out of Arizona, let alone off Mars. Travel held an air of excitement to her, but she suspected it would soon become wearisome. She wondered how Matthew lived with a ship as his home. No open sky or feel of the sun on your skin. She glanced at the meager rows of the garden. And very little soil between your fingers.

She had once provided a refuge for the Sparrow, a second home. A harbor in a universe of turmoil. And now that house was gone forever. She turned over the possibilities for the hundredth time. She could return to Mars, once it was safe, and rebuild, but it would never be the same. The farmhands would resow the fields when the proper season came, but she hardly needed to be there for that. She wasn't getting any younger, and there would come a time when she would only get in the way. Perhaps she already did. And then there was Antioch. Bishop Elias had offered her a permanent home and begged her to stay and teach. It was a tempting offer, but one she wasn't prepared to take yet. It would be like abandoning Albert on Mars.

Behind her, she heard Grace's comm. Elizabeth brushed the dirt from her hands and walked back to the center of the hold. "Ready to go?" she asked.

Grace nodded and pressed the control to lower the lift. "Davey says Yvonne's still dealing with the official side of things, but they're ready to accept the shipment."

Elizabeth wasn't impressed with her first view of Ceres. The hangar was little more than a warehouse with a retractable ceiling. It smelled damp and metallic, and there was a chill in the air. When the lift bottomed out, Grace pushed the refrigerated container out from under the shadow of the Sparrow. "Where are we going with this?" she shouted to Yvonne and Davey who were talking to the buyer. He waved them over.

"Here's your shipment," Yvonne said to a portly man with a suit and a sharply defined widow's peak.

"Excellent!" he said. "I'm sure you don't mind if we verify the authenticity of the ice before you leave."

"Naturally," Yvonne said.

"Very good. Mineral and trace element analysis will take two to three days."

Elizabeth saw the slight shift in Yvonne's posture. She must have been hoping to get out of here sooner. "I see," she said. "Well, the sooner, the better. Davey, Grace, give them a hand with the cargo." She passed a tablet back to the receiver and then turned away.

"Not what you were expecting?" Elizabeth asked.

"I'm used to a few hours wait in a situation like this, not a few days and..." She looked around and then hugged her arms to herself.

Elizabeth knew what Bright Crater meant to her. "In the meantime, what do we do?"

"We wait. I've let Matthew know we've arrived. I'll update on the delay later. They just got to Mars themselves."

"I don't see any harm in a slight delay," she said.

"A day on the ground is a day where we're spending money and not making it," Yvonne countered.

Elizabeth just raised an eyebrow. Matthew was right about her being driven. "Well either way, can we still make that stop by a commercial district? Everything on Enceladus was more expensive than I was willing to pay. Even the soap."

"I'll have to check a map to see exactly where we are, but there are a few areas of the city that would probably be safe enough. I have a list that needs addressing anyway."

"Not without me," Davey said as he and Grace rejoined them.

Yvonne scoffed. "I lived here with Tomas for two years and by myself for one. We'll be fine."

"And Matthew put me in charge of ground security," he said, shaking his head.

"Is Davey pulling rank?" Grace asked. "Because I'm going to enjoy watching him get shot down."

Elizabeth looked back and forth between Yvonne and Davey, wondering if there really was about to be an argument, but the woman sighed and nodded. "Fine. Grace, keep an eye on the Sparrow. We'll

293

be back in a few hours."

"Really?" she said, giving them all a withering glare. "You guys are going to go have fun, and you're going to leave me here."

"It's a supply run. It's not supposed to be fun. And remember, the last time we came to Ceres, you got lost on a weeks long side trip."

Grace kicked at the ground. "Just don't take too long." She turned and shuffled back to the ship, clearly not very enthusiastic about it.

"The day isn't getting any younger," Yvonne said. "Let's get moving."

A half-hour later, they pulled up to a commercial market. It had been a little uncomfortable for the three of them on the back of Davey's bike. His face had turned red when Elizabeth teased him about taking two older women out on the town, but outside of paying for a cab, they didn't have any other options. She watched the passing scenery as they drove through the narrow canyons of Bright Crater. She'd seen pictures of the crowded cities of Ceres before, but seeing it firsthand was a sobering experience. This was the underworld that Davey and Grace had grown up in. That Yvonne had lost her husband in. Mars had so far escaped most of the solar system's misery, but with a single misspoken word from a glib politician, war could change everything.

The market was built into a series of ledges extending up the wall of the canyon. Local boutiques were nested into the face of the stone, and street vendors peddled their colorful wares from carts. Elizabeth purchased a few personal effects as well as a viridian poncho. After visiting a few moons, it was becoming apparent that everywhere was colder than Mars, and it was no wonder Matthew never went without one.

"You done?" Davey asked as she rejoined him where he stood a little ways off.

"I have everything I need, thank you." She frowned and looked around. "Where's Yvonne?"

He gestured with his head toward the edge overlooking the canyon. Yvonne stood with her back to them, hands gripping the rail. Her posture was wrong, stiff and unnatural. "I think this is more your domain," he said.

Elizabeth patted him on the arm and joined the other woman. Neither said a word for several minutes. Elizabeth waited patiently, watching the lights of the traffic pass on the main road forty meters beneath their overlook.

"Like mother, like son," Yvonne finally said.

"You like the poncho," she replied. "It was always cold on Ganymede, and Enceladus and Ceres aren't any better. But no, we're only so much alike."

Yvonne raised an eyebrow but nodded. She turned again to the railing and pointed out the outdoor dining area on the level beneath them. "Thomas and I used to shop here," Yvonne said. She gestured at an outdoor dining area on the level beneath them. "We would always eat at that Italian place. Do you know what he would order every time? Chicken strips." She lowered her voice in a facsimile of a man's. "Why try something new when I know I'll love this?"

Elizabeth laughed softly at that. "When Albert and I first married, I was an adjunct professor at Flagstaff's local college. Most of our meals came hot from a microwave."

Yvonne made a surprised hum in her throat. "You've come a long way."

"I had to once Albert started drinking."

"I'm sorry, I didn't mean—"

"Ancient history," Elizabeth said, making a dismissive gesture. "That was a battle fought, lost, and then won at the last when Albert found his peace."

There was another cool silence between them, one that Elizabeth was reluctant to break. The rush hour traffic had passed, and the noise of the street and the crowds had faded from a bustle to a steady murmur.

"And how did you win your peace?" Yvonne asked, her voice barely above a whisper.

"It wasn't easy. In fact, it nearly cost my soul."

Elizabeth looked to where Davey stood leaned against a light pole a short distance away. He gave her a questioning look. She smiled and mouthed the words 'It's all right' to him. Regardless of how good he was at reading lips, he got the message and relaxed. She looked back at the street below. "After Albert died and Matthew abandoned me for the priesthood, I hated even the idea of God..."

The proximity alarm went off, and Grace turned the volume down on the radio. She reached across to where her tablet sat on the couch beside her and pulled up the security system. She and Yvonne had figured out how to feed quite a few of the Sparrow's systems to a portable device. Either Matthew had no idea how to do that, or he'd never bothered.

Which meant she didn't feel the need to run to the cockpit to see who was outside. She pulled up the camera to see a man in a black cowboy hat standing expectantly at the bottom of the portside ramp. Whitaker.

"What's that creep up to now?" she groaned under her breath. She turned on the outside intercom. May as well ask him. "What are you up to, creep?"

Whitaker laughed. "A warm welcome as always. I'd like to have a discussion with Matthew. If you could tell him I'm here, I would greatly appreciate it."

Hmm. Okay, she was in a pickle. For once, it seemed like Whitaker was working on bad information, bad enough to be off on Matthew's whereabouts by several million kilometers. At least that meant that the ruse of them taking the commercial flight worked. If Whitaker hadn't seen it coming, surely no one else would. She wasn't about to let him in on the secret.

"Taking a nap. Or something," she said dismissively. "You can leave a message."

Whitaker frowned at the camera and took a few steps up the ramp.

"I can electrify that ramp, you know," Grace said, almost regretting warning him because it sure would be fun to do.

He stopped his advance but didn't retreat. "This is important, Grace."

"So tell me, and I'll make sure the relevant parties are informed."

He took a sudden step back. "He's not here?"

Oh, she'd messed up. "That's not—"

"He and Abigail went back to Mars. And here I came bearing proof of his killer's identity. I see that information reached him through other means." He saluted the camera. "Very well. Thank you, Grace you've been of great—"

The crack of a gunshot rang out. Whitaker's hat popped off like the wind had caught it, and he stumbled forward up the ramp. Grace nearly leaped off the couch. Had he just been shot? By who? But no, he was on his feet again. He reached for the hat, but someone in the distance shouted something indistinct, and he froze for a brief second. Then he turned and ran up the ramp.

"Grace! Open up! Now!"

"What's going on?"

"Please!"

She heard the panic in his voice. Someone worse than Whitaker was out there? She made a snap decision and ran to the airlock and mashed the panel to open it. Whitaker stumbled in and barely made it through before she closed it again. Grace got the briefest look outside at a small army of armed men before the bulkhead sealed shut.

She whirled on Whitaker and grabbed him with her bracelet, pinning him to the wall. "What's your game? Talk!"

"Those are Logan's men," he said, struggling against her invisible grip.

She let him go and ran back to the common room to pick up her dropped tablet. "If you do anything I don't like, I'll crush you like a bug," she warned as she adjusted the camera outside. "Umm not only is it Logan's men, but the jerk himself is standing at the front. And he has your hat."

"Let me see that," Whitaker said, coming up behind her.

Logan replaced his own hat with Whitaker's, frowned for a moment as if concentrating, and then shrugged. Whitaker visibly relaxed.

Grace hadn't missed that detail. "Looks like that's where you keep the Helm of Hades. Don't act surprised. We did our research after the hospital stunt."

"Guilty as charged. Thankfully it will take him some time to figure out how to use it." Whitaker said. "In the meantime..."

"Are you going to help me defend the Sparrow?" Grace asked. "Because if not, I'm going to lock you in a storage closet and forget about you."

The villain held out his palms and gave her a smile that looked almost sheepish. "Unarmed as always. I don't provide Matthew or Abigail any reason to consider me a threat to their safety, remember?"

"Matthew's right. You are useless." Of course, he'd never said that, but given the hurt look on Whitaker's face, it was totally worth saying. She grabbed her comm. The sooner Davey got here to give her backup, the better. She frowned when she only got static.

"They have a jammer," Whitaker observed.

"Thanks, I never would have figured that out if you weren't here to hold my hand. Do you really expect me to believe that you showed up literally seconds before these guys?"

"That's exactly what happened. Matthew's bad luck appears to have rubbed off on me."

"Weren't you the cause of that bad luck originally?"

That shut him up. Grace pulled the cameras back up. Logan stood in front of the airlock at the top of the ramp. Idiot. She had a response to that. With a few taps, she brought up the command to electrify the ramp. "Have fun," she said and pushed the button.

Logan didn't so much as twitch. He waved at the camera.

Grace frowned at the screen, wondering how'd avoided the debilitating shock. Honestly, did all of their enemies have to show up when she was on watch? At this point, it was only a matter of time before White Void made an appearance. Grace turned on the intercom. "You can stop waving. I'm not blind. If you want to talk, I'm listening. If you're after this jerk, I'm more than willing to hand him over for a price."

"Good to hear your voice, Ms. Anderson," Logan said. "And I'm sorry, but I have no use for that charlatan, though I won't mind taking him into custody. I'm here to borrow the Sparrow, but I promise to leave its crew unharmed and return it when I'm done."

"No thanks."

He shook his head. "I wasn't making an offer. You see, Cole made the mistake of allowing me on the Sparrow back at Ceres. He should have kept a closer eye on me because it was a simple matter to install a backdoor entrance in the computer." He motioned at the airlock, and to Grace's horror, it opened. "Now it's about thirty of us to the two of you. I'd rather you not put up a fight. I know what those miracles of yours are capable of, but even you won't win at those odds." He motioned to his men, and they charged up the ramp, weapons drawn.

Grace glanced at Whitaker. He wasn't in control for once, and the look on his face said he didn't care for being on the receiving end of a sudden twist. "You're not going to go down without a fight, are you?" he asked. She shook her head, and at that, he sighed. "I was afraid of that."

She shouldn't be here. It was madness, and only more grief could come of it, but Yvonne made a call and tracked down the one person that might be able to answer the question that needed answering. She sat alone in a booth at a diner on the south side of Bright Crater. The old clinic she ran with Tomas was less than two kilometers away. The rough neighborhood they'd lived in was making Davey more nervous by the minute. He and Elizabeth sat a few tables away, out of earshot, but nearby in case they were needed. Yvonne still didn't think she needed protection in a place she had lived, but there was no point arguing with him when he was in duty mode.

The diner itself was unremarkable, the kind that humanity had been building for over three centuries at this point, and served food greasy enough to induce a heart attack in a single visit. The walls were adorned with local memorabilia, most in need of a good dusting. She sipped at the tea she'd felt obligated to order while she waited, heart hammering.

Finally, a waitress approached the table and took off her apron. She was a young woman, probably in her early thirties, with beautiful olive skin. Yvonne had seen her only once before, three years ago. The woman slid into the booth across from her. "Ms. Naude. I gotta admit I never expected to see you again. There's not much we have to be friendly over."

Yvonne folded her hands together and then separated them, anxious. She shouldn't be here. "Ms. Scalone, thank you for agreeing to meet on short notice. I know that..." She trailed off, unsure of where to begin.

"Monica is fine," the other woman said. "And I have to admit, I was curious. You've every reason to hate me."

"And you me," Yvonne said.

"That's not as convincing a case. I'd be lying if I said you didn't make my life easier."

Yvonne hesitated at that. "Will you tell me about him?"

Monica's eyes widened in surprise. "Kevin? Why would you care? Why would anyone care at this point?"

She stared at her hands. "Just... Please."

"He was a terrible boyfriend." Monica shrugged. "That's for sure. We dated on and off again for six years. He always said he loved me, but we both knew he loved his damn job with White Void more. I tried to act like it didn't matter, the things he did, and maybe that says something about me, but when he finally killed your husband, I was done.

299

No more. I cut him off for good that time no matter how many times he came back begging." The woman leveled a stare at Yvonne. "His boss came calling after he died. Gave me a couple thousand dollars that he said Kevin was owed. He said you were the reason." She paused. "I said he probably got what he had coming."

He had got what he deserved. Yvonne knew that. Monica knew that. She looked at the table. "My part was a little more complicated."

Monica sighed and played with the ties of her wadded-up apron. "Was it? It doesn't matter at this point to me. I had feelings for him for years. Convinced myself I'd loved him on more than one occasion. But both of our lives are better for him being gone, and nothing you say, no twisted sense of pity is going to change that."

"So that's it then," Yvonne said. "He was just a monster and nothing more."

"Well..." Monica drawled. "I wouldn't change what happened. Don't get me wrong."

The diner's front door opened, and Monica gestured in that direction. A boy, maybe six years old, weighed down by a backpack that was too large for his tiny frame, ran in. "Mom!" he shouted as he dove into the booth and gave Monica a hug. Yvonne's mouth went dry, but she remained silent, not daring to interrupt.

"School okay?" Monica asked. The boy nodded with a smile that showed all his teeth. "Good. Head on to the back. Mommy's got to finish this conversation first and then you can tell me all about it." That wasn't to the kid's liking. His backpack had fallen to the floor, and he grabbed a strap and dragged it toward the back of the diner. "Pick that up! It's going to be filthy!" He whined but obeyed and disappeared into the back with slumped shoulders. Monica returned her attention to Yvonne. "My mother drops him off after school and my manager lets him stay in the break room till my shift is over. He's good to us."

"I can see that," Yvonne said. She waved her hand in the direction the boy had gone. "Is he..." She couldn't even bring herself to say Kudzu's birth name.

"Yes," came the simple reply. "I had Bryce a year after Kevin and I started dating. And that was the cause of the first of our many breakups."

Yvonne had nothing to say to that. After Tomas had died and she had saved Kudzu's life, she'd briefly met Monica when the woman came before she'd sent him to a hospital. The thought had never in her darkest

300

dreams crossed her mind that he might have been a father. She felt the old bitterness creep in that she and Tomas had never been able to have children. Even a man like Kudzu, or well, Kevin, had been a father.

"And if you have to know," Monica said, "the only reason I kept taking him back was for Bryce. I wouldn't say that Kevin was a good father, but I think he wanted to be. He always made Bryce's birthdays even if we were on the out at the time, even if I forbade him from showing his face. He loved his son, I think, more than he ever did me." She sighed. "Look. Ms. Naude, I don't know why you're here, but I can't help think you're looking for a reason to feel guilty. Don't. He deserved what he got, but if you gotta feel bad about something, Bryce is it. The one noble thought that Kevin ever had was that he wanted to be a good daddy and..." She shrugged and turned her face away. "He never got to do that. Just like everything else, he got in the way of himself. And that's the end of his story." She stood, tucking her apron under her arm. "If you don't mind, I'm going to go spend the rest of my break with Bryce."

Yvonne nodded slowly. "If there's ever anything you need—"

"We don't need your help, Ms. Naude. We've got a good life."

She pursed her lips. "I understand, but if that ever changes, you'll always have an escape so long as I live."

Monica nodded, but Yvonne saw in her eyes that she was only being polite. She turned and left, disappearing into the back of the diner. Yvonne stared after her, unwilling to move. After a minute, a soft hand landed on her shoulder and squeezed it gently.

"Did you find what you were looking for?" Elizabeth asked.

"My question was answered," she said, so softly that she could barely hear her own words. What that meant was a mystery she had not yet even begun to contemplate.

"I hate to interrupt," Davey said, "but we're going to need to go. "I can't get a hold of Grace."

"She's probably being careless," Yvonne said, but she did stand to her feet. "Let's go home." She felt Elizabeth's eyes on her, but she ignored them and walked through the front door out onto the street. She'd hoped to stop by the old clinic to see what had become of it, but that was going to have to wait for another time. As usual, they were rushing from one crisis to the next, even if this one was a teenage girl who had thoughtlessly left her comm in another room.

"See," Yvonne said as they entered the hangar. "The Sparrow is still sitting there in one piece." She'd felt the worry radiating off Davey as they drove back across town. At least it distracted her from her own troubling thoughts.

He didn't sound convinced. "She still hasn't answered the comm," he said, as he pulled the bike up under the ship.

"Perhaps she decided to take a nap," Elizabeth suggested.

"She's a light sleeper," Davey said, a fact that Yvonne knew to be true. Another trait the kids picked up from their street days. He dug a fob out of his vest and activated the lift. "I swear if she's goofing off—"

"Then we'll take appropriate measures," Yvonne said.

When the lift bottomed out, they pushed the bike onto it and started the ascent into the hold. The conversation fell dead in the air. Davey and Elizabeth still felt awkward around her, but at least they'd had an excuse to ignore each other during the bike ride.

They crossed the plane of the hold, and Yvonne saw several things all at once. They were in the middle of a crowd of people, almost all of them were armed in combat gear, and Grace and Whitaker had been roughed up and handcuffed nearby. Davey drew his gun in a flash, but the subtle mechanical rustle of over a dozen weapons aiming at him caused him to have second thoughts, and he slowly set the revolver down.

Yvonne breathed slowly, trying to come to terms with the scene. If there was a way out of this, it was going to have to wait for a more opportune moment. Her eyes drifted to Grace and Whitaker, and she wondered just what he'd done to bring this onto them. "Are you okay over there, Grace?"

"I've been better," she said, her voice ragged. "I couldn't stop them, but I made them earn it."

"She did that indeed," a voice with a familiar British accent said, "a fact with which I'm rather annoyed." Alexander Logan stepped into view from behind a shipping container that hadn't been there this morning. "She killed three of my men and severely wounded six more. I'm sorry that they were rough with her, but she left me little choice."

"That's a pity," Davey said. "I would have killed a few more if you weren't such a coward to attack when only a teenage girl was left on watch."

"It's almost as if that was deliberate," he said, almost playful. "Let some useful information fall into the right hands, insinuate that the Sparrow was being tracked, and Cole and the Shield Maiden rush back to Mars." He stepped forward to retrieve Davey's gun. "You being absent was a bonus, though I very much doubt you would have affected the outcome." He stopped in front of Elizabeth. "New recruit?"

"Old recruit to be precise," Elizabeth said. Yvonne felt herself smiling in spite of the situation and not just for Elizabeth's cheeky response. Despite Logan's masterful job at maneuvering them, again, his intel wasn't perfect if he hadn't been expecting Elizabeth's presence. They had beat him at Ceres. They could beat him again.

"What's one more prisoner? Lock them up."

Yvonne struggled as men grappled her from behind. "What's this about?" she asked as they were stripped of any useful equipment.

"As I already told Grace, I need the Sparrow. You will be kept in confinement for now and released in a few days when my need has passed. Well, maybe not the one you call Whitaker. I may dispose of him out the airlock when this is over, and I'll hardly be the only one to celebrate his demise."

Whitaker hadn't said a word through any of this. His cold eyes merely shifted back and forth as the conversation ebbed and flowed. It looked like he had been severely beaten. He was dragged after the rest of them to the foreign shipping container. As Yvonne was forced through the entrance, she realized that it was a furnished prison cell, complete with bunks and a small private bathroom.

"You'll notice I even made an attempt to see to your comfort," Logan said when the last of them stumbled in, and the barred door was shut. "I wasn't expecting the old recruit or the trickster to show up, so I'm afraid you'll be short a bed. Knowing how virtuous this crew is, you'll all volunteer to sleep on the floor."

"Your generosity knows no bounds," Yvonne mocked. "I'll need a first aid kit from my cabin. Second one on the right," she said and turned her back on him. "Grace, let me look at you."

"I'm fine, I promise." Grace tried to lay down on one of the bunks, a difficult task considering her arms were twisted behind her back and cuffed with multiple sets of binders. To Yvonne's surprise, she still had her miracles. Grace saw her staring. "They couldn't get them off, and I wasn't going to volunteer to help. So they had to improvise after they pinned me." Yvonne knelt by her and began to probe at her cuts and bruises. Nothing severe, though several were still slowly oozing blood.

Davey was near frantic. "I'm sorry I wasn't here, sis."

"There wasn't anything you could have done. We were overwhelmed when he let himself in. Logan said something about a backdoor program he installed at Ceres."

"Wonderful," Yvonne said. That would be a fun problem to deal with on a future day.

A few minutes later, to their surprise, the first aid kit was delivered by a messenger. Yvonne set it by Grace, but the teen just shook her head. "He needs it more than me." She inclined her head to the furthest corner of the cell, where Whitaker sat silently with his eyes closed. Even from here, Yvonne could see the severe laceration at his hairline. Logan must have really had it out for him.

"Grace says I need to take a look at you," she said, kneeling by him.

He opened a single eye. "I'll live."

"I believe I'm the only one professionally qualified to make that judgment," she retorted.

He coughed out a single laugh, but his shoulders slumped in acceptance. Besides the cut, and several more like it, he had three broken fingers, a possibly fractured ulna, a sprained ankle, and a dislocated shoulder. She did what she could for him, stopping the bleeding and wrapping the ankle and fingers. For the shoulder, she recruited Davey to help her reset the joint. Whitaker bore it with hardly a grimace and no complaints, despite the extreme pain he was most likely experiencing.

As they finished, they were interrupted by the rumble of the engines.

"It seems we're leaving Ceres," Elizabeth said.

Yvonne shook her head. "Not yet. They'll need me for that. Logan's little program may have given him control of the Sparrow's security, but the frameshift device is on an isolated system. It's a quirk in the design of the Model 42."

Davey tried to pace the cell, but Grace put a stop to that as soon as it started. "There's not enough room."

"Sorry. I just don't know what to do," he said.

"Nothing," Whitaker said, "until we know what Logan's plan is. Then we reevaluate."

Davey didn't seem impressed. "And just what are we going to be able to do from this cell?"

Whitaker stared at him for a moment and then shrugged. "Depending on the stakes, I can have the Sparrow destroyed."

Yvonne's blood boiled. It was enough to have one mad man on board, but how had they gotten so unlucky to have two? "So Logan takes over our computer," she bit out, "and you've smuggled a bomb aboard, is that it?"

"It's nothing so primitive," he said. "And I rather hope that's an end we won't reach. I intend for all of us to walk away from this, minus Logan and his men."

They fell into silence. Outside of wringing more information out of Whitaker, which seemed unlikely at the moment, there wasn't much else to talk about, and if Yvonne had to guess, they were all going to be stuck in close quarters for the foreseeable future.

Sometime later, Logan reappeared outside their cell. "Ms. Naude, if you'll come with me, please."

There were armed men, so she didn't bother to protest. They herded her up the ladder to the main deck. When she reached the common room, she whistled in appreciation. "You weren't kidding about Grace causing you trouble." The room that had been so big a part of her domestic life for the last couple years had been utterly destroyed. Smashed furniture, broken appliances, dented walls, bullet casings and holes everywhere. A few of Logan's men looked to be getting started on cleanup, but it was going to take hours.

"She effectively put a third of my team out of commission," he replied. "And then we couldn't even relieve her of her weapons without irreparably harming her." Yvonne didn't mind at all that he sounded tired and frustrated.

They passed through to the cockpit. Yvonne's eyes flitted across the navigational displays. They were in orbit over Ceres. "No doubt you want me to access the frameshift," she said. "I don't think I will."

"I think you'll see my side of things," Logan said, "I can have a tug here in a couple of days in the worst-case scenario. I'll still get the Sparrow where I need it, and you only lengthen your internment. Or you can unlock the system, and you and yours are treated well and eventually released."

"And what do you need the Sparrow for?"

"I'm not interested in death and body counts. You know that."

"I know that thousands died when the Prodigal detonated at Ceres."

He shrugged and leaned against the doorframe. "And tens of thousands more would have died and a city burned had I not interfered. What I want with the Sparrow is irrelevant to whether or not you unlock the frameshift. I'm going to ask again and I want a straight answer. Will you cooperate, or will I reconsider the respectful treatment of your crew."

She gave him a hard stare. A delay could put enough of a monkey wrench in his plans that they could find a way to escape or foil it. But then a delay he wasn't expecting could be far more devastating than the one he was. She leaned over the side console with the frameshift and unlocked it, making sure her body blocked their sight of the screen.

"Happy?" she asked.

"Overjoyed," he slid into the copilot's seat and nodded at the man in the pilot's. "Let's get out of here. Is the heading set?"

In the split second she'd been in the system, she'd cleared the most recent diagnostic on the system warning screen.

The lattices in the frameshift were still cooked from frame-skipping. She'd been babying them for months, keeping to slower speeds that wouldn't cause a burnout. It was an expensive repair they'd been putting off for a later day. The pilot leaned back and she stepped away as he keyed up the frameshift, setting a speed that would lead them to dropping out in a couple days. It was standard procedure if you didn't want to crawl across the solar system.

Only when they dropped out this time, they'd do catastrophic damage to the entire system.

She smiled grimly to herself as she was escorted back to the hold. Maybe there would be a way to capitalize on the delay, or maybe it would just be a nuisance to their captors. Either way, it gave a few more days for Matthew and Abigail to figure something out. Once they realized the Sparrow had dropped off the grid, it was only a matter of time before they were on Logan's trail again. She just hoped it would be fast enough. But that meant that they would have days of boredom, in a cramped cell, with Whitaker of all people. Days alone with nothing but her thoughts to accuse her.

As she tried to sleep that night, one thought refused to be silenced. Like a tiny flame, it burned into her sanity. Monica had answered her question. The man that killed her husband was a human being.

When she finally did fall asleep, she dreamed of a boy that had lost his father.

Wormwood: Part 3

———— ◀◗▶ ————

I.

Elizabeth Cole knew with certainty that her son was gone when he failed to message her on Christmas Eve. It was his habit to sit down after every mass he gave and write to her. And he never once missed. She waited up long into the night, knowing it was futile. A rational part of her argued that a distraction had arisen or that he had been delayed. Perhaps Hueso Rojo had attacked Villa María on the holiday, hoping to catch them off guard. But then Matthew would still have sent the briefest of messages if it were humanly possible. Perhaps there was still a chance that any moment now, her comm would ping, and he would let her know that he was okay.

But in her heart of hearts, she knew. There would be no happy ending for Villa María, and Matthew would die the senseless death of a martyr.

She kicked the covers off her bed and crawled out, knowing that sleep would not come that night. It was the last straw. The final test had been failed. The God that had taken her husband from her had also taken her son. She pulled on her clothes and stumbled through the dark house and out the back door into the night. A faint spot of light shone in the sky, its journey across the firmament discernible. Like a cold eye, Phobos, stared down on her, uncaring.

She passed her garden and continued toward the fields of grain, only making it halfway before stumbling to her knees. It would be easier if her tormentor didn't exist. But no, she had seen the way Albert was transformed into something new and better. There was no mistaking that. And he had made her promise to try and believe in that same God.

308

She gripped the ground with her hands as sobs wracked her body. And how hard she had tried, for Albert, for Matthew. For her own supposedly eternal soul. But she'd had everything taken from her. Her family, her life. Gone. Gone like so much dust. And now she was utterly alone and bereft.

Like the biblical Job, she looked to the heavens and cursed the day she was born.

II.

Her prayer went unanswered, though whether or not that was merciful she was doubtful. Mars continued its revolutions around its axis as it spun through the universe and no message's from Matthew ever arrived. Christmas passed, cheerless and unwelcome, and it wasn't until the start of the new year that what she already knew was confirmed.

One morning during breakfast, there came a knock at the front. She pulled the belt of her robe tighter around herself and opened the door. On her porch stood a man she had never seen, but knew at once. He looked to be near seventy, with warm mahogany skin, dressed in the robes of the church. His face was cast down and filled with sorrow.

"Bishop Elias," she said, surprised at the poison in her voice, "have you come to tell me how my son died?"

His eyes welled with tears and he nodded. "He died in the service of our Lord and Savior Jesus Christ and in the service of the people of Villa María."

The words rolled off of her, naked truth that she had already seen. "Have you come to deliver his body so that I can bury him beside his father?"

The bishop bowed his head. "In the past, the cartels have negotiated with us on such issues. But they have rebuffed our best efforts."

"My son gave them hell and they take their revenge on him even in death."

"He seems to have done just that."

There was an awkward silence in which Elizabeth counted to twenty. "So why are you here, Bishop?"

He looked her in the eye. "Because Matthew asked me to come if something were to happen to him."

She let a long sigh hiss through her lips before standing wide of the door and gesturing inward. "You know, considering you're the one that shipped him off to the Slaver's Moon, I don't think there's anything you can offer me." It was a harsh rebuke, especially considering he had come all the way from Ganymede to see her, but this man had caused her nothing but grief. She owed him nothing, and he owed her a son.

She led him to the kitchen. "I'll offer you a cup of coffee, and then let you have your sermon. Then you will be free of your duty to Matthew." She started the coffee, having already drained the first carafe. How dare this man come here? She wanted nothing to do with God or His so-called church, ever again. Her trembling hand slipped, and the carafe hit the countertop hard, shattering and slicing her finger.

She cursed softly and stuck the finger to her mouth. And now she was speaking like a sailor in front of a priest, which, for some arcane reason, bothered her. "Sorry," she mumbled.

"What was that?"

She whipped her head around to find the bishop had lingered in the hallway staring at the wall of framed photos. They were arranged chronologically, starting from a picture of Albert and her shortly after they had started dating, up through Matthew's birth and school years. There was a noticeable dearth during the worst of Albert's alcoholism, though there were several at the end of a smiling and happy family shortly before his death. The last was Matthew's graduation from seminary. The photo was her only connection to the event since Ganymede was too far a journey from her responsibilities, and she had little desire to visit the people that had stolen her son.

The old man was crying softly. "I'm... I'm sorry," he said. His face screwed itself into one of anguish, and his hand touched the wall as if to brace himself. For the space of a heartbeat, she felt a pang of remorse for her treatment of the bishop. Perhaps she had misjudged him. At the very least, it was clear that he cared for Matthew deeply, regardless of his role in her son's death.

"I was only saying I had broken the carafe," she lied. "Let me get it cleaned up, and I'll get another started. You can have a seat at the table."

Wordlessly she swept the pieces into the trash, glancing again at her finger. It was just a scratch. She'd have to check the floor thoroughly later. It took her a few minutes to get the fresh pot started and finally take a seat opposite the bishop. She regarded him for a long moment before asking the obvious question. "Why did Matthew send you here?"

"Perhaps," he said slowly, "he thought you would need someone when you heard the news."

She looked away. "I've been grieving since he missed his last message. So if you came to see me cry, you've missed it." Or he would miss it the moment he left her alone. "Go ahead then. Go ahead and tell me how this was God's plan, and if I just believe it'll all make sense and make me a better person."

After a long pause, he cleared his throat. "Do you know, Mrs. Cole, that I've been rather angry with God over this?"

Her eyes snapped back to his, expecting to see them downcast, but they met hers without hesitation. "I didn't know you were allowed to be angry with God."

"Allowed?"

She frowned. "Christians aren't supposed to sin."

"Since when does anger equate to sin?"

She opened her mouth but then closed it again. She was being baited into a theological discussion. This was why Matthew had sent the bishop. Didn't he guess that she was tired of trying? That his death would be the final footstep along the path of rejecting the very thing he had given his life for? Instead, she stood up to pour the coffee. "How do you like it?"

"Black, please."

Well, at least they had one thing in common. She passed him the mug and then resumed her seat, unsure why she didn't bid him a good day and end this charade.

"Do you know the story of Jacob?" he asked.

She raised an eyebrow. "You mean from the Bible?"

He nodded.

"Mostly," she said, "though my familiarity is from a literary perspective of the book of Genesis more than from any understanding of spiritual teaching. Jacob was the trickster, if I'm not mistaken."

For the first time that morning, Bishop Elias cracked the smallest of smiles. "Along with his mother, father-in-law, one of his wives... They were a messy family, and that's an understatement. But Jacob was a complicated man, certainly more than just a trickster."

Elizabeth gestured for him to continue, having no idea where this was going.

"That, of course, is true of all the men and women of the Bible. The narrative tells us more about their faults than their strengths. They were, after all, only human. And do you know how God's people got their name?"

She stared at his hands. To her surprise they showed the calluses of one who knew hard work. Context and a dim memory indicated that it had something to do with Jacob, but she couldn't recall the details.

"Jacob had not seen his brother Esau, whose birthright he had purchased and whose blessing he had taken from their father through guile, for twenty years. He sent messengers ahead to Esau only to find that his brother was approaching with four hundred men. Jacob, reasonably assuming his brother was coming for blood, prepared for the worst. The night before the fateful meeting as he waits in solitude, he is confronted by a man who wrestles with him."

"I remember now," Elizabeth said. "And the suggestion is that it was more than just a man."

"Indeed. Whether it was an Angel, God himself, or as some believe, a yet unrevealed Christ, Jacob wrestles through the night with a divine messenger, and though it seems he overcomes him at daybreak, the man touches his hip and injures it. Afterward, Jacob asks for the man's blessing, and then the man declares that Jacob's name will now be Israel."

"It's a peculiar story," she said. "Coming upon a man and wrestling with him in the night feels like something out of a pagan mythology."

"Jewish and Christian scholars have debated it for ages," the bishop agreed. "But difficult as it is to parse, it is an important passage, for God named his people Israel after the incident. Israel, in Hebrew, means struggle with God. You see, when Jacob met with God that night, he was at the lowest point of his life. He thought that all of his family, his servants, and possessions would soon be slaughtered or stolen in retribution for past actions. All through the night, he wrestled with God, and yet all it took to be defeated was for Jacob's hip to be touched. God, despite having all power and sovereignty, allowed Jacob to struggle against him in the dark. God welcomes the confrontation, as he welcomes our struggles, our accusations, our finest reasoning. They are no threat to him. After all, we have those faculties because we are but a pale image of him."

She turned that over in her mind. "And the hip?"

Bishop Elias smiled softly. "None who contend with God come away unchanged. Jacob walked with a limp for the remainder of his days as evidence of the encounter. And that was only an outward proof of the changed man that Jacob was. Never again did he resort to trickeryhen he met with his brother Esau, it was with humility and open arms." He cleared his throat. "All this is to say that, yes, I am angry with God. I loved Matthew dearly and wish that he had listened to me and left Villa María before the end. But God does not forbid my anger or accusation. And I know that in the end he must by his nature overcome them. I will be humbled before Him."

Elizabeth looked away as her own bitterness threatened to choke her breath. "Were it so easy."

"It never has been. Most turn away, when they find that to contend with God will be a difficult thing. It is easier to choose yourself and your own means, limited as they are, rather than be ultimately overcome. But no one who has ever been overcome by and changed by God is worse for it."

III.

Bishop Elias stayed on Mars for three more days. Each morning he arrived at the Cole family farm, humbly accepted a cup of coffee, and then stood his ground as Elizabeth Cole made her argument against the creator of the universe. Like a prosecutor, she built a case against the goodness of God. In a universe where the good suffer and the evil prosper, how can there be a loving God? It was an ancient complaint, but its potency has never diminished in the eyes of the suffering, nor would it until the ending of time.

Elias made his defense, his arguments also born in antiquity. For the philosophers and theologians that came before him had spent thousands of years on that very accusation. Indeed, those very disciplines existed merely in the hopes that men might begin to answer that question. And yet, even Elias was aware that there was no sure answer, for the human mind, made in like fashion after God's, was subtle in its cleverness. Reason and argument can ever be found to circumvent reason and argument.

They spoke of unmoved movers, holiness and depravity, and will and sovereignty in light of a maximally great being. In some phases of their discussion, Elias merely taught, and Elizabeth listened. In others, she disagreed with great violence, and his words felt clumsy upon his lips. But there was one discussion that he felt landed between the cracks of her armor.

"I sometimes wonder that people focus so much on the evil of the world," he said on the third day.

She frowned in response. "I fail to see how one could ignore it."

"I'm sorry. I didn't state that well. I sometimes wonder why people focus on evil as if it were rare, or a novelty. They ask how there can be a good God when there is also evil. But I think they have the starting point backwards. Because evil is ubiquitous. It is the standard. Life is full of suffering. Rather than asking why there is evil in light of a good God, I wonder if more people should question why there is any good at all if there is not a loving God to invade the darkness of this universe. If not for a God of like character, then where does goodness come from?"

There was a distant look in her eye, like the beginning of an understanding, but time was out, and Elias' flight to Venus came sooner than he liked. He bid Elizabeth Cole a final farewell, doubtful that he would ever see her again in person, and begged her to contact him if she was ever in need. Though he dearly wished they could continue the conversation from afar, he would not do so unless she desired it. As he left the atmosphere of the red planet, he said a final prayer for her in the hopes that she would find peace, one way or another.

IV.

Life continued on the Cole farm despite Elizabeth being the last of that name. With Matthew's death, the bloodline that came with the name was ended, but Elizabeth would endure for a time yet. And the words of the bishop lingered, troubling her soul.

What did it mean to struggle with God in a time so far removed from the Middle East of long ago, where brothers fought over blessings and a herd was the greatest fortune a man could own? Was it shouting at the night until your throat was raw and eyes emptied of their tears? Was it a worm that festered in your heart and made itself at home until it had eaten away all that was rotten? Or was it waiting for a quiet voice in the dawn and a calm assurance that this sunrise would not be the last?

For Elizabeth, it was all of those things in turn, though she failed to mark their passing, and it was only some weeks later, when she lay on her back beneath a broken tractor, frustrated that it had died for the second time that season and her mechanic was out of town, that she came to an understanding that she was going to be okay. There was order to the universe, and that order was good. Despite the chaos that had rocked her life, there were distant lands that remained untouched by her storms, and further still perhaps a green country where even Albert had found his home beyond all that harried their troubled race. And if he and Matthew had found safe harbor, then she must be content.

She wiped her hands and sat up, setting aside her wrench. She had passed from one state to the next, though the final stage of the struggle ended in a gentle whisper. No fire in the sky or thunder of heaven. Just a quiet exhalation that it was over, or rather only beginning. At the very least, she could accept that the God of her husband and son was not a cheat or a liar. Perhaps someday she could even call him good.

She put away her tools and closed up the barn. There was a sandstorm coming, and soon the highlands would be engulfed by the tempest. The late afternoon sun was already shrouded and pale by the outermost bands of dust. There would be no work for many days.

In the morning, she slept in, a rare thing for a farmer, enjoying the deep darkness brought by the storm and gentle creaking of the old house, and when she woke, she had received a message from an unknown comm number.

I'm okay, Mom, but it may be some time before you hear from me again. I've got some things to sort out. Stay safe. I love you.

And she wept for joy. Content, and at peace for the first time in her life.

Chapter 13: Scylla and Charybdis

The public demonstration of the Phobos Platform brought terror across the surface of Mars. It wasn't a single demonstration, but several scattered across the red planet. Derelict ships were set up within sight of colonies, both opposed to and part of the Highland Treaty Organization, and obliterated from orbit.

The HiTO calmly proclaimed again their new era of security. They would protect nearly the entire planet from the low altitude moon. But even within their members there were detractors, and anti-war protests formed overnight. Nonmember colonies struggled in their response. The French colony of Nouveau Lyon immediately agreed to sign the treaty, handing over what little military power they had to the organization.

But there were some who made plans in secret. Churchill, long sympathetic to the plight of Kyoto, signed secret pacts with Rhineland and Españito. If the time and opportunity arose, they would fight for Kyoto and her people.

And so the colonies prepared for their first war, splitting off into factions, even as the twilight of civilization bore down upon them all.

Johann Michaelson Kinn
Author of Rumors of the First War
Died 125 AM

The door to the prison container in the hold of the Sparrow opened bright and early the next morning, and one of the terrorists pushed a handful of military ration packs through with his boot. "Nothing else till tonight," he said and slammed the door shut.

Davey gave it a ten count to let the guard get out of earshot before grumbling. "Wonderful. I needed to lose weight." He stooped to pick up the rations and distributed them to his fellow prisoners, deliberately leaving Whitaker for last. The lowlife sat legs crossed and back against the wall, obviously in pain, but too stubborn to say anything about it. Davey dropped the plastic-wrapped packet at his feet. "Breakfast is here." Whitaker slid the package to his side but didn't so much as look up at him.

"He's still in a bad way," Yvonne said, tearing into her own from her cot.

"He's just grumpy because he's used to getting his own way," Grace said.

"And for someone who was treated so poorly, you're not making it any better," Elizabeth chided her.

Yvonne sighed at the crumbly bar from her pack. "This is only just better than our ration bars."

"But at least they are feeding us," Elizabeth said.

Davey nodded in agreement. Leave it to Elizabeth to be the optimist. He doubted many terrorists bothered to take care of their hostages, and yet Logan had prepared them their own little prison. He still had doubts about whether or not he would actually turn the ship back over to them without a fight, but it beat starving. "So any guesses as to why they need the Sparrow?"

"It's a good ship," Yvonne said, "But hardly anything special in and of itself."

"Unless they want to pretend to be the Sparrow crew," Elizabeth suggested.

"Hmm," Davey said. "That's not actually a bad thought, but the illusion is going to break the second they disembark." He turned to Whitaker. "Anything to add?"

The man shook his head. "I know as little about this as you do." He reached for his meal, wincing as he tried to tear into it with his injured wrist.

Elizabeth was right. He really had been through a beating. "Hold on," Davey said. "I'll get it." He took it from him and opened it. Whitaker nodded in thanks and then went back to his silent brooding. So much for making an inroad there. He sat beside Grace on her bunk and opened up her package as well. Her hands cuffed behind her back made it impossible to feed herself. "How are you doing?"

"Not gonna lie," she said. "My shoulders and arms are killing me, I hardly slept, and if I have to stay like this for multiple days, I'll lose my mind."

"I'm sorry," he said. "If there was anything I could do, I would. You ready to eat?"

Her face fell. He knew how embarrassed she was to be fed by hand. "Let's just get this over with."

After they finished, Davey dumped their trash outside the bars of their cage. Let their captors clean up the mess. Now it was just a matter of figuring out how to waste time until something changed. As it was right now, Davey saw no way out of their current confinement, and even if they could escape the cage, they were stuck on a ship somewhere between the planets with a couple dozen angry Abrogationists. That sounded like a good way to be ushered out the airlock for a quick and painful death.

"Maybe they'll let us borrow our own checkerboard," he said absently.

"Better settle in," Yvonne said. "This is going to be a long trip."

He frowned at her. "Did they say where we were going when you were in the cockpit yesterday?"

"No, but I might just know something they don't. We're going to—"

"Don't say it!" Whitaker snapped. "Whatever it is, just don't." He pressed his good hand to the wall and lifted himself to his feet. "At least not until I've checked for bugs." He began to run his good hand along

318

every seam in the walls, methodically working his way around the room.

If you were going to go to the trouble of preparing a cell like this, it made sense to have a microphone listening to them. They probably didn't have someone listening at all times, but if something happened, they could go back and check the recording. "Is there any way we can help?" Davey asked.

"Unless you have experience sweeping a room for covert electronic devices, then no. When I'm finished, we can talk."

Davey sat back by Grace. She gave him a look like she was thinking something sarcastic, but he just shook his head. There was no use in poking the dragon if you're stuck in the same room with it. A few minutes later, Whitaker gave a small grunt of triumph. "Found it. Built into the post of the bunks." He pulled out a wire and bent it back and forth repeatedly until it broke. "Give me a few to make sure there aren't any others." When he was finally satisfied, he slumped back into his spot. "There's no telling how long it will be until they realize. We may only have a few minutes, or they might not ever discover if they don't think they have a reason to check in on us. Ms. Naude, you may continue, but keep your voice down in case someone approaches the door."

"We're going to have a burnout," she said. "In the next day or two. And when we do, the frameshift lattices will be fried permanently. The whole system will need to be rebuilt, and we'll be dead in space, probably waiting for a tow since it'll take a full-service maintenance bay to replace, and that will gain us at least a couple of days, maybe more."

Whitaker leaned his head back against the wall. "From your frame skipping stunt," he mused. "This changes everything."

"Care to enlighten the rest of us?" Yvonne asked.

"Remember how you accused me of smuggling a bomb aboard?"

She nodded.

"I told you it was nothing so barbaric. My ship, the Imperious Doubt, is autonomously following us, wherever we're headed."

She scowled. "I've never heard of such a system. It sounds pricey."

"Earthtech. It was obscenely expensive, and even then, it's extremely limited." He looked between them. "But if we're dropping out of frameshift and stationary, relatively speaking, it may provide a method of escape for one or more of us."

"Supposing that you really can engineer an extraction," Yvonne said,

319

"someone will need to stay behind, or we lose a valuable inside perspective. I'm not abandoning the Sparrow to Logan."

He shook his head. "As one of the only two pilots present, one of us will have to fly my ship. If an escape ends in a fight, I don't fancy my survival chances, given my injuries. Logan won't hesitate to slaughter me like an animal if given an excuse."

"I can fly," Davey said casually.

Whitaker cocked his head. "So the irascible teenager grows up. How many hours do you have behind the helm? I don't know that I trust my ship to a greenhorn."

Davey shrugged, trying to look unconcerned. Honestly, the last thing he wanted to do was fly an unfamiliar ship. That sounded about as much fun as dodging thumper fire while naked, but he was going to do what he had to either way. "I don't think we have a choice."

"No, I don't suppose we do," Whitaker agreed. "Grace, if your hands were freed, could you break out of this prison?"

"I doubt I could get through the walls," she said, sitting up a little straighter. "I won't know about the door until I try it. But its bars are a different story. Davey, go test them for me."

He crossed to the door and gripped the bars in his hands, giving them a tug. "Feels pretty solid to me."

"I wasn't expecting you to bend the steel yourself, dummy," she said, staring at him. "Are they part of the door? Separate but welded?"

He peered closely. "Light weld job. If I had to guess, they extend down into the door."

"It's possible I can work at the bars and bend them, but that would take time," Grace said.

"Then we may have to stage a breakout when they open the door," Whitaker said. "When we drop out of frameshift, they'll probably come for Yvonne."

"And we still need to, you know, actually get these cuffs off me," Grace said. "If you haven't forgotten that tiny detail."

"Easily surmounted when the time comes," he replied.

"How about now," she said. "They're killing me."

He shook his head. "We can't risk them discovering you're free."

Grace opened her mouth to protest, but Elizabeth laid a hand on her shoulder. "He's right, Grace. I know you're hurting, but—"

"Fine," Grace growled. "I just hope the blood returns to my arms when they're needed."

"So Grace and Davey make an escape attempt," Elizabeth said. "Supposing that's successful, where do they go?"

"The Guild," Davey said without hesitation. "If the Sparrow's dead in the water, maybe we can get backup and meet you at your destination. We'll be able to work that out from navigation on your ship."

Whitaker smiled one of his obnoxious smiles. "And I'm set up to track the Sparrow anyway. If we make a stop and keep moving, you'll be able to follow and update your friends."

"You and Logan both, huh?" Yvonne said, shaking her head.

He held both his palms up, then winced and lowered his injured arm. "You didn't think my ability to find Matthew whenever I wanted was just luck, did you?"

"Unbelievable," Grace muttered.

"And utterly necessary," he retorted, falling back into his smug self for the first time. "And it's a good thing I thought so far ahead, otherwise where would we be?"

Davey rolled his eyes. No wonder this guy got under Matthew's skin.

Matthew tipped his hat to Thompson's secretary, Sheila, as he rounded the corner. Given how little regard he had for Barclay's administration, she was probably his favorite person on the government payroll right now. "Is the minister available?" he asked.

"I wasn't aware that we were asking for permission now," Abigail said.

"He'll appreciate that you are," Sheila said with a wink. "But I'm afraid he's still with the other ministers in the war room for the Phobos demonstration."

Abigail stopped short and frowned. "That was over an hour ago."

"Come now," Matthew said. "I'm sure the testing of a new superweapon has the bureaucracy patting itself on the back." He could imagine Thompson bored out of his mind in a room with politicians and military brass, and he was a little ashamed to admit that he found the image funny. He was trying to get along with the lawman, at least while they were working together, but they weren't exactly on a first-name basis.

"Would you like to wait in his office?" Sheila offered.

"If you don't think it will be too long, and you don't think your boss will be too angry."

"He's always angry," she said, stepping from behind the desk and opening the door for them. "But he and I both know you're not going to do anything untoward, and if he throws a fit, I'll remind him about the importance of keeping appointments."

"I see who's in charge here," Abigail said, giving her a thumbs up.

The office was dark, the lights off and the shades pulled. Matthew flipped the overheads on and raised the blinds. The seventh story window gave a spectacular view of the northern side of the city. Miles away, outside the dome of the colony's environmental shield, a massive column of red dust lingered in the sky from the weapons test. He and Abigail hadn't been in position to see the actual demonstration, but they'd watched the public broadcast in stony silence.

"There's nothing you can do about it," Abigail said. He turned as she pulled back the steel ball of the Newton's Cradle on Thompson's desk. It fell with a clack and the ball on the opposite side lifted in perfect obedience to the law of conservation of momentum.

That was something there was too much of on Mars, Matthew thought sourly. Momentum. Too much that could only lead to one destination. "Stein is our quarry. If we take him down and convince him to betray Logan, then we'll be done with it. At that point, it'll just be a gun pointed at Mars, without someone that actively wants to pull the trigger."

"Who's pulling triggers?" Thompson asked. Matthew turned to see him entering the room. "I should say something about you two in my office, but frankly, that seems like too much to bother with."

"At least we're punctual," Abigail sniped.

"I'm sorry," he said, his tone indicating anything but apology. "You weren't stuck with the Joint Chiefs of Staff caught in a feedback loop of self-congratulation." He tugged at his tie, loosening it, and then laid his suit jacket on the corner of his desk. "You two turn over any stones?"

"We checked, but no one we know has ever even heard of Stein," Matthew said. "I warned you most of our contacts were on the straight and narrow."

"Never hurts to try."

"What about the satellites?"

"I should have the report waiting on me," he said, sitting down and

322

pulling up his monitor. He frowned. "Or not. Let me check on that."

Abigail caught Matthew's eye. He shrugged. They were waiting on Thompson either way at this point, whether they wanted to work with him or not. May as well make the best of it.

"So how's President Barclay taking this?" he asked.

Thompson looked up from his screen as he finished typing out his message. "Threatened to fire me for not involving the Office of Colonial Intelligence or the boys in Defense. Threatened to fire me for a hairbrained operation. Threatened to fire me for failing to apprehend Stein. For insinuating that half the Department of Defense might be crooked. For Stein's involvement with the Phobos Platform. Have I missed anything?"

"Not one to see reason then, is he?"

He shook his head. "Not when the suspect is connected to so many state secrets."

"How's he taking my involvement?"

Thompson chuckled. "You're kidding, right? If he knew I was working with you, my family would be on the street tomorrow. That interview caused a public backlash against Phobos. They've been trying to get a lid on the PR problem for weeks. And I don't have a shred of sympathy for him there. My men are going to be working overtime because of the protests the demonstration will inevitably cause."

Matthew smiled, pleased, that at the least, the populace wasn't thrilled with the HiTO's threats. He also filed away the details that Thompson had a family. Not what he had expected, but then he hadn't ever thought about it either. "Glad I'm a popular man."

"Well, if you ever think about running for office, you'll be a shoo-in. The public eats up anything they can about you." He curled his fist.

"I take it something is wrong?" Abigail asked.

"Intelligence has the satellite imagery but doesn't want to give it to me because the skyhopper left Arizona. It's outside my jurisdiction now." His fingers raced across the keyboard.

"So is that it then?" Matthew asked. "Are we done?"

"Let me rephrase my request to my dear friend over in OIC."

Matthew crossed his arms. "Do I even want to know?"

"Consider it the median point between a threat, a bribe, and calling in a favor. No, you don't want to know." He finished typing and leaned back in his seat. "You hear from your crew yet?"

"Nothing," Abigail said. "Our broker is trying to get security footage from the hangar, but the client is already mad that the Sparrow disappeared before they'd been released."

"I'm sorry to hear that," Thompson said formally.

Matthew closed his eyes and tried to push back the wave of anxiety. They had plenty of enemies on Ceres, and elsewhere for that matter. And the timing couldn't be worse. But his crew was competent, and he could only pray they'd make it through. It was his mother he was losing sleep over.

"Oh," Thompson said. "Lookie here. I've got my satellite imagery." He paused as he clicked through image after image. "The skyhopper went to ground in the industrial sector of Doch Rossiya." He smirked at Abigail. "You know the last time you were there, I had trouble getting you out."

"But can you get us back in?" Abigail asked.

He waved her off. "I'll do better and take you myself in the morning."

Abigail opened the door. "I'll go call Milena to see if she's still in on the hunt."

Matthew crossed his arms and turned back to face the other man. "I thought this was outside your jurisdiction. Not worried about President Barclay?"

Thompson stood and fixed his tie and grabbed his coat. "You're looking at the only person in the administration that I trust right now. And much as I hate to admit it, you're the only outsider I trust with the skill set to take Stein down. I may just hang for it, but Stein's going to beat me to the gallows if it's my last case as Minister of Law."

Matthew nodded and then, on impulse, offered his hand. "We'll get him, and hopefully Logan too."

Thompson raised an eyebrow and sighed before taking the hand. "Either I'm getting idealistic in my old age, or you're rubbing off on me."

"I don't recommend you make a habit of that. People try to kill me pretty much every other Tuesday."

"I'll keep that in mind. Pack your bags and brush up on your Russian. We'll be on the first train out in the morning."

Nearly a full day after they made their plans, Grace felt the brief moment of disorientation that signaled they had dropped out of frameshift. If Yvonne was right, there was a piece of smoldering equipment in forward engineering, and they had no time to lose.

"It's time," Davey said. "Free my sister."

Whitaker moved from his position on the ground to sit by Grace. "Now about that magic trick," he said with a grin, as he peeled back the skin on his right forearm to reveal a smooth metal surface.

Davey's mouth dropped open. "Has that always been fake?"

"I wasn't born with it if that's what you're asking."

"Very funny. More earthtech?"

"Top of the line. And part of the reason I stay out of fights. I'd rather not lose the other one. First time it hurt like the devil." He opened a compartment in the arm and pulled out a small laser cutter.

Grace turned her back to him to let him get to work. She almost told him to watch what he was doing, but she really didn't want him distracted when he had a laser pointed at her. Adding laser burns to arms that hadn't gotten blood in two days wouldn't make their escape any easier.

Yvonne and Elizabeth shifted to block the view from the door. "You seem to have a steady supply of earthtech," Elizabeth said.

"It's all in who you know," he said. "Give me one more moment. Got it."

Grace pulled her hands to the front and nearly cried in pain as she moved them freely for the first time in two days. "Thanks," she mumbled. "Let me see the door." She pushed past the women. She raised her left hand, ignoring the sharp stabs in her muscles, and grabbed one of the bars with her bracelets to give it an exploratory pull. It didn't budge, but the door itself shifted. "No chance. Solid welds and I'll make a lot of noise if I even try. What about your laser?"

"The battery won't last long enough to get through that much steel," Whitaker said. "If you can't break out, we'll have to wait until they come for us. It won't be long." Grace shuffled to the rear of the prison and put her arms behind her back to conceal her freedom. Whitaker dug a metal cylinder out of the cavity in his arm and passed it to Davey. "Here's my beacon. When you're clear of the Sparrow, my ship will pick you up."

A gruff voice came from beyond their cell. "On your feet."

Grace could just see the pair of guards outside. "Is there a problem?"

Yvonne asked as she turned and folded her arms.

"Mr. Logan wants to have a word with you, Ms. Naude. Everyone else, step away from the door, please." He gestured his rifle to emphasize the point. Grace readied herself as Elizabeth crossed to sit beside her and gave her a wink. She took a deep breath.

The door swung open. Grace grabbed one of the guards and threw him with bone-shattering force into his comrade. Davey was out the door like a shot and fumbling for their weapons mere seconds later. Grace bounded after him, and despite all of her best instincts screaming that it was a terrible idea, she shut the door. Much as she wanted to fight and retake the Sparrow, there were too many enemies to risk it, especially with nonfighters like Elizabeth and Yvonne. Someone had to escape to get help.

Grace saw three more terrorists dive for cover the second she appeared. She couldn't resist the smug smile that crept across her face. They'd respect her now. The only problem was that they'd have backup swarming down that ladder before they knew what was happening. And then Grace would be overwhelmed again with more targets than she could swat away.

"Grace, move!" Davey was already backing towards the lockers that held their pressure suits, keeping Grace in between him and the hiding terrorists.

She backed toward him, eyes searching for anyone getting a brave or stupid idea. So far, they were all keeping their heads down. She risked a quick glance at Davey. He already had their suits out and was prepping his. "Make it fast," she said.

"What do you think I'm doing?" He shoved his legs into the suit. "Taking a leisurely stroll?"

"They're coming down the ladder, so any faster would make our odds of not dying go up." She grimaced at the stream of men coming from the main deck. This was going to take too long. "Please tell me you're almost done."

"Close enough," he said, latching on his helmet.

"Then give me cover," she said and started working on her own suit.

Davey hefted his scavenged rifle. "Keep your distance!" he shouted. "My sister made a mess of you last time, and I'd hate to punch the rest of you full of holes."

"There's nowhere to go," a voice said from the ladder well. As she pulled the suit over her waist, Grace glanced over her shoulder to see Logan duck behind cover. Of course, if he was dumb enough to expose himself, she'd take a few extra risks to rid the universe of that slime. Unfortunately for the rest of the human race, he had more brains than that. "Even if you make it out of the ship," he said, "as the pressure suits clearly imply, there's nothing within millions of kilometers. This is your last chance to avoid certain death."

"Or you could just surrender to us," Davey suggested.

"Is that honestly the best taunt you've got? You've been listening to too many radio dramas."

"I think they're underrated. Maybe give them a chance."

Grace clipped her helmet on. She nodded at Davey, and in unison they hit a switch on their suits. Air rushed from the compressed canister as they pressurized. "Thanks for letting us stall, you thruster nozzle." She reached out with her bracelet and hit the panel for the main lift some distance from her. There was a mechanical groan as it started to lower, and the environmental shield snapped into place. "How long does the lift take to bottom out?" she whispered to Davey.

"About thirty seconds."

"We don't have that long."

"Take them now!" someone shouted. "Before they escape."

Grace grabbed Davey by the hand, and they ran, closing the four-meter gap and diving through the shield just as bullets began to shatter around the invisible barrier provided by her bracelet. Grace looked up as faces appeared overhead. She wrapped her arms around Davey and molten fragments splattered from blocked gunfire. Any second now, the air would be ripped from around them, so their attackers wouldn't risk coming through the shield. But Grace couldn't help but hear Matthew's warning that her bracelets couldn't protect her indefinitely.

Were they almost at the bottom?

The sound of the gunfire nearly disappeared as the lift cracked into open space. There was a faint rumble still transmitting through the metal of the ship, the lift, and up into their boots, but it was a lot less terrifying than the deafening barrage it had been. The crack widened until it was big enough to squeeze through. Davey yanked her hand, and together they slipped out of the Sparrow.

They were free. Her magnetized boots stuck to the hull and she let her body hang slack in the zero gee. "Test. Do I have you?" Grace said into the suit-to-suit comm.

"We're live. Hurry. They may suit up and try to follow. And if they borrow one of our suits, they'll be on the same frequency." Davey reached a tether from his suit and clipped it to Grace's.

Ready?"

"On three. One. Two. Three."

Hand in hand, they demagnetized their boots and pushed off the hull, aiming for the black of space. Grace gritted her teeth as she watched the Sparrow start to recede. She'd feel better if they'd had time to grab their thruster packs to put some distance between them and the ship. Their warm bodies would show up on the scope for several minutes, and there was a small window where they could be chased down. Being separated from the ship without any means to return to it also brought a shiver of fear. It was a worst nightmare scenario for any spacewalk, and they'd just done it deliberately.

But the Sparrow sat silent and unmoving as it slowly receded. The only sound was her own breath and occasionally Davey's when the comm picked it up. "Pretty wild, huh?" she said, mostly to hear her own voice.

"If Whitaker was lying about his ship, this is going to be a bad way to die."

"I trust him. He had nothing to gain by sending us off to suffocate."

Davey grunted. Here between the planets, there was no rescue. No way anyone would find the two lost siblings if she was wrong. A needle in a haystack didn't even begin to describe the scale of how small they were in the universe.

"Hey, look at that," Grace said. The Sparrow's main engines lit up and it accelerated away until it was just a pinprick of light amongst the stars. "I guess Logan thinks he just executed us."

"Whitaker said his ship would keep its distance until he gave the signal at our escape. It should be on approach now."

"Just how many controls were on that little beacon?"

"I didn't get a good look. But we'll have time to poke at it later." Grace saw him smile through the faceplate. "And we'll be able to explore his ship. He's probably hiding all sorts of secrets."

"It's probably booby-trapped."

"You'd think he'd warn us if that was the case."

Twenty minutes later, the lights of a ship approached them. They had seen it once before after the adventure with the Mosaic frigate when Whitaker picked up the rescued salvage team. Of course, Grace hadn't had any need to pay attention back then, and now she had a few more years of experience in appraising ships. The Imperious Doubt was easily larger than the Sparrow and more heavily armed. It would probably qualify as a Patrol Craft rather than a Utility Vessel, like the Sparrow. And like everything else that Whitaker owned, it was very modern and high tech.

"You know," Davey said. "I have no idea how we're going to get in safely without a thruster pack."

"Let's just see what happens."

The Doubt slowed its approach and turned its port side to face them, steam thrusters firing to make fine course adjustments. It lined up and crept ever closer. When the airlock opened right in front of them, Grace was hardly surprised, but she was impressed. The precision required for the computer to pluck them out of space like this was unreal.

And then she realized they were about to have a rough landing. "Uh... Davey."

"Yeah I see it," he said. "And I'm not happy about it."

The airlock engulfed them and gravity hit, dropping them upside down to the floor. Grace lay on her back, head spinning and arms no longer hurting, but now starting to feel like overcooked noodles.

"Come on, sis," Davey said. "We've got to find the cockpit and get out of here. If the Sparrow sees us and comes back to investigate, I'd rather not get blown up."

"Or worse, let Whitaker's ship blow up the Sparrow. I have a feeling it might defend itself." That's all it took for Davey to jump to his feet and frantically bang the airlock controls to let them into the main part of the ship. He disappeared as soon as it opened. She sighed and tossed her helmet aside and followed after him. As usual, they were in way over their head.

The three remaining prisoners were dragged out of the cage, rather roughly this time, and thrown to the floor of the hold. Elizabeth winced as she hit the ground and cradled her knee. She bit her tongue to keep from making a sound. Avoid attention. So far, the terrorists were almost entirely ignoring her. It was probably best if they never realized that Matthew Cole's mother was in their power. Whitaker was drawing most of their ire, and they recognized Yvonne as in charge when Matthew wasn't around. Rather than being his mother, she was just a nameless old woman.

And that gave her power. They didn't know that she was an excellent shot and had no qualms about fighting for those she cared about. If the opportunity arose, she would be the last person they considered a threat, a mistake that might prove deadly.

Yvonne wasn't worried about any such anonymity. "Is this really necessary for two old women and a washed-up con artist?"

"Where are they?" Logan asked, his voice cold and soft. "I know they aren't stupid enough to throw their lives away like that."

"We told them not to go," Yvonne said. "Why do you think we remained behind? And if you wanted them back, why did you sentence them to their death by burning the engines?"

He shook his head. "You care too much for them. If they were dead, you would be grieving. Not playing coy."

Whitaker made a show of picking himself up into a sitting position. A quick glance was all Elizabeth needed to see that his shoulder had been dislocated again in the fall. She wasn't looking forward to helping Yvonne put it back in its socket. He cleared his throat. "If you're so certain, then where are they? You're an awful lot of talk right now for someone that's just murdered two kids in the middle of nowhere."

Logan paced in front of them, hands folded behind his back. "Thanks to your little trick sabotaging the frameshift, we're stuck waiting on a tug. I have men scouring the hull as we speak. They can't have much air and will have to sneak back inside soon. And if there are any hidey-holes for them to disappear into, I suggest you tell us now. It may just save their lives and keep us from tearing the Sparrow apart while we wait on the tug."

Yvonne shrugged and Elizabeth shook her head. "In case you've forgotten, I'm new."

Logan stopped in front of Whitaker and used the heel of his boot to push the man back to the ground. Despite her distrust of the man, Elizabeth couldn't help but feel sympathy as he cried out and curled in on his shoulder. Logan didn't give him a heartbeat to recover. "And what do you have to do with this? The one that always has wheels turning within wheels. What parlor trick did you use to spirit those two away?"

Between shallow breaths, Whitaker managed a response that was cryptic even for him. "I have the... Had the Helm of Hades. Not the Merkabah. Moses never worked the bugs out of that one, if Josiah Carver is to be completely trusted." He shrugged. "I don't, personally, but then I don't think he lied about it either."

Logan didn't appear to be amused. "I'm not interested in mystical nonsense."

"Neither am I, but Moses at least found such foolery to be a useful naming scheme for his toys. Alas, I don't have the power to translate a pair of dumb kids out of your reach, and if I did, I promise you I would have sent you into the depths of space instead."

"Make him regret that sharp tongue of his," Logan said, turning away. "And find those kids!"

Elizabeth turned away as Whitaker was kicked savagely. Sharing a cell with a man that had caused so much pain to her son was disturbing, but no one deserved such dehumanizing treatment. When they were thrown unceremoniously back into their prison, he landed hard on the floor and didn't even try to pick himself up.

She bit her lip and gently roused him. "Come on. Let's get you onto the cot."

He glared at her, which she ignored, and she helped him roll himself up onto the bed, where he curled into a ball, injured shoulder up. She looked over at Yvonne, who sighed.

"We have to reduce that shoulder," she said softly.

"I'd rather die right now," he said. "Thanks for the offer though."

"I'm not offering euthanasia," Yvonne said. "Matthew would disapprove."

After a long moment of silence, he sat up and leaned against the wall. "This better have been worth it."

"They'll come through. You'll see." She gave Elizabeth an apologetic look. "I may need your help with this."

That's what she had been afraid of. She grimaced and rolled up her sleeves.

By the time Grace caught up to Davey, he had already made it to the cockpit. Her jaw dropped as her eyes fell on the state-of-the-art consoles. "Flippin' shiny. I never knew the Sparrow was such a piece of junk."

Davey frowned at her and then went back to the main console. "It's not junk. It's just an older and much sought-after classic. And technically, this is an even older model, closer to how they built them in Moses' day. They're too expensive to build these days."

She slid into the seat behind him and to the right. Rather than a single copilot's chair, there were two behind and to the side. "Since when are you an expert on ship models?"

He shrugged. "Benny's right. The Venus Circuit is really cool when you get into it. I've got the Sparrow on scopes. They're still running hot and moving away. In a few minutes, we'll be able to fire up the engines without risking them spotting our heat signature."

Grace swiveled her chair to her console and pulled up navigation on one screen and the scopes on the other. This was so much cooler than the Sparrow. "Well first, let's figure out where we are and where the Sparrow is likely heading." The navigational chart populated, and the answer was immediately obvious. "Just over a day out from Mars," she said. "Unless they're stopping briefly and moving on, there's no doubt. Convenient, since Matthew and Abigail will be waiting for them."

"Without a ship," Davey said thoughtfully. "But at least they're on the right planet." He facepalmed. "There's just one problem. I don't know his comm number."

"Yeah, we might have an issue there." Matthew had been pestering them both to memorize his number for some time, but neither had ever gotten around to it. Spending the effort to memorize a thirty-two-digit number-letter sequence had hardly seemed like fun.

"And we'll even deserve the lecture this time. Okay, plan B. Whitaker has to have it in the computer somewhere. Let's see. Communications. There we go."

She turned to look over his shoulder as he tapped through a few screens. A promising solution turned into disappointment in only a few seconds. The equipment all seemed good, but the address book showed empty. "What's with that?"

He hefted the cylinder that Whitaker had given him. "Security, I bet. This thing acts as a beacon that lets the Doubt follow along, and even acts as a passkey to some extent. But it won't get us into Whitaker's personal files or contacts."

"That's a stinker. I bet we could find all sorts of juicy information on that creep." Which gave her another idea now that she stopped to think. It would have to wait until they actually had a plan. "What about heading to Mars and just tracking them down?"

"And how do you propose we do that?"

Okay, good point. Mars was a planet, and even one of the colonies would take them forever to search. She looked at the navigational chart again. They could always return to Antioch, but that would waste days of time, and the Sparrow would probably beat them to Mars. Who else did they know that they could get to quickly enough to make a difference? The answer hit her like a meteor strike. "Gebre'elwa."

"What about her?"

"Her home base. It's on an asteroid that shares Mars' orbit, right? I know I heard Yvonne talking about it."

"That would cover all our problems," he admitted, coming over to her display. He gestured at the empty space behind Mars. "It used to be a pirate base, so it's not on the public registries."

"Could we just go look for it?" she asked. "Start at Mars and work back half a million kilometers at a time."

"Sounds tedious."

"I'm waiting for a better idea."

He shook his head. "Let's go to Mars." He went back to his station and prepped the Doubt for the trip.

"And you really know how to fly this thing?" she teased.

"I actually think it will fly itself. It's going to take half the fun away and make it too easy. Go ahead and pull up the tracker on the Sparrow if you can."

She was half worried that that system would be blocked out too, but when she pulled it up, it showed exactly one frequency being tracked, one that happened to be only a few thousand kilometers from them. Maybe Whitaker set that up through his little cylinder remote before giving it to them. Or maybe they had no idea how any of this worked. "Alright. It's done. We'll lose it once it's out of range, but as soon as they get close to a comm satellite, the tracker will update us. Do you need anything else from me?"

"I'm good. We'll be frame shifted in just a few minutes. Why?"

"I'm going to go explore."

He spun on her and frowned. "Hey, be careful. You said yourself that there could be traps. And we don't need you-know-who mad at us for screwing with things."

"Relax. I'm just going to learn the layout of the ship. We're going to have to sleep and eat here for at least a day, you know." He sighed and gave her a quick nod of the head. She just laughed. "You keep reading your nerd books, and I'll make sure to take care of the practical stuff." And with that, she left the cockpit before he could get in another word.

Her current deck didn't have much to see. Aside from the cockpit, a long corridor ran toward the aft before reaching a lift. "It's a good thing Yvonne isn't here," she said, "because she would demand we put one in the Sparrow." At the lift, separate halls split to starboard and port, leading to a thumper turret at each end. Grace keyed up the lift and saw there were two more decks, one above and one below. She tried up first but was annoyed when she was forbidden access. The bottom floor had a small bunk room, kitchen, as well as most of the engineering areas, and a small storage room.

But she couldn't get that top floor out of her mind.

If there was one thing she'd learned from living on the Sparrow for a couple years and on the Duke's Habitat before that, it was that the official ways to get from place to place on a ship or station were never the only ways. There were always crawl spaces, hidden ladders, ventilation ducts, and more.

The challenge took her about twenty minutes to solve. One of the engineering compartments had a display connected to the main computer, something else the Sparrow could have used to make life much easier during repairs. From there, she pulled up a complete schematic of the ship and found her solution. She keyed the intercom. "Hey Davey, I'm turning off the fans for the air recycling for a few minutes."

"Grace. Please don't mess around with—"

"It'll be fine."

The duct would have been a lot easier to shimmy through a few years ago before she'd grown those last few inches and passed Davey, but she made it work. There was a single awkward corner at the junction on the third deck where she almost chickened out, but her curiosity got the better of her, and she forged ahead. By the time she kicked off the grill and pulled herself out into the hall of the third deck, she was sweating and filthy. The third deck turned out to be the smallest with only two doors. Behind one was a spartan bedroom. Short of going through Whitaker's drawers, she wasn't liable to find anything of interest there.

The second door turned out to be far more intriguing. It revealed a well-furnished office, complete with a massive hardwood desk that held a commanding view of a huge window looking out to space. Unfortunately, the computers up here were locked to personal information too, but after a couple of minutes of poking around, she found something that she felt was important.

It was a framed photograph, old and somewhat faded, of a teenaged Whitaker and what could only be an older sister. She was bound to a wheel-chair complete with neck support, but she had a mischievous smile on her face. Grace suddenly felt like an intruder and almost turned away but knew that this was an opportunity she couldn't pass up. Gingerly, she flipped the frame around and saw a few words scrawled in a thin and unsteady hand.

Love you brother, even if you are a jerk sometimes.

She'd need to find a way to record this so Matthew could see it later. Much as he tried to act like he wanted nothing to do with Whitaker, Grace knew better. Once they'd been friends, and she thought that deep down, Matthew still felt some responsibility toward the other man, if only so he could understand him better. But that was tricky given how secretive Whitaker was. This was proof that he had a past and the first real clue about it.

Thankfully, by the time they reached Mars, they came up with a better idea than searching for 'Elwa's base blindly. At one of the Freeport's in orbit, they were able to get in contact with the Broker's Alliance and send a message to Benny. It was from a source he wouldn't recognize, so there was a chance he would ignore the unsolicited message, but they got lucky. After a bit of back and forth explaining what was going on, he gave them the orbital coordinates they were looking for and promised to let 'Elwa know they were coming. He also gave them Matthew's contact number.

Davey rerecorded the message a half dozen times before pressing send. Matthew's response when it came was the predictable freak out, but he agreed with the decision to rally the Guild through 'Elwa. So for now, they were to proceed as planned. He and Abigail hadn't caught their assassin yet anyway but were hot on the trail. Davey couldn't really imagine what Matthew was feeling, knowing that his mother was being held captive by a terrorist. Logan was effectively off the grid until the Sparrow got back into range of a comm relay and the tracker began transmitting again. It was a waiting game no matter their course.

A little more than two days after fleeing from the Sparrow, The Imperious Doubt arrived at the small asteroid base. To Davey's eye, it was little more than a hangar and some living space. Warm light escaped from windows dotting the surface of the rock. Ironically 'Elwa's ship was far too large for the hangar and floated beside the base, connected by a slender docking tube. He reached for the comm and flipped it to an open frequency. "This is Davey Long, aboard the Imperious Doubt. I believe we're expected."

There was a long enough pause that he started to get uncomfortable. Grace made a face. "You sure we have the right address?"

"That's the Queen of Sheba. We'll give them a minute, and I'll try—"

"Davey? Grace?" came 'Elwa's voice. "Are you alright?"

"We're fine," Davey said. "But Abrogationists have taken the Sparrow and have Yvonne and Matthew's mother."

"That's what your broker tells me. Come aboard. The hangar is clear for your landing. I expect to hear the full story as soon as possible."

The hangar was big enough for two of the Doubt, and thankfully he was able to land it without incident. He hated to imagine how angry Whitaker would be if he scratched up his ship. 'Elwa and her men met them at the bottom of the ramp and led them to a comfortable sitting room. It had a wide observation window with a distant view of pale red Mars. As expected, she offered food and drink, which they gratefully accepted, having spent two days scrounging what little was available in the Doubt's storage. Whitaker's food stores were clearly that of a bachelor.

"Now," 'Elwa said when they were situated, "tell me everything." They gave her the story, from their capture on Ceres to subsequent imprisonment and escape. She paced the whole while, and when they finished, she stared out the window. "And they are heading for Mars, you say?"

"I can't see any other destination," Davey said. "We know he's threatened the grav plate factory in Kyoto. Maybe he's finally making his move."

"That's in my mind too," she said. "Though I can't see how the Sparrow fits into this puzzle."

"We couldn't figure that part out either," he admitted. That was just like Logan. One step ahead until he was ready for his plan to go into action. Maybe their escape would give them a fighting chance.

"So what are we going to do?" Grace asked.

"I've summoned the Guild members that have ships. The Queen of Sheba and Shotel Squadron are standing by. The Qolxad, under my son's command, will be here within the day, but the Jade is too far to be of assistance. The Red Dragon is en route from Venus, and the Azure Dream from Io." Davey wasn't familiar with the Azure Dream. It must have been one of the crews that Julia had recruited. She continued. "Assuming you pick up Matthew and Abigail and have a fully staffed ship, we will have a fleet of five ships and one squadron of interceptors ready to deploy anywhere on Mars."

Davey sucked in a breath. "And the other crews are okay with this? There's no money to be made here, and we have no idea what Logan's got up his sleeves."

'Elwa waved him off. "If not for a moment like this, then what was the Guild of Lanterns built for? If the Martian colonial governments are too busy fighting amongst themselves to see the approaching storm, then the freelancers will stand in the gap." She smiled wryly and winked. "Besides. If that factory falls, then all our profits will suffer."

Davey couldn't help but smile. Ultimately, freelancers weren't too different from mercenaries. Maybe some of them had hearts of gold, but they still needed those payouts to keep flying.

"We'll be ready," he said. They'd get back in contact with Matthew and make a plan, decide when and how to pick him and Abigail up, and then take the fight to Logan. Along the way, they'd have to figure out how they were going to save Elizabeth and Yvonne. And stop Logan from attacking the Kyoto factory and hastening the extinction of the human species.

There was never a dull moment, that was for sure.

Chapter 14: Devils at Odds

There will always be a tension between the concepts of justice and mercy, for they are seemingly at odds with one another. In our self and for ourselves, we will always desire the latter, for in justice, we receive what we deserve, which will never be to our liking. But in the universe at large, we crave justice.

There are of course only three logical conclusions to reach about justice in a universal sense, and through the ages, systematic structures of belief have codified each. The first is that justice is karmic, that each will receive what is due in this life. Harm one and harm will be visited upon you. But a cursory glance can see that this most certainly is not universally true, though it may apply in individual circumstances.

The second is that justice is meted out after one leaves this mortal coil. But if that is the case, it cannot be proved with any certainty, and the dead do not come back to report either way. The first and second systems of justice are not mutually exclusive, and a man may be punished for his crimes in this life, and further in the next.

There exists a third possibility, that there is no such thing as justice, but in that direction lies madness and nihilism, and if there are no scales to weigh the actions of men, then all is permitted, nothing is forbidden.

Woe to those who adopt this view of justice, for they stand before an abyss such that even the best intentions may not prevent their fall into destruction.

Luther Schultz
Judge, Rhineland Federal Court of Justice
Died 50 AM

Damon Stein peeled back the bandage on his side to inspect the bullet graze from last night's encounter with the Gaucho and Shield Maiden. They'd followed him from Arizona and ambushed him on the street in the middle of the night. In a humiliating defeat, he'd lost four men and two vehicles to the pair. He covered the injury and lowered his shirt.

He should have been annoyed that a man he'd been hired to kill was now hunting him, but instead, it was the most deliciously thrilling thing that had happened in years. The pair were either terrifyingly good or insanely lucky to get away with assaulting a team of veteran commandos like his. Probably both. Stein pulled on a combat vest and loaded it with ammunition. Cole would have to be dealt with and soon. Much as he would love to drag the game out for the sheer enjoyment of a challenge, the longer it went, the more likely the Gaucho might get the upper hand.

He needed a reversal. A weak point to hit and draw Cole out. Unfortunately, he'd already exploited both Elizabeth Cole and the broker, and most of Cole's allies were elsewhere. Perhaps giving the little colony on Ganymede a visit would provoke the confrontation he was looking for. But that was millions of miles away, and they were both here. Still it was a practical solution for a last resort.

But the Shield Maiden, she had a past in Doch Rossiya. The old crone had been her broker. He smiled as he holstered his pistol and slung his bag across his back. Now there was an idea. After all, she had a part to play in this as well, and if he was burning bridges, that was one he could bring down in flames.

Threaten the crone, draw out the Shield Maiden, kill the Gaucho and fulfill his contract in front of the crone, and then kill her for good measure. There was a delightful poetry to all of it. Then he could turn his attention to the Abrogationist.

And then he'd be free to make new enemies.

He opened the door to the main hideout. His dozen remaining commandos looked up, poker games and newspapers forgotten. He smiled, knowing they'd be more interested in an operation than hiding out for another day. His handpicked team was a special brand of amoral psychos.

"Load up," he said. "We have a target."

Tatiyana Medvedev felt her grip slipping, everything she cared about sifting through her fingers. It was like sand. No matter how hard she tried to hold it, it escaped, falling down the hourglass to pool at the bottom. Most of her life was down there now, and her gnarled hands couldn't turn the glass back over.

On her screen was the resignation of another of her freelancers. Fallen in love and getting married. Ellie's letter reeked of false gratitude and self-righteous nonsense. Like the rest, she had used her until she no longer needed her and then abandoned her like so much refuse. She closed her screen and leaned back in her chair, squeezing her eyes shut to will away the tears of anger. Ellie deserved no emotion from her, the ungrateful little whore. There was nothing any of them could offer her. They were no better than men. Nothing but disappointment and betrayal.

She reached for her cane and slowly stood to her feet. Her cave-like office felt dark and constricting for once. Perhaps letting in a little of the afternoon light would be calming to her nerves. She hobbled to the window and pulled the curtain back, wincing at the sudden brightness.

This was Abigail's fault. She'd taken that girl in, given her a long leash and built a mighty reputation for her as the Shield Maiden. An invincible woman of steel. And she'd squandered it, throwing her lot in with that priest. Ever since then, her empire had been crumbling. Her girls no longer thought they needed her and struck out on their own or turned to new lives altogether. Even her eldest, Milena Drugova, was drifting away, caught up in the priest's ill-fated guild. But they were all wrong. No one cared for them like she did.

That was why she hired that filthy assassin to kill Matthew Cole. She would never soil someone she cared about with a mission so distasteful.

But like all men, even Stein had disappointed and Cole survived. Worst of all, the animal was off his chain, if reports from Arizona were to be believed.

She closed the curtain and shuffled back to her desk. Much as it pained her to do so, she would need to be honest with Ellie in her reply. She stared at the screen and began to type her response.

Dearest Ellie,

I struggle to find the words to convey my disappointment in you. I had thought you wiser than to throw away everything we have worked for over the past four years. I have labored endless hours to find clients for your unique skills, and this is how you repay me? By leaving me on a whim for a man you hardly know, who can scarcely care for you? This simply will not do. I do not accept your resignation, for I know in my heart that you will reassess your foolish decision and come to regret it.

She paused briefly, considering how to phrase the next passage, but her thoughts were interrupted by a noise somewhere in the building. She touched her comm. "Natalya? What is going on? Natalya. Answer me at once."

Gunfire erupted when the manor's automated defenses activated. She could hear the motion tracking canons in the main lobby. The building was rocked by an explosion, and one of the cannons fell silent.

The door slammed open and Natalya ran into the room. "Mistress! They are here for you. You have to get out now. I'll try and stall them."

Tatiyana shook her head gravely and waved her cane in her stewardess' direction. "Fleeing is not within my physical capabilities anymore. I shall not be run down like an animal but will face death with the poise and dignity required of one of my stature. Still, I should rather you not be here when that happens, my dear. And even then I don't intend to succumb, not if you can bring aid."

Natalya's eyes widened. "Then you mean to stall with—"

"Yes, dearest. You must find help, or else I fear I shall perish." She felt under her desk for the concealed release. The hidden escape passage opened behind her. "Hurry, or else we will both be caught. And then what should become of me?"

The young woman made as if to protest, but then slowly nodded and backed toward the opening. "I'll... I'll call anyone I can. Ms. Drugova is back in town."

Tatiyana smiled. "It will take more than Milena Drugova to repel this assault." Another explosion rumbled through the building and the second cannon went silent. "Leave me."

Natalya disappeared, pulling the door closed behind her. She stared after her for a moment before turning to face the entrance to her office. She rose slowly to her feet and moved to stand in front of her desk. She straightened her formal pantsuit and stood tall, like the empress of a great empire.

She wasn't surprised when the door opened and Damon Stein marched in. There was that same madness in his eyes that she had seen when she hired him months ago. What had seemed useful at the time had turned its blade upon her. He smiled as he looked around the room. "I was expecting more of a fight. Surely one of your famed freelancers is hiding behind the curtains."

"What is it that you want?" she asked, ice in her voice.

"Bait to dangle in front of my prey. I thought you'd be pleased to see Matthew Cole die for yourself."

Was Abigail near enough to come to her assistance? Would her dearest even come considering their last parting?

"Should I die today," she said, slowly and evenly, "a file will be published to incriminate my many enemies. Among which you're numbered. I don't hire scoundrels without insurance. I have long and detailed proof of your history with a certain Abrogationist. Every colonial government in the solar system will put a price on your head so high that you won't be able to wake up in the morning without a bounty hunter knocking on your door."

He shrugged, wholly unaffected by her threat. "I've been in need of a career change. Call the Shield Maiden."

"If she comes, it will be of her own accord. We've had a falling out of late." She reached to the neck of her dress and pulled at the silver chain, tugging the heavy metal cube out to lay on her chest. She fingered it idly and smiled. "I have not reached my current status without learning a few morsels of wisdom. One such truth is to never play another's game," she said. "And if you must, add your own rules."

Stein drew his weapon and aimed it at her face. "Hands at your side, old woman."

"You need bait. If you kill me now, you have nothing." If Stein

342

thought Cole would come to her aid with the Shield Maiden, it meant they were at hand. Abigail would come back to her, just as she always knew she would. And if the priest ended up being a useful tool in the end, well, she could admit to being wrong just this once. It wouldn't stop her from disposing of him eventually, but even the lowest animal can have a use. She raised the cube again.

His fingers tightened around the pistol. "I need backup!" he shouted.

"I don't like the odds you've presented me with. It would take a miracle to rebalance them in my favor." A cruel smile tugged at her lips. "Thankfully, that's just what I have."

His eyes registered shock and he dropped the gun and dove for her, but it was too late. She pressed one side of the cube and heard a click. Lines of light ran along its outer edges as—

Abigail was out of sorts when it came to helping Matthew. He'd been worried enough when the Sparrow was merely off the grid. But knowing his crew and mother were in the hands of his greatest enemy, conveniently with Whitaker of all people, had made him sullen. It was like suddenly being face to face with Matthew as she'd first known him. The man with quiet secrets and a past he never talked about.

Another woman, one with perhaps more developed emotional skills, might know how to peel back the layers and comfort him. She hadn't had any practice in the nurturing department. She could crush enemies with her bare, suited hands, but offering encouraging words that actually landed home was like trying to walk with her useless legs. She'd never felt so inadequate.

And she hated it.

For the time, they'd crashed in Milena's nest, the same one Abigail had visited months ago. The surveillance specialist was the only thing giving them a fighting chance at finding Stein, and the only reason they'd nearly closed the noose on him last night. It had been so very close, but his men were good, and unlike most of their enemies, worked together as a single unit, using tactics to their advantage. Stein had a few less men than he'd started the evening with, but he'd survived.

Matthew paced the length of the living area. Annoying as it was, she didn't dare ask him to stop. "Hey," she said. "It'll be okay."

He paused and very nearly glared at her for a moment before his fists unclenched, and he kept pacing. "We're out of time. Davey will be here in a few hours."

She raised an eyebrow in question. "I would have thought you were more interested in saving the others. Saving your mom."

"I am but we can't ignore Stein. He might know what Logan's planning and the intel could make all the difference. If we're ready for him when the Sparrow arrives, we'll have a better chance at saving them."

"I get that, but it's going to be okay," she said, mostly because she didn't know what else to say. Which made her feel like she was babbling, something else she hated.

From across the room, Milena called from her little fortress of surveillance equipment. "I'm on Stein. I've never had a target shake me yet, and I don't intend for it to start now."

"You can't take Stein on your own," Abigail chided.

"Please. I know my business. In fact..." She trailed off as her comm chirped. "Hello? Hold on, slow down, Natalya. Are you safe? Is the... Okay. Yes, I've got access to the cameras at her manor. Who do you think set them up?" Abigail glanced at Matthew briefly. He'd stopped pacing and was watching Milena with curiosity. "Inside cameras are down," Milena confirmed. "I've still got a view of the street. Yeah, I see them. Two outside at the front door."

Abigail cleared her throat. "Is there something you need to tell us?"

Milena waved her off. "Forty-one minutes. Understood. I'm sending you Abigail. I'll be in touch." She closed the comm. "Mistress Medvedev is under attack."

Abigail frowned. "I'm not sure she's going to be happy to see me."

"We can go check it out," Matthew said. "We have a few hours, and you wouldn't want to leave your old broker out to hang."

Milena shook her head and smirked. "You might if you knew the things she said about you."

"Be that as it may..." he said.

She cut him off. "You've got a better reason than the goodness of your priestly heart. Look at this."

He and Abigail crossed the room to look over her shoulder. She recognized the front of Mistress Medvedev's manor. There were two armed men who obviously weren't supposed to be there. Matthew recognized them first. "We saw them last night. With Stein."

"Why would Stein attack Medvedev?" Abigail asked, suddenly feeling her stomach drop.

"I don't know, but you have less than forty minutes to get there," Milena said.

"And then what?"

"I have no idea, but Natalya was very strict about the timetable. The Mistress seems to have had an ace up her sleeve to draw things out. I'll be on the cameras and provide support, though you'll be on your own when you're inside."

Matthew cocked his head. "Let's go."

To say that Abigail was conflicted when they loaded into Milena's van was an understatement. Over the months, she'd come to reevaluate her relationship with Medvedev. While she was certainly grateful that the woman had given her a chance and helped her find her career, she was more and more sure that it had always been for her own sake. There was something needy about the Mistress, something grasping, like a spider. Maybe webs were easier to see at a distance.

"Unless we're just going on a cruise," he said as he fired up the engine, "I'm going to need directions."

From her position in the back, she tried to lean forward so she could see between the front two seats out the windshield. "Take the next right and then keep going until you hit the big roundabout with a terrifying number of lanes."

"Sounds fun," he said, his tone implying the opposite. "Call Thompson and have him meet us there."

After Thompson was updated and plans made to meet them around the block from the manor, she told Matthew everything she knew about Medvedev, the house, and its layout. Admittedly they were going in pretty much blind, outside of the limited intel Milena would be able to provide. There was no telling how many enemies there were, or just how Medvedev was buying time.

"Back entrances?" he asked.

"Probably, but I'm not familiar with them. Even when she first took me in, I tried not to spend much time there. The mistress has an absolutely charming personality. Get over a lane. You need to take this right. And if you get the joy of meeting Mistress Medvedev, you'll know exactly what I mean."

"Is it true she's a misandrist?" She sighed and opened her mouth to answer, but he kept going. "There were rumors. Not saying I believe them or anything, just saying they were out there."

"Matthew. You're not offending me. Maybe she has something against men, I don't know. Milena told me there were stories that she killed an ex-lover years ago. But even if that isn't true, she does have something against you. Just a warning."

He grunted. They were nearing the destination. She directed him down a few more roads, noting the roundabout with the statue of Mussorgsky that stood as a landmark. They'd be there none too soon, with only ten minutes on the bizarre timetable that Natalya had given them. Matthew pulled the van over, and she climbed out the back. This was their last chance to catch Stein before they had to rendezvous with Davey.

The last chance to catch one mad man before the more dangerous one arrived.

"There you are," Thompson said, slipping out of a side alley. "After how insistent Sharon was on the schedule, I'd have thought you would have been more punctual."

Matthew only grunted as he did a quick check on his revolver and the ammunition stores hidden in the vest beneath his poncho. His hands moved on their own after having done this hundreds of times. "You're welcome to storm the manor by yourself if you're up for it."

"Very funny. I'll watch your back, but I'm not meant for the front line."

Plus, you have a family to make it home to, Matthew thought to himself. "Abigail, do you have Milena on comm?"

She nodded. "She's talking to Natalya, who's hiding nearby. We have seven minutes."

"Until what?" Thompson asked.

"She doesn't know. Something special with the security system, maybe." She hefted her shield off her back and deployed it. "Let's get moving." They moved down the sidewalk in a staggered formation, Abigail in the front, with Matthew a few paces behind and to the side. Thompson was further back, hand nervously perched near his holster. Matthew hoped the man wouldn't have to use it. "Milena says there are still two armed men at the door," Abigail said stopping just short of the corner.

"They'll see us quickly then," Matthew said.

"It's not far from here," she said. "I'm going to charge them. Get ready." He gave her a nod, and she breached the corner, breaking into her thunderous gait. Matthew followed, revolver drawn. It took his roving eyes a precious second to lock onto the two men further down the sidewalk. One drew his weapon and opened fire on Abigail, the second did the more prudent thing and retreated into the building. She reached the foolish one in seconds and sent him flying into the residence across the street and then turned and faced the door, shield at the ready.

"Here's where it gets nasty," Matthew said.

"Expect targets on the upper floor," Abigail said. "The pillars will give you cover." She turned to Thompson. "Maybe wait out here and make sure no one follows us in."

"Don't have to ask me twice," he shrugged. "Take him down."

With another nod, she charged, smashing the hardwood door with her shield, ripping it from its hinges and sending it flying into the manor. Matthew followed hot on her tail, using her for cover as his eyes struggled to adjust to the dim light. The gunfire started less than a second later, pinging harmlessly off the shield.

"Moving left," she hissed.

He moved with her until she reached the row of thick support pillars holding up the second floor. He took cover behind the first and then waited a moment as gunfire continued to track her. She was homing in on a poor soul bunkered out near the bottom staircase while keeping her shield angled to block fire from above. With a swift movement, Matthew leaned out from cover to return fire to the upper floor.

The answer was immediate and the barrage of bullets had him back into cover as showers of plaster rained around him. He'd seen three targets. He quickly used a speedloader and then stepped out on the other side of the pillar and dropped one before they could draw a bead on his new position. Then he was back into cover to dodge the return fire. As they learned last night, these weren't your average goons. They were fast at acquiring targets and almost as fast at firing on them.

"Abigail, some help, please!"

She ran across the foyer and jumped, grabbing the upper floor and crashing through the rail. Stein's men scattered, wisely unwilling to go toe to toe with the Shield Maiden. Matthew used the opportunity to drop another while the last one beat a hasty retreat out a nearby window. "Come on!" she shouted, pointing at a hall on the second floor. He ran for the broad set of stairs in the middle of the room and then flinched when he heard a gunshot behind him.

"You should watch your back," Thompson said from the door, nudging the body of the man he'd shot. "Turns out, they had three outside."

"I appreciate the save," Matthew said, giving a quick salute.

"Return me the favor and bring me Stein."

"Matthew," Abigail said suddenly from the top of the flight. "You need to come see this."

He caught the uncertainty in her voice and took the rest of the stairs two at a time. When it opened onto the upper floor, he stepped past Abigail to look down the hall she guarded, stopping abruptly.

What was he even looking at?

Partway down the corridor, there was a faintly shimmering wall of distortion. Beyond were two more of Stein's commandos, apparently frozen in place just turning to enter an open door at the end of the hall. It was as if someone had stopped time completely inside a bubble, or rather, since that was physically impossible, dilated it to an infinitesimally slow pace.

"What are the odds that Medvedev is in that room?" he asked quietly.

"That's her office. Matthew, what's... how is that possible?"

He approached the shimmering barrier, mindful not to get too close. He had a strong feeling that subjecting his body to two different time scales as he crossed into the field would lead to a nearly instant, grisly death. "I was hoping you'd be able to tell me. This has to be one of the miracles. And if I had to guess, based on what I'm looking at and reading Josiah Carver's writings, this is the Song of Brahma."

Abigail shook her head. "That's news to me. Let me check with Milena, see if she knows anything about this."

"I don't think there's time. I would guess our deadline has to do with this field expiring."

"And the clock is almost up," she said. "Can you shoot them?"

"Probably not. Best case scenario, I could prime bullets to hit them. As soon as a bullet passes the barrier, it'll slow to a stop. More likely, I bet it will be destroyed on the gradient between the two." He drew his revolver and emptied it, alternating between the two. On impact, each bullet seemed to dissolve into a spray of molten dust that froze a mere inch into the affected area. He calmly reloaded his gun. "Disappointing, but I'm not surprised. In fact, I suspect that's how Grace's bracelets intercept incoming fire."

"Localized reference frame differentials," Abigail said. "This is way above my pay grade."

"That's why they call them miracles." He grabbed his comm. "Milena, what's our timer looking like?"

"One to two minutes," came the crisp reply. "Best guess, owing that Natalya was also guessing."

"Thank you." He turned to Abigail. "Looks like we have to wait patiently then. Get ready."

Barely forty seconds later, there was an audible pop, and the barrier disappeared. The entire manor groaned, and Matthew realized that the field had probably sliced through the structure of the building, doing massive damage.

The bullets harmlessly fell to the ground in molten spray, and the two men, already in motion before time had been altered on them, continued into the room before Matthew could react. Abigail lowered her shield and charged, and he followed in her wake, knowing he was about to come face to face with the man that had put a bullet through his chest.

It would take a miracle to rebalance them in my favor." Medvedev said, smiling in spite of the danger. "Thankfully, that's just what I have."

Stein's eyes registered shock and he dropped the gun and dove for her, but it was too late. She pressed one side of the cube and heard a click. Lines of light ran along its outer edges as—

—there was a brief moment of disorientation, not unlike during a frameshift, and a loud popping noise. The house groaned and shifted beneath them as Stein reached her, kicking aside her cane and twisting her arm behind her back. She started to cry out in pain, but then bit it off, refusing to show weakness in front of such a degenerate creature. Then he pressed a cold knife to her throat, and she stilled. Two of his men ran into the room.

And then her lost daughter Abigail charged in with the force of a thousand war hammers, and she smiled. Even if she didn't make it out of this, she would die with the satisfaction of knowing that Abigail had come home and that she would destroy Stein for his transgressions. She grimaced as the priest appeared behind Abigail. But then she had no more time to drown in her hatred for the man because the knife pressed harder into her throat. Abigail and the priest slid to a stop as she felt a slick drop of blood trickle down her neck.

"That's right," Stein said. "One more step and the witch dies. Stand right there. Cole, drop the weapon unless you want this horrible old hag's death on your conscience."

Tatiyana stilled her breathing. No, there was no escape for her. Perhaps leaving the priest with a burden of guilt would be the best ending. A brief struggle would end her life. But no, she wouldn't do that to poor Abigail. Not if she could help it.

"So how does this end?" the priest asked. "Perhaps there's a way we all leave this room alive? Then you and I can continue our chase elsewhere. There's no reason to involve Medvedev."

Stein laughed. "There's every reason to involve her. She hired me to kill you."

Tatiyana felt Abigail's eyes land on her and pass from shock into anger. 'How could you?' was the unspoken accusation. She'd seen that look before. Once, long ago, her partner Mara had given her such a look. Dearest Abigail, you were always mine. Just like my Liam. Even in betrayal. She choked in fury at the cruelty of it all. Because just like Liam, Mara, and so many others, she couldn't keep those she loved within her arms. They turned to ashes and drifted away.

"Now that we're all on the same page," Stein said, "we can discuss the path forward. You see, I'm not quite done yet, Cole. Much as I'd love to finish what I started, I don't see any way to put another bullet in you that doesn't end in your partner separating my head from my body."

That would be an acceptable outcome as far as Tatiyana was concerned. Everyone dead but Abigail, and even her soul weighed down by the guilt of her betrayal. There would be justice in that resolution.

"Name your terms," the priest said. "If the woman walks free, I may give you a head start. A very short one."

Stein's other hand reached around Tatiyana and pulled the chain from her neck. "Hmm. You may be a man of your word, but I'm not quite crazy enough to think you won't kill me the moment I lose my hostage. Beck. Come here." He passed her miracle to the man that approached his side. "Here are the terms. I walk out a free man. Beck is going to stay here and activate the hag's parlor trick again. I'm not quite sure what it does, but it gave you time to get here, so I suspect it will also allow me a safe retreat."

"You're kind of throwing Beck to the wolves here," Abigail said.

"He'll surrender once I'm gone," Stein said. "And being as predictable as you are, you'll spare his life. When my fate eventually catches up with me, he'll be under lock and key when that happens. He's the lucky one that gets to live."

Medvedev spoke for the first time in several minutes, careful not to move her throat any more than was absolutely necessary. "He came here to kill me. Even if the butcher escapes, his lackey will cut my throat." She spoke with absolute certainty. Men like Stein didn't spare their enemies under any circumstance.

A new hand appeared at her throat as Beck and Stein traded positions. "But it's a chance the priest will take," Stein said. He pulled back the curtain, letting light into the room, and then smashed the window with his boot. "Cole, I expect to continue this at a later date." Then he disappeared over the seal, along with the third henchman.

"Beck," Abigail said. "If you put that knife down right now and let us go after your former boss, I'm sure the law will find some leniency. We can make a deal."

It was a vain effort. He would not betray his boss. Stein would only admit those that were absolutely loyal to his inner circle. This fool would die for him. From the corner of her eye, Tatiyana saw Beck raise his hand with her miracle.

Her end of days had come at last.

"Don't do it," the priest said, taking a step forward.

There was a soft click as the cube lit up—

—and then she gasped as the knife plunged into her throat, cold biting steel, greedily taking from her what little life she had left in her veins. She slipped from her killer's grasp and fell to the floor, landing hard on her side. The world became a whorl, impossible to decipher. She had the distinct impression that she was falling, and she nearly closed her eyes, damning the universe and all those that had abandoned her. But

351

then, for one moment, it cleared, and she saw Abigail's face, torn between grief and anger. And then she too was gone, and with a sigh, Tatiyana Medvedev closed her eyes and breathed no more.

The light coming from the window abruptly shifted when Beck activated the miracle, and an hour passed in the outside world. As he dug the knife into her old broker's throat, Abigail cried out in anger. In a single bound, she crossed the distance and backhanded the man with fatal force. He sailed across the room, dead before he hit the ground. No matter that Stein was right. They would have spared him if he'd surrendered.

But as she knelt by Medvedev, the floor gave out. Sliced apart by a second space-time gradient, this time in a slightly different spot, the tortured manor gave way under her impact as support columns shifted and floors sagged. Abigail wrapped Medvedev tight in her arms as they fell, and debris rained around them. They landed somewhere on the first floor, though a large part of the second was joining them. She hoped that Matthew wasn't caught in the ruin, of either the building or her early career.

After thirty seconds, the damage seemed to be done, and the collapse subsided for the time being. She glanced at the woman in her arms and tried to see if she was breathing or had a pulse. As far she could tell, she had neither, but she wasn't in the best position to check, half-buried in debris. She stood and began to push aside the fragments of twisted rebar, plaster, and concrete until she reached a door and wall that were relatively intact. This led to a hallway, and she finally recognized where she was. She jogged toward the main atrium.

It was crawling with dozens of Russian police officers. It was nearly evening now, and the blue and red flashing from emergency vehicles cast flickering lights into the manor's foyer. "I need a medic!" she shouted, then paused, realizing most of them probably spoke Russian. "Doctor!" The Russian word was close enough to English that they would all understand. The cry was repeated, only with more words that she didn't understand, and she gently laid Medvedev down. A few seconds later, a pair of paramedics appeared and knelt to work on her.

Abigail already knew the answer, but she needed to be here when it was declared. Despite the accusations of abandonment, Abigail had fulfilled her promise. When she permanently joined Matthew's crew, she'd promised to be there if the older woman ever needed her. And she'd made good on it. She just failed to make it worth anything.

The paramedics looked at her sadly and shook their heads.

Abigail nodded. "Spasibo." And then she turned away. Somewhere in this disaster she had to find Matthew, had to make sure that he was okay. She stood a foot taller than the sea of unfamiliar faces, looking around desperately and ready to charge back into the damaged part of the building, when she spotted him coming down the stairs with Thompson.

She couldn't help it. She grabbed Matthew in a hug and lifted him off the ground, cautious not to crush him or squeeze the air out of him.

He coughed once. "Glad you're okay. I take it that Medvedev...?"

"She's gone," she said, setting him down awkwardly. She looked at Thompson, "You called for the backup, I guess?"

"After you guys got imprisoned by whatever that field was, I decided it was time to bring in the local authorities. Unfortunately, Milena spotted Stein escaping. He's gone. Again."

She shook her head. "What a waste of time. This whole trip."

"We thinned his resources," Matthew said. "And I guess now we know who hired him to kill me."

She couldn't bear to meet his eyes. "I think I bear some responsibility for that."

"I don't have to tell you how foolish that thought is. But at this point, it's not about a contract anymore, it's personal."

"Isn't it always," Thompson said. "I know you two have a ship to catch, but the local authorities are going to at least need a statement."

"Sorry to have to bounce on you," Matthew said. "But if there's a chance we can catch Logan—"

"I expect you to take it. Let's get this over with."

The Queen of Sheba dropped out of frameshift in perfect formation with three other ships, the Qolxad, Red Dragon, and Azure Dream. Gebre'elwa stepped away from the front viewport and turned to her communications officer. "Open a channel to the fleet." She waited on confirmation before continuing. "Lantern Fleet, prepare to transfer to geostationary orbit nearest Kyoto."

"Understood," came the reply from the Red Dragon. "Any sign of our quarry yet?"

She glanced at another member of her bridge crew, who only shook their head. "Not yet."

"Pity," Ewan Hywel said. "Though I guess we'll be ready to intercept when they show their ugly faces."

"Qolxad, Azure Dream, are you ready for the transfer?"

"We're waiting on your order, ma'am," said Captain Dominguez of the Azure Dream. 'Elwa had only met Dominguez a handful of times, but the escaped slave turned freelancer captain had a sterling reputation. He was the sort that could always be relied upon.

She had the details on the orbital transfer sent over to the rest of the fleet, and when their window came, the fleet performed the burn in unison. She couldn't help but smile as she watched the scopes. She was used to maneuvers with the Qolxad, but there was something a little exciting about being part of a larger group. When the Sparrow showed, they would chase it down and force it to surrender. And when they had Logan, the universe would be that much safer for all of them.

She glanced at the time. Davey would be landing the Imperious Doubt to pick up Cole any moment now. She felt a stab of pity for the fractured crew and knew that Cole was probably near frantic for news of his mother and Yvonne. A crew was the responsibility of the captain, and even if it wasn't his fault, he would be losing sleep over it. Her thoughts drifted to Yvonne. The woman had been very indirect about what was troubling her, other than it was about her husband. 'Elwa hoped she would be able to find peace. It was hard to lose a husband. Worse to have him murdered.

They'd barely reached their target orbit when an officer called for her attention. "Ma'am, I've got a ping on the tracker!"

"Show me."

A diagram of local Mars space appeared, populated by various stations and its two moons. The Lantern Fleet appeared high in its equatorial orbit. On the far side of Mars was a glowing yellow icon representing the Sparrow. Now that the short-range transmitter was in range of the Martian comm satellites, they would get constant updates on its position.

"Orders?"

She sat in her chair and crossed her ankles. "Inform the rest of the fleet that we have the target on radar. And get a message to Cole. Track the Sparrow's heading and try to plot probable destinations. When we have that, we'll move to intercept."

Unfortunately, the Sparrow was nearly thirty thousand kilometers away, with a planet in between. They could perform a series of frameshifts away from Mars and back to close the gap faster, but Logan had quite the head start. It would be better to know where he was going and react accordingly.

"Ma'am...?" The navigation officer trailed off as if unsure of himself.

"Out with it, please."

"They're matching orbits with Phobos."

Matthew slung his bag over his shoulder at the sight of the Imperious Doubt descending through the Martian sky. The sun had just slipped beneath the horizon in Doch Rossiya. Thompson managed to wrangle a permit for the Doubt to set down, briefly, outside the city. HiTO airspace was tightly controlled these days, but that was doubly so in the Russian colony. Abigail joined him at his side. She'd been quiet since they'd left her old broker's manor. He guessed that despite her betrayal, she was grieving Medvedev's death.

"You going to make it?" he asked.

"I always do," she said, but then softened. "Thanks for asking. I always sort of knew she was a vicious old woman, but you want to give the benefit of the doubt to someone that does you a good turn. I'm still grateful for the things she did for me, but it does poison my memories. Now I'll always wonder what part of that was self-serving rather than genuine affection. I saw the look she gave you. I'm sorry about that."

Matthew took his hat off and gave it a shake. "If I let everyone that hated me get under my skin, I'd never have a moment's peace. It's not your fault."

"She tried to have you killed. Nearly did."

"And failed, thankfully."

The Doubt wheeled around on their position and settled a hundred feet away, blowing a cloud of red dust in their direction. Matthew turned his head away until it settled, and by that time, Thompson had joined them. "I'll keep my eyes and ears open," the lawman said, "but I expect that Stein won't risk stepping foot on Mars for some time."

Matthew put his hat back on and gave him a nod. "You heading back to Arizona now?"

"Time to see if I still have a job. I was hoping to have bagged either Stein or Logan as a peace offering before heading back."

"We're still after Logan," Abigail offered. Matthew raised an eyebrow at her, and she shrugged. "It would be nice to have someone along that can cut red tape."

The Doubt's ramp lowered and Grace ran down. "We've got the Sparrow on the tracker!" she shouted. "They just arrived in orbit."

Thompson looked at the Doubt, unsure for a long moment, and then slowly shook his head. "I'm not sure I'm going to be of any more use to you."

Matthew's comm buzzed, and he checked it. "It's 'Elwa," He answered the comm. "I'm here."

"Are you airborne yet?" she asked. "Because if you're not, we need you up here now."

He frowned and looked at the others. Abigail shrugged, and Thompson kept a poker face. "Davey just landed," Matthew said. "Has the situation changed?"

"I'm afraid so," she said. "The Sparrow has set course for Phobos."

And in the space of a heartbeat, Matthew knew Logan's plan.

"We're on our way. Move Lantern Fleet to a safe location as close to Phobos as you deem wise."

She acknowledged and cut the call.

Thompson unclasped his hands from behind his back. "On second thought, I'll take you up on that offer. As a cabinet member of the Arizonan government, I'd like to observe, and if necessary, advise the Guild of Lantern's actions in regard to the developing situation in orbit. If I can be of service, I will."

"We may need that," Matthew said. "As soon as we're aboard, see if you can get a warning to Phobos. And Abigail, you better apologize to Milena. It looks like we're abandoning her van out in the desert. Let's move."

The last few days had been hellish aboard the Sparrow. Whitaker's mood failed to improve. The additional kicks he had received when the destroyed microphone was discovered did nothing to aid that. Yvonne did what she could, but he was a mess. His arm should have been in a sling, and she was certain the injury would only worsen before it could properly be taken care of. Elizabeth mostly kept to herself, though she had a calm certainty that Matthew and the others would find a way to rescue them eventually.

Yvonne couldn't quite bring herself to share it. It felt more like a death sentence with an undetermined execution date.

It had taken nearly three days for a tug to get to them, and then it was still another day before they felt the subtle bump of the frameshift disengaging. "It appears we're here," Elizabeth said, sitting up from her bunk.

"We'll most likely be back on the Doubt's tracker," Whitaker said. He flexed his shoulder, testing its range.

"I recommend using the fake arm if you're planning to throw a punch," Yvonne said.

"Suggestion noted, though I will pick my fights carefully."

Twenty minutes later, Logan himself was at the door to their prison. "Ms. Naude, if you'll come with me to the cockpit."

"Need my help again?"

"Nothing of the sort," he said. "I thought you might appreciate the change in perspective."

She crossed her arms. "You want someone to gloat to."

He laughed and stepped away from the door as one of his men opened it. "Guilty as charged. Now, you will have to remain quiet, so for that, I'll apologize in advance." She jerked as strong arms pulled her from the cell and slipped a gag over her head. She rounded on Logan and made sure her eyes said everything she couldn't. "Time is short," he said and pressed her firmly toward the ladder.

They cuffed her once they made it to the main deck. When she reached the cockpit, her eyes widened. There was no doubt they were over Mars, no surprise. But in front of them hung a silent moon.

Phobos.

She kicked Logan and gestured at her gag. He glared at her but got the hint and pulled it down.

"Are you mad? You're going to get us all killed! The Phobos Platform is probably the best guarded military installation in the solar system."

He pushed the gag back into place. "Don't insult me. I have no intention of recklessly throwing all of our lives away. Political unrest and the threat of war are useful for the breaking of civilization and long-term goals we've achieved in recent months. But President Barclay made an offer I couldn't refuse."

The comm light pinged. Logan reached across the pilot and flipped it on.

"Unauthorized vessel, you are entering restricted space. Alter your course immediately or be destroyed."

Logan smiled. "This is Matthew Cole," he said in a fair mimicry of Matthew's Arizonan accent, "captain of the Sparrow, SPW 5840. I believe I have a standing invitation from President Barclay to visit the Phobos Platform."

"Acknowledged, please stand by."

Yvonne thrashed, but strong hands pulled her back into the corridor. "Ms. Naude," Logan said, "please don't make me remove you from the cockpit. I'm giving you the privilege of seeing the culmination of our work."

"SPW-5840," the comm crackled. "You are authorized for landing. Do not deviate from the course we're sending to you. A security team will meet you in the hangar to give further instruction."

"Appreciate it," Logan said. "We look forward to the full tour. Send the President my warmest regards and let him know he'll hear from me soon."

The pilot looked over at the navigation display and gave a thumbs-up as he altered course coming up toward the moon. Phobos was small, roughly a dozen kilometers across on average. Being tidally locked with Mars, one side always faced the red planet. It was that side they now approached. The moon had an eye of receding concentric rings nearly half a kilometer across dug into its surface, housing a deadly weapon that stared down on the colonies of Mars. An iris sank into the abyss at the center, a dark tunnel leading into the moon. The only way in, Yvonne realized, passed through the middle of the weapons array. Under normal circumstances, no enemy could ever hope to commandeer the facility without being blown apart. But the vigilant eye had let down its guard and invited an enemy to pass through it.

"Take her back to the cell," Logan said. "At least until we've taken control of the station. And when it's safe, we'll make sure our guests are given a front-row seat." He smiled in triumph at Yvonne as he pushed passed her into the hall. She resisted the urge to lunge at him. There was nothing to gain from lashing out right now. She would wait until the moment was right.

And pray there even was a right moment.

Chapter 15: The Gates of War

Everyone lost someone when Earth fell or at least knew someone that did. We'd only been in space a few generations and most of us still had family there. Most of us had been there. Back in those days, travel was cheap, and families could afford an occasional vacation to Earth. It was a way that we all stayed united, a heritage we shared, even if the stars were now at our feet.

Sometimes I try to imagine what it was like there after Moses left. How did they handle the world crumbling to war and chaos? What was lifelike for survivors of those wars? Did they think about us in the colonies and wonder about our fate too or was the daily struggle too much.

The truth is, we forgot about them, or else pretended that we had. What few ships tried to go home after Earth fell never returned.

So even though we all lost someone, we tried not to talk about them. It was just easier that way.

Hasani Shabani
Welder, Mbeya Ceres
Died 27 AM

The Imperious Doubt joined up with Lantern Fleet in a holding orbit some thousand kilometers away from Phobos. Matthew left Davey behind the helm, mostly to observe him. He was well aware Yvonne had been teaching him, but he wanted to judge his progress for himself. And since he'd been flying Whitaker's ship for a few days, Matthew didn't want to kick him out of the pilot's seat unless there was a reason.

"You know, you're making me nervous," Davey said without so much as a glance over his shoulder.

"Good. That's my job. But you're doing well."

"The Doubt is a dream to fly," he admitted. "So many routine maneuvers are automated. Orbital transfers, deorbit burns. It's almost too easy."

"Don't worry," Matthew said. "We're not trading in the Sparrow."

Matthew's comm buzzed. "It's 'Elwa. Go ahead and pull us into formation beside the Queen." He flicked the comm on. "We're here."

"I'm glad you could join us," she said. "My sympathies for the rough spot your crew is in. And your mother, of course."

"Thanks," he muttered. "What's the status up here?"

"We are awaiting your command."

Right. They were going to default to him because the guild was supposed to be his show. Never mind that his arm had been twisted into agreeing to the whole thing. "Have you set up a fleet channel?"

"Sending you the frequencies now."

He passed them through to the Doubt's computer and opened up a line to Lantern Fleet. "This is Matthew Cole aboard the Imperious Doubt. I've never heard of a group of Freelancers who have joined together for something like this. Maybe this is history in the making, but either way, I appreciate your willingness to serve your fellow man. Do a call out, so I know who I'm talking to."

"Gebre'elwa and the Queen of Sheba stand ready at your command."

"The Azure Dream under Captain Alex Dominguez is ready to go."

"Captain Tamru of the Qolxad is prepared to follow your lead."

"The Ddraig Goch and Ewan Hywels are ready as always. We're with you, Cole, and hoping you've got one of those plans of yours that wins the day."

"Not yet," he admitted. "But hopefully soon. I have a member of the

361

Arizonan Government aboard my ship. He's in contact with the administration. And as soon as we know what's going on, we'll respond accordingly. Standby for further orders."

He closed the channel and slumped into his chair. Davey gave him a stare. "What, you're not nervous, are you?"

"Of course I am. Logan is aboard the Phobos Platform."

"Maybe the defenders were able to fight them off. We might hear from Yvonne and Elizabeth and it's all going to be okay." Matthew wasn't a pessimist, but he couldn't quite get himself to believe it would be that easy. And with each passing second with no word from Phobos, that was seeming less and less likely.

Abigail and Grace entered the cockpit with a tray of snacks. Matthew grabbed a handful of salted peanuts, not remembering how long it had been since a meal. "This was all we could scrounge," Grace said, apologetic. "Whitaker eats worse than we do."

"Are we still waiting on Thompson?" Abigail asked.

Davey nodded. "Apparently, all things government waste time." He hit a key and a map of Martian space came up. "Meanwhile, we're less than two hours until Phobos has a line of sight on the Kyoto factory."

"Yes," Thompson said, entering the cockpit. "Which is why the Treaty Organization has a commando team en route to Phobos as we speak."

"They'll be dead men if Logan has managed to seize control of the facility. He's been on Phobos forty minutes already," Matthew said.

"A risk that soldiers take," Thompson said. "Their shuttle is ten minutes out. And I'd appreciate it if we give them that time before doing anything rash. Like staging an attack on an HiTO military base."

Matthew crossed his arms. "Time's ticking. We all know what the intended target is. Logan announced his plans months ago. The HiTO made the gun, they loaded it, and then they lost it. We're on a timer now, and if there's any hope the guild can stop that gun from firing, we intend to."

Thompson sighed. "I suggested such an attack was rash. I didn't say it wasn't the only reasonable thing to do. I don't know how quickly the HiTO will be able to muster a full-scale response, and through a miracle, you've already done so. Let's just hope it was a wasted effort."

Matthew turned to stare at Phobos, hanging in the distance. "We have to assume the worst," he said finally. "If the commando team fails, what are our options?"

"We threaten to blow it up. Get them to surrender," Grace said.

Abigail shook her head. "Five ships aren't enough to take apart an entire moon. Not before they have a chance to fire."

Grace brushed a strand of hair behind her ear, suddenly acting nervous. "That might not actually be true."

Matthew frowned and then wheeled on Davey. "What have you two neglected to tell me?"

"We've had the ship to ourselves for a couple days," he said, "and thought it would be smart to take a thorough inventory."

Matthew held his breath. He had a feeling he knew where this was going. Whitaker had insinuated years ago that he had an arsenal. He pulled up a munitions screen and leaned back so everyone else could see the readout. "As it turns out, Whitaker is packing some serious firepower."

"How serious are we talking?" Thompson asked quietly as he leaned in to get a look.

Matthew grimaced as he read the screen. "Three eight-hundred-kiloton nuclear torpedoes."

Yvonne, Elizabeth, and Whitaker were pushed unceremoniously down the Sparrow's ramp. The hangar around them was carved from the natural rock of Phobos and reinforced with steel girders. Besides the Sparrow, the only ship was a single small shuttle, the kind that could pack in fifty passengers. Which, Yvonne realized, meant that for safety reasons the entire installation had less than fifty crew, many of whom were probably technical rather than military. The Phobos Platform was meant to be defended from the outside, not the inside.

At the bottom of the ramp were the remains of a slaughter. Eight dead soldiers in the uniforms of three different Martian militaries. She recognized the Arizonan and Russian ones but couldn't identify the third. Probably another important signator of the Highland Treaty Organization. These men had been expecting Matthew Cole and came face to face with a barrage of gunfire. They were never even given a chance to fight back.

"I see you were polite with the welcome committee," Whitaker said, earning him an additional shove.

Yvonne glanced around the hangar memorizing every detail in the hopes that it would be useful in a hypothetical escape. Behind them, the hangar opened into the roughly one-kilometer tunnel through the moon, before exiting out to space. It was reinforced with support beams, and through the distant portal the dull red glow of the Martian surface was visible. She saw a few side doors, but only one major exit in the far wall. They were being directed toward it. The doors slid apart to reveal a wide clean hall, bearing a certain sterile military feel. Unfortunately, the scattering of bodies, some of them she recognized as former captors, did little to add to the charm. A series of metal barricades that had risen out of the floor for the defenders blocked three-quarters of the hall at regular intervals. The central hallway design, combined with the defenses, would have made for a formidable fortress that even a small group could hold for an extended period of time. Had the defenders not been taken wholly unaware and unprepared, of course.

Her eyes roved to the signage on side halls. Dormitories. A mess hall. A series of numbered tunnels, heading presumably into technical regions of the installation. It was a self-sufficient, if small, military base.

"I like to think Matthew might have had words about the security situation had he taken Barclay up on that offer sooner," Elizabeth said.

Yvonne could only shake her head sadly. Defenses are effective when approached by something they are intended to repel. An enemy was never expected to land on the Phobos Platform, for the entrance was in the iris of the weapon itself. Logan had simply out-thought the HiTO and sidestepped their preparations.

At the end of a hall, a set of stairs led up to a bulkhead door. They were marched up the steps, through the door that slid open at their approach, and into a large modern command center. A handful of Logan's men manned the various stations.

The man himself stood at ease, eyes on the central tactical display. He turned at their entry. "Welcome, to the Phobos Platform, and the crowning achievement of the Abrogationist movement."

They were made to sit in the middle of the room. Yvonne spat in Logan's direction. "Yours is a movement that devalues human life. It's a curse on civilization."

"Your opinion is misinformed. We aim to lower the grand total of human suffering. The colonies are doomed, but it will take centuries for

364

the last of them to slowly suffocate under the crushing weight of entropy." He approached and knelt in front of them. "Ours is imminently preferable to the haphazard plan of this meddler." He glared at Whitaker. "He who has caused immense suffering, who's propped up the slave cartels, assassinated the Caliph of Al Bakarj, who whispers in the ears of a hundred bureaucrats. Yes, I know all about you. Everything except your name and where you came from. You delay the inevitable and bring anguish upon humanity. The death toll of your passing is a dozen times mine."

"And yet because of my actions, there will still be a humanity," Whitaker said, devoid of expression. "I don't need to justify myself."

"Nor am I interested in hearing your vain attempts. But you will watch my victory." He turned to one of his men hunched over a console. "Is the ship in range?"

"Yes, sir."

"Activate the automated defenses then. Let anyone who thinks they can stop us find a swift death." On the main screen, Phobos turned gold, and a constellation of red lights winked into existence around it. Satellites perhaps? Yvonne also saw a rapidly approaching ship. "Put it on the scopes," Logan said. "I'm curious to see the Phobos Platform in action."

A secondary screen showed a view of the ship. Yvonne breathed a sigh of relief that it wasn't a model she recognized. Probably no one they knew then. Abruptly, Phobos turned red on the main screen, and there was a distant buzzing sound as the lights dimmed. The ship was utterly obliterated, any debris blasted out of view in an instant. It was almost exactly how Matthew had described the Guns of the Vatican, the Four Horsemen, in their escape from Villa María. Both were weapons of terrifying power.

"Very good. And that was only a limited fire." Logan said. "Transmit our list of demands to the HiTO."

"Petty ransom now?" Whitaker asked.

"No, but this will keep the entire planet occupied. And as for your little fleet of Guild ships..." He zoomed out the view to show a cluster of ships lurking in a nearby orbit. 'Elwa's super freighter stuck out like a sore thumb, betraying their identity. "They can't possibly assault this installation with that petty a fighting force. They'll never get through the defensive field, nor can they approach the iris without facing the weapon."

Yvonne stared at the five guild ships. Davey and Grace had made it. They'd brought help as promised and had come at the eleventh hour. Maybe the outer defenses were too tight. Maybe they didn't stand a chance. But Yvonne knew Matthew would keep trying until the bitter end.

Retired Commissioner-General Yuuto Kagurazaka thumbed the latest report from Milena Drugova. It seemed that her contract was finally at an end. When she had been hired, it was under the suspicion that Damon Stein was an intelligence asset that would likely be deployed against Kyoto or its allies. What she had discovered was far more useful, or so they had hoped.

He had given his blessing for her to work with Ryan Thompson, a man he had worked with on more than one occasion but had been much relieved when Cole had stepped into the picture. The new goal had been Alexander Logan via Damon Stein, and it seemed that that too had wound along to a dead end. They'd engaged Stein on three separate occasions, and the rogue agent had given them the slip each time. And now, just hours after his final slip, it seemed Stein had escaped Mars altogether. Drugova had footage from less than an hour ago of him hijacking a ship at the spaceport.

So that was the end of the line. He would negotiate final payment with the freelancer, and that would end the operation.

"You're supposed to be retired."

He gave his wife a sly smile as he set his tablet aside. "These are troubled times, and I would be remiss not to do my part, small as it is." And indeed it was small, though Drugova wasn't the only foreign asset he was in contact with. His status as retired would give them a buffer between themselves and the Kyoto government. Legally anyway. He was merely a middleman and nothing more.

"I foresee no further official communications today," he said honestly.

She gave him a knowing smile. "Do you know how many times I have heard that?"

"An embarrassing number of times." He leaned over in his chair and gave her a gentle kiss. "And I beg your pardon for each and every one that has pulled me from your side."

His comm buzzed and he pulled away to glance at it.

"Add one more pardon," she laughed. "Go ahead." She stood and walked toward the house to give him privacy. He had enough classified calls that she had long ago learned to leave before he even answered the comm. And judging from the caller, this was most certainly of that type.

"How may I be of service to you, Mr. Speaker?"

Saito Nakamura, Speaker of the lower house of the Diet, cleared his throat. "It's happening. Now."

"Excuse me?"

"Our sources within the HiTO have confirmed that they've lost contact with the Phobos Platform. We're hearing rumors that it shot down one of their own ships."

Yuuto's breath hitched in his throat. "We had best pray that they regain control."

"Indeed. Until we know what has happened, we must assume that we are the intended target. But there is more, and I wanted you to be aware. Chancellor Albrecht just gave the order. Rhineland and Churchill are on the way. And when they hit, we're going to join them."

The long-brewing war had come at last. They would have a short window to drive out the occupation, and in the meantime, pray that the Moon of Fear wouldn't rain death upon them all. It was a dangerous game, but Kyoto was ready to be free after months of living under the thumb of foreign troops.

"I appreciate the warning, old friend."

"Then, you will move to safety?"

"No, but at least this way, when the explosions start, we will not be caught off guard."

"Be careful, please."

Yuuto smiled. "Yes, of course. And thank you."

He ended the call and stood to his feet, folding up two of the patio chairs and tucking one under each arm. His wife must have been watching from a window because she appeared a moment later, a question in her eye. "The war has come at last," he said.

She nodded and offered to carry one of the chairs, but he adamantly refused. Together they left the grounds of their estate and hiked the short distance up a nearby ridge. The path was well-worn, as they had taken it many times before. When they crested the hill, the Kyoto grav plate factory came into view, not ten kilometers across a shallow basin. A formation of HiTO tanks rumbled across the plain, half as far away.

Saito would have wanted them to evacuate entirely, but what good would that be if they had no home to return to? They set the chairs under a small tree they had planted there years ago and had carefully tended in the bone-dry soil, knowing that visitors often enjoyed the view of the famous factory. Now it would give them shade from the sun as history unfolded before them.

Damon Stein ground his fist into the console of their stolen ship. Four men. He had just four men left after the disastrous incident at the Medvedev manor. The priest was more dragon than lamb, and their little chase had gone from a game to a fight for survival.

Which meant that all options were on the table.

He turned to his pilot. "Set a course for Jupiter. We're going to pay Antioch a visit."

He didn't wait for confirmation but rose and walked through the door to the passenger cabin of their shuttle. They would need supplies and more personnel, but those could be found in the Jupiter neighborhood. Right now, their best chance at survival was getting away from Mars and its orbit as quickly as possible.

"Hey, boss. You're gonna wanna hear this." Stein stopped in front of the man, a former colleague in intelligence that went by Cooper. He didn't say anything but only inclined his head to show he was listening.

"I've been listening in on HiTO comm chatter," Cooper continued. "In case they were mobilizing anything in orbit to intercept us. But I think they're going to be otherwise occupied." He grinned like a kid and Stein wished desperately that he would just get on with it. The smile faded and the man coughed. "They've lost contact with the Phobos Platform."

Stein's eyes went wide, and he ran back to the cockpit. "Belay that last order!" he said to the pilot. "We're going to Phobos instead."

"Are you mad? That thing will blow us out of the sky!"

"It'll do nothing of the sort. Logan's there. Right now. He must have found his own way aboard because I never turned over the backdoor passcodes to bypass the satellites and main weapon. They'll never see us coming. He thinks he can discard me and go on with the operation I planned for him. We're going to show him just who he betrayed."

The pilot shuffled nervously but reached over to the navigation display to pull up the needed flight path. Mars wheeled outside the window as they came around on the new heading and started the burn. Stein gripped the back of the chair and then turned. It was a pity he only had the barebones of his team left. They would have to strike like a meteor. Instantaneous, unexpected, and utterly deadly.

Sometimes the universe handed you a gift that was too good to turn down, even if it was probably going to get you killed.

Davey cleared the display on the thumper turret. "And then to mark a new target, you'll do this."

"That's not too hard," Grace said.

He nodded. "It is pretty easy. Once you get the hang of it, that is. And remember the biggest thing is to—"

"We know," Abigail said. "Don't shoot too fast, or you drain the capacitors."

He reset the system and leaned back. "I was actually going to tell you not to try and line up a shot with just visuals. Trust your instruments and get into a rhythm."

The Imperious Doubt was much more heavily armed than the Sparrow. It sported not only an aft thumper but starboard and port turrets as well as one under the nose. Their overlapping fields of fire meant that the ship had three-hundred-sixty-degree coverage. Davey was a veteran tail gunner, so it was decided that Abigail and Grace should take the wings. They were inexperienced, and Abigail had to rip out the chair, but they would have to make do.

Crash course concluded, they went back to the bridge.

Matthew looked up at their arrival. "Are you ready?"

"Doesn't matter," Abigail said. "We have less than an hour now. I'm guessing no one on Phobos was willing to talk."

"They didn't even acknowledge our presence," Thompson said.

"Even after I identified myself. We're broadcasting a warning and the terms of their surrender on repeat."

"So we're going to attack Phobos," Grace said slowly. "With Yvonne on Elizabeth still there?"

Davey watched the muscles tighten in Matthew's throat.

"We are," he said slowly. "Hopefully the situation will change, but until we threaten them..." He looked away. "We have to proceed."

"I've received my final orders from the administration," Thompson said.

"And those are?" Davey asked.

"Lantern Fleet is to stand down immediately." He smiled. "I say to hell with that. As a cabinet-level official of the government of the sovereign colony of Arizona, I'm authorizing a nuclear strike on Phobos."

"Do you have that authority?" Abigail asked.

He shrugged. "I do now."

"Then let's proceed," Matthew said. "Opening a channel to the fleet."

He stood and clasped his hands behind his back. The other ships wouldn't be able to see him, but Davey wondered if it gave him confidence. "This is Matthew Cole, acting captain of the Imperious Doubt. We are ready to commence the operation. Here's the situation. A formation of defensive satellites protects the moon, armed with either 40mm cannons or torpedo tubes. These defenses are automated. If we move smart and fast, we should be able to avoid most of their fire. Gebre'elwa has suggested that Shotel squadron be broken into four flight groups of three interceptors each, assigned to the Imperious Doubt, the Red Dragon, the Qolxad, and the Azure Dream. Interceptors will take shots at targets that present themselves, but their primary mission is to protect the larger ships from torpedoes, either by presenting a harder to hit target or destroying them before they can land a hit. The Queen of Sheba will remain just outside the range of the satellites, giving a safe retreat point and picking off torpedoes that chase the retreat."

"Our goal is to clear a path through the satellites to Phobos. Once there is a corridor to the moon, the Doubt will launch three eight-hundred kiloton nuclear torpedoes at Phobos."

"What are we hoping to accomplish there, Cole?" Ewan asked over the comm. "We can't strike the weapon-facing side of the moon without getting blown out of orbit. Are we just attacking the surface of the moon? I know Phobos isn't very big, but neither is an eight-hundred kiloton warhead."

"It's true. We have a fraction of the firepower detonated during the Ceres Incident. However, the geology of Phobos works to our advantage. It isn't composed of solid rock. It's a rubble-pile, a collection of smaller asteroids, drawn together by gravity, and covered with a thin crust barely a hundred meters thick."

"Dios ten piedad," Captain Dominguez muttered. "You're going to break up the whole moon."

"If Logan doesn't surrender, that's exactly what we're going to do."

How could they even be thinking about doing this with the Sparrow still on Phobos? With Elizabeth and Yvonne? Davey thought he knew Matthew better than most people. Maybe not as well as Elizabeth or Abigail did, but he'd made it a point to watch the man. Matthew would do anything to protect the people he cared about. It was something Davey idolized and tried to emulate. But this was almost the opposite of that. This would break him. Maybe it already was.

They could only pray that somehow, Logan would hear reason and surrender before they had to do something terrible.

"Watch over each other," Matthew said. "Stay safe. It'll be an endurance race to cut through the satellites, and if you get yourself killed, we lose firepower." He paused as if waiting for further questions. When the line remained silent, he offered a simple prayer, one Davey had heard him give many times before. "May the God of all mercies grant us protection in this our hour of need." He cleared his throat. "We launch the assault in one minute."

Davey tore his eyes away from him and left the cockpit with Abigail and Grace.

"We've got this," Grace said. "It'll be okay. Always has been."

He made his way to the aft turret and slumped into the seat. "But it might not always," he muttered to himself as he checked over his systems.

Matthew's voice came over the intercom. "Lantern Fleet. You have your orders. Commence the attack on Phobos. If they won't surrender, we'll blast it to pieces."

"You okay, Whitaker?"

He opened his eyes and looked at Elizabeth Cole. To his surprise, he read genuine concern in her features and not the begrudging pity he'd received from other members of the Sparrow crew. The Cole family really was something peculiar, especially because they had every reason to hate him.

Which gave him all the more motive to find a way out of this. Because the truth was, he liked them both. It was one of those irrational animal parts of his brain that wouldn't quite go away, and deep down he knew that he probably shouldn't wish it away. That was how dangerous creatures like Stein were born.

He twisted at his cuffs, testing them. His injured shoulder screamed in pain, but his prosthetic arm was another story. It was much stronger than a human arm, though he doubted it came anywhere near the crushing strength of the Shield Maiden. Using something for leverage, he might be able to snap the links connecting his wrists, but that wasn't an opportunity he was liable to get any time soon.

"The guild ships are advancing."

His eyes snapped up to the display. Cole wouldn't throw his life away on a vain attempt. He had a plan. The question was, what was it, and did it give them any openings to do something, anything, to stop the Phobos Platform from firing.

"The lead ship appears to be broadcasting on an open channel."

"I'm not interested in what Matthew Cole has to say," Logan said. "Empty threats and bloviations are not my concern right now."

Whitaker coughed politely. "He's in my ship. He has the firepower."

Logan stared at him for a long moment before turning back to the tactical displays. "The platform will automatically fire on any ship that approaches the iris. If they even break the horizon of the moon, they die."

"Uh huh," he said, in a slow drawl. "Well, in my defense, I did try and warn you, and I suspect that Cole did as well. Don't blame me when we're all sucking vacuum." Logan didn't respond, but his body language said everything. Whitaker's improvised plan was working. He struggled to his feet.

"Sit down," Elizabeth hissed. Yvonne eyed him in curiosity but didn't say anything.

Logan turned at the sound. "I should kill you for the nuisance you've been."

He deliberately gave him his cockiest grin. "But?"

"But you may have uses, assets I could absorb, so you get to stick around this miserable universe a little longer." He turned to the only other Abrogationist not at work in the control room. "Get him out of my sight. I don't care what you do with him, so long as he's gone."

Perfect.

He was pushed out the main door and nearly stumbled down the steps. "That was hardly necessary," he grumbled as he regained his feet. His heart was starting to hammer in anticipation of what he was about to do. Hopefully the adrenaline would keep him from passing out. "You can just point and I'll walk. I've been beaten enough times in the last week that you don't need to make further effort on that front." The short muscular man, whose name Whitaker had overheard as Benson, sighed and pointed at a door. "See. That wasn't hard."

It was an empty conference room, or maybe a briefing room, given the military dressings. Benson flicked on the lights. "Just don't do anything stupid."

Whitaker snapped his head back toward the door. "What was that?"

The man took the bait and turned to look. "What?"

Whitaker almost screamed when he used his prosthetic arm to wrench his other shoulder out of its socket for the third time. With the extra range of motion afforded to him, he pulled his arms over his head and tackled Benson before he could react. With his hands now in front of him, Whitaker was able to use the strength afforded by his prosthetic to good effect, wrenching the gun away from his enemy and then getting a hand on his neck.

"Sorry, Benson. you chose the wrong side."

He crushed the man's throat without a second thought.

Through clenched teeth, he got to his feet and closed the door. He would need a second prosthetic limb after this, and the doctor in the control room was going to be rightly cross with him. After breathing slowly and deeply for a couple of minutes, hoping at least some of the lancing pain in his shoulder would subside, he finally cursed under his breath and crawled to one of the chairs at the table.

He took his wounded arm and braced it along the metal armrest. He wrapped the short chain linking his cuffs under the bar, and then twisted and pulled up with his mechanical arm. The link popped, while the cuff bit deep into his flesh, drawing blood. What was more damage at this point? Especially considering he was free for the first time in days. He slid over to a nearby computer and booted it up, ignoring the arm hanging limp at his side. To his surprise, the computer wasn't locked. Either security around here was nonexistent, or else there was a full back door override in effect. That would explain how Logan seemed to have taken complete control of the Phobos Platform mere minutes after arriving. He could use this to his advantage.

The current system he was on didn't have control over anything important, but he was able to find camera feeds. Flicking through the facility, he took count of how many men Logan still had. Two in the hangar. Six in the control room. Two patrolling the main corridor. Three outside the dorms. He frowned. What were they up to?

On a hunch, he switched to the view inside the dorm entrance. It was barricaded shut and guarded by survivors. He smiled to himself at the potential of reinforcements. The only problem was that he had no way to get there safely.

"Cut across the outside of the satellite formation," Matthew said. "Try not to get too deep or you'll be cut down."

"Following in your wake twenty klicks back," Ewan said.

"Gunners, hit anything that's not ours. Is everyone ready?"

He heard brief acknowledgments from his own crew.

"Seven seconds till we cross into their range," Thompson said. "I'm marking close targets and passing them to the turrets now." They passed into the overlapping spheres of fire. "I've got six satellites firing cannons. One incoming torpedo."

"Shotel, see what you can do about that torpedo," Matthew said and spun the Doubt to face back out of the danger zone and gunned the engines. Their trajectory would take them on a sweeping arc through the outside of the satellites before rocketing them back toward the Queen of Sheba. In the meantime...

The thumpers opened fire.

"This would be easier if we were flying straight," Abigail said.

"That's how you get shot down," Matthew chided.

"It's kind of hard to hit a four-meter target that's fifteen klicks out," Grace growled.

"Welcome to my life," Davey said. "Target down."

They hit two more before leaving the danger zone. Matthew adjusted their course to make a pass by the Queen and come back around. "Shotel, how's that torpedo?"

"Firing on it now."

"Got it!" shouted another member of the flight team. "Coming around to rejoin formation."

Matthew glanced over at Thompson. "How did Lantern Fleet do on the first pass?"

"I'm counting eleven downed satellites." He grimaced and gestured at the bare scratch they'd made in the cloud of defenses. "We've got our work cut out for us."

They had thirty-two minutes until Kyoto came over the horizon of Mars. "Lantern Fleet, we're going to be a little short on time. As soon as you finish a pass, get set up for another. Stay safe, but clear that path. There are a lot of people depending on us today."

He ignored the warning in his mind about the people depending on him on Phobos. He could only hope and pray that Logan saw the danger or that they would find some way to escape. The stakes either way were higher than he could bear to think about.

Yvonne stared at the tactical display as the Guild ships slowly whittled away Phobos' defenses. It was a strange feeling to be rooting for them, knowing that if they won, she and Elizabeth would die. Dead at Matthew's hands. It was the right choice given the stakes, but it was still eerie. Another display in the command center showed a rapidly dwindling clock, counting down to doom for the Kyoto factory.

Or rather three of its five production lines. Precious machinery that could never be replaced. But there was no telling if Logan would keep to the original threat now that he could fire on any target on Mars. Maybe he'd take out the entire factory. Maybe he'd strike at other public infrastructure.

No, she was rooting for Matthew. She just hoped he could live with himself afterward.

"It's probably foolhardy to say that you don't have to do this," Yvonne said aloud. Logan took a few steps closer and raised an eyebrow as if to question her sanity. "Yeah, that's what I thought. Look, there's no way you get out of this alive without surrendering. If Matthew doesn't blast us to pieces, the Martian militaries will as soon as they manage to muster their forces."

"We're aware of the cost," he said simply and turned away.

Time for a different tactic. "I'm sorry about your fiancé. I lost my husband to organized crime violence too." Logan froze but didn't turn back around. "I know what it's like to feel that hate eat away at your soul."

"And yet you're a doctor," he said. "An upstanding member of society. While I became a terrorist. I don't think you understand—"

"I became a murderer," Yvonne interrupted. "I pulled the trigger, not knowing the gun wasn't loaded." She felt Elizabeth's eyes on her. "So, yes. I know what it's like. And I'm sorry. For myself and for you. I'm sorry that no one shared your burden so that you could bear it. I'm sorry that you think all of humanity is responsible for your loss. But you're not alone. Life is tragic for everyone."

"Is there a purpose to this little therapy session?"

She sighed and dipped her head. No, there wasn't any hope in it. No real goal. She felt Elizabeth shuffle closer to her, and the other woman's presence was a comfort. And that she would still offer herself now that she knew how terrible a woman she was. Just like Matthew and Abigail, once they knew the full truth.

Maybe it was because, in the end, she was right. They were all in the same situation. Broken people in a broken universe. The battle was opening your eyes and realizing that truth. Logan had seen but a fragment of it. That life was full of misery, but missed the fact that in the end, he was part of the cause and had thus become an even greater source of suffering. But it was most likely far too late for him. Her feeble attempt at pity couldn't reach a heart of stone.

"No," she finally answered. "I suppose there isn't much use. But if we're all going to die here together, I thought maybe you would take some peace in knowing that someone else understood you."

He turned away and the clock continued counting down.

Whitaker scrounged Benson's weapon and comm before stashing the body in a cabinet. At least it was a bloodless kill. The gun, a modern military rifle of Russian manufacture, would be nearly impossible to use one-handed, but he could always cross his fingers, pull the trigger, and hope the spray would find a target.

He was running out of time. Benson's disappearance would be noticed soon, and Whitaker would be discovered hiding in a briefing room watching the cameras. It would be a pathetic way to die. The single corridor design of the facility completely eliminated the possibility of sneaking around the patrols in the hall. Even if he got the jump on them and cut them down with gunfire, the whole facility would be alerted to his escape. So he was still stuck without a reasonable way to get to the survivors in the dormitories.

He grabbed Benson's comm and manually keyed a line to the Imperious Doubt. The call connected, but there was no sound on the other side. "Come on, Cole. I know you're there."

"Whitaker! Sorry, having a bit of a tense moment. Shotel Two watch out for that cannon fire!" Shotel Two?"

Another voice spoke up, "We've lost Shotel Two."

"Oh," Whitaker said. "I see that the Minister of Law is along for the ride. This is a lovely get together. Now, if you're not actually dying, will someone please talk to me?"

"Have you escaped? Cole demanded. "Where are Yvonne and my mother?"

"Still held by Logan in the control room. I got put in isolation for poor behavior. My captor has been dealt with, but I'm trapped. There are other survivors aboard the facility as well."

"Whitaker, if you have any shred of human decency, please, save my mother and Yvonne."

Whitaker sighed. "You found the nuclear torpedoes."

"Grace, we're losing air on the lower deck. Must have taken a hit. See if you can get it patched before we make the next pass. If not just close off the deck."

"You will use those torpedoes whether or not we make an escape," Whitaker said. He voiced it as if it were an order. If the damn priest's over-developed ethics made this more complicated...

"We'll do what we have to do. Stay safe. You do what you can."

"And I'm getting another call. Which means my escape is about to be discovered."

He cut the call and stared at the comm. They would come for Benson any moment now. He turned the comm off, shut the computer's monitor off, and swatted the light panel. There was only one place to hide in the room. Thankfully the cabinet was double wide and mostly empty because sharing a tight spot with a body was going to be unpleasant enough.

He barely managed to get situated before the door opened and the light turned back on. He held his breath, aware that his heartbeat thundered painfully in his injured shoulder. One moment lingered into several.

"They're not in here. Keep moving."

The light flicked off, and he started breathing again. Just for safety, he decided to give it a count of one hundred. And then he was still without a plan, other than that if he didn't come up with one, Cole was going to kill them all.

Ewan Hywel was sweating bullets. Truth be told, much as he loved the Ddraig Goch, it wasn't well suited to this sort of fight. Unlike the other ships in Lantern Fleet and even Shotel squadron, it wasn't armed with thumpers. He had two thirty-millimeter chain guns. Which meant he had to get closer, and his gunners had a harder time leading their shots to account for the kilometers of distance between their targets.

As a result, his dives into the cloud were deeper than the others. And they'd taken more than a few stray hits. Thankfully the Dragon was well armored, and nothing important had been damaged, but it was only a matter of time at this rate.

They would be the first Guild Lantern crew killed in the line of duty. Would that be an ignoble or heroic death? Probably both. Maybe if they won, history would memorialize the brave Welshmen that made it possible.

"Dragon, you doing okay? You've got a smoke trail coming from your starboard."

"Just fine, Shotel Five. Minor electrical fire. Nothing important." He hoped. "Get ready for our next pass."

They were making headway, but it wasn't going to be enough. In trying to clear a relatively safe path, their passes were taking them into more and more dangerous territory on the entry and exit, and while the gunners had been picking off any extra satellites they could get a mark on, everyone was getting a little cooked. And they had less than ten minutes left.

He pushed the throttle forward. "Dragon making a dive. Faster this time. We have to cut deep if we're going to clear a path."

They hit the danger zone, and a few nearby satellites opened fire with cannons. His own gunners returned fire. And then his co-pilot started shouting.

"Torpedo! Close! Two-hundred meters!"

"I see it but don't have a shot," Shotel Five replied.

Ewan's mind almost blanked, but out of the corner of his eye, he saw the torpedo's position and started a spin to give the gunner's a fighting chance at hitting it. They'd thought the defenses this far out had run out of torpedoes fifteen minutes ago. Apparently, one vacuum brained satellite had other ideas.

"Fifty meters!"

Ewan closed his eyes and heard the deep rumble of the chain guns firing.

The torpedo took a hit and detonated a split second early, just meters shy of their hull, showering them with shrapnel that sliced through the Ddraig Goch. Depressurization sirens wailed through the ship, and lights flashed all over his console. He hit the maneuvering controls to stop their tumble, but they didn't respond.

"Not good. Not good. Not good," he repeated over and over under his breath. They were deep in enemy territory with no way to alter course. He tested the main engines, breathing in relief when they responded.

"Lantern Fleet, this is the Ddraig Goch, we're hit and hit hard," He pushed the throttle to maximum when the ship's rotation lined up with their trajectory. "I've lost all maneuvering. I'm going to try and push through the field." He cut the engine as they spun away from their path to keep from slowing their velocity. "I'm turning my flight group of Shotel Squadron back over to Lantern Fleet. Good luck. And wish me some as well."

"Godspeed, Ewan," came Cole's short reply.

"Thanks," he muttered back, throwing the throttle to full as they lined up with their trajectory again. He dug an oxygen mask out of a nearby compartment. "What's the word?" he shouted at his co-pilot over the alarms.

"Rhydian and Evann are trying to lock down the air loss. Marten is checking on the maneuvering thrusters."

"We need maneuverability now." Ewan glanced at the tactical display. Red marks showed nearby satellites firing on them. He opened up the throttle again. The additional speed made it harder for the automated tracking systems to keep up with them, but that luck could only last so long. In fact, they were heading directly for a cluster of satellites. The straight-on approach would make them an easy target.

"Everyone," he said. "It's bad. Real bad, but if there's a chance, we're going to find it." The satellites were nearly in range.

"Cut the melodrama Ddraig Goch."

A trio of interceptors, Shotel Four through Six, blasted past them straight at the approaching cluster. "I told you to get out of here," Ewan growled.

"Not our style, leaving men behind," Five said. "Keep working that throttle. We'll fly escort until you're through the field, then rejoin the fight."

Ewan growled in frustration. Heading straight at those satellites was just as dangerous for the interceptors as it was for the Ddraig Goch. He primed one of his torpedoes, one of only two in their arsenal. Sadly, they weren't too useful against a swarm of satellites, but he could at least give the defenses one more target to shoot at. He released it just as they came around and it blasted ahead, quickly overtaking and passing the interceptors.

Shotel Four through Six opened fire just as the satellite cluster locked onto the torpedo. The satellites began to wink out on the tactical display. Then the torpedo disappeared. Then Shotel Five disappeared.

Ewan closed his eyes as their ship blasted through the debris of the battle. "What was Five's name?"

"Abel," came the solemn reply. "His name was Abel."

"Arglwydd, dyma fi. Ar dy alwad di," he sang softly. Shotel Four and Six took out a pair of torpedoes as he opened up the throttle one last time, finally clearing the field. Thankfully their trajectory had taken them up and over Phobos rather than into its line of fire. Their orbit was going to be a mess to sort out, but they would live, so long as they didn't have any fuel leaks catch fire. "We'll be fine. Go back to the fleet and avenge Abel for us."

"We'll do that, Dragon."

He looked at the tactical display one last time. It was frustrating to be out of the fight, but then the Ddraig Goch was lucky to be in one piece. A spot of movement on the scopes caught his attention. A shuttle moving toward Phobos. Civilian. "No, no, you can't do that," he muttered, trying to hail it on the comm.

It didn't answer. But the Phobos Platform didn't fire on it either.

"Must be more bad guys," said his co-pilot.

"Either way, it's not our fight." He switched to the local intercom. "Get your pressure suits. We've got major repairs on our hands."

Matthew cheered the survival of the Red Dragon but lamented the loss of yet another interceptor. They were now down four of the twelve. Regardless of the outcome, Shotel Squadron would be mourning the loss of friends and comrades tonight.

Unfortunately, they were all out of time, and while a corridor had been thinned, it wasn't clear. He pulled them out of their current pass, sweeping back out toward the Queen of Sheba and let its gunners easily pick off the pursuing torpedo.

"Queen of Sheba, I think we have to give this a shot, we've got less than five minutes until Kyoto breaks the horizon."

"If you fire that torpedo from a safe range, it will never make it. The defenses have been prioritizing our torpedoes over our ships."

"We could deliver it half-way," Thompson suggested. "Drop it at high speed and hope."

"I don't really see another option," Matthew conceded. "We couldn't even go for a suicide close range run, because the odds are good we'll need more than one in sequence to crack the moon, and if we don't make it out for subsequent runs, this was all for nothing."

"Deliver it half-way," 'Elwa said. That's your best hope. "Four minutes."

"Everyone hear that?" Matthew asked.

"Confirmed," Captain Dominguez said. "We'll make the run with you to divide fire."

"The Qolxad is not in a position to assist," Tamru said. "We'll finish our current run and hold by the Queen for subsequent passes."

"Everyone ready?" Matthew asked his crew. Grace, Abigail, and Davey gave short acknowledgments. "This is the one that has to count, so say your prayers that this torpedo lands." He thought about his mother and Yvonne still on Phobos. "And pray that when it hits, Logan sees reason and surrenders."

His breath shuddered. There was no other way. He could feel Thompson's eyes on him, but what was he going to say to the man? Argue that it was the right thing to deliver a nuclear strike on his own family?

"It's alright, you know," Thompson said. "I'd be doing the same thing if it was my wife or teenagers. And I can't imagine."

Matthew blinked the tears away. "Azure Dream I'm starting my run."

"In formation five hundred meters off your starboard."

Matthew opened the throttle to full, punching straight down the corridor. He hit the comm and called Whitaker. The seconds ticked down as he neared the release point for the torpedo. Sporadic cannon fire from the remaining satellites began to trace across their path.

"Answer already," he begged. Then there was a click as Whitaker picked up.

"This better be important."

"I'm about to launch a torpedo that may or may not make it to Phobos. Please tell me you have my loved ones."

"I'm afraid I haven't been able to move from my position. They're still patrolling the main hall and I— Wait. I'm hearing gunfire. It's coming from the direction of the hangar."

"That shuttle," Matthew mumbled. There was only one person he could imagine that could slip past the defenses and have the grudge to go for Logan. "Whitaker, I think Stein is there on the platform."

"Hmm. That's a strange turn of events. But it may be the distraction I've been waiting for."

"The nuclear strike may get their attention too," Thompson said. "Twenty seconds to release."

"And that's my signal," Whitaker said, cutting the call.

Matthew reached for the torpedo controls, but Thompson slapped his hands away. "I authorized the nuclear strike, I'm firing the torpedo.

382

You don't need that on your conscience."

Matthew nodded. "Thank you," he said and had never meant it more than in that moment.

Thompson launched the warhead. "Torpedo away," he announced softly.

Matthew waited until he saw it streaking ahead of them and pulled up, keeping the throttle wide open. Their arc and speed would take them up and out to safety. The Azure Dream passed them, picking off a pair of satellites in their path and then sped on ahead. "Give me the good news," he muttered.

"Torpedo is still on track. Twenty kilometers from Phobos. Fifteen. Te—" He broke off and Matthew already knew why. "It's gone," he confirmed.

Matthew sighed and threw his hat aside. "Lantern Fleet, the first strike was a failure. Form up for another run. We're going to have to release a lot closer to Phobos this time."

"We have no more time," 'Elwa's cool voice answered. "I'm afraid Kyoto has crossed the horizon. The Phobos Platform has line of sight on the grav plate factory."

Yvonne waited until the timer hit zero and then caught Elizabeth's eye. Every soul in the control room, prisoner and Abrogationist, had watched the Guild ships chip away at the defensive constellation. Logan was nearly frantic at the progress they were making. But it was too late. Time ran out, and the factory was in their sights.

"Fire as soon as you have a lock on the production lines," he said, a manic grin spreading across his face. "As promised, we're only destroying three."

Yvonne tasted bile in her throat and wondered how Elizabeth could remain so calm. The woman had lost everything and been dragged into hell itself.

"We're ready to fire."

"Do it," Logan commanded.

There was a faint buzzing sound and the lights dimmed, followed by a slight turn of her stomach as the platform's thousands of combined thumpers worked together to launch a single massive gravity gradient toward Mars. Nothing could survive a blast like that.

Logan had won.

The liberation of Kyoto began only ten minutes after Yuuto Kagurazaka and his wife reached the top of the ridge. Coming in low over the horizon from the west, a formation of ships and skyhoppers used the disarray in the HiTO's ranks at the loss of the Phobos Platform to make their strike. The first desperate wave went after the surface to air defenses, giving as well as they received. Room was made for a second wave, carrying ground armor and soldiers that were deployed to retake the factory. The sound of explosions and death rang across the valley.

All over Kyoto, the local militia was coming out of hiding, picking off HiTO patrols in the street, reclaiming public and government buildings, and hitting strategic targets.

It was a good plan, but a lot depended on what was going on in low orbit. Phobos would soon rise into the sky, and if the HiTO had regained control of the situation, they might rain precision shots on the reinforcements. Or worse, someone far more sinister would be behind the controls.

There was no silver lining.

And so Yuuto and his wife sat hand in hand, waiting for the moon to rise. It was appropriately named after a pagan god who brought the terror of war. When Phobos appeared over the horizon, they stood and turned to face it, waiting for whatever would come.

It fired.

Yuuto had time to see the distortion in space-time as it streaked from orbit. He pulled his wife to himself. If this was to be the beginning of the end of his homeland, he would not turn away from it.

Streaks of yellow ran across the sky as a field of energy appeared to stop the blast while it was still some distance from the ground. There was a flash of light as the distortion disappeared, and then all was still. A few seconds later, a crackling explosion like a thousand bolts of thunder rocked the valley, followed by a great wind. And then they wept that the factory still stood and hope remained.

The fighting in the basin was momentarily forgotten.

Gebre'elwa set her scopes on Kyoto and zoomed in as far as they could, expecting to see ruin and destruction. And then her jaw dropped open. "The factory stands!" she shouted. Perhaps the sacrifices already made would not be in vain. Her bridge crew turned to stare at her.

"How's that possible?" Tamru asked. "We all saw the weapon fire."

Matthew Cole's voice rang across the bridge. "I'll have to apologize for the deception, but I was sworn to secrecy. I met Pope Willems a couple of months ago, and he agreed that one of the Vatican's treasures would be better put to use guarding the Kyoto factory. Svallin's Mantle, one of Moses' miracles, has been safely hidden there for weeks." Her crew began to whisper frantically to each other. "Unfortunately, I don't think it will stop another shot like that."

"Then there's still time," 'Elwa whispered.

"We have a short window," Captain Dominguez said. "A thumper array that large is going to need a massive bank of capacitors. It's going to take a few minutes to cycle and fire again."

"Which means we have one last chance," Matthew said. "And this time, we can't miss."

The Arizona politician cleared his throat. "So if anyone has any ideas on how to make that happen, now is the time."

'Elwa looked around the bridge of her ship. At the faces of her beloved crew. This was who she was fighting for. And for her family. She quietly called up emergency protocols on her display and authorized an abandon ship order. Red lights began to flash and sirens wailed through the Queen of Sheba. Her bridge crew looked at her with questioning eyes.

She cleared her throat. "I know how we can deliver the payload."

Alexander Logan couldn't understand what he was looking at. The factory stood, untouched and unharmed. It was impossible. After everything he'd worked for. "Fire again!" he shouted.

"It will take at least ten minutes for the capacitors to recharge, sir."

"Then set it to automatically fire as soon as they're ready."

"Yes, sir. It's... It's done. The weapon will fire as soon as it's cycled."

Logan wheeled on the two women. "What do you know about this? How did Cole do this?"

Ms. Naude shook her head. "I'm as surprised as you are." The other woman, the quiet one, just shrugged.

This was a disruption but correctable. In ten minutes, they would fire again, and this time the Kyoto factory would fall.

His comm crackled to life. "Sir! We're being overrun in the corridor!"

He could hear gunfire over the background noise of the command center.

He stared at the comm as a snaking tendril of fear began to creep into his mind. They had lost the one the women had called Whitaker, though that wasn't his name. But given the extent of his injuries over the last week, there was no way he could cause that much trouble. This was something else. "What is going on?" he shouted at the comm.

But there was no answer.

And then he knew.

The only one that could get past the security was Stein. Stein, who had irons in all the fires, in all the departments of the Arizonan government. Who'd bribed and threatened key contractors in the Department of Defense to create backdoor keys for the Phobos Platform. The first, he had handed over to Logan months ago, the very one they had used to shut down all internal security and gain full access to the central system. The other could be broadcast to bypass external security.

Stein had claimed he was having trouble acquiring that second key. When their relationship soured, Logan had found a different way onto the Phobos Platform. Clearly, the agent had been lying. And now, because they'd already used the first key, they couldn't even lock the doors and seal him out of the control room.

"Damon Stein is here," he announced, a sudden feeling of calm washing over him. Perhaps because the end was already written on the wall in meter deep letters. "Guard the door." He walked over to the women and gestured for them to stand. "I'm afraid I owe you both an apology. I promised that you would live, and I can no longer guarantee that." He stepped behind them and unlocked their cuffs. "If you would take my recommendation, you will go find a corner to play dead in."

Ms. Naude gave him a withering glare. "Did you set loose an animal you couldn't control?"

"That is an appropriate metaphor, yes."

He drew his pistol and crossed to the furthest side of the room from the door. To his relief, the women did as he suggested and laid face down by the wall nearest the entrance. Probably so they could try to escape. The odds of anyone in the room making it off of Phobos alive were nearing zero at this point anyway. Let them make a valiant attempt.

The door opened.

Chapter 16: Mere Humanity

We live in a universe of consequence. This is among the hardest of truths for us to accept, for it demands that we take account for our actions. Cause and effect we can accept, and in fact, we learn at a very young age. When we cried as babes, our mothers fed us. But we do not learn consequence, for consequence involves a moral reckoning. We did not once consider that our mothers could have done with ten more minutes of rest. We only knew of ourselves.

That is the moral horizon that we must come to terms with. Our story is not the only one being written. There are others who must bear our actions too. And there is a chance they will not be pleased.

That is consequence.

The greatest tragedy of all is that virtue can lead to consequence as surely as vice. We're not promised a fair trial, and even the noblest deed may be rewarded with violence.

Col. Margaret Lanney
Arizona, Career Military Officer
Died 61 AM

The door opened and a canister rolled in, belching out thick white smoke.

"Hold your fire," Logan shouted at his men. "Don't give away your position until you have a clean shot." The only sound was the soft hiss of the smoke. His heart hammered in his ears as he waited for Stein to make his move. He'd have to come through the narrow doorway, and Logan's men would catch him in a crossfire.

Then an object bounced into the room. Time crawled to a stop as Logan realized what it was.

A grenade.

"Hit the deck!" someone yelled a fraction of a second before a deafening explosion shattered the air around them. The concussive force hit Logan like a battering ram, blowing him off his feet. He slammed into the deck and struggled to find the breath that had been forced from his lungs. His side and chest burned with fire.

Forcing his sluggish limbs to work, he propped himself up and tried to focus his eyes. He could barely hear the gunfire over the ringing his ears. Three men advanced through the fog. At least some of his men must have made it to cover because one of the intruders was cut down by gunfire. Logan slipped and fell face-first to the deck, grinding his teeth at the pain in his side.

Damn Stein. That he would catch up to him here in the hour of triumph. If only Cole had killed him months ago when he had first set him on Stein's trail. But he'd played it too subtle. A beer with the mechanic in Warszawa was supposed to have started the ball rolling. He'd thought that leading Cole straight to Arizona's corruption would put Stein on the run, but the timing had been wrong. The kid who actually took the job was too slow in finding the culprits. Then Cole had been shot a few days later. Damn them all. Everything had been so close to perfect. But now it was all coming apart.

His world had been falling apart for years. Ever since Alisa was murdered.

The gunfire went quiet.

One side or the other had won. Logan rolled over and propped his back against the workstation, eyes closed. He was too afraid to open them. He clutched at his side, where blood oozed from a deep wound. It wasn't the only one, either.

"Look who I've found."

The voice he'd hoped to never hear again.

"Pitting Cole against me was clever. It was almost enough to save your sorry life. But you both underestimated me. Time and again. And now the payment comes due."

Logan opened his eyes, knowing that it was better to face his death than turn from it like a coward. Stein looked worse than he'd ever seen him, clothes torn and dirty. Logan grinned and spit blood at Stein. Around the room, his men were dead, but since Stein was also by himself, it had been close. It had come down to the nearest point of balance and tipped in the wrong direction, and now it was just the two of them. Only Logan wasn't the one with the gun. Stein pointed it at his head, and a cruel smile spread across his face.

"Goodbye Logan. And good riddance."

Logan's courage failed, there at the bitter end when all his kingdoms crumbled, and he closed his eyes as a gunshot pierced the air.

Gebre'elwa clasped her hands behind her back. "That evacuation order isn't a suggestion," she told her bridge crew. "Move." Most of them began to obey and ran toward the Queen's escape shuttles.

Her first officer, a man half her age named Abraham, stood his ground. "Ma'am, if you think I'm about to let you do something foolish, then you have sorely misjudged my character."

"If you think I'm going to throw my life away when there are alternatives, then you're the one that's not thinking clearly."

"I'm not leaving without you."

She eyed him. "Very well." She reopened the comm to Lantern Fleet. "As I was saying, I know how we can slip a payload past the satellites. They most likely track targets by infrared, possibly prioritizing smaller targets in the hopes of shooting down incoming torpedoes. To get past them, we simply disguise our torpedoes with a bigger source of heat."

"A ship," Matthew said. "We sacrifice a ship and program the torpedoes to remain close enough that it can't distinguish between the two."

"We'll use the Qolxad," Tamru said without delay. "You can even fly it from the Queen with sequence rigging. No one has to go down with the ship."

"The Qolxad will never reach Phobos," 'Elwa said. "Whatever ship we use will have to fly straight and true to allow the torpedoes to stay close enough. And the Qolxad will be torn to pieces on that kind of flight path."

The comms were silent for a moment. "Mom," Tamru finally said. "You can't... The Queen is..."

"She has the tonnage to take a beating. She'll hold together, and she'll make it to Phobos." 'Elwa smiled grimly. "And she'll hit hard enough to make up for the lost nuke." More stunned silence from the comms. "I've already issued the evacuation order. Tamru, see to the sequence rigging. You'll be flying the Queen from the Qolxad. As soon as we're clear, set up the attack."

She turned her comm off. Her decision was final, and there would be no better plans with the resources and time they had. She took a last look around the bridge of her beloved Queen and then turned away, suddenly feeling very tired. Perhaps this was how she was supposed to feel at her age. Maybe this was an indication that at long last, it was time to retire.

"Ma'am?" Her first officer was at her side, offering her an arm.

"Abraham," she said, grateful he had waited on her. "Take me to my shuttle."

Whitaker watched on the cameras as Stein passed his door and proceeded to the control room.

"Only two men? My my, you must have fallen on hard times."

As soon as he dared, he slid out into the hall, and, with a quick glance in either direction, set off toward the dormitories. If he remembered, it should only be about fifty meters down the corridor on the left. He wove through the barricades, half expecting to come face to face with a hostile at every turn, but the hall was now eerily empty. Nearly everyone on the platform, on all sides, was already dead.

He reached the tunnel that led to the dorms and saw three fresh bodies at its entrance. Stein had cut down the Abrogationists guarding the survivors as well. Whitaker ran up to the door and pounded on it. "I'm friendly! You have to open up now." It wasn't until the words came out of his mouth that he realized how ridiculous they sounded. They had no reason to believe a thing he said.

"Okay. Let me try again. The real Matthew Cole is about to unleash a nuclear strike on Phobos and blow it to pieces because Abrogationists have seized control of it and are firing on Kyoto. If you want to live, you open this door." He heard a distant explosion. "Also, there's a rogue agent from Arizona making a mess of things. Don't ask. It's complicated."

No answer. He groaned as he tried to remember why he was wasting time on these people. Even with their help they probably didn't stand a chance at retaking the station. If they were hiding, they were most likely just scared technicians. It meant that Ms. Naude and Mrs. Cole were as good as dead.

Matthew Cole was not going to be happy about this turn of events, but sometimes life was unfair like that.

"I'm heading to the hangar," he said. "I'm tired and injured. Last ride out leaves as soon as the engines are hot."

As he turned away, he heard the door slide open behind him.

Yvonne curled in on herself when the grenade exploded. She was supposed to be playing dead, and the corpse she was pretending to be shouldn't move, but it was instinct when she felt hot fragments pepper her skin. Gunfire erupted, and she squeezed her eyes shut against the terror of it all.

This was the end of her story, here on a God-forsaken moon filled with madmen. It was a long way from growing up on Amalthea, a long way from falling in love with Tomas in a quiet corner of the library at the University of Ganymede. The life she'd lived had turned out to be a bigger adventure than she'd planned. After decades as a doctor, she'd found a new family, become a pilot, and fought the good fight. But in the end, that fight had caught up with her.

The gunfire came to an abrupt end, and she opened her eyes and tried to make sense of the disaster around her. Smoke lingered in the room, and broken tactical displays sprayed showers of sparks. In all the wreckage and ruin, only one man was left standing.

Damon Stein with his gun pointed at Logan.

"Goodbye Logan," Stein said. "And good riddance."

And then a single gunshot tore through the room, and Stein stumbled forward, shot through the chest. The gun fell from his hand as he half turned, confusion on his face. For the last time, his lips curled into a smile. "And they say there's no justice in the universe." Then he slumped to the ground and was still.

Yvonne turned her head to see Elizabeth clutching a weapon scrounged from one of the fallen. She was bruised and battered but stood steady. She threw the gun away and limped to Yvonne.

"Are you alright?"

"I've been better," Yvonne said, "But I'll live." She sat up and checked herself for injuries. She had multiple small wounds from grenade fragmentation but lying flat on the ground had probably saved them from the worst of that. She took Elizabeth's hand and stumbled to her feet, then winced and picked a piece of metal out of her arm. "We've got to get out of here."

"Can we stop the weapon from firing?"

Yvonne gestured at the sparking monitors. "There's no way anything in this room is functioning again. What's done is done." She hobbled over to where Logan was still leaning against a workstation. "Give me your comm." He coughed twice and pulled it from his belt, offering it to her without complaint. He'd had a much worse time from the grenades and was bleeding from several severe injuries. She took the comm but tossed it aside with a sigh when she saw it was no better off than its owner.

"This is our chance," Elizabeth said. "Maybe the route to the hangar is clear."

Yvonne looked at the other bodies, knowing someone would have a functioning comm, but it would take precious time to scavenge. "Grab a weapon and head that way. Carefully. I'll be just behind you."

Elizabeth raised an eyebrow in question.

"There's another survivor," Yvonne said.

"I see." Elizabeth stooped to pick up the rifle she'd used to kill Stein and limped toward the corridor.

"I'm assuming this is a joke," Logan coughed. "Surely you're only going to finish me off. Frankly, the universe would thank you."

Blood stained his satin vest. He'd been hit hard. She wasn't sure she could even save him with the medical supplies she kept on the Sparrow. He was a pitiful sight. "Once upon a time," she said. "I hated someone and almost lost my soul." She knelt by him.

"I assure you mine is long gone, and I'm not coming with you." He laughed bitterly. "Why would I? There's nothing for me out there. This was the last plan. The final scheme. Whitaker has spent the last year dismantling everything I've worked for. Your crew ruined my finances when you took that ship out over Ganymede. I have no more men. Maybe someone else takes up the Abrogationist cause someday. But until then, we're done. I'll wait here till the end and hope Phobos fires one last time."

She shook her head. "It's better to live than die," she said softly.

"Not when all you have to look forward to is a firing squad."

If he was going to be stubborn, then there was nothing she could do about it. She and Elizabeth together couldn't have hoped to carry him all the way to the hangar, not after the week they'd had. He was going to die here, alone and a fool. But still, there was one thing she still needed to know.

"Tell me her name."

He leaned his head back, but his eyes still tracked her. "Excuse me?"

"Your fiancé. What was her name?"

"What does it matter at this point."

"It matters more than anything else right now. This way, the last person that spoke to you will remember that your story was a tragedy."

He looked at her for a long moment, as if trying to understand her. "Her name was Alisa Smithson," he finally whispered, "and she was the most beautiful woman in the solar system."

She nodded. "Alisa Smithson. Goodbye Logan. I'm sorry that this was what your life became." She turned away from him and marched from the room without looking over her shoulder. She was the last person to lay eyes on Alexander Logan, Abrogationist, terrorist, and broken man.

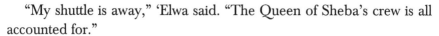

"My shuttle is away," 'Elwa said. "The Queen of Sheba's crew is all accounted for."

"We're finishing up with reprogramming the torpedoes," Matthew said, nervously tapping his fingers on the console.

"I hope you're almost done," Tamru said. "We're still on a timetable."

Matthew turned to look over his shoulder at Grace. She tapped away at one of the secondary consoles. "I'm working on it. Torpedo's are supposed to strike targets, not tailgate them. But there's enough settings in here that I can make it work."

Thompson frowned. "Are you sure I shouldn't take a look at what–"

"She's got it," Matthew said. "Of all my crew, she's the best at poking through computer programs. And she's smart. I trust her."

"I'll never understand you."

The feeling was mutual, but Matthew thought that was implied in their relationship.

"There," Grace said. "It'll try and keep fifteen meters from its target. Hopefully. And when the target stops suddenly, they'll evade and relock on Phobos."

"That will have to work," Matthew said. "Lantern Fleet, we're ready. We'll follow in the Queen's wake, match its speed, and then drop the torpedoes right on its tail to make sure they get locked into course."

"The Queen is lined up on impact trajectory," Tamru said. "Mom, if you want to give the order?"

There was the slightest moment of hesitation before 'Elwa issued the command. "Do it."

"Burning the Queen's engines now."

The kilometer-long super freighter's aft engines lit up and started it on its final voyage. A ship that large took time to pick up speed, but simple physics guaranteed that when it did it, it would strike with massive force. Matthew didn't even want to guess how much this would cost 'Elwa financially. A hundred million, at least. Probably more.

He angled the Doubt to follow in its path and pushed the throttle forward. "Davey, Abigail, we'll pass through the edge of the defensive field. Keep an eye on things, would you?"

Grace crept up behind him as they neared the Queen's aft. "You know if I messed up, we're firing a nuclear weapon at point-blank range."

"Did you mess up?" Matthew asked.

"No. But I recommend running away. Just in case."

"You people are insane," Thompson grumbled.

Matthew pulled the Doubt up to the Queen, right between her engines to avoid backblast. He let off the throttle and drifted to about fifty meters back. One of the thumpers fired at a nearby satellite, turning it into a short-lived fireball, quickly snuffed by vacuum. Matthew took a deep breath and let it slowly escape from pursed lips. This was it.

"Still want me to do the honors?" Thompson asked.

Instead of answering, he called Whitaker.

"Good news," Whitaker said, too cheerful for Matthew's liking. "I've made it to the Sparrow. Stein cleared my path. And I even played the hero and have seven survivors from the Phobos Platform in tow."

"And Yvonne? My mother?"

"No sign of them. I don't have any fighters, and I'm down to one functioning arm, Cole. I can't mount a rescue."

"I'm about to make another attack. This one won't miss. Everyone on that station dies."

"What do you want me to do?"

"I know you have a sister," Matthew said. "Would you go back for her?"

Whitaker's voice turned to ice. "You know nothing about me. Nothing about her."

"You didn't answer the question."

"Nor will I. None of the survivors are pilots. If I do something stupid, they die too. Simple math says I stay on the Sparrow."

Matthew clenched his fist and looked at the navigational chart warning of their upcoming crash into Phobos. "You have three minutes, twenty-two seconds."

"I have to wait either way," Whitaker said calmly. "If I leave too early, the array may shoot us down."

Matthew gripped the hair at the back of his head. He clenched his eyes shut.

"Do it."

Thompson sighed and, after a moment, pulled the trigger that sealed the fate of two people that Matthew loved.

"torpedoes two and three away."

Matthew opened his eyes, giving three seconds for them to clear the hull, and then turned the Doubt out of the field, pushing the throttle wide open.

"It worked!" Captain Dominguez said. "They're sitting right off the Queen's hull."

"And the queen is still accelerating," Tamru confirmed. "She'll hit like a comet."

Matthew could only breathe heavily as the tears began to fall. He felt Grace's hand rest on his shoulder. At least he wouldn't lose everyone. "Lantern Fleet, keep your distance," he said. "Mars is about to lose a moon."

Whitaker stared at the controls of the Sparrow, mind strangely numb.

Somehow, someone had been in his office. His key cylinder shouldn't have given access to the upper deck of the Imperious Doubt, but someone had been up there anyway. That was the only way Matthew could have known about Hannah. For a single terrible moment, he wondered if they had broken into his files. Then they would know everything. But that was impossible. They had only seen the picture and made obvious connections. Nothing more.

But the insinuation made him furious. Of course, he would go back for Hannah. He would walk into hell for her. Had been doing so for many long years. He thought back to the last time he had seen her. Long ago now, and yet not that long. Time was fickle like that. Physics made it so.

He swore at Matthew and the universe in general and left the cockpit. Seven sets of eyes stared at him as he ran through the common room toward the exit ramp. "I have to check on someone else," he muttered. "I'll be back."

He jogged down the ramp and into the hangar. The only sound was the hum of the Sparrow's engines as they warmed up. There was no one to stop him as he rushed toward the corridor leading into Phobos. He couldn't hope to go the whole way to the control room with the time he had, but he could at least—

Yvonne and Elizabeth emerged from the corridor, both a mess. Yvonne was bleeding from several minor injuries, and Elizabeth was limping badly and toting a rifle. Her other arm was slung over Yvonne's shoulder, clearly trying to keep weight off of one of her ankles. "Hurry!" he shouted at them. "There are nuclear torpedoes en route!"

"Hurrying isn't an option right now," Elizabeth said, wincing.

Whitaker rolled his eyes and took Yvonne's place, using his prosthetic arm to support Elizabeth's weight. "I've got her. Yvonne, the Spar-row's already warming up. She'll need a pilot familiar with her."

Yvonne jogged ahead toward the ship.

Elizabeth's arm gripped his bad shoulder, and he nearly cried out in pain. After all he had done for these people, they had better make it. They shambled as quickly as they could across the hangar, and when they reached the ramp, he breathed a sigh of relief. "I expect you'll tell Matthew about this."

She grunted at the exertion of climbing the incline but shook her head sadly at him. "Virtue isn't its own reward?"

They entered the airlock and Whitaker closed it behind them. "No," he said, "it isn't."

Once clear of the danger zone, they all crammed into the bridge of the Imperious Doubt, anxious to see what was about to happen. It was roomier than the Sparrow, but Davey thought Abigail's bulk still made it feel like a can of those cheap, over-salted sausages she liked.

Matthew had given them momentum that would keep them moving away from Phobos but spun now to face it. Then he wilted. Davey felt something unpleasant in his stomach, fear coiled with anger, and some-thing else. He couldn't imagine what Matthew was feeling with his mother still on Phobos. But he could at least grasp the beginning of it.

The Sparrow crew was the only family he'd ever had, or at least remembered, and Yvonne and Elizabeth were both like a mother to him. Yvonne wasn't exactly what anyone would consider motherly, not in the warm fuzzy sense anyway. But she was always there for him, al-ways someone to talk to, even with whatever problem she'd been deal-ing with since Ceres. And Elizabeth, was motherly and encouraging. Or maybe she was more like a grandmother. If Davey had any of those, he couldn't remember them either.

There would be a hole in the crew forever.

They watched in silence as the Queen continued its death dive into Phobos. Cannon fire raked at its side, and it even endured a couple torpedo hits, but it would take a lot of firepower to disable a ship that size. Even if its engines died, it would continue on its course with incredible inertia. Already, fires and smoke bled from the sides of the magnificent ship, and Davey wondered what 'Elwa was feeling watching it dive to its doom.

The comm pinged and Matthew answered. "Whitaker, you have to leave now. You've got about thirty seconds to impact."

"Hello to you too, Matthew," Yvonne said. "The Sparrow is just now lifting off. What's this about an impact?"

Matthew almost fell out of his seat. "My mother—"

"We're fine. A little worse for wear, but we'll live. Impact. Talk. Now."

"The Queen of Sheba and two nuclear weapons."

Yvonne was silent for a moment. "I'm getting the Sparrow turned around to leave the hangar. How much time do I have?"

Davey glanced at the navigation chart plotting the Queen's dive. They were out of time.

"Clock's at zero," Matthew whispered.

The Queen slammed into the side of Phobos like the universe's biggest hammer on its biggest anvil. Her bow plowed into the crust, sending rock spiraling into space before an explosion ripped apart the front module of the ship. The long spine buckled as the inertia from the massive engines on the back drove the Queen deeper. At this range, it was clear by comparison both how large a one-kilometer ship and how small a twelve-kilometer moon are.

"Firing the engines," Yvonne said. "We'll be out of—"

She was cut off in a squeal of static as two small nuclear warheads detonated in spheres of light. What was left of the Queen turned into shrapnel, blasting apart the surface of Phobos. Deep snaking fissures raced across the moon's face as its thin regolith crust collapsed.

Originally nothing more than an asteroid captured from the belt between Mars and Jupiter, tiny Phobos was a fragile thing, in too low an orbit. When humans first studied it through telescopes and probes, it already showed signs of impending destruction, stretch marks from enduring the tidal forces of Mars' gravity. Those greedy fingers of gravity were slowly pulling Phobos toward Mars. One day, in the distant future, Phobos would have crossed a line and been broken up on its own by the sheer forces of its mad orbit. Mars' equator would be pelted by some of the debris, and the rest would form a ring of dark rock around the red planet. That hypothetical was supposed to be millions of years away.

As the surface continued to break apart, Davey realized that they had moved that timetable up to now.

<hr>

When the moon shuddered for the first time, the Sparrow's nose had just pointed out of the hangar. The lights in the tunnel flickered briefly, and dust drifted off the walls, but the tunnel held. Yvonne took one last look over her instruments. Now or never.

"Firing the engines," Yvonne said. "We'll be out of—" A burst of static from the comms cut her off, and the lights in the tunnel went out permanently. She flipped on the Sparrow's exterior lights right as the moon began to shake violently and pushed the throttle as far forward as she dared. Rock formations half the size of the Sparrow broke off the wall and floated nearly free, Phobos' tiny gravity only barely altering their course. She spun around one, almost scraping the wall in the effort.

Whitaker stumbled into the cockpit, "What in... Oh my."

"Sit down and shut up!" The tremors intensified, and the straight tunnel began to warp visibly in shape as tortured rock splintered under immense pressure.

"Watch out for—"

"I said shut up!" Yvonne shouted as a sharp rock formation sliced through the tunnel threatening to block it entirely. They slipped past even as the Sparrow was showered with debris.

Then the largest tremor yet hit, and the exit disappeared entirely as the tunnel ceased to exist. Yvonne cursed under her breath and rotated the ship, using the throttle to kill their momentum. Behind them, the hangar shredded as if a pair of giant hands grabbed each end and twisted it in opposite directions. Whitaker whistled. She could agree with the sentiment as she turned back to face what used to be the exit, praying the maelstrom of destruction would clear it again.

Instead, the sides of the tunnel opened up, revealing dark fissures between the rocks. She picked the largest of these and nosed the Sparrow in. They were near the surface. All they needed was for Phobos to break apart enough to find it.

"You're insane," Whitaker muttered.

"It's either certain death or probable death. Take your pick."

They looped around a trio of rock fragments bigger than the Sparrow, wincing as a smaller one scraped down the hull. Their current pathway trembled and began to break apart and compress.

"There!" Whitaker pointed. "An exit!"

She saw it too. A brief flash of red. Mars. She hit the maneuvering thrusters and twisted in the right direction, nosing up the throttle. There it was. Two hundred meters ahead, a sliver of light, barely big enough for the Sparrow. And it was narrowing. She maxed the throttle, and the engines roared through the deck. It was going to be close. Way too close.

"We're not going to make it," Whitaker said.

"Ye of little faith." She rotated the Sparrow to slip through the crack and gripped the yoke till her knuckles were white. And then they were through. Mars stretched out before them, and it had never been a more welcome sight.

Lantern Fleet watched in silence as Phobos slowly gave in to the forces tearing it apart. As its center of gravity was disrupted and the shallow crust giving it cohesion disappeared, it ground itself to pieces, and Mars' gravity was already working to spread the remains out. Matthew kept his eyes glued to the scopes, praying for some sign of the Sparrow. He checked the comms again but was just met with a burst of static. It would be some time before the background radiological noise let a comm signal through. They'd learned that at Ceres.

"This is going to leave a mess," Grace muttered. She'd pulled up the navigation chart. "The computer is having a hard time tracking all the rocks out there." She tapped a key a few times. "Actually, navigation just crashed entirely. So... yeah. Stay away."

A few larger chunks had broken off of Phobos, perhaps half a kilometer across or larger, and were starting to drift away. Matthew watched as the last fires of the Queen of Sheba were snuffed by the grinding tempest. It was a ballet of destruction on a scale never before directly witnessed by mankind, the kind of thing astronomers only theorized about happening in the past or distant future. This may have been an entirely avoidable tragedy, but at least the astronomers were going to have a field day with it.

He checked the comms and found the static had begun to decline. "Sparrow?" he asked on an open channel. "Sparrow, are you out there?"

Silence and then a spot of distortion.

"Sparrow, are you there?"

"We... you Matth..."

"Sparrow, is that you?"

"We hear you loud and clear, Matthew," Yvonne said, and Matthew's heart almost stopped for the joy of the moment. "We'll loop around the debris field and join you."

"Is everyone okay?"

"We are. It's me, your mother, Whitaker, and seven other survivors." She gave the nervous laugh of one too tired to do anything else. "It is good to hear your voice. Is everyone there?"

"We're all here," Grace said. "Davey, Abigail, even Ryan Thompson."

"Sounds like you guys have a story too."

"You know what," Matthew said. "Change of plans. Head to Arizona. We'll meet up to swap ships at the Cole farm."

"Understood. See you soon."

Matthew flipped open the channel to the fleet. "Lantern Fleet. It was an honor to lead you today. Cliche as it sounds, humanity owes you all a debt."

"It was a pleasure to stand by your side," Captain Dominguez said. "And I'll gladly look forward to meeting you in person someday soon."

"Yeah, yeah," Ewan said. "Speeches and niceties are great and all, but I don't suppose someone could give us a tow. We're floating dead in space."

"Tamru," Gebre'elwa said. "Why don't you give the Dragon a tow back to the station before looping back for the escape shuttles. We have mechanics that can take a look at it. Matthew, drop by when you can. You and I have a lot to discuss."

"I'll do that," he promised. "Grace, plot us a deorbit trajectory for Arizona."

"Navigation is as effective as a brick right now, remember?"

"Right. We'll put some distance in between us and Phobos first."

What used to be Phobos was beginning to lose its shape as it expanded. Equatorial colonies would have to keep a close eye to make sure no larger fragments were pushed out of orbit. They would need to be redirected or destroyed before that happened. The skies of Mars would be forever changed by the destruction of Phobos. No longer would the colonists look up and see the moon cross their vision twice a day. Over the next weeks and months, it would slowly form a ring around Mars, narrow bands of dark rocks, a monument to the Battle of Phobos.

Matthew frowned as the Imperious Doubt put the debris field behind them. Not everyone was going to be happy about this change of fortunes.

A tense silence had fallen over the Kyoto factory. Whether through unspoken agreement or the panicked orders of superior officers, the fighting stilled, though smoldering wreckage gave proof to the violence that had disturbed the valley. Both the HiTO and liberating forces had retreated to opposite ends of the exclusion zone, though Yuuto Kagurazaka didn't doubt that at the slightest provocation the battle might be rejoined.

What would happen when the Phobos Platform fired again? It was the stroke of fate that all waited for. He knew that a thumper array that large would need time to recharge, but how long?

So he and his wife stood staring at Phobos when there came a flash of light, like distant fire against the moon. He held his breath, daring to hope that a stroke unlooked for had befallen the Moon of Fear. Perhaps the HiTO had rallied to retake their station. And yet the weapon might still fire.

And then his wife gasped. "Do you see it! Look, it's coming apart!"

He squinted because his eyes weren't nearly as keen as hers. And then he saw the cracks, great fissures forming in the moon. He sat back in the chair heavily, unable to believe what he was seeing. Someone had destroyed the whole moon? Surely the HiTO wouldn't go to such measures, but then who else had the firepower they had witnessed?

Over the next hour, they watched as Phobos slowly broke apart and the remnants crept across the sky. In the valley below both sides dug in, preparing for what, they did not know. As the sun set and Yuuto looked down on the valley, he wondered if life in his colony would ever go back to the way it used to be.

It was the dead of night when the two ships set down at the Cole family farm. Or rather what was left of it. When Matthew walked down the ramp of the Doubt, he saw for the first time the remains of his childhood home, burnt to the ground. In the ensuing months, there had been a dust storm, and the foundations were now half-buried. It was gone forever and lived only in memory.

But right now, he had loved ones he needed to see safe with his own two eyes.

As the Sparrow's ramps opened and long shafts of light spilled out, he ran across the ruined fields. Whitaker was first down the ramp, and Matthew checked his gait. The man's hat was low over his eyes, and one arm hung limp at his side.

"Well, Cole. This one wasn't very pleasant."

"I see you've been mistreated."

He grimaced and bounced on his toes. "Turned out that Logan didn't like me very much. But that's the price that a meddler pays."

"And you've recovered the Helm of Hades."

Whitaker tipped the hat at Matthew. "Logan couldn't figure out how to use it and had it stashed away in your cabin of all places. Lucky me, I found it before you did. Now, if that's all, I'll be taking my ship and leaving."

The man stepped past Matthew toward his own ship.

"Hey," Matthew said. "Thanks for getting them out of there."

Whitaker didn't turn. "I'm hardly the dashing hero that you are, but I did wait for them." And then he plodded across the dark field, disappearing into the night.

"I see he's in a good mood," Abigail said as she joined him.

"He has an excuse this time," Matthew said. A group of strangers was coming down the Sparrow's ramp, ostensibly the survivors of the Phobos Platform. He let them pass. This was Thompson's domain, and he could deal with them. The women he wanted to see were silhouetted in the airlock. He rushed to them, nearly tripping over his feet before he could pull them both into a hug.

Elizabeth laughed, and Matthew could feel her tears dampening his shoulder. "It's good to be home," she said. "We're okay, and, Matthew,

404

we still need to breathe. Don't crush us!"

"I'll be the judge of that," he said, but he did let off a little.

"Aren't you sentimental tonight," Yvonne said.

He backed away sheepishly and turned to Yvonne. She cast her eyes down. "Are you alright?" he asked softly.

"I will be. Ask me another time."

Cryptic, but that was the most optimistic she'd sounded in months. The others had gathered at the bottom of the ramp, and he led the women down to them. Grace was entirely too enthusiastic at the reunion, as was expected, demanding a group hug.

"Don't make this awkward," Abigail grumbled.

"Wouldn't be Grace, otherwise," Davey said.

And like that, Matthew had his family back. He'd do everything in his power to keep them from being separated again. Warm laughter bubbled up in the stories that others had missed. It seemed everyone had had their share of heroics, and Matthew's eyes widened to hear that in the end, it was his own mother that had killed Damon Stein. He hated that she had been dragged into this, and yet even she'd had her part to play.

The Imperious Doubt roared as it lifted off the ground, and Matthew reached up to hold his campero on his head as the backblast blew across the farm. He wondered briefly about Whitaker's sister and what her story was. It was an important detail and a clue to the mystery that was Whitaker's past. If only there were a way to follow it back to the man that was Whitaker, the real man, the one with a sister, not the arrogant manipulator that thought humanity was his charge to direct. He watched as the Doubt blasted into the sky, becoming a point of light, before finally turning away.

"I hope I'm not interrupting, but I thought we should have a word, Matthew."

Matthew left the crew to join Thompson a few feet away. "Of course. What can I do for you?"

"I've called for transport to pick up the survivors. They're from four different HiTO colonies, so it'll be a nuisance getting them home. Still," he said, "they're the lucky ones. The rest of their colleagues died."

He nodded. "Can I ask you something?"

"Don't see any reason to say no."

"If you return to Flagstaff, are you going to be okay?"

Thompson let out a short, bitter laugh. "No, I don't think so. My career is over, without a doubt. But before you make a stupid offer, I'm going to turn it down. I have a responsibility to return. I made decisions that have consequences, and someone has to give a full report of what happened to the Phobos Platform."

Matthew regarded him thoughtfully. In the dark, it was almost impossible to make out the man's expression. "You sure? You did what was right, and only a fool would argue."

"Morals are irrelevant when it comes to the needs of politics. I helped destroy a valuable HiTO asset. There's no proof it was ever commandeered by terrorists. No public proof, anyway. They'll deny everything. It'll be treason. We'll both be called Kyoto sympathizers."

"Both?"

"I wouldn't stick around Arizona if I were you."

"I'll keep that in mind."

"But," Thompson said. "I did want to ask a favor."

"Anything." And he meant it. Matthew knew he never could have pulled the trigger on those torpedoes.

"My future is in a cold prison cell at best. I've got a wife and two teenagers that may have hard times coming for them."

"If they're ever in need, they'll be welcome in Antioch."

"Good," Thompson said. "Good." He extended his hand to Matthew. "I don't know that I'll ever get the displeasure of working with you again, but at least at parting, I can say it was an honor to stand by your side."

Matthew grasped his hand. "The honor was mine, Ryan."

The crew shared a late-night breakfast, scrounged from supplies leftover from Logan's men. Much of the Sparrow's living area had been converted to support the extra personnel that had lived there for a week. It was going to be a mess to sort through the cots, personal effects, and equipment. Grace and Davey had already started dumping it all down the ladder into the hold just to make room.

But there was still plenty of coffee, which Abigail thought was the most important thing. Apparently, even terrorists needed a steady supply of caffeine. She sat in her wheelchair at the table, half slumped over

406

in exhaustion.

"Move over," Grace grumbled. "There's room for two to sleep on the table."

"Don't get too comfy," Elizabeth said. "Oatmeal is just about ready."

"Yay. Gummy, mushy oatmeal. Breakfast of heroes."

Matthew looked up from his tablet briefly, but then his eyes went back to whatever he'd been reading. "What's got you so engrossed?" Abigail asked.

He scratched at the hair on the back of his head. "The Martian news agencies have no idea what to do with any of this. In the last day, a war has started and then been abruptly derailed. A superweapon was fired but stopped through unclear means. Oh, and apparently someone blew up Phobos. It's just gone. Rubble now. And none of the governments are claiming responsibility. Any of you know anything about that?"

"Oh dear," Yvonne said, from where she sat nearby, already on her second cup of coffee. "It won't take long for them to connect the guild to Phobos."

"I already sent Julia a warning," he said. "We'll have to get with her and have an official statement ready. We won't cover up what we did." Abigail hadn't thought that far ahead yet. As much as Ms. Legs annoyed her, she was glad that someone had the head to deal with the public relations front. She'd probably end up hospitalizing the first reporter to ask her a question.

Davey chuckled and shook his head. "Hey, anyone remember when life was easy?"

"No," Abigail deadpanned.

"Breakfast is up," Elizabeth said. "Come get a bowl."

Abigail gripped the wheels of her chair to turn, but Matthew touched her shoulder as he passed. "I've got it."

"I'm not helpless, you know."

"And I know that better than anyone," he said, placing a bowl in front of her.

Grace elbowed her, and Abigail took that as a cue to change the subject. "How many satellites did you guys shoot? I got twelve."

"Eighteen," Grace said.

Davey didn't even bat an eye. "Thirty-one."

Grace huffed as she shoved a spoon of oatmeal into her mouth. "Not fair, you've had practice."

"And I flew the Sparrow through a collapsing moon," Yvonne said. "And Elizabeth took down Damon Stein, which you two failed to do."

Abigail opened her mouth to retort, but Elizabeth beat her to it. "It wasn't exactly a fair fight, and if I never have to touch a gun again, I'll be content. I'm going to have nightmares about this for months."

That put a damper on the competitive spirit, and they finished their bowls in silence. "Still," Matthew said. "I couldn't be prouder of all of you."

"Aww," Grace said. "Matthew's getting sappy in his old age."

"Watch it," Yvonne said. "Some of us are old enough to be his mother."

"And some of us are his mother," Elizabeth added.

Matthew yawned. "Speaking of age, I'm going to go catch the sunrise topside if anyone wants to join me. I may not ever get the chance to see the Martian sunrise again after today."

Abigail frowned at that. And then it clicked. They were going to take the blame. Not that they weren't responsible, but they would be held accountable. And maybe Matthew specifically. Her heart twisted in anguish. Being forced from your homeland was a pain she knew all too well.

"Wait, I'll join you," she said. Everyone else made excuses about wanting to get at least a couple hours of sleep, and Abigail rolled to her room to grab her suit. She'd just as soon not bother, but alas, the top hull was only accessible via ladder.

Matthew was already topside, perched on a hull outcrop, and facing the grey east by the time she made it up there. She thought about ditching her armor again but knew it was far too cold in the predawn to only be out in the athletic gear she wore under her suit. "Do you really think they'll blame you?" she asked softly.

"Thompson thinks so. He's expecting to go to prison, himself."

She whistled. "I'd say that's a miscarriage of justice, but I don't think my opinion is going to count for much."

He shook his head. "Do you remember the first time you faced death? Realized that you might not live to see another day? I like to think that exposes a person's true character. The colonies are having that moment right now."

"It hasn't been a pretty sight," she mumbled, thinking about the fighting in Kyoto. Reports said that several thousand died both at the factory and around the colony before the Phobos Platform put a stop to that. Even so, she doubted this was the end of the political turmoil on Mars. The box had been opened, and such things were impossible to close.

"Nations rarely have been," Matthew agreed, "but what's a nation except a collective of imperfect individuals."

"That spells doom for us all, doesn't it?" Yvonne asked.

Abigail turned in surprise, not having heard the top hatch open again. "Hey, umm, guess you changed your mind?"

Yvonne froze just shy of closing the hatch, a sly smile crossing her face. "Am I interrupting something?"

They were all comedians. Each and every one of them. And none of them were even the slightest bit funny.

"Not at all," Matthew said, saving her from having to come up with a witty retort. "Sun's not yet risen." The greys were shifting to the pale blues of the Martian sunrise. It was certainly pretty, but Abigail couldn't claim the attachment to it that Matthew had.

"I just..." Yvonne began, hugging her arms to herself. "I just wanted to apologize to both of you for everything."

Abigail shut her mouth, not really keen on broaching the topic. Sometimes it was better to let things lie rather than dig up old bones. Yvonne clearly didn't see it that way. Hopefully, this was the end of this season. They weren't going to chase her off for hiding a few skeletons. Matthew certainly wouldn't, and that meant that it was good enough for her too.

"I had convinced myself that losing Tomas wasn't that hard, that I was okay," Yvonne said. "That I had moved on. I tried to do something terrible. And I'm sorry that it became a thorn in the crew."

"What's done is done, but it's already been forgiven," Matthew said simply. "I've already deleted the security video from Ceres."

And that, to Abigail's immense relief, was the end of a conversation she was wholly unequipped for. She'd missed the old Yvonne and hoped dearly that this would signal her return. Though deep down, she knew it probably wasn't that simple. No one passed through storms unchanged. Nothing was ever easy, and it certainly wouldn't be for Yvonne. But at least she wasn't alone anymore. Abigail stood aside and gestured for her to join them, and after a moment of hesitation, Yvonne stepped past her to sit by Matthew as the sun rose slowly over the distant hills, filling the valley with light.

And then the lovely sight was interrupted by the chirp of Abigail's comm.

Wormwood: Part 4

―◁◍▷―

I.

No one got much sleep.

Abigail was called back to Doch Rossiya by Milena Drugova to deal with the fallout over Tatiyana Medvedev's death. No sooner was the sunup than Matthew saw Abigail off on a government train.

And when he returned to what was left of the farm, he got the dreaded message from Thompson. A warrant was out for both of their arrests. So far, it wasn't anyone else from the Sparrow crew, just Matthew and Thompson. The lawman said it would be the last they heard from him before he surrendered his comm and was taken into custody.

Matthew gave the order to pack up and leave, sending a warning to Abigail that she would need to be careful and find her own way off Mars as quickly as possible. While Yvonne was prepping the Sparrow for flight, he walked out across the barren fields. If he was never going to freely return to Mars, there was a place he had to visit one last time. He reached the red cliffs at the edge of the farm and the small grove of scraggly trees that took shelter beneath them. His mother was already at the tombstone.

Albert Cole
28-73 AM

He stood beside her and placed an arm around her shoulders, and she sighed into his embrace. There were a thousand things he could say, a thousand things he should say, but at the moment, they all felt like hollow words of mere sentiment. Elizabeth Cole would have to leave Mars for good this time. And it was his fault.

"I'm sorry," he whispered in her ear.

"Don't be," she said. "You have nothing for which to be sorry."

"Our home. Your life. I've taken it all away with the choices I've made."

"We all share in the chain of consequence that has led us here in this hour. You. Me. Your crew. Even your father. I can't help but think he'd be proud of you for those choices." He stiffened and she pulled away to look him in the face, a hand gripping each of his arms. "I mean it. I wouldn't have our life any other way."

"With everything I've put you through? A failed priest turned freelancer. I've destroyed your whole life."

"Well," she said, a smile tugging at the corner of her lips, "it certainly hasn't all been sunshine and daisies, and you've probably taken years off my life in worrying over you."

He grimaced. "Because I needed that reminder."

"Then let me finish. I wouldn't change a thing, not one lonely night without you or your father. Not the loss of the home in which we raised you. Not one bitter accusation against God over the course of my life. All those melt like snow when I see what you've done, the people you've saved. If I must suffer for a greater good, if that is what I was put in this universe for, then I can accept it with small complaint in the dark hours of the night. But the one that made me is greater than my grumblings. He will bear them, and I can be content."

He sighed and turned back to the tombstone. Despite her reassurances, he didn't think he would ever stop feeling guilty over the grief he had caused his mother. The grief his father had caused her. That was part of why he had originally become a priest. A misguided attempt at righting the wrongs his father had caused. But then as his mother had said, they all had a part in the chain of consequence that led them here. That was part of it.

So was Whitaker's betrayal.

And his father's alcoholism.

But his mother was somehow at peace with all of this. Maybe someday he would be too.

"I took Bishop Elias up on his offer to teach," she said. "I'll be staying at Antioch the next time you pass by."

That brought a smile to his face. It was as safe a place as any in this age. "And the farm?"

"Jonas and his wife will be purchasing it, save this grove which I'll retain. They can't afford the land outright, of course, but I've been working out a finance plan with them. The land will be replanted next season and the farm will continue. Just... Without the Cole family." As she said the last words, she began to tear up and Matthew pulled her into his arms again.

They looked at the tombstone one last time and then turned away in silence. There was nothing more to be said. Ahead of them, the sun continued to rise into the sky and the Sparrow's engines hummed. It would lead them away from Mars, and who could tell if it would ever bear them back?

II.

It took a long time to get all of their people Home. With the loss of the Queen of Sheba, Tamru was left ferrying not only the Red Dragon but the shuttles full of personnel from the Queen, as well as the surviving members of Shotel Squadron. Thankfully, the Azure Dream volunteered to help, and between the two ships, they got the job done.

Home, of course, was what they called the old pirate asteroid base. They'd debated on names for months before eventually settling on the obvious because, more than anything, that's exactly what it was. A Home for their families and the families of many of their employees. He disembarked from the Qolxad into the raucous noise of the busy hangar. The Red Dragon already had mechanics crawling over it like insects, and he stepped over to have a word with their chief.

"Are you the one I need to thank for this?" asked a voice from under the ship.

Tamru turned to see Ewan Hywel crawl out. His coveralls were already streaked with fresh grease. "You'll have to thank my mother," Tamru said, "but you and your crew are welcome here until you're ready to go. The cafeteria is on the house. Just ask around and someone will point you in the right direction."

Ewan looked a bit stunned, and he offered his hand before realizing he was a mess. "We'll be out of your hair as soon as we can. I'll let 'Elwa know how thankful we are."

413

Tamru shook his head. "Take your time. You're our guests." He turned and pushed his way through the crowded hangar toward the lift. Families were out in force to greet their loved ones, especially those of the Queen's crew. He made a mental note that he'd have to check on the families of the interceptor pilots that died and make sure they weren't lost in the bustle. Not everyone got a happy ending today.

The doors of the lift closed, insulating him from the chaos, and he punched in the code to the family's private floor. It opened onto a lounge filled with a sea of friendly faces, but his eyes roved until he found his wife, Naomi. They met in an embrace, and soon his teenage children were clustered around him as well. Homecomings were always a relief, but this was the first time he had left looking for a fight. It changed things and the breaking of the tension was sweet.

"Have you seen mom?" he asked Naomi.

"She went straight to her office."

"That's what I was afraid of. Go ahead down to the caf. We'll join you soon."

He kissed her and opened the door to his mother's office, knocking as he pushed it open. "Mother? Are you in here?"

"Yes, yes, come in." She was staring out the window toward Mars. "Well what is it?" she snapped when he didn't say anything.

He rubbed at the back of his neck. "I was just checking on you. We lost a lot today and I wanted to make sure you were okay. I'm surprised Mateo isn't with you."

"I sent your step-father to bring us something to eat. I'm not feeling terribly sociable at the moment."

"I understand," he said. As long as Mateo was coming back, Tamru would be content. He turned to leave but was stopped by a tired sigh from his mother.

"Do you remember what I said about closure, so long ago?" she asked.

So that was it. "Do you miss him right now?"

"The Queen was his idea, you know. He wrote up the business plan that was going to get us there. I just skipped most of the steps when we cashed in Captain Meriadoc's bounty. It's been over twenty years, but..." The moment lingered. "Watching the Queen go down felt like losing him again. The dreams we had together." She turned around, and her eyes shone. "Am I a terrible wife for missing my late husband?"

414

Tamru stepped around the desk and took her hand. "Mateo knows, Mom. You're always quiet around the anniversary of dad's death. We all understand. You said yourself that grieving doesn't ever truly end."

"Is that what I said? And you listened like I knew what I was talking about."

"I miss him too."

"And I wish I'd had a chance to meet Kofi," Mateo said, entering the office behind them. "Because he must have been a wonderful man to have made such an influence on you and the kids."

Tamru smiled as his mother tried to wipe away the evidence that she'd been about to cry. "Yes. Well. This is all very embarrassing now that you're both here to watch me cry over a ship and my first husband."

For once, she looked her age, and very tired after a long day. If he had anything to say, she'd be spending more time at Home from now on. She'd earned that at least. "Then I'll leave you two," he said. He opened the door to leave. "Get some rest."

He shut the door and left the office behind. It was going to be a long day ahead, dealing with the fallout, and an even longer few months. There was no way they could replace the Queen anytime soon. Perhaps they could purchase a couple smaller ships in the meantime to cover the lost business. But that sort of planning was for another day.

Today was a day to rest and mourn those that had been lost. That was how he found himself in the cafeteria with his own family, telling his kids stories about the grandfather they'd never known and the father he'd lost over twenty years ago.

III.

Abigail didn't dare leave Medvedev's manor, or what remained of it. Despite Milena's assurances that the government of Doch Rossiya had no interest in arresting Abigail, she wasn't going to take any chances. The sooner they could deal with the estate and be done with it, the sooner she could catch a flight off Mars and rejoin Matthew and the others.

And what a mess that estate was. And worse, it was all over Abigail's head.

Tatiyana Medvedev left no will, no instructions on what was to be done with her property, her businesses, her assets, her fortune. She had no family or partners in business. She'd never had much interest in paperwork, let alone the peculiarities of Doch Rossiyan law, but Abigail, Natalya, and Milena were left to protect the interests of the freelancers that used Medvedev as their broker.

Over a two-week period, Milena became the unofficial face of the Medvedev estate to the Rossiyan government, despite lacking official standing. Knowing the corruption in the judicial system, she was able to push for a hasty resolution that favored all involved. After receiving an enormous bribe, a judge made a quick ruling and closed the case. The businesses were given to the employees. All unrelated assets were to be sold, except for the manor. The vast majority of the proceeds and fortune were seized by the government, with the fraction that remained to be divided among the freelancers, who were known to be the mistress' favorites.

Milena began the work of transitioning from freelancer to broker. The manor would remain the property of the new management business to be helmed by Natalya and herself.

"Someone has to look out for the girls since Medvedev couldn't be bothered to," she said during yet another late evening in which they waded neck-deep through paperwork.

"You're sure this is the career you want?" Abigail asked, setting aside her tablet.

"Well, I'm not going to be able to run field operations forever, and given the opportunity that's presented itself, I can't turn it down. You might keep your own options in mind."

Abigail turned away so as not to show the nerve she'd struck. That wasn't a line of thought that she wanted to contemplate. Pretending it wasn't going to happen someday wouldn't stave off that eventuality, but it kept her sanity in check. "I'm going to catch one of the flights out tomorrow if you can get me an exit voucher."

"Easily. Rossiya's border is only locked down if you don't know who to approach. For someone that knows the bureaucrats, it's as porous as can be." She put down her papers and looked up to meet Abigail's eyes. "I do appreciate you coming."

"I didn't do much. You and Natalya took care of everything."

"Maybe I just needed a friendly face." She took on a somber expression. "I'm sorry about what the mistress did."

They'd found the records where Medvedev had hired Stein among a dozen other serious crimes. She hadn't even tried to conceal them. She'd never expected anyone to look through her files.

"She failed, or Stein did." Abigail tried not to imagine a world without Matthew Cole. "And in the end, her crimes found her out." She thought about the slender old woman that had died in her arms and couldn't help but shudder. Medvedev had had every worldly power and had died a beggar, desperate for what her money could never purchase. It was only as her freelancers compared notes that they all realized how deeply subversive the old woman had been. Perhaps that was why there always seemed to be a revolving door of new recruits joining and veterans leaving.

She hated how it put everything she knew about her old mentor in a new light. Without Medvedev, she might have never become a freelancer and likely would have never met Matthew. For that alone, she could be thankful to the old woman, at least on an intellectual level. But in her heart? Tatiyana Medvedev had sown only bitterness, and Abigail struggled not to turn it back upon the dead woman. She tried to pity her and remember that her actions had led her to an ignoble, if still just, ending.

"They found her out indeed," Milena said. "And because of what she did to you, the other freelancers voted you into the cut."

Abigail looked at her in surprise as she held out an envelope. "Medvedev hasn't been my broker for over two years. I don't have any stake."

"None of us do, legally, but the court ruled otherwise, and we voted to include you." She pushed the envelope into Abigail's hands, and she hesitantly opened it. "Inside are details on how to access the account with your share."

"How much?" She was almost afraid of the answer.

"Over half a million."

"Holy... I can't—"

"It's already done," Milena said. "You guys may need it anyway. The Sparrow's going to have hard times ahead. Consider this an apology from the Medvedev estate and a thank you for being among the good guys." She grinned. "Also, every one of our freelancers wants membership in the guild now."

Abigail tore her eyes off the envelope. "Even with Matthew labeled as an enemy of the state?"

"Are you kidding? He's practically going to be a folk hero to the masses after this. The tabloids are already comparing him to Robin Hood for destroying the Phobos Platform." Abigail shook her head but couldn't help but smile in pride. Matthew wasn't going to approve of this at all. Something she took great delight in. "Further," Milena said, "I thought that you should keep this. You're more likely to find use. And it's safer in your hands than with someone who doesn't appreciate how dangerous it is." She passed Abigail a small, sealed container housing a smooth metal cube.

Medvedev's miracle. It must have been found in the ruined half of the building. She carefully took the container, and its wondrous piece of technology, one last gift from her old broker. Unwilling, of course, but that was how all of her gifts came.

The next morning she left the manor, without a single glance over her shoulder, leaving the dead past to be forgotten.

IV.

It had been a simple request. She didn't expect Matthew to go out of his way to fulfill it so quickly.

Yvonne climbed off the back of his new bike and looked at him expectantly. He only gave a grave shake of the head. "This is your business. I'll be here if you need me."

The cold dark streets of Ceres had an unavoidable familiarity. Despite only living here for five years, her life was anchored around the events that had transpired here. It was the centerpiece of her years, with one life stretching out before and another life after. She lifted her eyes to the old storefront carved into the stone tunnel.

The windows had been broken out long ago. No doubt, anything of value had been scavenged from the clinic within days of her abandoning it. When Piggy had ludicrously proposed, and Matthew Cole swept in to give her a chance at a different life. She'd walked away, walked away from the profession she and Tomas had labored in, and become someone different. A pilot, a passable mechanic, a cook, a freelancer.

A draft blew down the dark street, and trash rustled at her feet. She hugged her coat to herself and pulled a small flashlight from her pocket, and shined it into what was left of the clinic. The waiting room was stripped of furniture, the walls stained with mold and decay. The humid tunnels of Ceres quickly destroyed anything that wasn't maintained. She pushed the broken door open, wincing as the corroded hinge whined a mournful note. It occurred to her that the clinic might not be totally abandoned. But Matthew was nearby, and after the dangers she had faced, stumbling onto a squatter held little fear for her.

So many memories assaulted her. From them scrounging funds to rent and finally purchase the location, to the hiring of an occasional employee when times were good, to the last birthdays they had shared together. And the people they saved. She pushed through the swinging double door to the back, into the open area that could be partitioned into rooms via a curtain. Those were torn down and either missing or piled in a corner.

This was the room where Tomas had died. There against the wall, he had bled out from a fatal wound while she saved Kudzu's life. In the pool of light from the flashlight, she imagined she could still see the bloodstains creeping ever outward. A wave of nausea washed over her, and she flicked off the light to stop the spinning of the room.

It had been foolish to come here. What was she proving? That she was someone changed and different? And to whom? Tomas was certainly long gone from this place.

"I'm sorry I couldn't save you both," she said to no one in particular. Then she frowned. "I'm sorry that... That life was hard, Kudzu. That you were a damn fool and left behind a son. That you couldn't get even that one thing right. And I'm sorry that I took away any chance you had left at that. Tomas was better than both of us, I guess."

She flicked the light back on and turned toward the office in the back. "But it's all wrong isn't it. And not just with me. It's been that way since the beginning." The sound of her voice made the dead clinic feel a little less empty, even if it did make her sound like a crazy woman.

The office door had been pulled off and leaned against the wall. She stepped through the entryway and wasn't surprised to find that, like everything else, it was in ruins. She looked through a twisted metal filing cabinet. Someone had used a heavy object to smash the lock apart. They were most likely disappointed to discover that it only held hard copies of medical records. But at the back was the very thing she was looking for. Taped to the rear wall of the cabinet was a picture of Tomas making a goofy face. He'd hidden it there one day, hoping she'd see it and laugh. It had taken her three weeks to stumble upon it. She'd never taken the picture down.

She rubbed at the tears running down her face as she peeled the tape back and took the precious photograph into her hands. Oh, Tomas. At least now I know what's wrong with me. That really was the mistake, thinking that there was a remarkable difference between Kudzu and herself. Maybe she hid it better, but in the end, they were both merely human.

And that realization, both in the heights and depths that simple word implied in all its mystery, made all the difference. That the image of the divine and the depravity of hell itself could be found in a single fragile vessel.

She pocketed the picture and carefully picked her way back through the clinic to the street, where Matthew sat leaning against the still running bike. He gave her an appraising look before asking, "Did you find what you were looking for?"

"I did. Or at least the beginning of it."

He smiled, perhaps understanding more than she had spoken aloud. He was good at that. "Then let's go home."

Epilogue

The Battle of Phobos was a way marker in the history of mankind, the end of one act in preparation for the next. Some thought that with the exit of Alexander Logan's particular brand of Human Abrogation the state of the colonies would improve. How wrong they were in their estimates of man's nobility. They always are.

The Highland Treaty Organization refused to withdraw from the Kyoto factory zone, despite the passing of the known threat, citing an uncertain future and the continual need for security, particularly in light of the destruction of Phobos. Kyoto's allies, designating themselves as the Allied Forces, an astute nod to Earth history, also refused to leave and two armed camps settled into a tense watch over the divided colony. In the name of protecting an essential asset, the shadow of a cold war fell across us all.

And in the skies above, Mars now missed one of its moons. More than just a navigational hazard, the remains were a danger to life and limb in those first few months, as some debris fell to the surface. A series of new craters ran along the equator. But once things settled, Mars was left with a beautiful new vista. Though nowhere near as bright or spectacular as mighty Saturn's, it was a favorite subject of many artists.

Ryan Thompson's actions in the battle were declared treasonous. The 'Man who destroyed Phobos' was sentenced to life in prison, despite mass staged protests. His family moved to Antioch to escape the public eye and I have had the pleasure of getting to know Emily and the twins, despite them attending the local Baptist church rather than the masses I conduct.

My student Matthew Cole became a wanted man, first by his home colony of Arizona and then by the Highland Treaty Organization. A resolution was drafted to outlaw the Guild of Lanterns from operating in member colonies, but the public outcry was absolute. Julia of Venus had done her PR work well, and through pressure from the public the Guild continued to run jobs throughout Mars, growing to be a household name in a matter of months. Still, there were more than a few bounty hunters who tried to take down their leader. They discovered that Matthew Cole was a dangerous man indeed.

Elizabeth Cole returned to Antioch. She was grossly overqualified to teach at our school, but our students benefited immensely. And it is a well-known fact that she keeps the most magnificent garden in all of Antioch. Her friends, of which I am blessed to be counted, regularly receive gifts of the finest produce in the Jupiter neighborhood.

And as for Yvonne Naude, Elizabeth assures me that she is at long last recovering from the malaise that had poisoned her heart. It pained me to see the crew so divided. But all harms can be healed, and the Sparrow is once again a family. Its matriarch runs the tightest ship in the solar system if the stories are to be believed.

The Battle of Phobos may have been a turning point for the colonies but it was also one for the Sparrow. Though they had always walked the straight and narrow, they were now at odds with the law. And that, though the greatest part of their journey was yet to come.

Elias of Callisto
Bishop of Antioch, Ganymede
Died 105 AM

Afterword

Thank you so much for reading *After Moses Wormwood.*
If you enjoyed it please consider leaving a review or rating by following the QR code below.

The adventures of the Sparrow continue in *After Moses Virtus.* Tragedy strikes and the crew is forced to split up, Davey, Grace, and Yvonne are stranded on Venus. When a violent revolution shakes the Venusian Empire, Davey may be the only one that can save the day.

Thanks again!

-Michael F. Kane-

Author Bio

Michael F. Kane cut his teeth on science fiction and fantasy. In fact, his first memories of Star Wars are his mother covering his eyes during the rancor scene. Later, he fell in love with the classics, Tolkien, Asimov, Herbert, and more. Somehow, despite the odds being stacked against him, he grew up to be a somewhat respectable human being. By day he's the music director at a mid-sized church, but at night he dreams of unseen lands and places man has never trod. Check out his website at www.Michaelfkane.com to stay up to date on his publishing adventures.

Milton Keynes UK
Ingram Content Group UK Ltd.
UKHW012009040923
428063UK00013B/469/J